SCAMMERS

ALSO BY J.T. GODDARD

Traces
Tracks
Piracy
Missing

SCAMMERS

A GAVIN RASHFORD NOVEL

J. T. GODDARD

To my brothers
Simon, Paul, Patrick, Michael
We've come a long way from Templestowe Crescent; you can take the boy out
of Leeds but you can't take Leeds out of the man
MOT

SCAMMERS

Chapter One

Staff Sergeant Gavin Rashford swore, flapping his hands and opening and closing his mouth rapidly. Tears welled in his eyes as he groped around for his can of pop. He had lost at least three of his senses but could hear laughter. He chewed furiously, swallowed, and gulped a drink, swilling it around his mouth. His vision cleared and he saw the giggling girls. The oldest was about six or seven, he guessed, and apparently thought that a man burning his mouth on a hot deep-fried scallop was really funny. Her little sister agreed. He glared at them, and they rushed back to their mother, who was sitting at an adjacent table.

The morning rain had dissipated but the pavement had been damp and steaming when he pulled off the highway just before one o'clock. He was hungry, and still feeling a bit hungover. He drove down the ramp and surveyed the array of fast-food restaurant options available. He settled on the one offering a scallop basket; 'when in Rome', he thought. Although even through his headache he remembered that he was in Nova Scotia.

He had parked at an angle between the building and the picnic tables, between a minivan and two Honda Goldwing motorcycles, and gone inside. There was no line-up, so he ordered his meal before going to the washroom. He had finished, washed his hands, and returned to the front area long before the young woman behind the counter called his number.

He took the cardboard box of food and some extra paper napkins, balanced his can of soda in the crook of his elbow, pushed open the door with his foot and found an empty table outside.

An elderly couple in bike leathers were chatting at an adjacent table, a map spread out between them. Further down the slope two children from the minivan laughed as they ran around next to their parents, who were still eating.

He had felt the sun on his neck as he opened the lid and the perfume of fried food rushed out to meet him. He speared a golden ball of batter with the small wooden fork he had been given, sniffed it without any idea of why he did that and popped it into his mouth. He had not expected the rush of superheated liquid that had embraced the scallop in its breaded casing.

The mother gathered her children in her arms, glaring back at the big man who had frightened her daughters. There was a steady drone of traffic from up on the highway. A plane on final approach to the nearby airport cruised overhead, the wheels already down. Rashford took another scallop, more carefully this time, and smiled to himself.

'At last,' he thought. 'Now I'm on holiday'.

The previous two and a half months had been busy. At the end of April, he had located Josee Whitecalf, a young Métis woman who had gone missing a few weeks earlier. It was now well into July. 'Time flies when you're having fun', he thought, although in truth he hadn't been having much fun lately. Josee had been abducted at the start of the university exam week and not found until almost the end of the month. The rush of meetings and reports over the next few weeks meant that May hadn't been too bad.

After a week of answering questions about how and why he had liaised with both an Indigenous 'socio-cultural support group' and a biker gang in the tracking and recovery of Josee, he had gone back to Wheatville for the convocation of his erstwhile girlfriend, Mandy. An old friend from Maple Creek, Bettina Blackeagle, had used her faculty status to procure him a ticket as her guest. This had raised many eyebrows and led to numerous amused glances and softly whispered comments. Bettina taught a Women's and Gender Studies course and was generally considered, by her peers and students alike, to be an uber-feminist, perhaps even a misandrist. Many had found seeing her escorted to a public event by a large, physically fit man with a 'number one' buzz haircut and an ill-fitting suit to be disconcerting on many levels.

After the ceremony, he had taken Mandy and her family, plus some of her friends, out to a fancy congratulatory dinner at the Ristorante d'Arno, an upscale eatery located in a renovated merchant's house on the river. Apart from wining and dining twelve people, an additional round of champagne had been called for because Mandy had won the President's Prize for the graduating student with the highest academic grade average. His credit card was still reluctant to re-emerge from his wallet.

Mandy had not wanted her parents to find out that she was in a relationship and had made him stay in his own room at the hotel that weekend. He had not been too surprised, however, when she knocked on his door at one in the morning and climbed into his bed. The following morning had been a mad dash to get showered and dressed before rushing to meet her parents, uncles, and cousins for breakfast. Mandy had pecked him on the cheek as they descended in the elevator, then asked him to wait a few minutes before joining the group.

The whole family was seated when he arrived, and it did not escape his attention that his friend Patrick York, a policeman from Barbados, and Josee's roommate, Petra Lahkshi, drifted in even later than he to join the breakfast. The tall Bajan and the slim Afghani looked deceptively like a couple until Mandy's cousin Shyanne looked up from under her eyelids at Patrick, and Shyanne's brother Pia took his hat off the chair he had been saving for Petra. The newcomers gave each of them respectively a bright hello, as though they had not seen each other since leaving the restaurant the night before, and they returned to staring at their eggs' benedict, hoping the steam would hide their blushes. Mandy's aunt elbowed her husband in the side and giggled.

"You owe me ten bucks," she said, nodding at the latecomers.

Rashford had not seen much of Mandy after that. She had gone to take her parents for a tour of campus, and after seeing them off for the drive back to Prince Albert she had made sure that her friend Josee was looked after and readied for the trip home. The young Métis woman was still traumatized by her recent experience of being kept captive and tortured, and tired easily. Petra had helped Pia load her into the back of his SUV and promised they would get her back to Wheatville safely. The two women shared a house, and Pia commented that he would drop by every day to check on them. Rashford knew that the heavily set leader of a Cree street gang would stand by his word.

Patrick and Shyanne had left as well, explaining that they needed to finalize details for their upcoming trip to Barbados. One of Pia's business operations was a travel agency, operated in partnership with a motorcycle gang, that offered cheap flights to the Caribbean for students. He had provided his sister and her friend with a good deal on business class tickets; they were leaving in ten days and taking Josee with them. The general hope was that Josee would find this a calming and relaxing break, away from all the bad memories. Rashford wasn't too sure. He had seen too many traumatized victims of crime, and knew that recovery would take a long time, with all sorts of unexpected triggers causing problems along the way.

Once everyone had left, Mandy and Rashford had sat in the hotel café and had a coffee. She was uncharacteristically quiet, even when he congratulated her again on winning the President's Prize.

"That opens up the graduate school opportunities for you, I'm sure," he said, cheerfully.

Mandy nodded.

"Yes. If I want to go through that door. I've got the tour to finish first."

Rashford looked at her.

"That's at the end of June, right?"

"Yes." She paused. "Are you still going to come out?"

"Of course. I'm booked into Halifax on the seventh, then I'm going to meet up with this police officer who's handing the cold case. The one that might be related to Marc Claydon."

"That beast."

Mandy was trembling with anger. Rashford reached across and held her hand.

"He's not been forgotten, you know," he said. "That's why I'm doing this follow-up."

She pouted.

"I thought you were coming to see me?"

He sighed, shaking his head at her ability to misconstrue even the most innocuous comment.

"I am," he said. "You know that. But I can't miss this chance, just in case it is related to what happened to Josee."

She nodded, mollified.

"I know," she said. "So, where shall we meet?"

"I thought I'd come to the show in, what's it called, Pictou? The last one you do in northern Nova Scotia. I've booked a cabin at a place near there for two nights, then we can get the ferry to PEI and join the others."

"It will be an early ferry, won't it? We've only got one night off, then we have to be at this Rollo Bay place, for the Fiddle Festival."

"Yes, don't worry. The ferry leaves at nine, we'll be there before noon."

"They're giving us a couple of camper vans for the weekend. I'm sharing with Monica. Where are you going to stay?"

"I'm not sure yet. There are a couple of hotels nearby, in Souris and Montague, or there's always Charlottetown. I've still got to book."

She scoffed.

"You'd better be quick. This concert is a big deal, everywhere is going to book up early."

"Don't worry, I'll figure it out."

"And have you booked a car? There aren't many available in the Maritimes, you have to book those ages ahead."

Rashford laughed softly.

"Mandy, calm down. It's all under control. I have travelled before, you know. You just worry about your playing. I'll see you after the show in Pictou."

She sighed.

"Promise?"

"Promise."

"I'll leave you a ticket at the box office, just give them your name."

"Thursday the tenth of July, right?"

She stared at him.

"Wednesday!"

He could only keep a straight face for so long, then laughed.

"I know, I know," he said. "I'm just teasing you."

She reached over and punched his arm. They sat silently for a few minutes, sipping coffee.

"Now what?" he said.

She looked at him.

"How long have you got your room?"

Rashford grinned.

"I wasn't sure what was happening today, so I'm booked through until tomorrow morning. Why?"

Mandy shrugged.

"I have to leave soon," she said. "I've checked out and left my bag at the desk. Now I have to wait for two hours before I can catch the next bus back to Wheatville. After that I probably won't see you until Nova Scotia. We're going to be really busy, practising and prepping for the tour." She rubbed the tabletop with her fingers.

Rashford decided to make it easy for her.

"So, what, you were thinking we might go to my room and say goodbye privately?"

She smiled.

"Something like that, yes," she said, and stood up.

Rashford stood as well. He put a ten-dollar bill under his cup, waving at the waitress to point it out for her, then took Mandy's hand and walked her across towards the elevators.

That had been nearly ten weeks ago. June had been pretty miserable, the days stretching out, the spring rains bringing layers of grey cloud. He had chatted with Mandy on the phone a few times, and they had managed one weekend together when the lead singer, Monica, had called a break from rehearsals so that she could rest her voice. Rashford had rented a room in Saskatoon, where they could wander the streets and be fairly confident nobody would know them.

He had booked them in at the Bessborough, a venerable old hotel near the river. Rashford had picked up Mandy as he drove past Wheatville, and they had spent two passionate nights in the Bridge City. One evening they went to the Italian restaurant in the faux railway carriages, each smiling at their own memories of previous meals there. Now, he was excited that he was going to be seeing her again.

He picked up his trash and took it to the bin, glancing across and pulling a face at the girls as he passed. The older one still stood behind her mother, using her for protection, but the younger giggled. Rashford walked back to his rental car and consulted the map on his GPS. He estimated it would take him an hour or so to drive to Pictou. He drove back to the highway, merged into the steady stream of traffic, and headed north.

As he drove, he marvelled at the dullness of the scenery. The road was edged with trees, with every so often an exposed rock face as the highway ran through a cutting. Sometimes there was a view down a valley, once or twice a river ran beneath him as he crossed a bridge, but mainly it was trees. And more trees. The road was mainly dry now, but every so often a car or a transport truck would speed through a lingering puddle, throwing up a spray which smeared his windscreen.

His mind drifted back to the previous day, which he had spent at the David P. McKinnon Building on Gottingen Street in Halifax. This was the red-brick headquarters of the Halifax Regional Police that his host, Constable Paula White, described as being 'in the middle of nowhere and the centre of everything'. She looked to be a few years younger than him, he thought, about five feet eight inches tall and with her hair pulled back in a severe bun. She had stood in her small office and clicked her computer back to a screen saver, then hurriedly scooped up some papers and a scarf from the ell-shaped extension to her desk. Laying out a city map on the now clear surface, she had pointed out the location of the building, then indicated the 'six cardinal points' of the area: The Commons, Citadel, Naval Base and dockyards, waterfront, ferry to Dartmouth, and downtown shopping area.

"We're Central Division," she said, "and seventy-nine per cent of our calls used to be from one of those areas, although things are changing now. The north end of the city is getting busier, and even the southern margins are seeing an increase in crime. East and West Divisions are also busy."

Rashford stood next to her and leaned over the map.

"Where was the girl being held?"

She pointed at an area in the northwest of the city.

"The 102 highway is the main corridor heading north-south, and the Bedford Basin here is the container port for Halifax. In between are Mount Saint Vincent University, here, and then lots of housing developments. She lived in residence at the Mount, but he took her to an apartment here, about two kilometres away. It's a development called Stonemouth Village, there are three hundred plus apartments."

"Are they expensive places?"

"Not really. They're not cheap, though. I guess you could say they are mid-range, although they would have been high-end when they were built. Nicely appointed. Good parking. Lots of trees. Easy access to both the downtown and to campus."

"And everybody minds their own business?"

"Pretty much, yeah."

"And you were on this case from the beginning?"

"God no. I was still at university then. I've only been in the police for six years. I got assigned this file a couple of years ago."

Rashford turned to her.

"Why? What happened to bring it back to life?"

"The media ran a story on outstanding police investigations. They called in with a FOIP request to see if we'd found anything and I got tasked with reviewing nine files. This was one of them."

"And had you?"

"What?"

"Found anything?"

She scoffed.

"Nobody had looked. At least, there was nothing in the file. Like I told you on the phone, all we had was a girl who said a guy had kept her captive for two days. He never touched her, just kept her chained up. Officers had been to the apartment and searched it, and all they found was that partial fingerprint on the toilet handle. That was never even entered into the database until I did the review. I wasn't expecting much of a result, to be honest. And then you called."

"On the phone, you said he'd paid cash for the apartment. How did that happen?"

"It turns out it was a private sub-let. Some guy from Dalhousie who had actually graduated kept renting his apartment and then sub-let it. This was the early days of Air B'n'B, there wasn't really any regulation around doing that. This Marvin Chesapeake guy paid him upfront for four months, until Christmas. He had an option on the winter term as well."

Rashford peered back at the map.

"This area is called Clayton Park?"

When White nodded, he turned to her with a slow smile.

"Well, well, well," he said.

She looked at him curiously.

"What?"

"The guy I'm looking for, he called himself Claydon, Marc Claydon. Or Claydon, Marc. That sounds a bit too much like Clayton Park to be a coincidence, don't you think?"

White shrugged.

"Perhaps. It sounds a bit like you're clutching at a straw, though."

Rashford stood upright, arching his back and rolling his shoulders.

"Yeah, maybe." He cleared his throat. "This fellow who had officially rented the place, the guy who had graduated. Do we know where he is?"

She nodded and went to her desk, where she rifled through some papers.

"Here we are. Stephan Maynard, now in Toronto, originally from a place called Ecum Secum."

"Ecum Secum? Really?"

"Yes, it's a small fishing village on the Eastern Shore. Anyway ..."

"Hang on. Ecum Secum? What kind of name is that?"

Paula White laughed.

"I had thought maybe it was the name of an old fishing captain, you know, from the eighteen hundreds. But it turns out it's from the Mi'kmaq, their word for the area was *ekemsagen*, which means 'red bank'. There must have been a sand bank or something there."

Rashford thought he quite liked her laugh.

∼

Inspector Jeremy Smithson was the Divisional Commander. Constable White had made the arrangements for Rashford to pay a courtesy visit and they were waiting outside his office promptly at eleven that morning. At the appointed time the door opened, and a civilian employee ushered them in to a small anteroom. She knocked on the inner door and a gruff voice indicated they should enter. The civilian opened the door.

"Constable White and Staff-Sergeant Rashford, sir," she said, shepherding them inside. She then left the room, closing the door gently behind her.

Smithson stood up and came out from behind his desk. He was a tall, bald white man in his early fifties, thin and sallow looking, wearing a sharply pressed uniform that seemed to hang off his shoulders, as though it were too big for him. He nodded at White and then shook hands with Rashford, at the same time indicating that they should each sit on one of the five club chairs grouped around a small table. Once they were settled, he spoke.

"Welcome to Halifax, Staff-Sergeant. I trust Constable White here is looking after you?"

"Yes, sir. Thank you, sir."

Smithson nodded.

"I understand you're looking for some help with a cold case?"

"Yes, sir."

Rashford explained the circumstances leading to the abduction of Josee Whitecalf, and the matching of a fingerprint believed to belong to the abductor with one collected by the Halifax Police in a case ten years earlier. He also noted the similarities between the two names, Clayton Park and Marc Claydon. Smithson looked at him quizzically.

"I'm still not sure how we might help," he said. "We have no further evidence as to who this fellow might be."

Rashford took a deep breath.

"Well, the thing is, sir, we do. But we can't use it properly, not in Alsama. I think you might be able to use it here, though."

Smithson raised an eyebrow.

"Go on."

"When we raided the house where Josee was being held, we surprised him. He hadn't had time to clear up, and we got some good DNA samples. Mainly saliva but some hair follicles as well. And semen."

Paula White sat forward quickly.

"He raped her?"

Rashford shook his head.

"No. We think he masturbated, thinking about her, perhaps watching her. We're not sure. There were tissues in one of the wastepaper baskets."

"So, what might we do with that?" said Smithson. "We've got nothing like that to compare samples."

"Yes, sir, I know," said Rashford. "But you do have access to IGG, sir."

"IGG? What's that?" Smithson looked at White. "Do you know what he's talking about?"

She nodded, then explained. "Only because he told me about it this morning, sir."

Smithson was mollified. He looked at Rashford.

"It means Investigative Genetic Genealogy, sir. Basically, you work with one of those commercial ancestry websites to compare the DNA evidence you have against the millions of voluntarily uploaded samples they have in their files."

Smithson shook his head.

"Is that legal?"

"Yes, sir, although you do need a judge's warrant. You have to prove you have good cause, sir, that you're not just on a fishing expedition. The judge reviews the case, and the evidence, and then you go from there."

"And the companies agree to this?"

"When there is good cause, yes, sir, they do. It gets results, sir. A few years ago, in Ontario, they solved a forty-year-old murder using IGG."

Smithson nodded.

"I remember hearing about that but remind me of the details."

"Yes, sir," said Rashford. "There were two murders in Toronto, about four months apart. This was back in the nineteen eighties. They had DNA evidence from the two crime scenes but no technology to compare it. Twenty years later, when the technology had advanced, someone checked the samples and discovered that the same perpetrator had probably killed both women. He'd raped them, and there were semen samples. So, they knew they were looking for one guy, for both murders.

"It was another twenty years before things developed enough on the tech front and they got permission to use IGG. Through that they made a match to what turned out to be the killer's great-grandparents. They got a genealogist involved, traced back the family tree and found the suspect. They took a DNA sample from him, and it was a hundred per cent match. Bingo."

Smithson looked at him.

"I don't understand, why can't you do this from Regina?"

"Because of Alsama, sir. Our genealogy data banks only have people from Alsama, not from Canada. We can't access the Canadian data banks; it would be a procedural nightmare. But you could."

Smithson scoffed.

"Maybe the West should have thought of that before they separated."

"Yes sir. That's political, sir. I have no opinion."

Smithson looked at him, tapping his fingers on his desk.

"It would be our budget, then?" he said.

Rashford nodded.

"Yes, sir. But according to the Halifax Regional Police website, sir, you have budgeted to follow-up three cold cases this fiscal year."

Smithson chuckled.

"Have we indeed?"

"Yes, sir. I'm hoping those cases have not yet been assigned, sir."

"I'll bet you are."

The Inspector got to his feet, signalling that the meeting was over. He guided Rashford to the door, then paused.

"I'll look into it, Staff-Sergeant. I'm not saying yes or no, and I'm making no promises, but I shall look into this matter. Make sure Constable White has your contact information and I'll let you know what I discover."

Rashford nodded.

"Yes, sir. Thank you, sir."

Smithson opened the door.

"You have a good day, now. Enjoy your holiday in the Maritimes."

As they walked down the stairs towards the back door and the car park Rashford turned to his escort.

"How did he know I was here on holiday?"

She shrugged.

"I'm guessing your superintendent told him, when she called to set up that meeting."

"My ... Didn't you set up the meeting?"

"Me?" she scoffed. "That's the first time I've had a conversation with the Inspector since I got here. I mean, I know him, and we say hello and stuff, but we don't chat."

"Interesting," said Rashford, pausing at the bottom of the stairs. He looked at the constable.

"He didn't look well, to be honest."

She nodded.

"He's not, not really. He had a cancer scare two or three years ago, lost a lot of weight and then the chemo took his hair. He's only been back at work for a couple of months. They say he's in remission but some days he just looks tired, like today."

Rashford scoffed.

"Mmm. Okay, so what happens now?"

White shrugged.

"Well, I have your cell number, when or if I hear anything, I'll let you know."

Rashford nodded.

"Fair enough," he said. "Thanks for the tour."

She smiled.

"You're welcome. What are your plans for the rest of the day?"

He looked at her.

"I thought I'd wander around downtown, the waterfront, you know.

See the sights. It's my first time in Halifax. I've got my hotel for another night and then I go to Pictou tomorrow."

She nodded.

"I'm off at five," she said, "if you'd like some company later? We could have dinner and a drink."

Rashford grinned.

"That would be great," he said. "Where should we meet?"

"What's your hotel?"

"The Waverley."

"The Waverley? Do you like blues music?"

Rashford nodded.

"Great," she said. "I'll meet you out front of your hotel about seven, if that's okay. There's a great little bar just across the street, it's got food, drink, and blues. Everything you need after a long day sightseeing. I don't think it will be too busy, but I'll book us a table, just in case."

They shook hands, then she went back up the steps and into the building while Rashford went to the car park and found his rental car.

Chapter Two

Now, as he navigated the junction at Truro where the highway from Halifax met the Trans-Canada, Rashford smiled as he remembered his evening with Paula. He had stepped down from the front door of the hotel and found her waiting on the sidewalk, wearing jeans and a sweatshirt, wrapped in a long, crocheted cardigan and matching toque. He had had a pleasant day wandering along the waterfront, enjoying the sunshine and the buskers, the temperature in the high twenties but alleviated a little by the breeze coming off the water.

He was glad he was now wearing a fleece jacket. The sun wouldn't set for another two hours but it had already dropped behind the buildings that rose up the steep streets to the Citadel, west of the harbour, and the air had cooled dramatically. She had shaken his hand and then led him across the busy street, imperiously ignoring the oncoming traffic, and in through the open half of a double wooden door.

The door looked heavy and old, and there was a plaque indicating that the building was a designated heritage property. Once inside, Paula spoke to the young woman standing at the cash register and then turned to the right, leading Rashford up some steps to a small, raised area. She shrugged off her cardigan and placed it and her purse on the back of a wooden kitchen chair, one of two placed around a small table nestled into the corner of the railing. She nodded at the chair opposite, so Rashford sat down. He saw that her hair, which she had let her down out of the bun, was shoulder length and cut to curl up at the ends. To his surprise he saw that, without the bulk of her stab vest and other police accoutrements, she was quite slim in build.

The young woman followed them to the table and stood patiently until they were settled. She placed two menu cards on the table and asked if they would like anything to drink. Nodding to acknowledge their order of a pint of Keith's Red Ale and a large glass of the house sauvignon blanc, she took the 'reserved' sign with her and went back down the steps. Rashford looked around.

To his right there were seven tables, all except one occupied. The crowd seemed to be of mixed generations. Four grey-bearded men with ponytails were sitting at a table across from the steps, deep in conversation as they huddled over a pitcher of beer. At the next table were three young couples who appeared to be of university age, the males with artfully crafted hipster beards and their partners an exotic blush of multihued hair and bright yellow lipstick. In the middle of the space two older women sat chatting quietly, each holding a glass of red wine, and a younger couple leaned against each other at the table up against the back wall. A quick glance over his shoulder had shown him that there were four people at each of the other two tables, but he didn't want to stare to make a full identification. Anyway, Paula White was looking in their direction, and he thought that she would give him warning if any trouble came from those tables.

He looked over the railing and realized that he was peering over the bar itself, which was below him, and then across the main room to an area in the far corner where microphone stands, and two large speakers, stood guard. The main room was busy, with customers walking about and greeting each other, some carrying drinks back from the bar and others waiting for table service. The young woman returned with their drinks and asked if they would like to order food.

"Please give us a few minutes," said Paula. She looked across at Rashford and raised her glass.

"Cheers," she said. They clinked glasses and each took a long drink. Rashford smiled in appreciation.

"That's a nice pint," he said. He picked up one of the menus. "Is there anything you recommend?"

Paula shrugged.

"It's all pretty good," she said. "It's not high cuisine or anything, just basic comfort food, but properly cooked and good portions. It's pretty famous for its ribs."

Rashford nodded and read the menu. They each pointed out a few things, and when the waitress returned were able to make their order with confidence.

"Calamari and barbeque skewers to share as starters," she confirmed, "then a small Greek salad for the lady and a BBQ rib sandwich with fries for the gentleman. It'll be about ten to fifteen minutes."

Rashford smiled at her.

"Perhaps you could bring us another drink, then," he said. "If we're going to be waiting."

She nodded, then walked away.

They had stayed for both sets, enjoying the food, the drink, and the music. Before and in between the sets they had talked about their lives, both in the police and before, and found they had a number of things in common and shared much the same outlook on the world.

Paula had spoken of her twelve years in the military police, which she had joined at age eighteen.

"I was proud to be a meathead," she laughed, "but in the end I decided I wanted something else. I left the army and took a year off, travelling, then went back to university and did a BA in Criminology at St. Mary's. After that, it was an easy transition to the civilian police."

"When you served, did you deploy overseas?" asked Rashford. She nodded.

"I was on Operation Athena, the first tour to Kabul, in zero four," she said. "Then I came home and didn't go back there, so I was lucky, I missed all the horrible stuff. The rest of my time I was mainly in Ottawa, although I did get to spend some time down in the States as well. What about you?"

Rashford shrugged.

"Nothing special, I guess. I didn't really know what to do when I left university, so that summer I just sort of bummed around for a bit. I worked at a couple of local feed stores, hauling bags around, and then when I thought that I had enough money, I took off. I figured it was going to be a whatchamacallit, a 'gap year'. Then nine eleven happened and I figured the end of the world was probably coming, so I might as well make it a gap life. Or something."

She laughed.

"So, this was what, two thousand and one?"

"Yeah. I graduated from university that spring."

She giggled and raised her glass to him.

"I was fifteen that year! You should have seen me with my friends, lowcut jeans and a popcorn shirt, frosted lip gloss, drinking alcopops and singing along to Nelly Furtado."

"That must have been quite the sight."

"I'm sure it was. Five or six of us, arm in arm, staggering down Kent Street after an evening at Myron's."

She turned pensive.

"I thought I was free like a bird, you know, even though now I realize that I had no idea what those lyrics meant. Anyway, I finished high school, then went to St.-Jean for BOTC."

"Botch? What's that?"

"It's an acronym. It means Basic Officer Training Course. It's run out of Quebec."

"Is that where you are from?"

"No, not at all. I grew up in Charlottetown."

"You're an Islander?"

"No, I'm a *Come From Away*. I was adopted, sort of like a down-market Anne of Green Gables. I didn't lose my parents, they lost me."

Paula was quiet for a minute, sipping her wine. Then she waved at the waitress.

"Another round, please," she called. She looked at Rashford.

"We're supposed to be enjoying ourselves, not telling sad stories. So, tell me a funny one. It's two thousand and one, the twin towers have fallen, then what did you do?"

"I'd worked all summer and after Labour Day decided to hitchhike to Vancouver, you know, see the country. But the first ride I got was going to Winnipeg, so I went east instead. I met a girl in Toronto, so I stayed there for about a week, but then she hooked up with someone else and I left. I thought I'd try to get to Vancouver, again. I was in Sault Ste. Marie on the tenth. I got a cheap room downtown, near the bus station. The next morning, I'd slept in a bit and went into a diner for some breakfast, about half-past nine. I can still remember it."

He shook his head, slowly.

"I walked in and there was dead silence. There was a TV up on the wall and everyone was watching it, nobody was eating. The waitress was standing in the aisle, holding a coffee pot at a weird angle and it was dripping onto the floor. The TV was showing that scene when the second plane crashed, the first tower is on fire and then you see the second plane coming in. It was like it was on a loop, over and over again."

He took a large swallow of the new beer the waitress had brought. Paula touched his arm.

"That's not a funny story," she said, quietly.

He nodded.

"Sorry, you're right." He shook his head, blowing air through his lips as he did so, making a rude sound.

"Let me tell you about the time I was on a bus and the driver punched a passenger and left him in the parking lot," he said. She laughed, so he continued. "We were up at Tunnel Mountain, near Banff …"

The waitress appeared and placed more drinks on their table, taking away the empty glasses. The band started to play and so they stopped talking for a while, drinking and applauding through the set. Their meals arrived and they ate, chatting easily about the food as they shared the appetizers and then focused on their main meals. More drinks were ordered and consumed, and their conversation bounced from topic to topic, both of them deliberately trying to up the humor of the evening.

At ten thirty Paula had stretched and said she was feeling tired, so they finished their drinks and Rashford called for the tab. She insisted on splitting the bill and after a short argument, one he quickly realized he wasn't going to win, he gave in gracefully. They each gave their credit cards to the waitress, who ran them through her machine, then made their way carefully down the steps and out of the front door.

The cool evening air felt cold after being inside the bar for over three hours. They walked arm-in-arm across the road and stood below the stairs leading up to the hotel.

"That was a lovely evening," said Rashford. "Thank you."

"Yes, I enjoyed it as well," said Paula, looking up at him. She pulled her cardigan closer to her body.

"Are you chilled?" said Rashford. "Would you like to come in for a minute, to warm up?"

Even as he said it, he thought it sounded a bit lame, but she just laughed. She reached over and patted his cheek.

"That's very kind of you," she said, "but here's my Uber. Enjoy your holiday and remember, if you get stuck on the Island, give me a call. I'm going to be at our family cottage for the last two weeks of July. It's on the north shore, near a place called Goose River. And I'll let you know as soon as I hear anything about the IGG."

She opened the door of the sedan that had pulled up next to them, gave him a final wave, and then closed the door. The car moved slowly off down the street. Rashford watched it disappear around the corner, and for a moment thought about having a cigarette. Then he remembered that he had quit, almost a month and a half ago now, so he turned and went up to his room. The steps seemed longer this evening, but perhaps the six pints of red ale had something to do with that.

He went to the washroom, then cleaned his teeth, then went to bed. As he lay there in a half-awake state, he thought first of Paula, and her laugh, and then of Mandy, and her sexuality. He was starting to feel aroused when he fell asleep.

～

Now he drove along the causeway next to the decommissioned pulp and paper mill, glancing across at the cormorants clustered on old jetty poles that emerged from the bay. At the roundabout he missed his exit and had to go around again, much to the consternation of the drivers behind him. Leaving the cacophony of horns behind, he dropped down the hill into the small town of Pictou. It was still only mid-afternoon so he thought he would do a reconnaissance first.

He followed the one-way system through the shopping area, locating the hall where the concert was going to take place, and then continued along the road leading along the harbour. He passed the country inn where he'd thought of booking a room, reflecting that it looked like a nice enough place, then turned left as instructed by his GPS and followed the road up the hill, turning right at the T-junction. It took him ten minutes to drive the eight kilometres to the lodge where he had reserved a private cabin for two nights. It was late enough that he could check in, so he took the key and drove along the gravel path until he found the correct building.

The inside was comfortable enough, he thought. There was a queen-sized bed with a big fancy duvet, and the windows from both the bedroom and the living room looked out over the water. There were two pushouts built off the living room, one a small kitchenette and the other an eating area with a table big enough for two people, and as well as the normal couch and arm chair the living room had a fireplace and a flat-screen television. All in all, he thought, Mandy would like this. Whistling to himself, he brought his bag inside and arranged his toiletries in the bathroom. He had a shower, then changed into clean clothes. Checking his watch, he saw that he still had two hours until the show started. He locked up the cabin and drove back into town to find something to eat.

It was a warm evening, and he was pleased to find a gastropub with an outside verandah. He was sitting quietly in the shade of the low-slung roof with his beer and a plate of fish and chips when he heard Mandy's laughter. He looked around and was about to stand up and call to her when he realized that she was with someone. Arm-in-arm with someone. Laughing with someone. Slowly he sat down and watched as they walked past, laughing together. He recognized the tall man walking with Mandy. It was Gary, he realized, the drummer from the band. As they went past, Gary leaned over and kissed the top of her head, and she giggled. They disappeared down the road, and Rashford sat, looking at his food. He drained his pint and ordered a second, then picked at his French fries as he processed what he had just seen.

~

The show was a wonderful success. The band had obviously benefited from their almost two weeks of being on the road. The music was tight, and the sound was good. Mandy prowled and flowed around the stage, pulling impossible notes from her fiddle. The crowd loved her, and she received a standing ovation at the end of each solo performance. At the end of the evening the band had to come back out for three encores, and even when the lights eventually went up the audience was still stomping and shouting for more.

Rashford made his way to the stage and had started to mount the stairs when he felt a hand on his shoulder. He turned and found himself face to face with a large man in a black leather jacket. Rashford realized that he was already on the first step, so the man had to be at least six inches taller than he was, which must have put him a fraction under seven feet. Not knowing quite what else to do, Rashford smiled.

"Hello," he said. "Can I help you?"

"The way out is over there, sir," said the man, not moving his hand. "Step down off the stage, please."

Rashford shook his head.

"It's okay," he said, still smiling. "I'm with the band."

The man looked at him.

"Where's your pass?"

Rashford reached into his pocket for his ticket. He sensed that the man stiffened, then relaxed when he pulled out the square piece of paper. The man gave it a quick glance.

"That's a ticket, sir. Not a backstage pass."

Rashford looked at him.

"This is all she left for me, at the door," he said, shaking his head.

"Who, sir?"

"Mandy. The fiddle player. Amanda Robicheau. She's my friend."

Rashford realized that he was starting to gabble but he could not stop himself. A few of the other late stayers from the audience were watching, elbowing each other and listening to the conversation. The security guard tightened his grip.

"You need a pass to go up there," he said, his voice dropping in volume. "Please step down, now."

Rashford straightened up, reaching to brush the hand from his shoulder. He forced himself to stay calm.

"Or what?" he said, looking straight at the man.

"Or we bring you down," came the response, as the man nodded to a second, equally large colleague who emerged from the side of the stage and walked towards them. "You don't really want that, do you?"

Rashford took a deep breath and stepped down to the floor level of the room. As he had surmised, he now found himself looking up at the man, who must have topped seven feet in height. The second man was more Rashford's size, about six feet five inches tall. The three formed a triangle at the bottom of the steps down from the stage, the two staring at him and he flicking his glance between them. He sensed another presence on the stage behind him and risked a quick look over his shoulder, then relaxed marginally.

"Seabass," he called. "Can you help me here, please."

He heard footsteps approach and felt a shadow cast by the stage lights fall on his back.

"Gavin?"

Rashford nodded.

"Yes. Hi. I was just going back to see Mandy and these gentlemen won't let me."

"He doesn't have a pass," said the larger security guard. "He's just got a ticket."

"I tell you, that's all she left for me," said Rashford.

There was a pause.

"Come on, then," said Sebastian. "I'll vouch for him. I know Mandy has been expecting him to be here tonight."

The two security guards shrugged.

"On you, mate," said the second one, and they both walked away. Rashford turned and went up the four steps to the stage, where he shook Sebastian's hand.

"Thanks," he said. "Where is she?"

"They're in the dressing rooms," said the roadie. "Follow me and I'll show you."

~

"I left it at the ticket office," said Mandy, her hands on her hips. "Didn't you ask for it?"

"I just gave them my name and said there was a ticket for me," said Rashford. "That's all they gave me. A ticket."

"A ticket and a pass," she said.

"I didn't ask for a pass."

"How did you expect to get backstage, then?"

Rashford shrugged.

"The way I do back in Saskatchewan," he said. "You know, climb on the stage and push though the curtains. I wasn't expecting you to have your own private stormtroopers."

She shook her head in exasperation, her voice low and precise.

"Honestly, Gavin, you just don't get it, do you? We're getting to be big stars, now. We've been on radio and television, and all our shows are sold out. We have to have protection."

They were standing in a hallway just outside the dressing room area. The rest of the band were inside, slouched on couches and mainly drinking from large bottles of fizzy water, although Mick the lead guitarist had already switched to beer. Sebastian was on stage, wrestling with cables and large speakers, and Nigel Woods the sound guy had nodded to them distractedly as he went out to the van, already playing a game on his phone.

"Protection?" he said, annoyed, starting to feel that he was getting blamed for this mess and not sure why. "And who protects you when the stormtroopers aren't there? Gary?"

Mandy stopped as though struck, her mouth open and her eyes wide.

"Gary? What do you mean?"

"I saw you two earlier, canoodling in town. You walked right past where I was grabbing some food."

She stared at him.

"Canoodling?"

He nodded, already regretting opening his mouth, but now not sure how to stop the words.

"You were arm in arm, and he kissed your hair."

She shook her head, slowly.

"You idiot," she said. "Is that what was bothering you? Look, he's got a partner. They're very happy together. We were just laughing about something he'd noticed over the past few days, that Monica and Seabass the roadie were meeting at odd hours, to 'test their connections', apparently. For heaven's sake, don't be so paranoid. And anyway ..."

She took a deep breath, and her voice seemed to drop another twenty decibels and become even more precise.

"And anyway, what if we were? Canoodling, or whatever you call it. What if he wasn't gay? What if we'd been having a quickie, just to let off steam? What's that to you? We're not married, are we? I don't watch over you and question everything you do, do I?"

He held out his hands.

"Look, I'm sorry. I've missed you, that's all. I've been so looking forward to seeing you, and I jumped to conclusions when I did."

She shrugged, reverting to a normal conversational tone.

"You don't own me, Gavin, and I'm not going to let you."

"I know. I know. I'm sorry. Come here. Please."

Mandy stood still for a moment, then stepped forward. He opened his arms and hugged her tightly, nestling his face in her hair.

"I've missed you so much," he said.

She thumped his chest with her hand.

"It's still just enthusiastic sex, Gavin," she said. "Remember? I can't do a relationship and my career as well."

The cabin served its purpose as a peaceful haven. They woke late the next morning and took their coffee down to the shore, where they sat on the granite rocks and looked at the gulls circling the inlet.

"You really did quit?" said Mandy, surprised that Rashford was only holding a cup. He nodded.

"Yup. May thirty-first."

"Why then?"

"It was World No Tobacco Day."

"Says who?"

"The United Nations."

She looked at him. "Really?"

"Scout's honour. You can look it up."

Mandy shook her head.

"Oh, I believe you. I'm just not sure why?"

Rashford shrugged.

"I'd been thinking about it for a while," he said. "Then one day I was channel surfing, and I came across this documentary about Big Tobacco. You know, how they fudged all those studies back in the fifties, made smoking sexy even when they knew it was causing cancer. Anyway, I watched the rest of the show, and at the end someone mentioned that there was a World No Tobacco Day, and it was celebrated on the last day of May. That was about a week away. I had just over half a pack left so I rationed them out and smoked my last one just before midnight on the thirtieth. Then I quit."

"Just like that?"

He sipped his coffee.

"So far so good, yes," he said.

She smiled at him.

"Are all your habits as easy to quit?" she laughed.

He rolled his eyes.

"Sadly, no," he said. "Some habits I just itch for all the time."

"You itch for them?"

"Yes."

"Would it help if I scratched that itch?"

He nodded.

"Yes, please,"

She stood up and slapped his shoulder.

"Don't beg," she said. "It's unbecoming."

Then she took his hand and led him back into the cabin.

When they re-emerged, it was almost noon. Mandy settled in the front seat of the rental car while Rashford drove aimlessly around, turning at random junctions and following the road for a while before turning again. They visited a lavender farm, amazed at the multiple rows of purple and mauve plants, the neat earthen mounds a rich brown against the freshly cut green grass. Mandy bought some bars of soap and a jar of honey, both flavoured with lavender, while Rashford bought three packets of seeds.

"These will go to Bettina, Gayle, and Sarah," he said, laughing.

Mandy nodded.

"Okay, but what about the Superintendent? Or Sheri?"

"I'll keep looking for something for them," he said.

A few turns later they came to a garden centre, where they wandered around looking at plants.

"That's beautiful," said Mandy, wistfully gazing at a metal obelisk covered in a vine. The obelisk was about a metre tall, and the vine cascaded around it, covered with a profusion of large red flowers that had a white centre with golden tipped anthers. Rashford leaned closer and peered at the tag.

"That's a Rouge Cardinal Clematis," he said. "Will it fit in your suitcase?"

Mandy scoffed, then pulled out her phone.

"Not likely," she said. "But I'll take a picture and see if I can look for one, when I get back home."

She clicked a couple of times, then had Rashford hold the tag so she could document that as well.

"The climate here is so much better than ours," she muttered. "They have proper seasons. Everybody talks about the fall colours, and the spring must be fabulous. I think we just have winter and summer, there's no real in-between."

"Well, don't forget construction season," said Rashford.

Mandy smiled.

"There is that," she said.

They followed a few more roads and ended up at the highway, where Rashford turned and drove back towards Pictou. As they came over the causeway Mandy pointed out a worn poster stuck to one of the road signs.

"No pipe in the Strait," she read. "That's what closed the mill, you know."

Rashford looked at her.

"What do you mean?"

"One of the local guys was telling us yesterday, at the sound check. There used to be a big pulp and paper mill here, apparently you could smell it for miles, but it's closed now. The company wanted to pump the wastewater straight into the Strait, if you see what I mean, and the government wouldn't let them."

"Straight into the Strait?"

Mandy giggled.

"Yes, but they're spelled differently. Anyway, they didn't spend the money to put in scrubbers or whatever, to clean the water, so the mill got closed."

Rashford nodded.

"I bet that's why there are so many cormorants," he said, gesturing towards the prehistoric looking black birds perched on the old jetty poles. "They must like unpolluted fish."

"There are happy fishermen, as well," said Mandy. "Especially those who catch lobster or who harvest oysters. It's only the foresters and mill workers who are not happy, the people who lost their jobs. The guy at the soundcheck told us that there's not a lot of other work around here."

Rashford stayed silent, not knowing quite what to say to that. When they approached the roundabout, he took the correct turning and drove down the hill, then took the first right and went along the waterfront, stopping alongside the harbour. They were next to a small jetty where a wooden ship was moored. Rashford pointed.

"Do you want to visit the ship? It's called the Hector. It's a replica of the ship that brought the first Scottish settlers here to Nova Scotia."

Mandy looked doubtful.

"It's got a nice little museum as well," said Rashford. "We can look in there."

Mandy sighed.

"Sure, if you want to," she said, and opened the car door. As she stood on the pavement she paused, looking around. Some voices started shouting and she hurried back inside the car, slamming the door behind her.

"What is it?" said Rashford, just as a group of young men and women surrounded the car and started banging on the windows.

"Amanda! Amanda!" they shouted. "Can I have your autograph?"

~

"Does that happen a lot?" said Rashford, once he had extricated the car from the raucous crowd. He had got out and calmed them down, then Mandy had opened the door and stood with them for a few moments, chatting. She had signed some notebooks, a t-shirt, and one young man's arm, then posed for selfies as they all flashed their phones. She had got back into the car and waved as Rashford had driven away.

"That's the first time," she said. "I mean, I've had people ask for autographs and pictures before, they did that in Saint John's and in Sydney as well, but not aggressive like that. That was scary. I'm glad you were there."

She patted his arm as he drove.

"I guess we'll avoid the museum and the ship," he said, laughing. "What do you fancy for dinner?"

Mandy shrugged.

"We can eat in," she said. "I saw a supermarket up by that roundabout where we came in, and we have the kitchen in the cabin. It would be good to cook something and not eat out in a restaurant for a change."

"Sounds good," said Rashford. He worked his way around the one-way system and then back up the hill, having to circumnavigate the roundabout again before finding the somewhat disguised turning to the supermarket.

"Look, there's a liquor store here as well," he said. "We're in luck!"

"Do you mind if I stay in the car?" said Mandy. "I should have brought some dark glasses and a hat, sorry."

"No worries," he said. "I'll be right back. Do you want anything special?"

"Not to eat. Whatever you get will be fine. I wouldn't mind some white wine, though. A nice Pinot Grigio from Florence if you can find one."

Rashford nodded, then left the car and dashed first to the liquor store, where he bought a bottle of Ermacora Pinot Grigio and another of

Lungarotti Torre di Giano Bianco, plus half a dozen cans of Keith's Red Ale. He dropped those back to the car before heading back to the store. When he got back a second time, he placed his full carrier bag on the back seat. Mandy sniffed as he put the bag, and his head, inside

"I went the easy route," he laughed. "I got one of those bar-b-que roasted chickens and a baguette, some butter, some mayonnaise, a ready-made salad with dressing in a little pouch, and some chips for dessert."

Belatedly, he saw the look on her face.

"What's wrong?"

Mandy was holding one of the wine bottles.

"This is from Udine, not Florence. Udine is up past Bologna and Venice. It's almost in Slovenia."

"It was the best pinot grigio I could find," he said. "The other one is from just south of Perugia. That's near Florence, isn't it?"

She looked at him.

"Near? It's over a hundred and fifty kilometers. That's like you saying the stage monitor at the Majestic was in the right place. It wasn't. It was near. Precision, Gavin." She shook her head. "That's what's missing sometimes. Never mind. A wine from Torgiano will be fine."

She returned the bottle to the bag with the others and leaned over to lay it in the back seat. Rashford stood up and closed the rear door, taking care to do so quietly, then put his head back and stared at the sky. He closed his eyes for a moment and took two deep breaths, then went round the front of the car and got back into the driver's seat. Slowly he exited the car park and turned left, away from Pictou and back towards the roundabout. Mandy looked across at him.

"Where are we going?" she said.

"I'm going to take the ferry road," he said. "I think there's a road from the terminal back to the lodge. If I'm right, then we'll save ourselves a trip through town in the morning."

They drove down the long stretch between trees, slowing down as they saw the first speed warning for the ferry and passed under the Three Brooks Road bridge.

"That's the road," muttered Rashford. "The exit should be somewhere here. On the right."

"This next one's called Ferry Road," said Mandy, looking at the GPS. "I think we take this and link up with the other one."

They did, and ten minutes later drove into the lodge. As they approached the entry, Rashford beat a staccato drum roll on the steering wheel.

"That will save us a lot of time tomorrow," he said. "The ferry is at nine, but all the guidebooks say you have to be there early, at least an hour and a half, because you can't make a reservation."

Mandy stared at him.

"Yes, you can. We did."

"You must have bought a ticket coming off PEI, then. There's no cost going this way, so you can't book. If you want a return leaving from PEI, you can get one as part of your ticket. But not going from here, one way. It's a free trip, but you have to take your chances with the queue."

Mandy shrugged.

"I don't know how we did it, but I know we had a reservation for this morning's ferry, for the van."

Rashford chuffed.

"Well, we don't, so we need to be leaving here just after seven tomorrow, to make sure we're on the nine o'clock boat. If we miss it, we'll have to wait until eleven thirty or something."

"We can't miss it," said Mandy, getting out of the car and stretching. "I have a sound check at one o'clock, you promised me I'd be there for it. Not near there, actually there."

"It'll be fine," said Rashford, picking up the bag of food and the bag of wine, kicking the door shut with his heel, and following Mandy up the narrow path to the cabin. As he went in through the door, his phone rang. He put the bags down on the counter and answered. Mandy had gone through to the bathroom and was calling out something about the towels, but he raised one finger in the air and held the phone to his ear. All he could hear was sobbing, words jumbling together.

"Slow down," he said. "Who is this? I can't hear you."

Mandy came into the room, holding a large fluffy towel in each hand. She looked across at Rashford, who waved his finger at her and pulled a face.

"Hello? Who is this, please?"

There was a pause.

"Roxanne?" he said. Mandy raised an eyebrow.

"Anne, what's the matter?"

He held the phone away from his ear as she gulped, noisily.

"You've got to help me," she cried. "Someone's murdered my dad."

Chapter Three

Mandy silently took the towels back into the bathroom. She went to the kitchen, ignoring Rashford as he paced around the couch, and re-emerged with a large glass of wine. She stepped past him again and went outside, taking her drink down to the rocks by the shore. Ten minutes later she came back in and carved up the cold chicken, lying slices of breast meat on one plate and a leg and thigh on another. She opened the bag of salad and divided it between the two plates, then squeezed some of the dressing over each serving. She cut a three-inch wedge from the pound of butter and put it in a small dish, then cut some of the baguette into slices and put it in a larger bowl. She finished her second glass in one long swallow, then took the glass, the packet of potato chips, and the wine bottle with her out to the rocks. She had eaten half the chips, and was on her fourth glass of wine, when Rashford appeared. He sat down next to her.

"Sorry about that," he said.

Mandy was silent. She picked up a small pebble and threw it, underarm, into the sea. It gave a splash as it disappeared. She stood up, then turned and looked down at him.

"If you've finished, dinner is ready," she said, and walked back into the cabin. Rashford sat for a moment, looking at the shallow waves rolling up onto the shingle beach and then running back out with a shushing sound. He gave a sigh, then got up and went inside. He found her in the nook, putting the plates on the table, so he went to the kitchen and collected cutlery, salt and pepper, some napkins, and the jar of mayonnaise. Mandy was already sitting at her place when he put them on the table.

"Thank you for your help," she said, tonelessly.

Rashford bit back his initial retort, and instead muttered a quiet "you're welcome." He went back to the kitchen and picked one of the cans of beer from the fridge, then took it and a glass back to the table, where he sat down at the other place.

"This looks great," he said. "Thank you."

Mandy shrugged.

"You bought it. All I did was put it on a plate."

She finished her glass of wine. He poured her a refill and realized that it was the end of the bottle. He quietly placed the empty on the table.

"What's the matter?"

She looked at him, and he saw that her mascara had run, thin black lines under her eyes.

"You tell me. She called you, not me."

He took a deep breath.

"Yes, Mandy, that was Roxanne. Sorry, I still can't get used to calling her Anne. She called me because she thinks her father has been murdered. The police have told her it was an accident, but she doesn't believe them. She's hired a private investigator and wants me to help him."

"How?"

"How what?"

"How does she want you to help him, and how did she know you were here?"

Rashford put down his knife and fork and looked at her.

"She didn't know I was here. She thought I was in Saskatchewan. She wanted me to call this fellow and ask him questions, to make sure he was doing everything properly."

"You didn't tell her you were coming east?"

"No. Why would I? I was going to be your personal groupie, remember, at your beck and call. I thought I might see if you'd be okay with me comping her and her mom, Sandra, with tickets to the show in Charlottetown on Monday, but I haven't done that yet."

He stood up, then went and kneeled next to her, hugging her tightly.

"Look, she is in the past, okay? She has her own life here, back in her home place. She has family and friends. She contacted me because she's frantic about her dad, the accident, all that. No other reason. For heaven's sake, I didn't even tell her that I'm going to be on PEI, because I wanted to check it with you first."

Mandy dug into her pocket and pulled out a Kleenex, which she proceeded to use to wipe her eyes. The mascara smeared in a thin arc. She blew her nose, then leaned into him.

"Sorry," she said.

He squeezed her again, then stood.

"Would you like some more wine?"

"In a minute," she said, choking back a laugh. "Maybe I'd better eat some food first."

They finished their meal and cleared up, then Mandy suggested they go to bed before she had anything more to drink.

"Otherwise, I'll just be going to sleep," she said, "and this might be our last night for a while."

"Why?" said Rashford, unsure where the conversation was going.

She huffed.

"Well, the next three nights I'm sharing a camper van with Monica in Rollo Bay, and after the Charlottetown and Summerside shows we've got gigs booked all across New Brunswick. We have a travel day on the ferry from Saint John to Digby, but this is our last day off until the end of the tour."

He nodded gravely.

"We should certainly not waste it, then," he said, leaning forward so she could put her arms around his neck. Standing upright, he cupped her bottom in his hands and squeezed. She wrapped her legs around his waist.

"Are you going to carry me to the bedroom and have your wicked way with me?" she asked.

"If you insist," he said.

The alarm function on his phone sent out an incessant beep just before six o'clock the next morning. Rashford jumped to his feet and looked at Mandy, who was still asleep. He went to the bathroom and came back, then pulled the corner of the covers down and shook her shoulder. She groaned and tried to pull the duvet back up over her head. Rashford held it down.

"Come on," he said. "We have an hour. We have to leave here at seven."

She lifted her head and pulled out the pillow, then flipped it so it covered her face. Rashford stripped the duvet completely off the bed, leaving her naked, only her head covered. Shaking his head, he walked to the bottom of the bed, drinking in the view. Then he leaned over, index finger extended, and slowly start to rub his finger tip up and down the sensitive sole of her foot. Mandy squealed.

"No tickling," she cried, curling her feet beneath her and simultaneously throwing the pillow at Rashford's head. "That's not fair."

"Up and at 'em, your ladyship," he said. "Your chariot leaves in an hour. Fifty-five minutes, actually."

"Don't shout at me," she mumbled, swinging her legs off the bed and standing up. She paused for a moment, head bowed, her hand on the mattress to support herself, and took a deep breath. Rashford grinned.

"Bathroom's clear," he said. "I've already washed up. I'll use the rest of that baguette to make some toast while you get ready."

"No food, just coffee," she said, walking slowly across the room and closing the bathroom door quietly behind her.

Rashford shrugged, then went into the kitchenette. He put the pre-packed coffee pouch into the percolator, added water, and switched it on. Then he ripped off a chunk of baguette and walked outside, chewing slowly. The sea was calm, and the tide was going out. He wandered down onto the sand, which was damp under his feet, and walked along for a few hundred metres.

A couple sitting on matching red Adirondack chairs outside the adjacent cabin called out hello as he passed, waving, and he waved back. A gull sitting on a pile of washed-up kelp shrugged itself to its feet as he approached, then lazily flew away. He reached the seaweed and turned, walking slowly back to his cabin. There was no sign of Mandy, so he poured himself a coffee and took it outside to one of their chairs, which were blue.

The sun had peeked above the wooded hills of Cape George to the east, and he relaxed as he felt the warmth on his face. He smiled, remembering the last – and only – time he had driven around Cape George, when he and Roxanne, as she was then, had made their way down to the beach from the lighthouse on the point. As he thought of that day, his mind naturally segued to the phone call he had received the previous evening.

"The police said that he must have had a medical problem, or else not been paying attention, and just caught the edge of the ditch and rolled the car. But they're wrong. He was healthy, and he's a really good driver. He was always really careful. Someone must have done something to his car."

Rashford had decided not to mention that her dad had now reached his early seventies and had perhaps not been as meticulous as he used to be. He also decided not to mention that the police would no doubt have had, sadly, a lot of experience in examining motor vehicle accidents. He knew that he had been to more than he wished to remember. Instead, he had cleared his throat.

"Look, this private detective you hired, he'll check into all that. But really, isn't it more likely that the police are correct? That this was just an accident?"

Anne had cried again.

"No, it can't be. Will you to talk to him and make sure he's looking properly?"

He had agreed to phone the man, who was apparently a retired police sergeant, and noted down his details. He had considered telling Anne that he was going to be on the Island soon, but then had decided not to until he had spoken to Mandy. He was glad he'd made that decision.

He checked his phone, discovering that it was already six thirty. He got to his feet and returned to the cabin. Mandy was still in the bathroom, so he packed up his things and put the left-over food into the green bin. The unopened wine he slipped into his bag. Then he knocked on the door of the bathroom.

"Twenty minutes," he called, receiving a muttered reply in response. He took his bag out to the car and placed it in the trunk. When he got back to the cabin, Mandy was standing in the front room, coffee in hand, looking out over the water.

"I'm nearly ready," she said, her voice scratchy. "I'll just be a minute."

He nodded, then came over and stood next to her.

"It's beautiful," she said. "I love the ocean. One day I'm going to live with a view like this."

They arrived at the ferry port at a quarter past seven. The woman in the toll booth waved them through, directing them to lane nine. Lane ten was already full, and there were already a number of cars in their line, so Rashford eased down the hill and joined the end of the queue. To their far left, seven cars were parked in lane fifteen, and to their right were a number of large semi-trailers, the drivers playing with their phones or snoozing with their heads against the window glass. Mandy put on a baseball cap and dark glasses, then eased out of the car.

"I just need to use the washroom," she muttered, and walked down the hill to the building that offered snacks, maps, and facilities to those who wanted them. Rashford stood by the car, watching the cluster of people who had walked to the concrete bollard that separated the parking area from the road that would carry vehicles leaving the ferry. They were standing apart, in ones or twos, sometimes nodding at newcomers but not talking to each other. They were smokers, he realized, and for a moment thought about going over to join them. Not to smoke, not really, but just to inhale, and to be part of the community.

Mandy returned looking a bit happier. She took a deep breath and then nodded towards the people by the bollard.

"They have reservations," she said. "Someone in the ladies told me."

Rashford looked.

"They're the smokers," he said. "It's not allowed on ferry property."

She scowled at him.

"Not the people, the cars. The ones in that last lane. They'll get on first."

He nodded.

"Yes, they'll be Islanders going home. They paid extra to have a reservation to come over this way, so they get a free reservation to go back. But we didn't come over, we're only going one way. You only pay to leave the Island."

She scoffed.

"How on earth do you know that?"

He shrugged.

"I was here before, remember. I've done this trip. When I went to Cape Breton."

Mandy smiled, sweetly.

"Ah, yes. With Roxanne or whatever she calls herself. I remember."

"It's Anne," he muttered. "Oh, look, there's the ferry."

He was grateful that she turned and looked, although he more than ever wanted to go over to the bollard. They watched as the ferry slowly eased into its berth, then after a great deal of clanging and banging the first vehicles started to drive over the corrugated metal ramp. The motorbikes came first, then the big transports and the logging trucks, followed by campervans and trucks pulling boats or trailers. Eventually there was a steady stream of cars, and before the last had passed an employee in a high visibility vest climbed down from their golf cart and started waving the cars in lane fifteen to move forward. Mandy muttered impatiently while they were loaded, and them with distress when the next group to be beckoned were the semi-trailers and the camper vans.

"There's not going to be room for us," she cried, sniffling. "Do something, Gavin. Go and tell them we have to get on."

"Just calm down," he said. "They have to load in a specific sequence, to balance the weight. There's lots of room."

She shuffled impatiently as the line of cars next to them started to move forward, then let out a sigh of relief when the worker waved at the cars in front of them. They drove down and across the corrugated metal, which bowed alarmingly, then they bumped onto the ferry itself and were directed down into the cavernous hull. Rashford eased down the ramp and was waved into the outside lane, then directed to pull up close to the car in front. He turned off the engine.

"Happy now?"

Mandy had the grace to look contrite.

"Yes, thank you."

He opened the door.

"Right, come on. Let's go and see if there's any breakfast left."

Mandy shook her head.

"Just coffee, please," she said. "My head still hurts."

"Self-inflicted," he grinned, and led her through the parked cars and up the long flights of steps to the passenger deck.

"Can you see if you can grab us a table?" he said. "I'll get your coffee, and my breakfast."

The journey across the Northumberland Strait was uneventful. It was calm, the ferry plowing through the gentle waves with ease. Mandy had taken one look at Rashford's plate, an 'Islander Special' of fried eggs, bacon, hash browns, and toast, to which he had added a liberal sploosh of ketchup, and quickly excused herself to go outside. He had finished his meal and then wandered out to find her standing by the rail, looking out over the bow of the ship. She wrapped her arms around herself, running her hands up and down her biceps.

"Is that PEI, coming up?"

Rashford looked at the low ribbon of land emerging out of the horizon.

"I think so, yes. We should be there soon."

"I just saw another ferry, going the other way."

Rashford nodded.

"Yes, they have two, especially in the summer. They usually pass each other in the middle of the Strait. So, we must be over halfway there."

Mandy continued to stare out to sea. When she at last spoke, her voice was quiet and pensive.

"This is a huge weekend for me, you know. The Festival. There are going to be all sorts of people there, talent scouts, agents, managers. The band wants to do well, but I know that they are already looking forward to getting home. This is just a fun adventure for them. But for me, it's a chance to really make a go of things."

Rashford nodded, not sure what to say, or whether he should say anything.

"I know I am good, but so are a lot of people. That's only the starting point. Once you get there, then the real work starts. The hard work."

Rashford nodded, this time adding a vocalized hmm-hmm in agreement. She turned and smiled at him.

"I knew you'd understand," she said, then leaned across and kissed his cheek. "Thank you."

They stood silently again, watching the land draw nearer and details starting to emerge. A long red sandstone bank, a crest of dark green indicating trees, a lighthouse flashing its warning. Rashford cleared his throat.

"What do you really want?" he said. "Apart from a house looking over the ocean, that is."

She laughed.

"I want to be rich and famous, of course, who doesn't? And I want to be the best Métis fiddle player in the world."

Rashford rolled his eyes. He didn't particularly want to be rich and famous, and he already thought she was the best Métis fiddle player in the world.

"So, what's the first step? After being good, I mean."

"Being noticed, so that other people see how good I really am. And then getting better. Playing with better musicians, in bigger venues, with larger crowds. Getting paid lots of money to play. And selling lots of merch."

"Merch?"

"Yes, merch. Merchandise. You know, CDs, vinyl, t-shirts, children's clothes, jackets, hats, everything. That's where the real money is. And perhaps getting on tv, my own show. There are just so many possibilities. But first you have to be good. Then noticed. Then practice. Then get better. Then be noticed by more people. And so on."

Rashford shook his head, amazed that she had thought everything through with such clarity.

"And it all starts here, at Rollo Bay?"

"It all starts here."

He wished they still allowed smoking on the ferry. He needed a cigarette.

"I'll be back in a minute," he said.

He came back with two small coffees and a chocolate bar, which he broke in half.

"You have to eat something," he said. "You can't live on coffee."

She murmured her thanks and took a bite. Rashford ate his half in one swallow, then took a deep breath.

"So, is this you saying goodbye?"

She shrugged.

"I'm just being realistic. I hope we'll still be friends."

Rashford scoffed.

"Even when you're rich and famous?"

"Especially when I'm rich and famous. I'll still need friends."

He bit back his retort that she could always buy some. Instead, he simply nodded. She looked off to the right of the ship, where a group of large white birds with black wing tips were circling. One after the other they folded their wings and arrowed down into the sea, surfacing a moment later. They sat on the waves for a moment, then flew up and rejoined the flock.

"Aren't they beautiful?" she said.

He nodded. "They're gannets, fishing."

She huffed.

"Plenty of fish in the sea," she said.

He was considering a response when the tannoy blared the information that they would soon be docking at Wood Islands, and that all drivers should return to their cars. They took their coffee and walked carefully down the steps back into the hold, then sat in the car in silence. There were some loud clangs as the ferry docked, and then the front hatch opened up and light flooded in. A man in a high visibility jacket waited a few minutes, listening to a two-way radio, and then opened the bar that extended across the opening. He waved at the first car in line, and it moved forward. Rashford started the engine and followed the traffic up the ramp and into the sunshine.

They drove past the long line ups of vehicles waiting to leave the island and turned right onto Route 315. Mandy looked at the GPS.

"It's about fifty minutes," she said.

Rashford nodded.

They drove without speaking, each looking at the scenery. Rashford sighed when they passed two dogs copulating vigorously in the driveway to a farm. Mandy giggled.

"That looks enthusiastic," she said.

Rashford drove on.

At the gate to the Festival Grounds, they were stopped by a man holding a clipboard. Standing outside a small ticket booth, he was shirtless, his arms and torso covered in tattoos, and incongruously wearing a large floppy brimmed hat.

The man leaned into the driver's side window.

"Only artists allowed just now," he said. "The gate doesn't open until five."

Mandy reached into her purse and held out a laminated card to the man.

"I'm playing," she said. "Amanda Robicheau."

He checked his list, then nodded. He looked at Rashford.

"I'm with the band," said Rashford, wondering how many more times he would get to say that. For some reason he thought of Sarah, wearing her inappropriate dress and hanging off his arm as they entered the Majestic. He smiled.

The man looked back at his list.

"It's okay," said Mandy, matter-of-factly. "He's not staying. He's just dropping me off."

"Fair enough," said the man, waving them through. "The campers for the performers are up there to the right."

They drove across a large grassy area that would undoubtedly soon be a very busy car park, but which presently looked just like a field. There were twenty or so camper vans parked in two long lines, most with cars or motorbikes in close proximity.

"There's our van," said Mandy, pointing along the second row. Rashford drove up and parked next to it. He turned off the ignition and they both sat quietly for a moment.

"Will you come to the show in Charlottetown?" she said.

He looked at her.

"Can I?"

She pouted.

"Don't be silly. I'll leave you a ticket at the door. And a pass."

Rashford nodded.

"Can I bring Anne and her mom?"

"Yes, of course. I'll leave four tickets, in case one of them wants to bring a friend."

"Thank you."

There was an awkward silence. Mandy picked at a fingernail.

"And if you manage to get to any of the other shows, just text me before, and I ... no, wait. There's Mick. Just a minute."

She got out of the car and waved at the lead guitarist, who had just stepped down from the camper van and was lighting a cigarette. He waved back.

"You made it, then. We were getting worried."

"I'm here," she said, then moved towards him. Rashford could hear them talking but not make out the words. Mick nodded, then handed Mandy his cigarette and went back inside the van. A few minutes later he came out and took back the cigarette, giving her something in return. She walked back to the car and climbed into the front seat.

"Here," she said, handing him a laminated card like the one she had shown at the gate. "This is an all-access pass, good for any of the shows on our tour. You just come to whichever ones you want, enjoy the music, then show this and come backstage afterwards."

"No stormtroopers?"

She laughed and punched his arm.

"No stormtroopers, promise."

Rashford nodded.

"Thank you."

She leaned over and held his face in her hands, then kissed him. She leaned back.

"It was just enthusiastic sex, Gavin. And it was good. And if you come and see me after one of the shows, who knows? We might do an encore."

He smiled.

"That would be good," he said, then leaned over and kissed her as completely as he had ever kissed anyone. Eventually she pushed him away, at the same time brushing a tear from her eye.

"Off you go," she said. "I have to get my game face on."

He nodded, then got out of the car and retrieved her bag. He saw that Gary had come out of the camper and was standing next to Mick, watching them. He handed the bag to Mandy and gave her a quick kiss on the cheek.

"Knock 'em dead," he said, then waved at the men before getting back into his car. As he drove away, he glanced in the mirror and saw Mandy looking after him. She waved, then turned and went to meet her bandmates.

Chapter Four

The drive to Charlottetown took just over an hour. Rashford paid little notice to the scenery or even the other traffic. He knew there was a ninety kilometres per hour limit on the Island so he set the cruise control at a steady ninety-eight, believing that any police who noticed him would give him the normally allowed plus ten percent grace period. He didn't see any marked cruisers, although he was sure there would be ghost cars mixed in with the regular traffic. The farms and forests blurred by as he remembered some of the special times he had shared with Mandy.

The day matched his mood. Clouds had been building since late morning and were now billowing up over the Strait. Some had segued from white to grey, others were morphing into a more ominous black. The light on the fields made the crops stand out crisply against the red soil. He passed a herd of cows all lying down by the fence, which he remembered his grandmother describing as a sign of rain to come. But perhaps that was just on the prairies.

At the outskirts of the city, he pulled off at the second roundabout he encountered and parked at a Tim Horton's attached to a gas station. He sat in the car with his coffee and an apple fritter and scrolled through his phone looking for last minute accommodation bargains. He knew better than to walk off the street and pay the rack rate. Sure enough, he found a special discounted rate at a hotel near the downtown and immediately booked it.

He put the address into his GPS and then drove over the Hillsborough Bridge into Charlottetown itself. His eyes blurred as he saw the cormorants sitting on the stone pillars, all that remained of the old railway bridge, and he heard Mandy's laugh as she talked about pumping wastewater straight into the Strait. Shaking his head, he focused on what the GPS was telling him, and eventually pulled into a budget hotel just off one of the main streets, at the edge of the downtown core.

Once he had checked in and unpacked his toiletries, he sat on the bed and considered his options. He thought about not connecting with Anne until the next morning, and simply having a quiet evening in the hotel, but he knew he would probably go out to eat and there was too high a chance he would bump into her or her mother. Shaking his head at himself, he picked up his phone.

Anne was both surprised and ecstatic that he was in Charlottetown. At first, she did not believe him, asking him to look outside his hotel window and describe the weather. It was only after he had described the clouds, and what he thought was the threat of rain, that she believed he was actually in the city. She gave him her address and insisted that he go round immediately.

Rashford grabbed his jacket and walked down the street, passing a large Chinese restaurant and an office complex before coming to a small parade of shops. He crossed at the traffic light and in the next block, between a coffee shop and a natural foods store, he found the door she had mentioned. He pressed the bell and heard her voice on the intercom.

"It's me, Gavin," he said, and there was a click as the door unlocked. He walked up the stairs and at the landing saw two doors, one each to left and right. Her name was printed on a small card next to the left-hand door. He squared his shoulders, took a deep breath, and knocked.

She opened the door slowly, looking up at him with inquiring eyes. She scanned him from head to toe, then nodded, as if confirming something to herself.

"You haven't changed," she said, and stepped forward into his embrace. He held her tightly for a few moments, breathing in the scent of her, feeling her start to convulse as she started to cry. He pushed her away and at the same time took a step back, holding her shoulders as he did.

"I'm so sorry about your dad," he said.

She shook her head.

"Thanks. But it's not that."

"Why? What's the matter?"

"I'm just so happy to see you," she sniffled. "Sorry."

She stepped back and wiped her eyes.

"I must be a sight," she said. "And where are my manners? Come in, come in."

She reached behind him and pushed the door closed, then ushered him into an open kitchen area, divided from the large living room by an arched doorway.

"Don't worry about your shoes," she said, as he paused and started to bend down. "You'll see in a minute; I've got a dog. Here, give me your coat."

As if on cue, a loud bark reverberated through the apartment. Anne told it to shush and lie down, and there was a low rumble followed by a heavy thump. Rashford looked around and noted the two metal dishes placed on a small mat against the wall. One held water, and one was empty, but what concerned him was the size. Both were quite substantial dishes, alongside which lay a green striped blanket. He shrugged off his jacket and gave it to Anne. She hung it on a hook, one of three screwed into an old wooden panel and displayed next to the door.

"Mom will be here in a minute," she said. "Can I get you a tea? Or coffee?"

"Tea would be good."

"Go through," she said, "I'll just be a sec."

She ushered him into the brightly lit room. He watched her bustling around, hearing the rushing of water as she filled a kettle and then the quick roar of a gas stove. He looked around, noting the two comfortable armchairs, the small two-person couch, and the round table surrounded by three wooden dining chairs. There was a television, and a small chest of drawers with three china figurines on top, but no bookcase.

The front wall had two tall sash windows, one with a small air conditioning unit held down by the lower pane. The windows looked down on the street and across at three buildings that, in his quick glance, seemed to house a clothing store, a florist, and various offices including a hairdresser. A large piece of woven fabric hung on the side wall, the one with the door by which he had entered. He saw another door further along the back wall, at the end of the kitchen, and then a second side wall covered with large abstract mural paintings.

Anne stepped through the arch, carrying two large mugs of tea.

"Still milk but no sugar?" she said. Rashford nodded, taking the offered drink and waiting for directions. She pointed at one of the armchairs.

"Sit there," she said, and went to the one opposite, curling her feet under her and cradling the mug in both hands. He looked at her.

"You've changed your hair," he said.

"Gosh, you must be a detective," she laughed, lifting one hand and running it over her head. Her bright red curls were gone, replaced by a light blonde tousle cut with an emerald-green streak running over her right ear.

"I couldn't be a red-haired girl called Anne any longer," she said. "Not here. I was getting teased too much, and after a few months, all the suggestions that I must be getting excited for Halloween parties got a bit boring. So, I changed it."

Rashford nodded, lifting his mug.

"Anyway, I hear that you like blondes now. Is that true?"

Rashford choked on his tea. She waited until he got his breath back and then smiled.

"It's okay, I'm not a witch. Bettina told me. We chat every couple of weeks."

He nodded,

"So, really, you knew I was in the Maritimes?"

"Well, sort of. She said that she thought you were going to be following the band for a bit of their tour, but she didn't know for how long."

"Why did you pretend to think I was still in Saskatchewan?"

She shrugged.

"Why didn't you tell me you weren't?"

They looked at each other. Eventually, Rashford nodded.

"Pax?" he said.

Anne smiled.

"Pax," she agreed. "Let's start over."

Anne didn't want to talk about her father.

"Let's wait until mom's here," she said. "You can't do anything right now, anyway. Let's talk about other things."

Over the next twenty minutes they chatted and brought each other up to date on their lives. Anne explained that she had found a job quite easily, there were lots of possibilities as long as you were willing to work for minimum wage. Finding an apartment that she could afford had been harder, but the one she was in had been available for a good price because it was on a busy street, had no elevator access, had only the two windows in the front, and at eight hundred square feet was quite small.

"I'll give you a tour when mom gets here," she said. "She can look after Wakoshi so he doesn't get too excited."

"Wakoshi? Like the Cree, for fox?"

"Yes. I named him after Bettina's dog, but he's male, so Fox Woman didn't sound right."

Rashford chuckled.

"Fair enough," he said. Then he had a thought.

"He's not the same breed as Wakoshi-Mitimoye, is he? I don't really like Dobermans."

Anne laughed.

"Gosh. No," she said. "He's much scarier than that. Anyway, where was I? Oh yes, my job."

She spoke about her work at a boutique, selling 'new to them' clothes on consignment. The work paid minimum wage with a commission, and the hours were good, plus she picked up shifts at the bar where her mother was now the general manager.

"So, all in all, I make enough to get by," she said, "and I don't go out much. So, it's all good. Anyway, enough about me, what about you? Why are you here?"

When Rashford started talking about his presentation at the university, and all that had led him to the Maritimes, Anne was not surprised that Mandy had split away from Rashford but was surprised that she was still going to leave tickets for them at the Monday night show.

"She must be a good person," she said, "as well as a sensible one. How she managed to stay with you for so long is beyond me. You're so pig-headed sometimes."

Rashford was surprised at the accusation.

"I am not. I'm just logical. Things happen for a reason, and in sequence, and you just have to get those right. It's not the details."

"Exactly," said Anne, picking up the mugs just as the doorbell rang. She walked past the door and pressed a small buzzer that was wired into the wall, then took the mugs into the kitchen. She had just re-emerged when there was a perfunctory knock and then the door flew open. Rashford got to his feet as Sandra came in, slamming the door behind her, and rushed over to give him a big hug.

"Hi mom," said Anne.

Sandra spoke into Rashford's chest.

"Hello Anne, isn't it great to see Gavin again?"

"Yes mom."

"Have you given him a cup of tea?"

"Yes mom."

"Did you remember, milk but no sugar?"

"Yes mom."

"He feels thinner, did you feed him?"

"No mom."

Sandra sniffed, stepped back from Rashford, and turned to glare at her daughter.

"Why not? What else have you been doing that would be more important?"

Anne shook her head, laughing.

"We've had a cup of tea and talked, mom. That's all. He's not even been here for half an hour, yet. I've not even shown him around."

Sandra huffed.

"Has he met Wacky?"

"Not yet. I wanted you here first. Wakoshi likes you best."

"Yeah, right."

Sandra got up and walked over to the closed door, calling softly.

"Hello Wacky, how are you? Wacky Wacky Wacky, kiss kiss kiss."

Rashford heard an excited yelp and the sound of a wagging tail thumping against the floor. He nervously sat straighter in his chair, not quite sure what to expect. Sandra opened the door and a salt and pepper coloured blur exploded out, banging through her outstretched arms and heading directly at Rashford. He jumped to his feet as Anne stepped in front of him and scooped up the frantic animal. She hugged it close to her chest, laughing. Rashford took a deep breath.

The dog squirmed and quivered as it tried to escape from Anne's grasp, then settled down, panting lightly and staring at Rashford. He hesitantly outstretched his hand and received a lick for his bravery. Emboldened, he stepped forward to scratch Wakoshi between the ears. The dog growled and he stepped back quickly. Sandra scoffed.

"Don't be silly, Wacky," she said. "He's a friend. Look."

She walked over and reached up, scratching her fingers through Rashford's buzz cut. Anne giggled as Wakoshi tilted his head to one side, his eyes bright and inquisitive.

"Try again," she said.

Tentatively he reached out. The dog followed his hand with its eyes but did not growl. Sandra murmured encouragements and Rashford slowly ran his fingers through the wiry fur. He applied pressure with his fingertips and Wakoshi arched his neck and pressed up into Rashford's hand.

"Now we're good," said Anne, and bent over to place the dog on the floor. It sniffed at Rashford's ankles, then followed Sandra to the couch. She sat down and the dog stood on its hind legs, it's front paws on the seat cushions. Sandra laughed and boosted him up next to her. He leaned into her side and watched Rashford carefully.

"What is it?" said Rashford, following Anne's direction and returning to his armchair.

"A miniature Schnauzer," she said. "They're usually really friendly but he sometimes gets nervous. I rescued him from the pound, and I think he'd been abused before they got him."

"How long have you had him?"

"Just a few months. I got him in the early spring, they thought he was about six years old. He's still getting used to people."

Sandra scratched under the dog's chin.

"He's just beautiful, aren't you Wacky? Here, say please."

She brought her right hand out of her pocket and held it over the dog, who promptly rolled over, side over side, to the edge of the couch, then rolled back and sat next to Sandra, one paw outstretched.

"Good boy," she said, putting a small piece of dried biscuit into Wakoshi's mouth. Anne huffed.

"You spoil him too much," she said, rolling her eyes at Rashford. "He's like all males. Offer him a treat and he'll do anything to get it."

Rashford grinned.

"Sounds right to me," he said.

Over the next hour, they drank tea and chatted, and then Anne started suggesting that she should start making an evening meal, and that Rashford stay for supper. He agreed, so Sandra said she would take Wakoshi for a walk, inviting Rashford to join her, and once the dog had done its business, she let him hold the leash while she used a blue plastic bag for pick-up. They circled the block, down past the theatre and the ice cream shop, then back up past the bookstore and round to the hairdresser Rashford had seen from the apartment window. It was a twenty-minute walk because Wakoshi kept sniffing at everything, fixed or mobile, and once fronted up to a large shaggy German Shepherd that tried, imperiously, to ignore him.

By the time they had returned to the apartment, Rashford clearly understood that Anne had established a happy and productive life in Charlottetown, and that although Sandra really liked him, he had better not disturb her daughter's equanimity or else people would find his various body parts washed up on secluded beaches around the Island. As they climbed the steps back to the apartment, they were greeted by the smell of seafood and garlic. Sandra nodded approvingly.

"Shrimp and pasta," she said, smiling. "Good food that."

Anne stopped stirring the wooden spoon around the deep-dish frying pan long enough to point to the selection of beer cans, wine bottles, and glasses on the counter.

"Red, white, IPA and red ale," she said. "Help yourselves."

She laughed.

"And you, lie down."

Wakoshi didn't move, sitting by her feet and staring up at the counter. She shook her head and reached into a bowl of dog treats, then walked over and placed one carefully on the green blanket. Wakoshi followed and scarfed up the treat, then circled the blanket a few times before lying down with a great sigh.

"White wine, please," said Sandra, when Rashford looked at her inquiringly. He nodded and poured her a glass, then a second glass for Anne when she smiled and nodded as she walked back to the stove. He clicked open a can of Rabble Rouser red ale, murmuring apologetically as it sprayed over the countertop. He poured most of the beer into his glass and then mopped up the rest with a dishcloth he found hanging over the tap.

Anne shooed them over to the table and brought out their plates, placing them carefully. She returned and brought out a third, plus the salt and pepper. Sandra clicked her tongue in appreciation. Rashford nodded, admiring the mound of rotini flecked with garlic and onion and dotted with large red prawns, all coated in a white sauce. Anne lifted her glass.

"To old friends," she said, clinking against first Rashford and then Sandra, "and family. Now eat, before it gets cold."

Rashford tasted his food, then added a little salt.

"Are these local prawns?"

Anne scoffed.

"No, they're not found here. There is a fishery up Labrador way, but you can't find local prawns on PEI. These are from Argentina. They practice eco-fishing down there, so these are wild caught but in an environmentally sustainable way."

Rashford decided not to ask about the environmental cost of transporting frozen prawns eleven thousand kilometres. He simply nodded and continued eating.

"Do you have any bread?" said Sandra.

Anne shook her head.

"Sorry, I had the last slice for lunch. I wasn't expecting company."

"Mmm. Never mind."

They continued to eat.

Rashford cleaned his plate, put down his fork, then waited until the other two had finished before he spoke.

"So, what's all this about your dad?" he said.

Anne gulped and started to tear up, but Sandra just straightened her back and looked at him.

"It was an accident," she said.

"Mom ..."

"That's all it was, Anne. I know it's hard, my girl, but these things happen."

"No! He was too young; he wouldn't make that sort of mistake. He was a good driver."

Rashford looked from one to the other.

"I'm not making any assumptions," he said. "Can one of you just tell me what happened?"

Sandra shrugged.

"His car crashed, and he died."

Anne burst into tears.

"You're so cruel," she wailed. Wakoshi walked over from his blanket and rubbed up against her ankle, but she ignored him, so he reared up on his hind legs and put his head on her knee. Only then did she scratch between his ears.

"It's not cruelty, Anne, it's just truth. These things happen in life."

Anne continued to sniffle, so Rashford focused on Sandra.

"What do you think happened?"

She shrugged.

"I only know what the police said. They told me that Marc was either driving too fast for the conditions or was distracted by something, anything. Whatever, he caught the edge of the road, lost control, and the car went into the ditch, and hit a power pole. And he was killed."

Rashford nodded, ignoring the sounds coming from Anne.

"And you've asked someone to check into this for you?"

"A private investigator, yes. Anne found him online."

"Is he from here?"

"Oh, yes, we stayed local. He used to be a police officer here before he retired and started his own agency."

Rashford felt a rush of envy. At one point he had considered exactly the same kind of career switch. What must it be like, he wondered, to have your own freedom to pick and choose cases, the flexibility to spend whatever hours you wanted on one investigation. And, if he was being honest, the ability to work within your own parameters, without having a boss like Chief Superintendent Pollard breathing down your neck the whole time, complaining about budgets and resources and targets.

"Would I be able to meet him?" he said.

Rashford walked into the Pho restaurant at noon the next day. He scanned the nearly empty room, his gaze glancing over three couples and a table of four. A young Vietnamese man came up to him, nodding and asking if he wanted a table for one. Rashford shook his head.

"I'm meeting someone," he said. "Perhaps he's not here yet."

The young man looked at him.

"Are you Mister Rarsfred?" he said.

"Rashford, yes."

"Come, please."

They walked down the centre aisle to the back of the long narrow dining room, past three elaborately designed privacy screens. At the last table, sitting with his back to the wall, was a man who stood up as they approached. Rashford shook hands, pleased to note that the grip was firm but not crushing. His host obviously had no need to engage in the macho statement of strength enjoyed by some would-be alpha males.

"Jim Preston," said the man, "pleased to meet you."

Rashford nodded, taking in the nondescript nature of the man, who was in his mid-fifties. He wore a pale cotton shirt with a faint stripe under a light summer jacket. He appeared shorter than Rashford by six or seven inches but looked to be carrying about the same amount of weight, albeit distributed differently. His hair was a mousy brown and spiked out haphazardly, as though he had stopped for lunch on his way to the barber.

Preston sat down, gesturing for Rashford to do likewise, and studied his guest. He recognized the symbolism of the brush-cut hair, and the muscular body indicated a person who worked out regularly.

"You're a Mountie?" he said, once the waiter had placed two glasses of water on the table and left them with the menus.

"No," said Rashford, nodding his head at the same time and laughing at the confusion on Preston's face.

"I used to be," he said. "Before Alsama. Then I switched to the North-West Mounted Police, but we call ourselves 'Gaffers'. The RCMP still use the term 'Mounties', of course."

Preston nodded.

"Of course. 'Gaffers', eh? I've not heard that before. Why do you call yourselves that?"

Rashford shrugged.

"No reason you'd have known it," he said. "It's not really caught on yet. It's to honour our first commissioner, back in the eighteen seventies. Sir George Arthur French. When it was being discussed, someone noticed the initials. We thought 'Gaffers' sounded better than 'Frenchies'."

Preston laughed.

"Yes, I can see that." He picked up the menu. "I can recommend any of the noodle soups. I like the Special Pho but they're all good."

"Sounds good to me."

Preston nodded, then waved his menu in the air. The waiter came over and took their order, then left them again. Rashford looked across the table.

"What about you?" he asked.

Preston coughed.

"Spent thirty years on the job, retired on a sergeant's pension, got bored after a year and started my own agency.

Rashford smiled.

"Freedom, flexibility and no bosses," he said, enviously.

Preston looked at him and scoffed.

"Bills, deadlines, and screw-ups," he said. "I've been doing this for just over two years now and this is the first case that didn't involve a wandering spouse or an insurance scam. The grass isn't always greener, you know."

"No beautiful blonde clients and belligerent baddies, then?"

"Hah! I wish. Nope, just the daily grind of hoping someone will call with a job, and then the unremitting boredom of doing that job. Like I said, this is the first time that there might be some actual investigating involved. Ah, here we are."

Their bowls of noodle soup arrived, streaming and aromatic, and they spent the next fifteen minutes slurping and digging through the liquid with their chopsticks, trying to catch elusive slices of beef amid the clumps of rice noodles. Once they had finished, they ordered some green tea, then Rashford asked the question they had both been expecting.

"Thank you for seeing me on a Saturday," he said. "What's the story here, then, as you see it?"

Preston covered his mouth with one hand as he used a toothpick to dig out a piece of something from his upper molars. Popping his cheeks and sucking in through his teeth, he put the toothpick on the edge of his saucer.

"The facts are simple. An older gentleman was driving along a rural road. He crashed. He was dead when the first responders got there, probably from impact but they're checking to see if there could be a medical reason. Your friend, Anne, is, or was, his daughter. She can't believe it's an accident and wants me to look into it."

"What do you think?"

Preston shrugged.

"It does seem pretty straightforward," he said, nodding. "The police say that he caught an edge, ran off the road, and was killed on impact when he hit a power pole. I've been out to the scene, and it looks plausible. He came off at the end of a straight stretch and just before a pretty tight left-hand bend. I asked around and locals said he's the third fatality there in the past five years."

Rashford nodded.

"I'm sure you still have contacts in the local force," he said. "Did they see any anomalies at all?"

Preston smiled.

"Yes, and no," he said. "I do have contacts, and the main one said there were no anomalies. 'Open and shut', he reckoned. It's interesting, though, ..."

He paused, drank some tea, then put down his cup and called for the bill.

"I'll get this," he said. "It's a receiptable expense."

Rashford waited while Preston paid, then got up and followed him outside. It was only once they were out on the pavement that he spoke.

"What was interesting?" he said.

Preston pulled out his cigarettes and offered him the packet. Rashford shook his head.

"I quit."

Preston scoffed.

"Good for you. I keep thinking about it, but ..." His voice cracked as he coughed, his shoulders shaking. He blew out a deep breath, then took a long drag. "I like the taste," he finished.

Rashford laughed.

"Go on," he prompted. "What was interesting?"

"My old partner, she said that she'd heard there was a lot of brake fluid sprayed everywhere. The responding officers say it was an old car, his brake hoses must have chafed and frayed, then burst in the crash. Anne picked up on this and won't have anything to do with it. She says there's no way her dad would have missed that. According to her, he was meticulous about keeping his cars in good repair, he did all his own mechanical work."

"What does the police mechanic say?"

"He says that it looks like the hose broke alright, but that must have been during the crash. If the seals on the master cylinder had dried up or the hose burst before that, the driver would have noticed that he had no brakes, he'd have been pushing the pedal to the floor."

Rashford thought for a moment, then nodded to himself.

"Do you have a tame mechanic, someone you trust?"

"Of course."

"Do you think you can get the car released, and have him look at it for us?"

Preston shrugged.

"I can ask," he said.

Rashford thanked him, relieved that he could now face Anne and tell her he was doing something. He gave Preston his phone number and was promised an update on Monday. He checked his phone and saw that it was only one o'clock. He had been invited to meet Anne and Sandra for supper at a local gastropub but that was not going to be until seven, so he had nearly six hours to kill. He walked up the street to his hotel, retrieved his car from the car park, and drove back to Rollo Bay.

Chapter Five

That evening Rashford reported back to Anne and Sandra. They had been able to secure the table in the bay window of the pub and were relatively isolated from the crowd. Once they had ordered drinks to accompany their fish and chips, he told them about his meeting with Jim Preston.

"So, now what?" said Anne, tapping her fork on the table.

"Now we wait," he replied. "Like I said, Preston is going to see if the police will let us recover your dad's car, so we can have a mechanic look at it. At some point there will be an autopsy that will see whether your dad had a medical issue, a sudden heart attack or whatever, but that might take some days. There's not much else to do right now."

Sandra nodded.

"Thank you for speaking with the investigator," she said. "What else did you do today?"

Rashford drank some beer.

"I, umm, went out to Rollo Bay," he said.

Anne looked at him, one eyebrow raised.

"How was that?" she said.

He shrugged.

"Okay, I guess."

"Did you speak to your friend?" said Sandra.

He shook his head.

"No, I didn't get the chance. When I got there, she was playing on one of the stages, jamming and talking with some other fiddle players." He reached into a pocket and pulled out a creased piece of paper. "I wrote down their names on the program."

He read off the names.

"Tim Chiasson. Keelin Wedge. Cynthia MacLeod. Richard Wood. They're all top players here on PEI, apparently. Anyway, there were so many people watching them, I could hardly see her. Then Mick tapped me on the arm."

Sandra looked at him.

"Who's Mick?"

"He's the lead guitarist for their band. I guess he'd seen me standing at the back of the crowd, so he'd come over to say hello."

To say hello and to commiserate, Rashford remembered. The man had dragged him off to the edge of the event ground, to a marked off smoking area, and lit a cigarette. He had raised an eyebrow when Rashford declined but had not said anything. He asked Rashford what he was up to but had not waited for an answer before talking about the festival. The band had played one show on Friday evening and been well received, he said, and they were looking forward to their second set on Sunday evening.

"But that's not the main story," he'd said, lighting a second cigarette. "They just love Amanda here. That's the second technical circle she's been on today. I'm worried she's going to go solo before we even play tomorrow, let alone before we finish the tour. We're toast if she leaves us, man. You've gotta say something."

Rashford had mumbled something to the effect that Mandy was her own boss and would do her own thing, but Mick wasn't listening.

"She respects what you say, man. She has to stay with us until we get to Halifax. After that, good luck to her. But if we show up without her, we're gonna get killed. Seriously."

Rashford had laughed but had eventually agreed to speak with Mandy about her plans. He and Mick had listened to the rest of the show, admiring both the individual virtuosity and the collective integration of the five musicians. At the end, after rapturous applause, the group had walked down from the stage and disappeared into the restricted area behind. Mick had said he could take Rashford back to try and find her, but Rashford had concocted a prior appointment and said he was looking forward to the Charlottetown concert.

"See you on Monday," he'd said, and left after again promising Mick that he would speak with Mandy after the show. Now, he repeated the invitation to Anne and her mother.

"We're going to have four tickets," he said. "Is there anyone else you'd like to invite?"

The women looked at each other. Sandra shrugged.

"Not me," she said, then smiled at Anne. "Maybe Darryl?"

Anne looked doubtful.

"I can ask them," she said, "but I'm not sure whether fiddle music is really their thing. Where is the band playing, anyway?"

"Some place called Roadside or Trailer Park or something. I'll have to look it up."

He went to pick up his phone, but Anne stopped him.

"Do you mean Trailside?"

"That sounds right, yes."

"And we have four tickets to a sold-out show?"

"Yes."

Anne smiled.

"It'll be a blast," she laughed. "We can go a bit early and get something to eat before the show, they have a decent menu."

The Trailside turned out to be a converted ballroom on the ground floor of a recently renovated hotel. They entered through the lobby, with the café area on their left, then passed through a door into a generous space already filled with chatter. They were led to the front of the room, to an empty table with four chairs. They were directly next to the stage, the speakers looming above them on their metal posts. Sitting down, they looked around.

"Great seats, thank you," said Darryl, their eyes shining with excitement. Rashford saw that there were different sized tables, with two, four, six or more chairs at each one. Anne noticed him looking.

"It's ticket only," she said, "so they know in advance how many people are coming, and the number in each group. The tables are made up to fit."

Rashford nodded, then shifted on his chair. Anne laughed.

"The chairs are all different," she said. "It was a gimmick at their old venue, and they just repeated it here. Ah, thank you."

She broke off as a young woman dropped menus onto their table and asked them if they'd like a drink. Once they'd ordered, she left, and they studied their options.

"Chicken mac 'n cheese?" said Rashford, doubtfully.

"Yeah, that's what I'm having, it's really good," said Darryl. "So's the fish taco."

Sandra and Anne nodded at the suggestion. When the waitress came back with their drinks, they ordered. Rashford asked for a burger.

"Chicken," said Anne, making a clucking sound.

"No, it's beef," protested Rashford, and everyone laughed.

They chatted as they ate and drank. A mixed tape of older and contemporary music played softly over the speakers; the words distinct but not overpowering. A young couple came up to Anne and said hello, she introduced them as people with whom she had gone to school, and an older gentleman stopped on his way back from the washrooms to shake Sandra's hand.

"I was sad to hear about Marc," he said. "I'm sorry for your loss."

Sandra nodded and mumbled her thanks. When he had left, she wiped her hand on a paper napkin.

"At least I know he washed his hands," she said.

Rashford looked at her and grinned.

"Maybe," he said.

Anne and Darryl laughed, but Sandra just shivered theatrically and rubbed her hands more vigorously together. They had finished their meals and ordered a second round of drinks when a bearded man in a plaid shirt came out of the crowd and walked onto the stage. He stood at one of the microphones and looked out at the room.

"Welcome to Trailside," he said. "Thank you for joining us for what promises to be an exciting show. Tonight, we're delighted to welcome the Bridge City Rollers, all the way from Saskatoon, Saskatchewan. And as those of you who got to Rollo Bay for the festival this weekend already know, we have a special treat in their fiddle player, Amanda Robicheau."

A few people in the audience whooped and hollered. Rashford wondered what Monica, Jody, Mick, and Gary thought about Mandy being singled out for special attention. He decided that he would use that question as his way into the conversation he had promised to have after the show. For now, though, he sat back and got ready to lose himself in the music.

The host finished his introduction and clarified a few house-keeping matters before leaving the stage. The lights went down slightly, and Mick came out from a side door, followed by the rest of the band. They took their places, Gary started to beat out a soft rhythm on the snare drum and Jody joined in with a base line before Mick sent out the opening riff of their first song, and Monica's voice sailed clearly over their heads.

They had changed the set list, Rashford noted, for the band were only two minutes in when a long, drawn-out note from Mandy's fiddle echoed around the room, getting louder as she emerged from the side door and joined the others on stage. Her hair was piled up in a majestic beehive style, like a blonde Amy Winehouse, and she was wearing a black and white checked dress with a large chunky belt. As she started to play, stomping her boots on the wooden floor, the crowd started to roar. Sandra put her hand to her mouth, Anne grabbed Darryl's arm, and Rashford smiled.

Their ears still buzzing, Rashford led his table companions to the side door. People were milling around, chattering and laughing, some still sitting at their tables and drinking. A wiry man in a neat grey suit stepped in front of them and barred their entry into the back room.

"It's okay," said Rashford, holding up his pass. "We're friends of the band."

The man did not move, but he took the pass and examined it carefully. Only then did he nod, reaching behind him and knocking in a complicated and obviously rehearsed sequence. The door opened and another, rather larger, man looked out. The first man handed him the pass and the door closed.

After the longest two minutes that Rashford had ever experienced, when they stood frozen in place under the implacable gaze of the thin man, the door opened again. The large man nodded and the one in the grey suit stepped aside. Sandra stepped confidently through the door, Rashford a step behind, and after a quick look at each other Anne and Darryl followed.

The back room had three couches and a variety of armchairs scattered around, with two tables up against the back wall crowded with bowls of snacks and bottles of wine and water. A variety of beer and soft drink cans were sitting in a metal bowl full of ice, and a bottle of gin stood on the floor next to Monica. She looked up as they entered, her confusion at seeing Sandra quickly settled once she noticed Rashford.

"Gavin," she called, waving a large glass in his direction. "Welcome, welcome. Come in and have a drink."

She took a large swig and reached down for the bottle, topping up her glass with a healthy splash of spirits. Rashford walked over and put his hand on her shoulder, bending down to kiss her hair.

"What a great show," he said, standing up, clapping, and looking around. "Well done, guys."

Mick waved a beer bottle at him to acknowledge the compliment, and Gary reached across to give him a complicated handshake. Rashford laughed and nodded at Jody, who smiled back and raised his can of cola.

"Who are your friends?" he said.

Rashford coloured slightly.

"Sorry," he said. "Please let me introduce you to my friend Anne, her mother Sandra, and their friend Darryl. Guys, this is Monica, the lead singer, and Gary, the drummer, and over there are Mick the lead guitarist and Jody the bass player."

Everybody smiled and nodded at each other, before Anne asked the question that everyone was thinking.

"Where's Mandy?" she said.

Mick coughed through his mouthful of beer.

"Sorry, I need a smoke," he said, and went out of the room via a back door. As he left, he held the door open, and Mandy entered, pulling pins out of her hair so that it cascaded around her shoulders.

"Gavin!" she called, almost running as she crossed the room and threw her arms around his neck. "You made it! Sorry, I was just in the washroom. Do you have a drink? Who are your friends?"

Rashford repeated the introductions and Mandy smiled as she shook hands, gesturing to the tables.

"Please, help yourselves," she said. "There's way too much here for just us. Come on."

They moved across as one and each took a drink, then looked at each other. Monica asked Darryl what they thought of the show, and Darryl stood starstruck as they struggled to respond.

"It purred like a perfect engine," they said at last. "Sometimes racing, sometimes idling, always just motoring along smoothly. Brilliant."

"Thank you," said Monica, smiling.

Slowly the group dispersed, like a flock of pigeons separates and settles once the sense of danger has passed. Rashford watched and listened as Sandra walked to Jody.

"Who are your people?" she said.

He smiled.

"Nêhiyaw. Saskatchewan nitohcîn. Treaty Six. Jody nitisiyikâson. You?"

"E'pite's. Wejiey Eskasoni. Teluisi Sandra."

They looked at each other and laughed before reverting to English. Rashford shook his head and looked for Mandy, only to find that she had taken Anne's elbow and guided her to a corner. He heard a chuckle and turned to see Gary.

"You're in deep doo-doo now, man," said the drummer. "Those two are going to be swapping the gee-gees."

"Gee-gees?"

"Gavin gossip," said Gary, wiping his eyes as he shook with laughter. "Here, have a proper drink."

He passed over a tall thin bottle containing a dark liquid.

"Ironworks, man, from Lunenburg. Best black rum I've ever tasted, not including the secret stuff my dad used to bring back from home, Mont Verde in Saint Lucy parish, of course. Help yourself. There's plenty more where that came from, someone gave me one after our show and I bought a case."

He laughed from deep in his belly and once they both had drinks, toasted Rashford. They both tossed back the shot and Gary poured a second round.

"How's the tour been so far?" said Rashford.

"Pretty good. We had a good time in Saint John's but I don't think anyone there will remember our set. It was foggy as hell and most of the crowd were drunk. When we got to Nova Scotia, we went down the south shore a bit, Lunenburg and Bridgewater, down to Yarmouth. From there we drove all the way up to Cape Breton and back. We played Sydney, Baddeck and Antigonish before we got to Pictou. Then the Festival, and now here. We're basically halfway through the tour now."

Rashford nodded.

"How's Seabass doing with the gear?"

"He's been pretty good. I think he's fallen in love with Monica but otherwise he's okay."

"And that sound guy. I forget his name, Neil or something …"

"Nigel. Nigel Woods."

"Yeah, right. Nigel. How's he doing?"

"He isn't. We sent him home yesterday. He pissed everybody off at the festival, kept moving the gear belonging to other bands, and when he wasn't working, he was playing games on his stupid phone. I don't think he spoke to anyone for two days. The last straw was when he used someone else's pre-sets on an amp when Mandy was playing, she had so much feedback it was kind of cool, in a weird way. She didn't like it much, though."

"I can imagine," said Rashford, ruefully.

"Yeah. Remember the monitor placements?"

Gary laughed and poured another round of rums.

"Anyway, instead of taking his licks like a proper soundie, you know, accepting responsibility and saying sorry to the superstar, he mouthed back at her. She fired him on the spot."

"Can she do that?"

The tall Black man shrugged.

"Right now, she can do whatever she wants. Mick's terrified that she'll quit before we finish the tour, so he won't go against her. Me and Jody, we're just background, we don't count."

"What about Monica?"

"Shit, man, she's only got three switches right now. Singing her soul out on stage, getting hammered by gin after a show, and getting pounded by Seabass whenever she's off-stage and sober. I tell you, man, life on the road can be brutal."

He raised his glass in a sardonic toast and they both emptied their glasses. The drummer got to his feet.

"That'll do me, bro. Time for bed."

"Where are you staying?"

"Here. We've got rooms upstairs, in the hotel."

Rashford laughed.

"That's convenient," he said.

"Yup," said Gary. "See you in the morning if you're still around."

"What time are you leaving?"

"Not until eleven. It's only a short drive, apparently, so we'll get there for lunch before we do the sound check. Ciao."

He waved broadly to the room and walked back towards the main area. The large man on security duty nodded at him before opening the door and speaking briefly to the man in the grey suit. Gary left, and the door was closed and locked behind him. Rashford got himself a can of ginger ale from the dish and found an empty seat. He sat down and waited for something to happen.

It was nearly half an hour before Mandy came over and sat on his knee, throwing one arm around his neck and nuzzling at his ear. To his surprise, Anne followed behind and did the same thing from the other side. Rashford froze, not sure what to do and deciding that speaking wasn't really an option. Mandy giggled.

"We had a good chat about you," she said, blowing softly on his right earlobe.

"I always thought take-away Chinese was good enough for you," said Anne, blowing on the left.

     J. T. GODDARD

"You never told me she was the one who taught you how to drink tea."

"I didn't know you could jig."

He tried to move his knees apart so he could stand up.

"Why did you not tell me you preferred beer to wine?"

"You never tried to pressure me into a relationship."

He tried to shake his head free from their embrace.

"We've never made love in the open."

"You never did ..."

Rashford took the only route available to him, and the women squealed as they rolled off his knees and to their feet. Anne stomped her foot, and Mandy put her hands on her hips.

"Tickling is *not* fair," she said. "That's cheating."

Rashford took a deep breath, getting to his feet himself.

"Okay, you two, what's going on?" he said.

They looked at each other.

"Nothing, just girls chatting," shrugged Anne.

"We thought all you guys liked the idea of two girls at once," said Mandy, fluttering her eyelashes.

Rashford opened his mouth but couldn't think of anything to say. He was relieved when Sandra came over, a star-struck Darryl by her side, and asked Anne if she'd like to meet Jody. They left and Rashford stared at Mandy.

"Two together?" he said.

She laughed.

"Sorry, it was a silly idea. We were just playing with your mind."

She reached up and kissed him on the cheek, taking him by the arm.

"Let's go for a walk," she said.

Rashford waved to Anne, who nodded as she waved back and then returned to her conversation with Jody, Sandra, and Darryl. Mandy led him across towards the security guard. The big man opened the door and spoke briefly to the man in the grey suit, who nodded and stood aside as they stepped out, then followed them across the now empty room. Once in the lobby he waved them towards the glass revolving door, stepping out in front of them and looking around before they left the hotel. Rashford was not surprised when he saw the man was starting to walk behind them, at a respectful but actionable distance of about ten metres.

"You get used to it," said Mandy, clinging to Rashford's arm. "Just ignore him."

"Really, a bodyguard?"

"My manager insists."

"The band has a manager now?"

"No, not the band. Just me."

Rashford was silent as he processed that information. They walked down towards the recently refurbished Province House, then zig-zagged around the edge of the historic centre of Charlottetown and made their way to the waterfront. It was only once they were leaning against a fence, looking out over the boats and seadoos moored in the marina, that Mandy spoke.

"Say something," she said.

Rashford shook his head slowly.

"I'm not really sure what to say," he admitted. "Why don't you just tell me what's been going on?"

She leaned in closer and spoke so softly that he had to bend his head forward. He listened as she told him about the wonderful people whom she had met at the fiddle festival, and how one of her new friends had introduced her to their manager. That person was not looking for new talent themselves but introduced her to someone else, and they had hit it off immediately.

"Phil is such an amazing person," said Mandy, looking up at last. "We sat up until two in the morning, talking about their career and how they got into management, and then about me and what I want to do. I've signed a three-year contract."

She squared her shoulders as she spoke, almost as though she was expecting a negative response. Rashford just nodded.

"Three years starting when?"

"August first," she said, relaxing. "I figured I owe it to the band to finish this tour, and anyway Phil needs to get some paperwork together so that we have all the details worked out."

Rashford thought for a moment, then spoke.

"But ...?"

She looked at him.

"What do you mean?"

"There's always a but," he said.

Mandy smiled, then nodded. She reached up and put a finger to his lips.

"Let me finish, okay?"

He nodded.

"But ... well, but this means I won't be going back to Saskatchewan after the tour. I'm meeting Phil in Halifax after the last show, and then we're going to go to Toronto together. I'm going to be based there for a while."

She removed her finger so he felt he could now speak.

"Have you told the band, that you're not going back with them?"

She shook her head.

"No, I don't want to upset them. I thought I'd wait until we'd done the last show."

Rashford scoffed.

"Can I make a suggestion?" he said.

"Of course."

"I think you should tell them as soon as you can. And," he continued, putting his finger to her lips, "let me finish. I think you will be surprised how happy they will be. Not that you're leaving them, of course, but that you're going to finish the tour. I think some of them are worried you're not going to keep playing with them."

Mandy stared at him.

"Why would they think that?"

"Well, why do you think. Look at you, Mandy. You're playing with the best fiddlers here on PEI. You're the star of the show and getting mobbed by fans everywhere. You've been given a bodyguard, for heaven's sake. Mick and Monica and the rest, they're not stupid. They know you've got something they don't have, that star quality that will take you to the next level. Yes, I know you work hard, and that's part of it, but you also have talent. And because you haven't been telling them anything, they're expecting the worst."

"Really? I hadn't thought of it like that. I was trying not to hurt them."

"So, tell them that. Please."

They made their way back through the well-lit streets. It was nearly two o'clock in the morning and the bars were starting to empty out, clusters of inebriated people laughing and shouting to each other. They walked past a well-lit and crowded Chinese take-away and stepped into the street to avoid a large group arguing over whose taxi had just arrived. Outside the coffee shop beneath Anne's apartment, Rashford stopped. He turned Mandy to face him.

"We're nearly at your hotel," he said. "Do you want me to drop you off there, or do you want to come to mine?"

Mandy looked at him.

"I have to meet everyone for breakfast," she said. "Especially now I've got something to tell them."

Rashford nodded, waiting for her to wish him good night.

"Do you think you'll be able to join us?"

"For breakfast?"

"Yes."

Mandy waited.

He shrugged.

"Sure. What time?"

She smiled and linked her arm in his.

"It's only five floors down," she said, smiling. "Why don't we see what time we get up?"

Chapter Six

Rashford waved as the van pulled away from the curb. Mandy was sitting in the front passenger seat, looking straight ahead, but Gary flashed him a thumbs up from the second row, where he sat next to Jody. Monica and Mick were in the last seats, with the gear carefully stacked behind them. Seabass was driving. He stopped at the traffic light, turned left and drove out of sight. Rashford stood for a moment, then walked the other way.

Over breakfast Mandy had spoken to the band about her plans. Heading back to the buffet, Mick had slapped Rashford on the shoulder in appreciation. Jody was the only one who had spoken, looking directly at Mandy as he did.

"Tênikeh," he said. "We knew you would walk the correct path."

'Maybe you did,' thought Rashford, 'but Mick didn't.'

He told the waitress that he didn't want the buffet, just coffee, then sat next to Mandy. In addition to her normal fruit and yoghurt, she had brought a slice of toast, and he took a quarter piece to chew on as he listened.

Mandy continued to talk about her future, reiterating that she wanted the tour to finish well because that would be a good springboard for her solo career. Rashford could see from their increasingly restless body language that the others were starting to get fed up with having a single-subject conversation. He kept trying to intervene and change the subject but was unable to do so until he mentioned Josee. Immediately Mandy turned to him.

"You've heard something?"

Rashford nodded.

"Not directly but it's related," he said. "I got a message from my contact in Halifax, they are going to include the Claydon case in their review of cold cases, using this new genetic tracking technology."

"That's fantastic," said Mandy, her eyes shining.

Gary looked across the table.

"What new genetic tracking technology?" he said.

Rashford explained how the process worked and described how the police in Ontario had made an arrest based on forty-year-old evidence. He gave them a brief summary of what had happened to Josee and found that they had already heard most of the story from Mandy.

"So, now you'll be able to find that bastard?" she said.

Rashford shrugged.

"Eventually, perhaps," he said. "First, we have to get Regina to approve this as well, although I think my Chief Superintendent will be on side. When they approve it, we'll have to make arrangements to courier the samples down to Halifax, and the police there have to get a judge to agree to them making the approach to the companies. Then the companies have to agree to this as well. If all that goes okay, we can make the submission and the process itself can start."

Gary scoffed.

"That sounds like it might take months, man."

Rashford nodded.

"I'm sure it will. Don't forget that it's summer as well, so people might be on holiday. I don't expect to hear anything until the fall, if we're lucky."

Mick scratched his head, his voice gravelly.

"If there's a match, then what happens?"

"I'm not exactly sure," said Rashford. "In Ontario, the company found a match, well, not really a match but more of a link, with a distant relative, and told the police. The police then had to hire some genetic scientists to trace back from the distant relative to the nearest relative, which turned out to be the brother of the suspect. That all took months as well. Even then they couldn't make an arrest, they had to get a judge to approve their request to mandate the fellow into giving a DNA sample, which obviously he didn't want to do. It was only after they got that approval, and the sample, and had the sample tested, that they could make an arrest."

Monica leaned forward.

"So, you don't think your case will be wrapped up next week?"

Rashford laughed.

"Gosh, no. I probably won't be the one to arrest him, even if we do find him. The local police will do that. And once they have him, we'll have to extradite him to Alsama. If he won't go willingly then there will be another court case, another delay, while we get the judge to agree that the charge is serious enough for extradition to be warranted. Even if everything goes at what passes for warp speed in the legal system, I don't think it's likely that he'll go on trial until next spring. At the earliest."

"Why is it all so slow?" said Mandy. "Poor Josee, that will mean she'll have been suffering from this for a year, before he goes to trial. It will bring back all her bad memories."

Rashford nodded.

"It will, for sure, especially if he pleads not guilty and she has to go to court."

"He can't plead not guilty; we all know he did it."

"Knowing it and proving it are two different things," said Rashford. "And until we can prove it, he's presumed innocent."

"That's ridiculous," said Mandy. "It's not fair."

"It is if you're me," said Gary, running his hand over his scalp. "I'm glad there are these checks and balances."

Jody nodded.

"Too many of our people have been pushed through the system without having their rights protected," he said. "You know that's true, Mandy."

Mandy flushed.

"I guess," she said. "But it makes me so mad. We know he did this horrible thing; he shouldn't be able to drag it out."

Mick coughed.

"If he drags it out long enough, he'll get off," he said. "That happened to a mate of mine. They did him for possession with intent to supply, but it took so long to get to court that they had to let him go. He was pretty chuffed. Mind you, he was on bail for almost three years, had to wear the bracelet, couldn't go on holiday or nothing."

Rashford nodded.

"The presumptive ceiling, it's called," he said. "A case has to be heard within thirty months of the charges being laid."

Mandy looked at him.

"That's two and a half years," she said. "Surely you'll have him by them?"

Rashford shrugged, not bothering to remind her that they had to find and charge him first, before the clock started.

"I hope so," he said.

He had been pleased to receive the text message from Paula White. She had told him that Inspector Smithson had approved the case being assigned as one of the three cold cases to be followed-up in the current fiscal year, and that she had personally submitted the request to Chief Superintendent Pollard as her last act before going on holiday. She had then sent him a second text, telling him that she was going to be driving up to the family cottage in a few days and that if he was still on PEI, he should let her know. He hadn't mentioned that one to Mandy.

As he walked down Queen Street, he checked his phone for other messages. Apart from a request that he send his bank details to the Taxation Department of a company he'd never heard of so they could issue him the refund he had apparently forgotten about, there was an automated weather advisory that a heat warning had been issued for the entire Island. There was also a note from an unknown number. He clicked on that one and saw that it was from Jim Preston. The message just said 'call me', so he did.

Preston asked him where he was, and they arranged to meet at a coffee shop down near the dock.

"There are no cruise ships in today," said Jim, "it should be pretty quiet."

Rashford walked down to the big red sign that showed Islanders what year it was, in case they'd forgotten, and after turning left ambled along the boardwalk behind the hotel. He passed the shops and bars of the Peake's Quay district, named after a businessman in the early eighteen hundreds who had shipped produce from the wharf. Now the area was a tourist magnet, not only during the day but also in the evening, when the bars were jammed with young people. In the late morning sun a young woman in a long skirt wailed from the small covered stage, accompanying herself on a guitar, seemingly oblivious to the fact that nobody was listening.

He turned past a fancy-looking apartment building, waving to the people on balconies who were looking out across the small marina, then found himself at what looked like an old brick warehouse. The plaque on the door told him that the building dated from the late eighteen hundreds and had originally been used to polish the brass fittings on locomotives, back in the time when there was a railway service on the island. There was a small outside seating area that was full, even in the heat of the day, so he pushed open the door and went inside.

The interior was busy as well but, thanks to the air conditioning, much cooler. A number of people were standing at the counter, either in line to order or waiting for their drinks, and as he stood by the chalkboard sign that told him to wait to be seated, he looked around. Most of the tables were full with couples or what looked like groups of friends, all chatting away. Only one table was an oasis of calm, the hulk of Jim Preston seeming to keep away sound itself. He looked up from his phone and waved at Rashford, who stepped into the room.

Immediately a young woman stopped him and asked him to wait to be seated, informing him that it might be a while as they were very busy today. She was carrying two large bowls of milky coffee and seemed to dare him to bump into her. He smiled.

"I'm just meeting my friend, over there. The guy on his own."

She looked across and then sniffed.

"Good. Tell him to order, will you. He's been sitting there for ten minutes, I had to turn people away. We're not a place just to watch people, you know."

Rashford waited for her to stamp her foot but instead she simply drifted across the room, coffee bowls held high, gliding between tables with a smile and placing the drinks in front of a young couple. They barely glanced up from their laptops to acknowledge the delivery, but she still smiled and then moved to the next table, picking up the dirty cups left by two older women who nodded as they walked away.

Rashford walked over and sat opposite Preston. He shook hands and looked over the other man's shoulder, the brickwork framed by two large windows. He smiled to himself.

"What?" said Preston. "Why are you smirking?"

Rashford huffed.

"You might be retired but you're still a cop," he said.

Preston looked around, then back across the table.

"Whatcha' mean?"

"Oh, you know. Back to the wall. Light shining straight in on my face. It's like being back in one of our interview rooms."

Preston laughed.

"Old habits, I guess," he said, but didn't offer to trade seats. Rashford looked at him.

"I've got a message for you," he said. "From that young woman who works here."

"Sharon?"

"I don't know her name. The young brunette over there."

Rashford tilted his head and Preston glanced across.

"Yeah, that's Sharon. She can be a bit prickly sometimes. She's my niece and hates to admit that she's related to a cop. Ex-cop. What did she say?"

"She told me to tell you to order, you were taking up space she could use for other customers."

Preston scoffed.

"Just like her mother. My sister is all about the money as well. Come on then, what would you like?"

Rashford picked up the menu that was on the table, smiling to himself as he read the introduction.

"What's amusing you now?" said Preston.

Rashford waved the paper at him.

"It says here that this coffee shop is, and I quote, 'the perfect spot to study, people watch or catch up on work'. Your niece just told me the opposite, that this is a place to drink and eat, not just a place to watch people."

"Contrary, just like her mother. And here she is."

Sharon smiled sweetly at the two of them, holding her tablet ready.

"Hello Uncle James," she said. "What would you and your friend like today?"

They each ordered a latte and Preston asked for a chocolate croissant, only to be corrected by Sharon that these were really *pain au chocolat,* in the Parisian style. Rashford flashed back to Mandy's 'no crumbs' rule and immediately ordered one for himself as well.

When she had left, the two men looked at each other, and then both spoke at once.

"Going to be another hot day," said Preston.

"What did you want to talk about?" said Rashford.

They chuckled, then Rashford held up his hand.

"You first," he said. "Why are we here?"

Preston nodded.

"I heard back from ..." he started, before his voice was drowned out by a loud clanging and banging noise, as though metal plates were being ground together. Rashford turned and looked over his shoulder to see what was making the commotion but couldn't see anything. He turned back just as the noise ended. Preston started again.

"I heard from ..." The loud screeching resumed. Rashford glanced around and saw that nobody else was taking any notice, other than stopping their conversations for a moment and using the pause to sip coffee or bite into a pastry. When the noise stopped, he interrupted Preston, who was trying to start his sentence for the third time.

"Hang on," he said. "What the heck was that?"

Preston shrugged.

"Oh, I forgot. You're new here, aren't you? You get used to it. It's the bread slicer."

"The bread slicer?"

"Yes, as well as the pastries they sell breads, and if you want it sliced, they'll do that for you. Someone must have just bought two loaves."

"It sounds like it's got rusty gears."

Preston scoffed.

"You should have heard it when they had the coffee grinder in here as well. Now, that was noisy. At least they've taken that away. And they don't slice too much bread, just a few loaves a day. Ah, here we are. Thank you, Sharon."

Once she had left, Rashford sipped his coffee, which was hot and rich in the most satisfying way. Preston took a huge bite from his pastry and chewed slowly, flakes sticking to his lower lip and dropping down onto the table. Rashford tore his in half, a stick of chocolate to each side, and took a small bite from one end. He swallowed and then spoke.

"Go on, then. Who did you hear from?"

Preston was still chewing as he spoke. Rashford looked into his latte as he listened.

"The police have said it's okay for us to take the car, as long as the insurance agree. They don't need it anymore and it's just taking up space in the pound."

"What did the insurance company say?"

"The agent I spoke to said that they've written it off and are going to take it to the junkyard. I asked if we could deliver it there for them, via a trip to our own mechanic."

Rashford grunted.

"What did he say?"

"He's checking with head office, apparently. I explained what we wanted to do, and why, and he didn't seem to think that it would be a problem. But he wanted someone else to sign off on it. He said he'd get back to me by Thursday."

"Okay. Good."

They finished their coffee and licked their fingertips before using them to pick up the crumbs of pastry from their plates. Sharon reappeared at the table.

"Can I get you anything else?"

"Just the bill, please," said Preston. "One check."

She nodded and took away the empty cups and plates, then returned with her tablet. She tapped on it a few times and then held it out to Rashford.

"Here you go," she said.

Preston reached forward.

"No, I'm paying," he said.

Sharon looked at him in surprise, then handed over the tablet. He tapped on the tip option and passed his card over the reader, which pinged. Sharon raised her eyebrows at Rashford as she recovered the tablet.

"You must be important," she said, grinning. "Or else he wants something. He never pays if he's with someone."

"Give me that back," growled Preston. "I want to change the tip amount."

She laughed and leaned over to kiss the top of his head.

"Thank you, Uncle James," she said. "Have a nice day."

When they were outside, Preston lit a cigarette.

"Whatcha' going to do now?" he said.

Rashford shrugged.

"I'm not sure," he said. "I think I might stick around for a couple of days, until we get the car to the mechanic. I've got nothing planned, though."

He paused, thinking.

"Do you know a place called Goose River?"

"Up on the north shore?"

"Maybe. Are there cottages up there?"

"Probably. They're all over the island. Why?"

"Oh, I might go for a drive around. I know someone who's staying in that area."

Preston nodded.

"It's a nice drive," he said. "Do you have a map?"

Rashford shook his head.

"No, but I've got GPS."

Preston chuffed.

"Come with me," he said.

They walked across the grass to another long brick building and paused so Preston could finish his cigarette.

"This is mainly for the tourists off the cruise ships," he said, picking up the butt and placing it in a metal garbage bin. He led the way inside and they entered the foyer, where two women sat at a desk and greeted visitors. Preston nodded at them and asked for a map, then guided Rashford to a table.

"You have to see the whole island to appreciate it," he said. "If you just follow your GPS, you'll miss half the good stuff. Here, look."

He spread out the map and then used his finger as a pointer.

"We're here," he said. "You have to head out of town on the Two, towards Mount Stewart. Then follow it all along here, until you get to St. Peters. Then once you're over the bridge and past all the little shops, keep straight instead of turning right. You'll take the Sixteen and go up to the north shore. And Goose River is here, see."

Rashford nodded.

"How long will it take?"

"It depends how often you stop, but about an hour should do it. You'll be back by dinner, unless you do the whole circuit and head out to East Point."

"Maybe next time," said Rashford.

As Rashford walked up to the road he was struck by the simple beauty of the large Mi'kmaq cultural centre on the corner. There were lots of huge windows providing views over the street and, he thought, probably out to the harbour as well. A certain curvature to the building that made him think of Kôhkum Christine, the grandmother of Bettina Blackeagle. As he walked back into the town, he thought more about his idea to drive out to visit Paula White and heard the old Cree woman's voice in his head, telling him that perhaps what he saw as spur of the moment might be considered invasive by someone else. When he turned the corner onto

Queen Street, he saw a metal bench anchored on the sidewalk. He sat down and took out his phone. His call rang unanswered, so he left a brief message to say he was in Charlottetown, and then continued to walk up the hill towards his hotel.

He had got to the bus stop area outside the Confederation Centre of the Arts when Paula phoned him back. They chatted briefly about the beautiful weather before Rashford mentioned that he was going to be at a bit of a loose end until Thursday. She was silent for a moment, then spoke.

"We've got a family thing going on today," she said. "It was my dad's birthday yesterday and things are still a bit hectic. Most people are going to be leaving either later today or tomorrow morning. Why don't you come for lunch tomorrow? We can go for a swim in the afternoon, or a walk on the beach."

Rashford agreed and listened carefully to the directions he was given, promising to be at the cottage around noon the next day. As he crossed the street and then started up towards his hotel, he thanked the spirit of Kôhkum Christine for guiding him away from what could have been an awkward situation.

He kept on the opposite side of the road from the building where Anne had her apartment and had gone another block when he heard the sound of a fiddle. Looking up, he realized that he was outside an Irish pub, and that it was open for drinks and food. He also recognized that he was hungry, having only eaten a quarter piece of toast and a *pain au chocolat* that morning. He pushed open the door and walked inside. There was a large open area with a bar, people milling around and talking, some playing darts, but the music was coming from upstairs. He saw some steps and climbed up, exiting through a nondescript door.

The upstairs room was smaller. There was a balustrade running away from the door, with a slightly raised area behind that was dotted with tables. A corridor-like track in front of him led across the carpet, with the balustrade to the left and a level area to the right. This was also packed with tables, beyond which was a small stage, on which three musicians were playing. Along the far wall a raised wing linked the stage to the upper eating area, the floor made of exposed wooden planks like a summer boardwalk.

As he glanced around, he realized that there was a podium to his immediate left, behind which stood a crisply dressed young woman. He automatically scanned her, noting that she was tall and slim, with a white golf shirt hanging outside her khaki shorts. She had the most amazingly pink hair he had ever seen, hanging in bangs over her face as though she was a 1930s film star.

"Just for one, sir?" she asked. He nodded, and she led him along the corridor between the balustrade and the tables and up to the boardwalk, where a number of smaller tables lined the wall. Some of them had a single customer, others a couple, but none were as jammed or animated as the tables on the main floor.

"What's this, the wall of shame?" he joked. The woman nodded, straight faced.

"If we run out of space and another single person comes in," she said, "then you might have to share the table. Are you okay with that?"

"Sure," he said. "Just make sure it's someone nice, okay?"

She shrugged.

"Luck of the draw, I'm afraid," she said, but Rashford thought he could detect a smile. "Enjoy your meal. Your server will be with you presently."

She walked purposefully away. He watched her go, then turned his attention to the stage, where a fiddler and a saxophone player were exchanging riffs, to the counterpoint of an acoustic guitar. He focused on the music and was startled when a voice in his ear asked him if he would like to order. It was a younger woman, wearing a tight green tee-shirt and a short black skirt. She was apparently dressed for tips, as she had obviously forgotten to put on a bra before going to work. He asked for a beer, anything that was local and on tap, and she told him the Barnone was popular, so he ordered a pint of that.

After she left to get his drink, he scanned the menu. It was Taco Tuesday, apparently, but that did not appeal, and he wanted something more substantial than the punningly named Aer Wingus. He considered the baked beans on toast with chips for a moment but settled on the Irish Boxty. The green tee-shirt reappeared and leaned across to place his beer on the table, brushing against his arm as she did so, then took his food order and left again. The musicians finished with a flourish, receiving a round of applause as they left the stage. Rashford sipped his beer and grinned, feeling relaxed as he sat back and surveyed the crowd.

The Irish Boxty was as advertised, a thin potato bread pancake shaped like a tart and stuffed with a rich beef and vegetable stew, served with a healthy portion of chips, as the pub called its French fries. He ate slowly, savouring both the food and the music. The saxophone player had returned, this time accompanying a woman who sang sultry songs with a smoky voice. Rashford wished he were a promoter; he would have hired them both on the spot to play at the blues bar he had visited in Halifax. That reminded him of Paula.

He was thinking about her, and how she would really feel about him dropping in for a visit, crossing that line between professional and personal, between work and play, when his phone buzzed. It was a short text message from Paula, asking if he was free to chat. He texted back '5 min' and then returned to his plate. When he had finished the stew, he waved to the server and she came to his table, and in response to his question explained where the washrooms were. After walking past the pink-haired movie star and out into the short hallway, he stepped to the end of the corridor and stood outside the men's toilet. Paula answered immediately.

He could tell from the static that she was driving, something she confirmed by explaining that she had been 'voluntold' to bring two of her uncles into town to catch their flight home.

"I'll be at the airport in about half-an-hour," she said. "If you're free we could meet?"

Rashford smiled at the indiscreet hollering that he could hear in the background. Paula shushed them and said this was a work call, a statement greeted with obvious derision. She apologized to Rashford, explaining unnecessarily that the phone in the car was on hands-free speaker. He decided that he could only make things worse, so he did. The roar from the passengers when he told her that he was in the pub and had a spare seat at his table was enough to convince him he'd made the correct decision.

"Half-an-hour," he confirmed, then went back to his table and ordered a second pint.

The lady with the pink film star hair came over to his table with a smile.

"I'm afraid you're going to have to share your table," she said, then stood aside as Paula came forward. Rashford stood to greet her and then staggered back half a step as she punched him in the shoulder. The pink hair lady burst out laughing.

"Ow, that hurt," he cried. "What was that for?"

"For the last half-hour I've just had," she said, sitting down opposite him. She looked up at her guide.

"Thank you for bringing me over," she said. "I'll have whatever he's having."

"I'll tell your server," the film star said, still giggling. "Have a good visit now."

She left them and Rashford sat down, still rubbing his shoulder.

"Nice to see you as well," he muttered.

She glared at him.

"Do you know how much innuendo and insinuation two sixty-something year old half Irish uncles can fit into a thirty-minute journey?" she said. "Especially when they're both half-cut from the night before and had to have a jigger for lunch to calm their nerves before being driven by a woman?"

Rashford shook his head, trying to look contrite.

She huffed, then looked around.

"I've not been in here for years," she said. "How was your lunch?"

"It was good," said Rashford, thrown by the change of conversational direction. Paula nodded, then smiled up at the green tee-shirted waitress as a pint glass was placed in front of her.

"Do you still have sweet potato fries?"

The waitress nodded.

"I'll have those please, with some mayonnaise as well as the curry dip. Oh, and it's all on his bill."

The waitress grinned.

"Right back," she said, and walked away.

"Make sure you give her a big tip," said Paula. "She's obviously cold in that tee-shirt."

Rashford felt himself flush.

"If you say so," he said. "I hadn't noticed."

She scoffed.

"Cheers," he said, raising his drink in an attempt to redirect the conversation. She lifted hers and they clinked glasses.

"Sláinte," she said, then took a long swallow.

They looked at each other for a long moment. He imagined this was what an errant soldier must have felt like when confronted.

"Can we start this again," asked Rashford.

He saw her lips twitch. He cleared his throat.

"I'm sorry if I embarrassed you in front of your uncles," he said.

Another twitch.

"I am glad of the opportunity to buy you lunch."

A third twitch, accompanied by a silent wave of thanks as the bowl of fries and two side-dishes of sauce were placed before her. The waitress padded away.

"I hope we can still go swimming tomorrow."

The twitch became a full-blown smile. Paula shook her head.

"Apology accepted," she said. She took another drink, then wiped her lips with her napkin before reaching for a fry and dipping it in one of the sauces.

"Ach, I gave them as good as I got, all good fun," she said. "Here. Help yourself. How's the music?"

Rashford gave a sigh of relief, then reached for the fries and started to talk about the blues singer and the saxophonist, who had now been replaced by two young women who looked like twins and accompanied themselves on guitars.

It was nearly an hour later when Paula got to her feet.

"Sorry," she said, "but I'll have to be getting back. Are you still okay for tomorrow?"

Rashford agreed that he was and recited the directions she had given him. She nodded, then waited while he paid the bill. The girl in the green tee-shirt glanced at the tablet when he had tapped his debit card, asking if he needed a receipt, and smiled broadly when she saw he had tipped her twenty-five per cent of the bill.

"You made someone happy," mused Paula, as they walked down the stairs and out to her car. She reached up and patted him on the cheek. "Thanks for lunch. My treat tomorrow."

She climbed into her car, a somewhat battered Toyota Corolla, and drove away with a wave.

Chapter Seven

The drive out to St. Peters was straightforward. He went past the blueberry fields and the forests, and the roads leading to fish plants and wharves, not slowing down even as he went parallel to the scenic footbridge shown on all the tourist brochures. It was painted a bright purple colour and, because it crossed a creek that ran perpendicular to the road, it framed a photographer's dream view of the large bay serrated by mussel lines.

As he came down the hill into St. Peters the eleven o'clock news interrupted his enjoyment of Ravel's Bolero on CBC Two and he realized that he was far too early for his invitation. He pulled off the road onto a gravel parking area and got out to explore the tourist shops that had been converted from what looked like old fishing shacks. He poked through a variety of souvenir lighthouses and trays of fudge in one store, examined sea glass earrings and hand carved gulls in another, and bought an ice cream cone in a third. This he took outside and ate while looking down the bay towards the small gap where he assumed the estuary met the sea.

The long lines of what he thought were mussel socks glinted in the sun. He turned slowly, noticing the white painted church and the large brown building that looked like a school and hulked over the community. Then he got back in his car and drove on, ignoring the main road as it curved to his right and instead following a smaller one up the hill, past first the building and then a farm field that appeared to be used as an airstrip. The windsock was wilted in the heat.

He drove slowly, trying to delay his arrival, and had time to indicate and turn into the driveway with a hand-painted 'Folk art here' sign nailed to a piece of two by four that was impaled in the grassy verge. It wasn't the words that had attracted him, it was the large blue arrow skillfully carved and painted to look like a bird, wings folded and beak directing visitors up the drive.

The gravelled track led between a variety of trees and shrubs up to an old farmhouse, in front of which stood a small mini barn with a bright red door. The door stood open, so he got out of the car and crunched across the gravel, looking inside and finding the building empty. Nobody came running down the drive to meet him, no dog barked. A hand-written sign pinned to the door invited him to go in and look around.

After pausing for a moment, he went inside and walked around between the heavily laden shelves. There was the scent of pine in the air, which he soon traced to a series of cut rounds decorated with burned drawings of lighthouses and cliffs. On a table there were egg cartons cut into strips of two, the tops painted various shades of brown and pink to represent nipples, and colour photographs haphazardly glued to blank greeting cards were displayed in an old shoe box. The table wobbled when he picked up the box to examine the pictures. An array of polystyrene fishing floats was propped against the back wall, underneath some polished beach pebbles nestled in multihued macrame hanging baskets, and a number of acrylic paintings on wooden board were hanging from randomly placed nails.

As he came back towards the door, the last two tables held his attention. On one there were three more of the carved bird signs, the first a close replica of the one in the driveway, which he now identified as a blue jay. The second was a crow, glossy feathered and with a startling eye, a bird he had seen everywhere on the island. The third was bigger, a large white bird with a yellowish head, black feet and wingtips, and a huge dagger like beak. A gannet.

Rashford picked it up and held it, turning it around in his hands, feeling the edges of the feathers and the weight of the wood. The bird had been captured in a dive position, its head and neck outstretched, and its wings folded flat against its back. He looked at the price and gulped, then carefully returned it to the table as he remembered Mandy's comment on the ferry and smiled. There might be plenty of fish in the sea, but some were definitely out of his league.

On the last table were laid out a series of art works, bright blue and white in colour, some whimsical in design and others recognizable as feathers, rabbits, whales, and so forth. One in particular struck his eye, an image of Prince Edward Island as viewed from space. This was a bit larger than the others, the island coloured blue but covered in the shapes of flowers and feathers, as though they were cut-outs on a photographic background. He turned it over and saw that this was a bit more within his budget.

Holding it carefully he turned towards the door, wondering whether he ought to just leave some money somewhere. He had already seen the roadside stands selling new potatoes at eight dollars a five-pound bag, two bags for fifteen, and marvelled at the honesty boxes left unattended in each small booth. Admittedly they were nailed down to the wood, they were not free-standing, but all the same he could not see that the notion of leaving money and vegetables, or art works, lying around unattended would take off anywhere else in the country. It seemed a business approach fraught with complications.

He stepped outside, still holding the artwork, and was relieved to see a young woman walking towards him. She had long hair in different shades of what he assumed was an expensive version of blonde, the intertwined strands of amber, copper and honey pulled back into a ponytail. She was wearing dungarees and Rashford was pleased to see that she was smiling, not holding a shotgun or accompanied by a large dog. He nodded a greeting to her as she arrived.

"That's one of my favourites," she said. "Good choice. Although the gannet is good as well."

He looked around, perplexed, and she laughed.

"There are two cameras in the store," she said, "and another one with a motion sensor down by the gate. They're hooked up to a computer in the house. I can watch you come in and have a look around, but I don't have to leave my workshop until I see that you're ready to leave. It gives you some privacy to browse. I always find it so annoying in shops, when they are constantly asking if they can help you. Don't you?"

He did, so he nodded, but at the same time he wasn't sure whether he appreciated being spied on either. He glanced around the barn but could not see any sign advising that there was video surveillance in operation. The woman must have read his mind.

"There's a sign by the gate," she said. "On the post opposite the blue jay. It tells you that there are video cameras here."

"I didn't see that," admitted Rashford.

"I've only been open a couple of weeks," said the woman. "Do you think I should put another sign up here?"

Rashford nodded, explaining that most people would be looking at the blue jay sign, not at something on the other side of the driveway, and so a reminder notice would be useful. She thanked him for the idea, then pointed at the artwork in his hand.

"Do you like it?"

"I do, but I can't figure out what it is. It's not a painting or a drawing, is it? And it can't be a photograph. Is it a print of some type?"

She laughed again.

"It's a bit of all the above," she said. "It's called a cyanotype. You know blueprints, what they use for buildings and so on?"

Rashford nodded.

"Well, blueprints used this process, more or less. They were invented by Sir John Herschel almost two hundred years ago."

"Herschel? I thought he was an astronomer."

"He was, but he was also an inventor. You coat the paper with the chemical solution and place different objects on the treated area and put the whole image outside. The area exposed to the sunlight undergoes a chemical reaction and goes blue."

"Hence blueprint," said Rashford.

The women bobbed her head excitedly.

"Exactly. And cyanotype. So, with this one, I painted the map area with the solution and then put a whole bunch of things on top, flowers, seeds, blades of grass, whatever. They blocked the light to different degrees, so you get this nice variation in tone and colour. I exposed it on a bright sunny day, et voila."

Rashford studied it more closely.

"I've seen photographs like that," he said. "Old ones, in a book."

She nodded.

"Probably Rayograms," she said. "They were done by a guy called Man Ray, back in the nineteen twenties. He put objects on photographic paper and exposed the image. It's the same principle."

Rashford held the paper out in front of him and looked at it again.

"Can you frame it?" he said.

"Of course. Well, I can't but you can. I don't do framing yet. You should use museum quality or archival glass, though, otherwise it might fade. Any decent frame shop can do that for you."

Rashford looked at her and smiled.

"Sold," he said. "Do you take debit?"

"Of course," she said, and rummaged in a drawer before pulling out a point-of-sale responder. She switched it on.

"It'll just take a sec to connect with the Wi-Fi," she laughed. "We're a bit in the woods back here."

Rashford looked around, noticing the thick brush that grew right up to the cleared driveway.

"Are you from around here?" he said.

She shook her head.

"No, we're from the other coast. Nanaimo, actually. We moved here last fall, but I just got the shop set up at the beginning of the season. Ah, here we go. You can tap or insert, please."

Rashford took the unit and checked the amount, then tapped his debit card against the item. He gave it back to her.

"Thank you," she said. "Would you like a receipt?"

He shook his head and reached out to take back the cyanotype.

"I assume it's a gift," she said. "Are you shipping it anywhere? Do you need it to be rolled in a tube?"

Rashford nodded.

"Yes. I'm visiting a friend and I thought they might like this."

"Let me pack it for you," she said, going to a back table and getting out some plain brown paper. "Just to protect it."

"I'm going to hand-deliver it," he said. "Just flat will be fine."

As she worked, he glanced around the shop again.

"Do you do all this?"

She laughed.

"No, my partner is the wood carver, and our kids do the folksy stuff. They're teenagers so they have fun, and it's good for them to be creative."

She carefully taped down the folded edges and handed the package to him, together with a business card.

"I hope the recipient enjoys it," she said. He smiled back.

"I'm sure they will," he said, tucking the card into his wallet.

He found the stake with the blue civic number sign at his third attempt. On the first pass he drove past the church manse before he realized that he had come too far. He had turned around in the church parking lot and driven back for two kilometres without seeing the sign, and so turned again to retrace his route. When he found the civic number, he saw that it had been half-obscured by fresh vegetation and wondered if he should say anything to Paula. If there were an incident, he thought, then first responders would probably prefer a clear view of the property numbers. There again, most of the numbers along the road were similarly hidden, and she was a police officer herself. Perhaps, he thought, the people in the community of Goose River simply liked their privacy.

Not that he had found anything that might remotely be called a community. He had passed a sign indicating he was there, and then a few kilometres later another sign indicating he was somewhere else, but between the two signs there was no actual village, nor even a coalescence of houses which collectively might deserve the name 'hamlet'. There were only a series of metal mailboxes nailed to stakes along the edge of the road. Once he had found the correct driveway, he travelled for almost five hundred metres along a rutted track leading through a stand of tall pine trees. Most of these were equally spaced, as though part of a plantation, with random gaps where it seemed trees had been removed.

He emerged into a larger clearing and the track ended in a gravelled area where cars could be parked, behind which stood a long low cottage with small windows and a flight of steps leading up to what appeared to be a front door. There was a sense of space beyond the building. He parked on the gravel between the Corolla he had seen Paula drive the previous day and a large SUV in the Audi family. Walking across to the bungalow he passed by a flagpole displaying both the maple leaf and the golden lion and oak tree emblem of Prince Edward Island. He walked up to the door and knocked, initiating a loud chorus of barks and howls from inside. He heard footsteps, both human and animal, and then the door opened.

Paula had shed her work skin altogether. She was wearing sandals, a pair of cut off shorts, and a t-shirt, and was bending down holding the collar of a large black dog that seemed desperate to make his acquaintance. He held the wrapped cyanotype up in the air out of reach and edged past, hoping she could maintain her grip until he had placed the gift on the table. She did, and he turned just as the black dog woofed and leapt towards him.

Rashford braced himself but the dog skidded to a halt and sat at his feet, its tail wagging furiously and its hind quarters vibrating with hope.

"Here," said Paula, throwing him a dog biscuit. He caught it and presented it, on his open palm, to the dog. At the same time, he scratched between its ears, and the dog sat quietly while crunching on the treat.

"What's his name?"

"Her. He's a she. Her name is Cilla. My dad's a big fan of the Liverpool sound."

Rashford had no idea what she was talking about, so he just nodded, then laughed out loud when she stood up straight and he saw the design on the front of her t-shirt. It was a rear view of a young red-haired woman in braided pigtails, wearing a straw hat and holding a beach bag, who was walking away from the viewer down towards a beach and throwing her black bikini top off into the dunes. Paula grinned at him.

"I got it a couple of years ago at the Farmers' Market in town," she said. "It's clever, isn't it?"

She put on a police officer's voice.

"I am obliged to inform you that this is not, I repeat not, intended to represent the ubiquitous Anne of Green Gables. That would require the designer to have authorization, which they do not. This is just a picture of a girl going to the beach."

"If you say so," Rashford chuckled. She walked up and shook his hand.

"Welcome to the cottage," she said. "Let me show you around."

The layout was quite basic, Rashford thought. In addition to the large living room, which included an open kitchen, there were two bedrooms, one at each end, a bathroom with a toilet and a shower, and a small office that looked out over the ocean. After taking a quick peek in each room, they walked to the big picture window and looked out. In front of them was a large area of unkempt lawn, extending from the cottage to a low picket fence. Beyond the fence, the sea.

Paula opened the back door, and they stepped out onto a wooden deck that ran the length of the house. Cilla dashed out in front of them and ran into the middle of the lawn, where she promptly lay on her back and rolled about ecstatically, paws in the air as she writhed around. The roof eave was extended, and the deck was both shaded and cool. They went down some rough steps onto the lawn, which Rashford realized was not grass but rather a thick covering of some type of creeping plants. As he followed her, his nose picked up a variety of sharp scents. He stopped and breathed in deeply. Paula laughed.

"It's a mixture of different herbs," she said. "They're drought and people tolerant. My dad thought this would be better than a lawn. You don't have to water it or mow it and it smells great when you walk across it. There's purple carpet thyme, winter lemon savory, and English mint, plus whatever comes in on the wind. They started off in patches but they've all kind of intermingled now."

They got to the fence and stopped. The lawn continued for another couple of metres, and then stopped at what appeared to be a cliff edge. They were looking out over the ocean, but from a height of about a thirty metres. Rashford glanced at Cilla, who was sniffing around behind them.

"Don't you worry about the dog going over the edge?" he said.

Paula shrugged.

"A bit, but she is trained. We put in one of those invisible fences, it follows the fence line so she has the visual awareness of where she might get a shock. And she's smart. She remembers."

Rashford looked back out to sea.

"Wow," he said. "What a view."

Paula nodded.

"It was even better twenty years ago," she said. "We had another thirty or forty feet of lawn to play on. We're going to have to move the fence back again at the end of the season, before the winter storms."

She saw the confusion on his face.

"Erosion," she said. "It's always happened, of course, but the last decade or so it's been getting really bad. We've had three big hurricanes in the past few years, although they call them post-tropical storms. Dorian, Fiona, Michael, they each took big chunks of land."

"How does a hurricane erode the land? Surely the wind won't knock down the rocks?"

"It's not the wind directly, it's the waves. We get big storm surges and they cut into the sandstone at the water line. It gets undercut, then the stuff on top collapses. And we've lost another metre of lawn. My dad's talking about moving the cottage further back into the trees."

Rashford turned and looked at the cottage, which was a good thirty metres away. He shook his head.

"You might lose all this?"

Paula scoffed.

"Yup. The last storm, eighteen cottages just disappeared. They were down at shore level, of course, but all the same. The water just came up over the dunes, then out again, taking the buildings with them. That was up west but it could happen here as well."

"That's incredible."

"Global warming," she said, looking back at the sea. "Things are getting weirder all the time. The tourists love days like this, hot sun and warm water, but these used to be special. Now we have a month or more of days like this, there's no rain, it's really hard on the farmers."

"We get really wet springs now," he said, "and then tornadoes in the summer. In Alsama, I mean."

Paula nodded.

"It's all over. I think it's like the earth is tilting, everything is moving north. The fishers are catching fewer mackerel and haddock, those have all gone to cooler waters, and instead they're seeing sharks and seahorses and things like that. We get strange birds, like egrets and cardinals. I saw on Facebook that one woman in Souris had a Baltimore oriole in her garden all last winter."

They walked back over the scented lawn to the cottage and went inside. Paula asked if he would like a lemonade and while she poured two glasses, he picked up the cyanotype from the table.

"Gosh, it's beautiful," said Paula, once she had finished telling Rashford there had been no need for him to bring her a gift and then unwrapping the package. She looked up at him, her eyes shining.

"What on earth possessed you to get me this?" she said.

He shrugged.

"You seem to like the Island," he said, "and you like the blues. Plus, I forgot to stop for wine or chocolates."

She shook her head and chuckled.

"Well, it is absolutely gorgeous," she said. "Thank you so much. I'm going to rewrap this and put it away, so it doesn't get damaged. I'll take it down to Halifax with me, for my apartment."

She reached over and patted his cheek with her fingers.

"Thank you again," she said. "It really is beautiful."

Rashford smiled, pleased he had made her happy. He looked out of the front window, the sea a long flat horizon beyond the lawn and the fence.

"So is this place," he said. "But where's the sandy beach we're going to walk on?"

Paula laughed.

"I know, we're a bit high up here, aren't we? Don't worry, it's close by."

After finishing their drinks, she pulled some cheese, lettuce and slices of cold meat from the fridge and made sandwiches. They ate at the small table on the back deck, protected from the sun, and she made him laugh with outrageous stories from her time in the military. When they had eaten and cleared everything away, she walked him out to her car. Cilla sat at the top of the steps, watching anxiously, until Paula gave a shrill whistle. At this the dog bounded down and leapt into the back seat of the Corolla.

"We could walk," Paula said, "but it's a bit too hot. Especially for coming back up the hill. And Cilla loves a car ride."

The dog leaned over from the back seat and nuzzled Rashford's neck. He laughed and batted her away. Paula drove them out through the trees, explaining that her father had planted them after buying the property thirty years earlier.

"He was going to harvest them, but Hurricane Fiona thinned them out for him. He lost nearly a third of the plantation. It's taken years to drag them out and clean everything up."

She turned left to follow the main road through of series of winding curves down some gentle hills. At the bottom the road crossed over a small creek, and just past the white metal railings she turned left onto an unmarked track that wound through thick forest. They passed a number of small roads, driveways perhaps, and emerged into a small sandy area, a turning circle of sorts, where she pulled to the side.

They got out of the car and Rashford looked around. In front of him was a large sand dune, separated from the woods behind by a flat area with stagnant pools and low-lying vegetation. There was no wind down in the hollow, and he immediately felt the humidity bring droplets of sweat to his face and his back. The spruce trees at the edge of the woods were curved and twisted, sculpted by the wind into shapes from a fairy tale. He swatted at a dozen mosquitos that seemed to have been waiting in ambush.

"Where is this place?" he said.

Paula laughed.

"We call it Secret Cove," she said, "although I don't know if that's a name on any map. It's what we call a locals' beach, no tourists ever come here."

She pointed at two ruts that ran from the parking area and parallel to the dune for thirty or forty metres before disappearing into the scrub and marram grass.

"That's a track down to the cove for vehicles, people use it to go down and collect seaweed. We'll go this way, over the footpath, it's quicker. Come on, there are no mozzies on the other side."

She led the way to a narrow path trampled over the dune. Rashford followed. Cilla ran ahead and disappeared.

"Why do people collect seaweed?" he said.

Paula stopped and looked at him. She shrugged.

"Some use it as fertilizer," she said. "On their gardens. Others use it as insulation, for the winter. They pile it up around the house and it keeps the snow and ice away from the foundations. That's the way they used to do it, back in the day, and it still works."

Rashford caught up to her. She was standing on the crest of the dune and in front of him he could see a long arc of white sand, stretching to the distance in both directions. He was awed by the view. Suddenly they heard a male voice.

"We missed the tide," it said. "Sorry. We'll try again on Friday."

The voice echoed, sounding as though it was coming through a speaker phone. A louder but more normal voice replied.

"Right, I'll tell mom. But she won't be happy."

"Can't help that," crackled the response.

There was silence. Rashford and Paula looked at each other; she shrugged. A movement caught Rashford's eye, and he saw a tall, heavy-set man emerge from a gully on the dune. Despite the heat, he was wearing a red and black flannel shirt. The man looked at him, so he nodded a greeting. The man nodded back and completed the zipping up of his fly before turning and walking down the sand and out of sight. Rashford turned back to Paula, who was looking the other way and watching Cilla. He didn't think she had seen the stranger.

Paula whistled and Cilla stopped, looking back up to the dune, then turned and raced off down the beach, tracking a seagull that kept flying fifty metres and then stopping for a rest. Rashford laughed, watching as a line of large white birds flew along, moving from right to left down the coast. Every so often one folded its wings and dived into the sea, leaving only a small splash, then resurfaced and sat for a moment before flapping back into the air and rejoining the parade. Further out there was a regular stream of birds heading the other way. Paula pointed at them.

"They're gannets," she said. "Those ones out there are going back to start again. There must be some fish running, maybe herring. They follow the line of the current that runs offshore, that's where the fish find food, and the birds find the fish."

Rashford could not believe beauty of the place. The sun was shining, the water was flat calm, and the light glistened off the dunes. There were no people on the beach. He took out his phone and stood on the crest, the sea and sand running in front and behind him on one side and the spruce woods on the other.

"Would you take my picture, please?" he said. "My friends back home will never believe this."

As he passed her his phone, they heard a vehicle engine and looked back, but there was no other car in the parking area. The engine got louder and Rashford sighed, sad to be losing the perfection of an empty landscape. He smiled towards Paula, and she took a quick series of photographs. The engine revved louder and then started to recede. Paula gave him back his phone.

"Sorry," she said, "I took a few because the truck was in the middle ones."

Rashford turned and saw the rear tray of a pickup truck disappearing into the trees.

"They came up from the cove," said Paula. "I'm sorry, I didn't see them until it was too late."

Rashford shaded the screen with his hand and glanced quickly at the photographs. In some he was smiling, in others there was a distinct impression of Paula's finger. The best one was one of the photographs that had the truck in the background, an older woman staring out of the passenger window. Rashford assumed the man in the plaid shirt was driving.

"These are great," he said. "Thanks. I'll take more on the beach."

They walked down the path through the dunes and emerged onto the sand.

Paula laughed as Rashford walked into the water, gingerly testing the temperature of the gentle waves by standing on one leg and extending the other forward. Satisfied, he stepped in, and splashed alongside as she walked down the beach, carrying his shoes and socks. Suddenly he stopped and grimaced.

"What's that?" he said, pointing at a red gelatinous mass that was pulsating in the water.

"It's a jellyfish," said Paula. "We get lots of them, they wash up on the beach."

Rashford looked at it dubiously.

"Do they sting?"

"Not really. Just step over it. If one of the stingers gets you, it's just like brushing against a nettle. Nothing serious."

"I think I'll walk around it," he said, and stepped out onto the beach. He had only walked three or four steps when he stopped suddenly.

"Oh, yuck," he said.

Paula laughed.

"They get washed ashore and stranded when the tide goes out," she said. "You have to keep an eye out for where you're walking. At least they don't sting you when they're dead."

She kept walking while he washed the gunk off his toes before following her. He took his shoes and socks back, then took off his shirt and carried that as well. The sun was warm but a light breeze kept the temperature comfortable. Cilla came racing up and nuzzled at Paula, who brought a dog treat out of her pocket and gave it to her. The dog dashed off again and they chatted as they walked along, talking about the benefits of separation that had happened in Alsama.

"I sometimes wonder if it will happen here," she said. "People are pretty mad at central Canada, especially Quebec and Ottawa, and we've always had a stronger affinity to the northern U.S. The Boston States, they used to call it. Lots of people went back and forth for work."

"Here PEI," said Rashford, "or here Maritimes?"

She nodded.

"Here Maritimes, I think," she said. "Did you know, we're the smallest jurisdictions but we've got the fastest growing population in the country? And we're getting bigger. Some people are coming from the big cities, they're looking for peace and quiet. Others are coming home, they worked away but now want to be near family. And there are lots of new immigrants, who think this is the best place in the world. For a while, anyway."

"What do you mean?"

She shrugged, then pointed to an area up by the base of the dune.

"Let's sit over there," she said. "It will be out of the breeze."

They walked over and sat next to each other. Cilla came racing up and then lay down next to Paula, who sat hunched forward, her hands clasped around her knees. Eventually she looked across at him.

"People think Maritimers are really friendly," she said. "They are always welcoming, they invite you to parties, all the rest of it. And that's true, if you're a tourist. But if you move here, if you come here to live, then it's different. They don't invite you to their homes, they don't need to, they have enough family and friends. And heaven forbid you suggest they change something, that maybe something could be done differently. All hell lets loose."

Rashford nodded, and she continued.

"New immigrants have it the worse. They're coming here from the most awful situations, whether its war or a poor economy or climate change or whatever. They get here and just want a quiet life, a decent job, a good education for their kids. Then people start to complain. They're speaking foreign languages in public, they're taking jobs from Islanders, their kids work too hard in school and win all the prizes. It just goes on. So, they leave, head off to Toronto or wherever, and things settle down. For a while. But that's changing."

"In what way?"

"I think that over the years enough immigrants have stayed that there are now these small communities, people who share the same culture and language, and so the new arrivals are feeling more at home. And they're growing those communities. It makes me laugh, actually. I was talking to this one guy, he's from one of the Caribbean islands that's been swamped by rising sea levels and stripped clean by hurricanes, so he came to Canada. He told me that he couldn't believe how much empty land there was, fields just growing weeds, old farmhouses abandoned and derelict. He thought he could bring his family and make a living."

She sighed.

"I had to explain to him that the fields were on a farrow rotation, and next year they would have potatoes or corn. That the houses were empty because the old people had moved into the city, but their kids came out every day to farm. But you know what?"

"What?"

"When he was talking, I was reminded of my history books. How the first settlers from Europe thought that the land was empty, and they could fill it by cutting down the trees, planting crops, building houses. They just ignored any indigenous people they met, or else tried to kill them. What if that's the next step, for us? What if we get so many new people who won't accept that land can be owned by large offshore corporations or used for monocrop agriculture? You can feed a big family if you have a hundred-acre farm, and that's the size of some of our fields."

Rashford stared at her.

"That's pretty revolutionary talk," he said. "Do others share it?"

She scoffed.

"You'd be surprised," she said. "More and more people are getting fed-up with off-Island ownership and big agribusiness. We have high rates of autism in our kids, and some say that could be because of the sprays and chemicals that are needed to grow perfect potatoes or whatever. When there's a big rain and the water runs off the fields into a river or lake, there are often huge fish kills. That stuff's being used on our food!"

Rashford patted her arm. Cilla opened an eye and looked at him.

"It's okay," he said, "I'm not going to hurt her." He leaned over and put his arm around Paula's shoulders. He pulled her towards him, but she resisted. He stopped and looked at her.

"No?" he said.

She nodded.

"No, best not," she said.

He put his hands back on his lap. They sat together for a few minutes. Eventually he spoke.

"Would you like to go for a swim?"

She looked at him, tears prickling from the corner of her eyes.

"No, best not," she said.

"Paula, what's the matter?"

She sniffled, then wiped her eyes with her hand. She reached out and scratched Cilla between the ears, then looked at Rashford.

"I like you," she said, "but there's something you should know."

He shuffled back a few inches and half-turned to face her.

"What's that?"

She took a deep breath.

"I'm divorced," she said.

Rashford stared at her, then laughed.

"That's it? Why is that an issue?"

"It was a difficult separation."

"What happened. Was he violent? Is that what you're worried about, being abused again?"

She shook her head, chuckling softly.

"No, nothing like that."

"What, then?"

"My spouse came home from work early one day and found me in our bedroom, trying on some new red lace lingerie and some high heeled shoes. I was still an MP then and we were living in this cramped apartment on the base. We didn't have much money, so they were pretty mad. But there was more than that."

Paula was silent. Gently, Rashford prompted her.

"What else?"

"My spouse, her name was Liz. My name was Paul."

Chapter Eight

At eleven the next morning, Rashford met Jim Preston at a different coffee shop, this one in a storefront half-way up Queen Street. He had spent a restless night, mulling over what Paula had told him. She had explained that after she had got divorced, and left the military, she had decided to live as a woman. The people who knew were small in number. A person from Human Resources at the Halifax Regional Municipality, and the Police Chief, her parents and uncles, and a few people who lived a similar life.

"You remember Phillipa," she said. "The front-of-house hostess at the pub, with the pink hair?"

Rashford did.

"Well, they're part of my community as well," she said. "I often visit them if I go into town."

He was suddenly angry.

"What, was their name Phillip? Is that the trick? You just put an 'a' on the end of your name and suddenly you are a part of some secret society?"

Cilla looked at him, surprised by the abruptness of his tone.

"Don't be upset," Paula said. "I wasn't trying to trick you."

"Why didn't you tell me earlier, then?"

Paula stared at him.

"I don't go around telling everyone," she said. "I thought I would only be seeing you that one time, when you came to check into our cold case. Then it was impromptu to see if you wanted to go for a drink and listen to some music. But I thought that would be it. I didn't know you would come up here. I didn't know that I would get to like you. And there was never a good time to tell you, so I didn't. But when you tried to make a pass at me, I had to tell you."

Rashford realized that he was angrier at himself than he was at her. He had walked her back to the car, Cilla plodding alongside, and at the cottage he had said a quick hello to her parents. They had just arrived back from town, bringing with them some fresh ingredients for a lunchtime salad. He had eaten with them, and then pleaded another appointment to avoid having to stay longer. On the drive back he had mentally reviewed all the women he knew whose names ended in 'a', trying to determine if any of them might be part of the community Paula had mentioned. He had got back to his hotel, taken a long hot shower, and spent the evening in the bar.

Now he walked into the tiled white space of the coffee shop and saw that he was the only customer. He ordered a latte and then sat at one of the tables, his back to the wall. It was only a few minutes before Jim Preston walked in. They nodded at each other, and the older man went to the counter. After he had ordered he came over and shook Rashford by the hand, laughed at the seating arrangements, and sat down. Rashford noticed that he angled his chair slightly as he sat, so that he was partially facing the door.

"What have you been up to?" said Preston, looking at the menu and then putting it back on the table with a shake of his head.

"I went out to Goose River," said Rashford, lightly. "Had lunch with my colleague from Halifax and then we went for a walk on the beach."

"How was it?"

"It was good."

Rashford pulled out his phone and tapped on the Photos icon. He pulled up the first of the pictures Paula had taken on the dune.

"Look at those," he said. "There was nobody on the beach. It was just stunning."

Preston scrolled through the photographs, smiling, then suddenly stopped and scrolled back. He angled the phone, as if to get a different view.

"It can't be," he said, softly.

"What?" said Rashford, leaning over and taking his phone back. He looked at the screen. The picture was the one of him on the dune, with the truck driving out of the cove behind him and the elderly woman staring straight into the lens.

"I know her," said Preston. "Holy shit."

Rashford looked at him, then leaned back as a smiling waitress placed a latte in front of him and a double expresso in front of Preston. He glanced at the waitress's name tag and saw that it read Roberta, so he studied her more closely. She rolled her eyes as he very obviously stared at her breasts but didn't say anything. He picked up his latte and took a sip.

"Who is she?"

Preston gulped down half his expresso in one mouthful. He put down the small cup and laid both hands flat on the table.

"She was a witness in my last case," he said. "One I never solved. One I've been thinking about ever since. Except maybe she was more than a witness."

Rashford stared at him.

"Go on."

Preston shook his head.

"No, you go on. Tell me where you were, what happened, did she say anything. Tell me everything. Tell me."

Rashford sat back, surprised by the vehemence of the words and the intensity of the gaze. He described the secret lane, the sand dunes, the man taking a pee, and then the truck driving out as Paula took his photograph. Preston nodded throughout.

"High tide on Friday, eh?" he said, bringing out his phone and tapping on the search engine function. "Hang on a second. Ah, here we are. Six thirty-seven tomorrow morning."

He looked back across at Rashford.

"How long did it take you to get there?"

They drank their coffee slowly, talking quietly. Rashford agreed to be ready at five the next morning, to drive out to the dune, but Preston would not give him any more information.

"I need to check a few things first," he said. "I'll tell you on the way out."

"Okay," said Rashford, accepting that fact and changing the subject. "So, what's the scoop on this car?"

Preston shrugged.

"Just what we asked for, really. We'll go up to the impound lot and sign for it, talk to the driver, and follow the truck down to this mechanic I know. He's not sure when he's going to get round to it, he's pretty busy and this is a freebie, so I don't want to push it. The insurance guy said that as long as we got it to the wrecker by Monday or Tuesday, we'd be okay."

"Fine," said Rashford. "Shall we walk up to the hotel and get my car?"

"Nah," said Preston. "I'm parked just outside. Let's finish our coffee and then we'll head up. The tow-truck guy is waiting for us up there, anyway. He's not going anywhere. No rush."

They sat chatting, glad of the cooling effect from a small air-conditioning unit sitting behind the counter. Rashford kept apologising for not hearing something Preston said, or only half-hearing it, but did not admit that his mind was still swirling from what Paula had revealed. Eventually Jim Preston put his cup down.

"I understand you don't want to talk about it," he said, "whatever it is. And that's fair. But let's not pretend that you're talking to me, because you're not. Finish your coffee and let's go and get the car sorted, then you can have the rest of the day to figure out what you need to figure out. As long as you're up to speed tomorrow morning. I'll need you on all cylinders."

Rashford nodded, tipping his cup to get the last dribbles of foam and then standing up.

"Sorry," he said. "I'll be fine tomorrow."

Preston chuffed, and they walked out into the sunshine. He led them over a cross-street, muttering about the lack of parking in the downtown, and then flipped out a key ring. He depressed the button and there was an answering beep from the other side of a large panel van. As they came past the front of the van, the car beeped again, and the lights came on.

"Automatic remote start," said Preston, proudly.

Rashford stopped walking and his mouth dropped open. His eyes widened.

"This is yours?" he said.

Preston chuckled.

"Yup, this was my retirement present to myself. I've always wanted one and I thought, dammit, if I don't get it now, it'll be too late."

He ran his hand over the dark blue bonnet.

"Isn't she gorgeous?"

Rashford nodded, then followed Preston's gesture and went to the passenger door. As they got in and fastened their seatbelts, Preston kept talking.

"All paid for as well. I got a golden handshake and used that, so I don't have to worry about this beauty eating into my pension."

He engaged the gears, and the engine gave a throaty roar, then settled down to a steady rumble. Rashford felt the sun on his head and wished he'd worn a hat. He put his arm out of the window and let it flop down the side of the door. Preston looked over his shoulder and started to back out into the traffic. A group of young men walked past on the sidewalk, one of them flashing a thumbs up at Rashford.

"Honking car, dude," he said to the laughter of his friends.

Rashford waved back, then settled into his seat as Preston drove his Jaguar E-type convertible down Queen Street, steadfastly ignoring the waves and catcalls he received.

The formalities at the impound lot only took a few minutes. Preston signed the appropriate papers and then chatted to the police officer on duty while Rashford went out to find Marc Gaudet's car. The lot attendant had the reference number scribbled on a piece of paper and soon indicated a small sedan. Rashford did a walk around as the tow-truck driver maneuvered his vehicle into place, attaching chains and placing the ramps as he wanted them. In addition to the stove-in front end, Rashford noticed that the windscreen was cracked and broken.

He walked back to the office and waited outside, running the palm of his hand along the roofline of the Jaguar. The driver of the tow-truck pulled up and beeped the horn, so Preston finished his conversation and walked down the steps, wiping his brow. He climbed into his car, beckoning Rashford to do the same, and they followed the truck out onto the road before joining the perimeter highway.

"Why didn't the airbags deploy?" Rashford asked.

Preston looked at him.

"I think the car is too old," he said. "I don't think it had them. But that's a good question for John."

"He's the mechanic?"

Preston nodded, concentrating on his driving. Rashford enjoyed feeling the wind in his hair.

"Does your head ever get sunburned?" he said.

Preston laughed.

"Yes, but it's worth it."

"How many months do you drive it?"

"Three or four, that's all. Just the summer and maybe a month into the fall. It's no fun when it's raining, I don't like it when I have to put the top up."

"Do you have a garage for it?"

"Not at home, but yes, there's a place where they store stuff over the winter. Cars, camper vans, boats, you name it. She goes in there once the weather turns. Ah, here we are."

He turned off the road and down a narrow lane between a steel fence and some concrete blocks. The lane was rutted, and clouds of dust thrown up by the tow truck obscured their vision. Rashford coughed as they emerged into a wider area filled with cars. There was a large metal-walled building with a faded notice informing potential customers that provincial vehicle inspections were carried out inside.

Preston parked in front of steps leading up to the door that gave entry to a small office. They left the tow truck driver starting to lower the ramps and went inside. The counter still supported a plexiglass screen, a remnant memory of the pandemic. A small window looked into the workshop, where two cars were raised on hoists, and a panel van stood waiting by the big rolling doors. Behind the screen, a lady sitting at a desk looked up from her paperwork.

"Hello Jim," she said. "Long time no see. Whatcha' you been up to?"

"Hi Donna, still looking good," he said. "I'm keeping busy with this and that, you know? How about you?"

She smiled.

"Crazy busy and the lad left, he couldn't hack the hours, so John's by himself. He says you've got a mystery for him?"

Preston laughed.

"Well, he keeps reading them, I figured it's about time he solved one."

He turned as a tall man in a blue boiler suit came out from the workshop, nodding at Rashford and shaking hands with Preston.

"Hi Jim, what's going on?"

Preston explained the background to the accident, stressing that Anne and the police disagreed on the cause. Rashford provided a bit more context, and John slowly nodded. He lit a cigarette, offering the pack around. Preston took one with thanks.

"Basically, then, you want to know if there was anything mechanical that could have caused him to go off the road. Is that it?"

The two men nodded.

"Okay, I can have a look. It won't be until over the weekend, mind. I'll come in on Sunday and put it on the hoist. Where is it now?"

Preston gestured outside.

"It's in the yard. He's about to drop it."

"Hang on," said John, opening the door and stepping outside. "Oy, Mickie, not there, mate. Just a sec."

He came back in and went through into the workshop. Donna looked up from her desk.

"Close the door, will ya. You're letting all the heat in."

Rashford pulled it closed, seeing John and the tow truck driver standing and gesticulating. The driver went back to his cab and the ramps started to whir back up into place. John went around the back of the building and then emerged in the silver van Rashford had seen at the back of the workshop. The tow truck was backed in and halted.

They watched through the small window as John supervised the offloading of Marc Gaudet's car. He signed a piece of paper handed to him by Mickie, who then drove away. John returned to the office.

"Okay, I can use my winch to drag it from there to the hoist," he said. "But I wasn't going to push it in from outside, not in this heat."

He lit another cigarette, not offering one this time.

"Anything else?"

Rashford coughed.

"Um, that car. It's a Toyota Camry, right?"

John nodded.

"Can you find out why the front air bags didn't go off. It looks like he went through the windscreen."

John scoffed.

"That's easy. It looks like it's an early nineties model, they didn't have air bags then."

"Oh," said Rashford.

He spent the rest of the day sitting in his hotel room. Jim Preston had dropped him off and he had declined the offer of a game of pool in one of the local sports bars. Instead, he had sat on the bed and stared into space, trying to figure out why he was still feeling so upset. After an hour, he took the filter out of the in-room coffee percolator and let the hot water run straight into his cup, in which he had placed a tea bag. He let that steep while he scrolled through his phone, then took his cup over to the chair by the window and dialed. Bettina answered on the first ring.

"Hello?"

"Tân'si," he said.

"Mânan'tow, ki'ya maka?" she replied. "Gavin, is that you?"

He agreed that it was, and they exchanged pleasantries for a few moments. He was saddened to hear that Kôhkum Christine was back in hospital, and that this time it looked serious enough that if she left, it would only be to a hospice.

"I just can't care for her," said Bettina, tears in her voice. "Even if I quit my work, I still couldn't do it, I just don't have the training. Even the community nurse tells me that my nôhkum needs full time medical care."

Rashford sympathized with her and told her that as soon as he got back to Alsama, he would drive out to Maple Creek to visit.

"Tê'nikeh," she said. "I know she would love to see you."

There was a lengthy pause. Bettina cleared her throat.

"How are things going for you out there?"

Rashford sighed, then spoke softly.

"It's all a bit, umm, mixed up," he said. "I'm not very happy."

"What's wrong?"

He scoffed.

"How much time do you have?" he said. "That could take a while."

Bettina made a tsk-tsk sound, then hardened her voice.

"Tell me," she said.

And he did, starting with the growing disagreements with and eventual separation from Mandy. Bettina pointed out that the two of them had never really been in a proper relationship, so 'separation' was perhaps too strong a word, and anyway if Rashford had listened to her in the first place he would have realized that a girl twenty years his junior was never going to be a good fit for him.

"But she was," said Rashford, smiling to himself and eliciting a ribald chuckle from Bettina.

"What else?" she said. "Have you seen Anne, or Sandra?"

Rashford explained the phone call he had received from Anne, and the steps he had taken to meet with the private detective she had hired. Bettina was interested to hear that they were looking into the circumstances of the accident, but more interested to hear about Anne's apartment and the behavior of Wakoshi.

"I've talked to him on the phone," she said, laughing, "but I've only had Anne's descriptions to help me visualize what he looks like."

They chuckled together at Sandra's threat to dismember him if he upset Anne, although Bettina did caution him that Kôhkum Christine had sensed something deeper when she had met Sandra in Maple Creek.

"She thought Sandra was a keeper of the old stories of the Mi'kmaq," said Bettina. "What some call a knowledge keeper and others call a witch. So be careful not to upset her."

Rashford assured her that he had no intention of upsetting either Anne or Sandra, he was just trying to give them some help and support at a difficult time. Bettina was relieved that he thought that Marc Gaudet had died in an accident.

"That will be hard for Anne," she said, "but in time she will come to terms with it. It would be terrible if there was some other cause."

He agreed with her, at the same time stressing that as far as the private detective was concerned, the investigation was open until he could prove something one way or the other.

"What about that police person in Halifax," she said. "The one you were going to visit and talk to about Marc Claydon. Did you have any success?"

Rashford took a deep breath, trying to think what he should say. He decided to start with the easy stuff, and shared the news that the Halifax police were going to be trying to identify Claydon through a review of DNA samples submitted to commercial ancestry sites. Bettina had heard of Investigative Genetic Genealogy and was interested in learning more about the process. Rashford told her what he knew, and then listened as she asked him the question he had been dreading.

"Sandra told me the beaches down there were beautiful," she said. "Did you walk on one yet?"

The floodgates opened. Afterwards, he wasn't sure whether he had been hoping for the question, or whether Bettina was also a witch and had identified which button she needed to push. He talked for nearly twenty minutes, Bettina not interrupting except to make encouraging sounds. As he spoke of sitting with Paula and Cilla on the beach, he stopped sniffling and broke into tears.

"I'm sorry," he huffed, crying and blowing his nose at the same time. "I just feel so stupid."

"Why do you feel stupid?" she asked.

"It's like there's this whole world of people out there who are different," he cried. "And I had no idea. Paula. Linda Benoît at the university. The front-of-house person at the pub. Where have they all come from?"

Bettina was quiet but firm.

"They haven't come from anywhere, Gavin," she said. "They've always been here. It's just that now you're seeing them."

He thought about that, still sniffling.

"What do you mean, it's me that has changed?"

She chuffed.

"To some extent, yes. I think that through Mandy and her friends you met a whole bunch of people who you wouldn't normally interact with. I don't mean that in a negative way, it's just that, well, you're a cop, and normally people try to keep away from you."

She paused, waiting for him to say something, but he didn't.

"I think that society has changed as well, and people are more comfortable being themselves now. More than they were thirty years ago, anyway, when we were young. I don't remember any gay or lesbian or trans or two-spirited or whatever people in my school, do you?"

Rashford laughed.

"None at all, no. Well, there was one guy who was pretty effeminate, we used to call him names and tease him a lot."

"Exactly. If you go to a school now, though, things are a lot more open. Well, they are at the university, anyway. I don't know about grade school."

Rashford was silent.

"Gavin, are you still there?"

He murmured that he was.

"This Paula, did you like them?"

"Yes," he said, without hesitation. "Right until they told me who they were."

"Why did that change them? They were still the same person, weren't they?"

Rashford did not answer.

CHAPTER NINE

Rashford was waiting outside the hotel when Jim Preston pulled up at five the next morning. He climbed up into the cab of the red pick-up truck and nodded at the detective.

"No E-type today?"

Preston huffed.

"No, it would stand out a bit on the north shore," he said. "Anyway, I don't think it would have the clearance for that track you were telling me about."

They turned onto a cross-street and then into a twenty-four-hour coffee shop.

"Large double double," said Preston, speaking into the grill. "And ..."

He waited, looking at Rashford, who leaned across him and called "large two milk please."

"Anything else this morning?" said the disembodied voice.

"Yeah, I'll take a blueberry muffin as well." He glanced at Rashford, who nodded. "Make that two."

"That'll be seventeen fifty," said the voice. "Come on up."

"I remember when that would be under ten bucks," muttered Preston, reaching into the small storage space under the radio in the centre of the dashboard. He pulled out a twenty-dollar bill, then wound down his window and gave it to the young woman who confirmed his order.

"Keep the change," he said, ignoring her surprised look as he drove to the second window. They waited a moment and then the screen window opened, and their coffees were passed over, followed by a small brown paper bag. Preston murmured a thank you and then drove back onto the main street, taking a right then a left before heading out of town on the St. Peters Road.

They finished their muffins before navigating the last roundabout at the edge of the city and settled into a steady cruise up the highway. Rashford sipped his coffee, then turned to his driver.

"Come on, then, Jim," he said. "Tell me what this is all about."

Preston scoffed.

"It was my last case," he said. "There was a tall ship in to one of the harbours down east, they were using it to host a dinner, a fund-raiser for one of the local orchestras or something. A group of yahoos robbed the dinner and got clean away with it."

Rashford glanced at him.

"How did they do it, and how much did they get?"

"They dressed up as pirates and made off with nearly a quarter million in cash and jewels."

"Holy shit," said Rashford, snorting coffee out of his nose.

"Exactly. We got there the next morning; they'd basically locked everyone up below decks for the night. It was a very clever heist, nice and simple, robbery in plain sight. When we were doing the interviews, we only got one coherent description of the people involved. From an old lady who called herself Muriel Stanhope."

"The woman in the truck," guessed Rashford.

Preston nodded.

"Indeed. The problem was, when we went to do a follow-up, we couldn't find her. False address, nobody by that name in the records, the usual sort of scam. Just a dead end."

"Did anyone inherit the case?"

Preston huffed.

"My partner, Janet Parsons, she tried to keep it going for a while. But we had no suspects, and not even any good leads, so it soon drifted to the back of her desk. I called her last night to check, she told me that there hasn't been any progress since I retired."

"Interesting. Do you think this woman was involved?"

"I honestly don't know. She was robbed like everyone else, but she gave us a false name and address. She described the gang members and seemed to have a bit of a salacious history herself, but then she just disappeared."

"Until now," said Rashford.

"Until now, yeah. To be honest, I thought she was a tourist and had gone back off-Island. I had no idea she was living here."

They turned off the main highway at St. Peters, the security lights on the small tourist shops the only illumination as they came around the head of the bay. Three fishing boats carved straight line wakes down the bay, heading to the open ocean.

"Lobstermen," said Preston, nodding towards them. "Sailing to meet the sun."

Rashford shivered and shook his head.

"Not for me," he said. "I mean, it would be okay on a flat calm day like today, but not with any kind of waves, no thanks."

Preston laughed.

"It's only flat calm here because this is a protected bay," he said. "Out there I would think there's a swell running, there usually is. There's probably fog, as well. That's common in the summer, especially after a cold spring like this year. The water's still cold, see, so you get fog in the morning when the air heats up."

Rashford stored away this knowledge and looked out of the window at the green fields. As the road levelled out at the top of the hill, he looked over to his left and saw the bank of fog lying just off the shore. Preston chuckled.

"Told you," he said. "We might get some in the dips as well."

They drove along the coast road for fifteen minutes, not talking, before Rashford cleared his throat.

"What are we actually going to do here," he said. "What's the plan?"

Preston shrugged.

"Look and listen," he said. "This is just an intelligence gathering mission. Don't be seen or heard, and don't be a hero, okay?"

Rashford nodded.

"Fair enough," he said.

The road at the turnoff to Secret Cove was shrouded in fog. Preston turned in, then stopped.

"How far is it, do you remember?" he said.

"About five or six hundred metres," said Rashford. "Maybe a bit less."

Preston nodded.

"Okay then, we'll find a place to stash the truck and walk in. I don't want them looking for us."

"I remember there was a turn-off about a third of the way in," said Rashford. "Paula said it went to a summer cottage owned by some Americans, they're only here for three weeks a year. In August."

Preston put the truck in gear and drove slowly along. They saw the track cutting off to their left, a thick rope strung across with a 'No Trespassing' sign hanging from the centre. Preston stopped the truck, then climbed down and walked over. He waved back at Rashford to indicate he should stay in the vehicle, then lifted one end of the rope off the post and threw it to the ground.

He returned to the truck and drove over the rope, continuing around a corner so the main trail was out of sight.

"Some security," he said, walking back and re-hooking the rope. "Come on, then."

They walked down the track towards the dune, the fog a damp miasma that subdued even the light. At the dune Preston paused, looking at the ground.

"It looks like they're not here yet," he said. "Where did that fellow have a pee?"

"Up here," said Rashford, leading the way up the narrow gully worn in the sand by generations of beachgoers. At the crest he stopped, pointing off to his right.

"He was down there."

Preston nodded and left the path, walking carefully through the sand and the marram grass along the ridge. Rashford followed. They came to a small dip and half-slid down, ending in an oblong gulley. Preston walked to the seaward end. He motioned Rashford to join him.

"Look," he said. "That must be the cove."

The fog gave a translucent shimmer to everything. They could see a few waves breaking softly on the sand, but the ocean disappeared from view within a few metres. The beach ran beneath them and continued for another thirty metres, then stopped at a narrow rivulet that ran down from the dune. On the other side of the stream was a jumbled array of brown rocks, followed by what appeared to be a wider passage of water. Beyond the creek, the dune curved to seaward.

"Tide's coming in," said Preston, nodding at the stones. As Rashford looked, the water around them swirled and rocks seemed to be getting smaller. He looked back at the beach, and saw that the waves were closer now.

"This will do," said Preston. "I'll just go and clear our track."

He picked up an old branch that lay in the gulley. It had a small array of side branches, but no leaves. Mystified, Rashford watched him climb back up the side of the gully. Five minutes later he returned, bent over with his back to Rashford as he reached the lip. He was sweeping the sand, Rashford realized, as Preston edged slowly back into the gulley, swishing the branch from side to side behind him.

"It wouldn't stop a proper spotter," said Preston, throwing the stick down. "But it will make us harder to find. Listen."

They could both hear the sound of an engine coming along behind the dune. They stayed still until it had stopped, then Preston edged forward and peered around the corner. He came back to Rashford.

"The truck is there," he said. "They've backed it onto the beach. Now, we wait."

They sat down on the sand, hands around their knees, the mist slurring the outlines of everything in sight. Neither said anything, each leaving the other to their thoughts.

It was thirty minutes before they heard the sound of another engine. Rashford stirred, but Preston motioned him to stay still. The noise was soft, disorientated by the fog, and Rashford was unable to determine whether the muffled rumble was behind him or ahead. Preston tapped him on the arm, pointing his chin out to sea.

Rashford watched the low white fishing boat emerge from the fog. A man was standing in the small shelter that served as a wheelhouse, with another in the open cabin behind. Rashford watched as the driver, or perhaps 'pilot' he thought, slowly eased on a handle and the boat came almost to a stop. The man moved his hand again, water swirling from the rear of the boat, and then the vessel turned towards the sea and the bow disappeared into the fog. The man in the open area raised his hand and the boat stopped again, then slowly reversed, emerging back into full view. The arm was raised again, and the boat stopped, the motor idling gently.

The man in the back leaned down and then stood back up, holding a large blue plastic container. He threw it overboard, where it landed with a splash and then started to sink. A rope snaked out behind it, and then a white buoy with two pink stripes around the neck popped over the side. The buoy submerged for a moment and then resurfaced, gyrating madly. The man bent down and then emerged to throw a second container over the side.

When there were six buoys bobbing in the water the man in the back walked over to the cabin and tapped the pilot on his shoulder. The engine engaged, the boat started to move forward, and the two waved back towards the shore as they disappeared into the fog. Rashford looked at Preston, eyebrows raised, but the older man again indicated that he be silent. They heard a splashing sound and Preston nodded, then started to crawl up the side of the dune. Rashford moved to follow but was waved back, so he sat down on the damp sand and waited. The splashing continued.

After a few minutes, Rashford could no longer bear the suspense. He crawled to the mouth of the gully and carefully peered around the corner. He saw a man moving from buoy to buoy, the water almost reaching the waist of his one-piece wading suit. He was holding a metal chain and moved like a cartoon robot, slowly and with his arms stretched out to help him keep his balance. At each buoy he reached down and pulled on the line that led to the sunken container, bringing in the slack and exposing a narrow oval carabiner which he attached to the chain. Once he had hooked all six buoys, he stood further off the shore and waved.

Rashford heard an engine start, then a grinding and rattling noise. The chain went taut, and the man let it go. The buoys started moving and the man followed the outermost one in towards the shore. He disappeared from Rashford's sight, so he sat back on the sand and waited for Preston to reappear.

At length Rashford heard the rustle of vegetation and the detective slid carefully down the bank to his side. He held his finger to his lips and pointed to his watch, then flashed an open hand twice. "Ten minutes', thought Rashford, so he nodded, then sat quietly again. The rattle of what he assumed was a winch ceased, and they heard a vehicle door slam. The engine revved more loudly, and they listened as it drove up the track and then, as the sound diminished, into the woods. Preston waited until the full ten minutes was over before he spoke.

"Got 'em," he said. And pulled out his cigarettes.

~

Rashford waited while the detective smoked his cigarette. The smoke hung in the air, and Rashford had to force himself not to ask for one. He tried to be patient but eventually his resolve broke.

"What did you see?" he said, testily.

Preston smiled.

"I saw, and I got proof," he said, reaching into his pocket and bringing out a square object, about the size of his fist. He noted Rashford's bafflement and laughed.

"It's a camera," he said, "but modified. Camera shutters make a click, even those on a modern phone, so this has a home-made rubber baffle to mask the sound. I can take pictures even on a quiet beach at dawn and nobody will hear a thing. And I did."

Rashford nodded.

"That's great," he said. "Pictures of what?"

"Pictures of the boat coming inshore, and the boxes being thrown into the water. Pictures of buddy pulling up those boxes and storing them in the back of the truck. Pictures of Muriel Stanhope standing in the tray of the truck, stacking the buoys neatly. Pictures of the truck driving away. I got all the proof I need."

Rashford looked at him.

"Proof of what, though?"

Preston laughed.

"Of smuggling, of course."

Rashford shrugged.

"Not in my world," he said. "First you need to find out what was in those boxes. They could have been dropping off picnic lunches for all you know."

Preston nodded.

"Oh, I know all that. But this is the proof that she is involved in something, and I have the name of the boat and the registration number of the truck, so I should be able to track her down at last. Once I find out who she is, then I can figure out the rest of it. Come on, let's head back to town."

They climbed back up the side of the gulley and Rashford had just reached the top of the dune when a flying black missile exploded against his ribs. He stumbled backwards and fell back into the gulley, winded and pinned by the weight on his chest, feeling a stabbing pain in his shoulder. He opened his eyes.

"Cilla," he said, "for God's sake."

He pushed the dog away and tried to get up without having his ear licked. Paula appeared at the top of the ridge, standing next to Jim Preston. Rashford could hear them laughing.

"I'm sorry," called Paula. "She must have got your scent; she just took off on me."

Rashford stood and brushed the sand off his clothes, Cilla prancing around him and jumping at his waist. He scratched her ears and told her to sit down, but she ignored him. The other two slid down the side of the gulley and joined him.

"Good grief," said Paula. "Are you okay? You're bleeding!"

Rashford tried to see behind himself, twisting his shoulder towards him.

"There. Your shirt is ripped. Oh, I'm so sorry. Cilla just got so excited."

"It's only a scratch," said Preston, peering at the wound. "A bit of antiseptic ointment and a band aid and you'll be fine.

Paula scoffed.

"And a new shirt," she said, before focusing on Preston.

"Hello. I don't think we've met."

Rashford introduced them and they shook hands. Paula looked at him inquisitively.

"I didn't see your car," she said. "Where did you park?"

Preston coughed.

"Ah, it's an old truck but it's mine, you know. I parked it up a cottage lane so it wouldn't stick out on the main road. I don't want some yahoo coming along and stealing it."

Paula looked at him, then nodded.

"Not many people down this cove at seven in the morning," she said. "That's why I bring Cilla down now, she can run forever on the beach."

Preston grunted.

"I, um, I take photographs," he said. "I asked Gavin here to show me this place at sun-up."

Rashford scratched Cilla's ears, enjoying hearing Preston trying to talk his way out of the situation.

"Really," said Paula. "Did you get any good ones?"

"Just one I'd like to print," he said, unlatching the back of the baffle to reveal a small point and shoot camera. He clicked on the photo display icon and held the screen towards her.

"That looks like a North Lake boat," she said. "They fish for lobster in this area, all the way over to the Covehead Light. He's in pretty close, though. It gets shallow inshore."

Preston nodded.

"That's what I was telling Gavin," he said. "I was going for a shot of the sun coming through the fog bank and then suddenly that boat appeared."

Rashford had had enough. He pointed at Paula as he spoke.

"Jim, she's a cop. She knows that's a pack of bull."

Preston looked from one to the other.

"A cop? Where? Not on the Island."

Paula chuckled.

"No, from Halifax. You?"

"Used to be, here. I was detective sergeant when I retired."

She nodded to acknowledge this fact.

"And embarked on a new career as a storyteller?"

Preston flushed. Rashford decided it was time to intervene.

"I think I'm the common denominator," he said. "Jim, Paula here is working on a cold case that seems to tie in to one I'm working on out west. Paula, Jim is a private investigator now, and was hired by an old friend of mine to look into her father's death. We're out here on something totally unrelated, something that came up when you and I were out here on Wednesday. Here, look."

He brought out his phone and scrolled through the photographs she had taken of him on the dunes. He passed her the phone.

"That woman, the passenger in the truck. Jim thinks he knows her."

They walked along the beach as Jim explained the story of the pirate raid on the gala dinner. Paula had heard some of the story, her parents had regaled her with it the previous Christmas, but she did not know all the details. Rashford kicked stones and pebbles along the beach, Cilla racing after them and throwing up a rooster tail of sand as she skidded to a stop. After forty-five minutes they turned and walked back, the dog still running in long ovals between the eroded edge of the dunes and the gentle wavelets of the shallows.

At the small parking circle, Paula dug into the glove box and produced a tube of antiseptic ointment and a box of band aid plasters. She laughed as she passed the plaster strips to him and he grinned when he saw the cartoon dinosaur images.

"I had them when a couple of my nephews came to visit," she said. "They're always getting into scrapes. Here, let me help."

She carefully applied the ointment and then stuck on two large plasters.

"That should be okay now," she said. "What do you think?"

Preston nodded.

"He'll be fine," he said. "That T-Rex will scare any infection away."

They laughed and shook hands again. Cilla climbed into the back of Paula's car and immediately went to sleep, her head on her paws. Rashford and Preston refused Paula's offer of a ride and walked down the track behind her, turning up the driveway and unhooking the rope barrier once more. As they approached the truck, Preston beeped the automatic lock and the lights flashed.

"No remote start?" laughed Rashford.

Preston shook his head.

"Nah, that's only for the Jag," he said.

They backed down to the lane and refastened the rope behind them before driving out to the highway. As the truck labored up the hill, Preston turned to Rashford.

"That friend of yours, Paula," he said. "You know she's a guy, right?"

CHAPTER TEN

They were back in St. Peter's and driving past the row of tourist shops contrived to look like converted fishing shacks before Rashford spoke.

"How did you know?"

Preston kept one hand on the steering wheel and used the other to shake a cigarette out of its packet. He threw the packet down on the seat between them before taking a lighter from his breast pocket. He dropped the lighter next to the packet, inhaled deeply, then opened his window a few centimetres before turning to Rashford with a shrug.

"Oh, you know, the basics. Voice. Walk. Physical structure and musculature. Adam's apple."

Rashford stared at him. Preston returned to watching the road.

"Fuck it," said Rashford, picking up the cigarettes and taking one. He leaned back against the seat, closed his eyes, and let the smoke slowly stream out of his nose. Preston chuckled.

"Just don't blame me," he said. "That was an act of individual choice."

Rashford nodded and took another drag. Preston turned up the hill past the old church and Rashford gestured back across the bay.

"What's that big brown building?" he said.

Preston glanced across and then back.

"That's the climate change research centre. It's a university thing. They've got classrooms, accommodation for students and profs, everything, including one of the biggest collections of research drones in the country."

"Really? Why?"

"They use them to survey the coastline, keep track on erosion patterns, that sort of thing. The island is basically a sand dune in the sea, you know, and every time there's a storm, we lose a bit more of the place."

Rashford blew smoke out of the window and nodded.

"That's what Paula said. She said they've lost nearly six metres of their property over the past few years, and during the last big storm eighteen cottages disappeared somewhere."

"That was up west," said Preston. "I remember that."

"Up west? What do you mean, like Alberta?"

Preston laughed.

"No, that's out west. Up west is the western end of the Island. So right now, we're down east."

Rashford shook his head.

"Madness."

"It gets better. If someone moves to Moncton or Halifax, or goes there for shopping, then they've gone over the Strait. But if they get sent to the federal pen, then people say they're accrost the water. Amazing thing, language."

They crested the hill and started down the long curve. Preston cleared his throat.

"It's not a big deal, you know."

Rashford chuffed.

"How would you know?"

Preston spoke quietly.

"Have you ever been to Tahiti?"

"No."

"There are people there called *mahu*. They were born as boys but raised as girls, wearing women's clothes, doing women's work."

"Why?"

"I'm not sure. The point is, they weren't necessarily homosexual. Some had wives, children. They just dressed differently."

Rashford stared at him.

"I'm not sure I understand your point."

Preston scoffed.

"The question you have to ask is, can they do the job? If they can, then it doesn't really matter what gender they are or want to be. I'm guessing you just found out. How did you know?"

"I didn't. She told me and I freaked."

"Why? It's good that people are free to be themselves. At the turn of the millennium, this place started getting a reputation for being gay-friendly, you know. There were rainbow flags everywhere. We elected a Premier who was openly gay. The word got out, as these things do, and the marketing folk started to build on that. Every second tourist ad started to show same-sex couples. And the sky didn't fall in. Live and let live."

"But how can she, he, they … what do I even call them, for god's sake?"

"If the preferred pronoun is 'she', why can't you just use that?"

"Because they're not … Oh fuck, I don't know."

Rashford dropped his cigarette butt into the old coffee cup that served as an ashtray and shook out a new cigarette. He inhaled the smoke deeply.

"I've missed these," he said.

Preston laughed, then picked up the packet and put it back into his pocket.

"Buy your own if you want any more," he said.

Preston pulled into the parking lot of Rashford's hotel and turned off the engine.

"Let's get a bite," he said, "and figure out what the heck's going on here."

He pointed down the street and they started to walk, Rashford noticing that they were once again passing Anne's apartment. Preston had pulled out his phone and was speaking quietly. They stopped in front of a small restaurant and stood in the shade of the awning while Preston finished his call. He then ushered Rashford inside and nodded at the man who stepped out from behind the counter, wiping his hands on a cloth.

"Hello Joseph," he said. "We're going to be talking business. May we have a table outside at the back, please?"

The man nodded and led them past the tables of other diners, up a few steps, and then through a door that led them outside. Nobody had been seated in this area, which was shaded from the sun by a pergola covered in vines. Joseph indicated the six wooden picnic tables dotted across the red gravel.

"This area is not open yet," he said. "Sit where you want."

Preston selected the table in the centre of the space and sat facing the restaurant. Joseph followed them over, placing two menus on the table. Preston raised his hand.

"We'll need one more, please," he said.

Joseph nodded.

"And to drink?"

"Just soda water for me, please," said Preston. "You?"

Rashford nodded that he would have the same, then picked up the menu.

"Hope you like Lebanese food," said Preston. "This is the best in town."

Rashford looked at the options.

"I don't know much about it," he said. "I didn't know it was a thing here."

Preston chuckled.

"We're not just fish and chips, you know, good as they are. I'll order, if you're okay with that?"

"Sure," nodded Rashford, looking around. "Are there lots of Lebanese people here?"

"There's been a big Lebanese community here since the late eighteen hundreds, almost a hundred and fifty years. They came because there were troubles at home, the normal stuff. Religious persecution, political rivalry, over-population, things like that. They thought there would be better opportunities here, so they came, settled in, had families, became part of the community. Now they're mainstream. We've had two Premiers who were of Lebanese descent."

Joseph returned with their drinks, including an extra glass.

"Will you order, or wait for your friend?"

"I'll order," said Preston. "We'll have a mezze lunch, please. Yabrak, falafel, large tabouli and large fattouch, hummus, three orders of kibbie, and some shankleesh. And some lemonade, please."

Joseph nodded and left them alone. Rashford raised an eyebrow.

"Mezze?"

Preston nodded.

"It's like a shared meal," he said. "They're all small plates and you pick a bit from each. It's a lot more fun than just getting a chicken shawarma or something. It takes a bit longer to prepare but you're not in a rush, are you?"

Rashford shook his head.

"Nope, I've got nothing planned," he said, then looked up as a slim Black woman came through the door and walked across the gravel. She slid onto the bench next to Preston.

"Hello boss," she said, punching him lightly on the arm.

Preston tapped her back.

"That was quick," he said. "I only just ordered."

She laughed.

"It's a quiet day, so far," she said. "It'll warm up through the afternoon."

Preston nodded, then gestured across the table.

"This is Gavin Rashford, he's a cop over here from Alsama. He's on holiday, but he's also working a case. Gavin, this is Detective Constable Janet Parsons."

They shook hands across the table.

"What's the case?" she said.

Preston chuffed.

"Hang on," he said. "Let's get some food first. Then we'll discuss business. Gavin, why don't you tell us what you think of the Island?"

For the next ten minutes they shared stories. Rashford talked about his first impressions of the people and places he had seen, and Janet Parsons made them laugh with stories from the court sessions she attended every Thursday. Jim Preston was just regaling them with details of a complicated case involving two cousins, a stolen pick-up truck and a misplaced goat when Joseph and a waitress returned with a series of plates, filling the table with wonderful colours and aromas. The pair made three trips, on the last bringing a large pitcher of lemonade as well as a mound of flat bread that was still warm from the oven. Joseph scanned the table and nodded, smiling, before leaving them to their meal. He quietly closed the door into the restaurant behind him. Jim Preston poured out servings of lemonade and raised his glass.

"To Friday afternoons in the summer sunshine," he said.

They clinked glasses, then served themselves from the array of foods on the table. Rashford tore off a corner from a piece of flatbread and used it to scoop up some of the cheese and herb salad.

"What is this stuff?" he said. "It's fantastic."

"That's shankleesh," said Janet Parsons, smiling at his enthusiasm. "Make sure you try the fattouch salad, that's really good as well."

"It's all good," said Preston, through a mouthful of falafel.

It was only once they had sated their appetites and were picking at the remains of the food that Preston brought the conversation back to business. He told Janet about the assignment he had received from Anne Gaudet, and how early indications supported the police assessment that it was a sad but simple accident. He also described how Anne introduced Rashford into the case.

Rashford explained how he was really on holiday to follow a band who were on tour, and there was a long divergence when it turned out that Janet Parsons was a huge fan of Mandy Robicheau and had attended both the Charlottetown and Summerside concerts. She peppered Rashford with questions about what Mandy was really like and made him promise to get her a signed photograph the next time he saw her. It took Preston some time to get the conversation back on track, a process only achieved when Joseph interrupted to see if they would like coffee.

Once that had been ordered and served, Preston took Rashford's phone and showed Parsons the photograph taken on the dune. She recognized the old woman immediately and listened carefully as Preston described their trip out to Secret Cove. He passed her his camera, and she scrolled through the pictures.

"You think this is smuggling?" she said.

Preston shrugged.

"It looks like it could be," he said.

She slowly shook her head.

"I didn't get the impression that she was an Islander," she said. "I thought she was a CFA."

Preston glanced at Rashford.

"Come from away," he said.

Rashford nodded.

"Are you from away?" he said.

Parsons looked at him in surprise.

"Why? Because I'm Black?" She chuffed. "No, I'm from Kings County. There have been Black people on the Island since the seventeen hundreds, a century before Confederation. My family came here in 1810."

Rashford looked contrite.

"I'm sorry, I had no idea ..."

Janet huffed.

"Not many people do," she said.

Preston coughed.

"Let's get back on topic, okay?" he said. "I don't know what she's up to, whether it's smuggling or not, whether she lives here or not, what name she might be using. The main thing, though, is that now I have a car registration as well as a boat identification. Those will help us answer the questions. I think you should be able to find out who owns those registrations, don't you?"

Parsons smiled.

"Of course. But how will that help you?"

Preston glared at her.

"Because then you'll share that information with me," he muttered.

Rashford laughed.

"That might not be kosher, Jim," he said.

Preston scoffed and shook his head.

"Maybe not in Alsama," he said, "but here we work with our friends and colleagues."

"Ex-colleagues," said Parsons, laughing. She turned to Rashford.

"Thank you for being on my side," she said. "This grumpy old man can't get his head around the fact that he's supposed to be retired. He thinks he can keep doing what he wants, and everyone will fall into line."

"What am I supposed to do, spend the day sitting in a coffee shop telling the same old stories to people who will pretend they've never heard them before?"

She shrugged.

"You could go fishing," she said, trying to keep a straight face.

He stared at her.

"How long were you my partner? Four years? Five? Have you ever heard me express the slightest interest in sitting at the end of wharf throwing worms into the sea? Have you?"

She shook her head, stifling a giggle.

"What about painting? Or growing roses? Or writing a book? You're always telling stories, why don't you write them down?"

"Nobody would believe them," he harrumphed. "But, if I did, the first one would be called 'The Case of the Ungrateful Underling That Forget Who Taught Her Everything She Knew'."

He reached for his coffee. Parsons smiled sweetly.

"Yes, boss," she said.

When Preston went into the main restaurant to pay the bill, Parsons turned to Rashford.

"Thank you for your help on this," she said. "That case has been eating away at him, he's convinced we were scammed."

"Are you?"

"No," she said, hesitating a little. "No, I don't think so. I think we were just unlucky. The gang hit the mother lode, and we've never found the money. Some of the jewelry turned up at a pawn shop in Edmundston of all places, but it had been through so many hands we couldn't trace the route. Jim was sure that Muriel Stanhope was involved but I don't think she had anything to do with them. I think she was just in the wrong place at the wrong time and was robbed as well. But I don't know who she was, or is, and I don't know what she's hiding or why she gave us false information. It would be good to figure that out, though, so thanks."

Rashford nodded.

"I got lucky," he said. "I just went for a walk on a beach, I had no idea there was a truck down there."

She smiled.

"Good luck, bad luck, who knows what will come our way?"

He smiled back, then started to get up as Preston reappeared. The older man waved at him to sit down.

"We have a couple of minutes," he said. "Joseph doesn't need this space until this evening. Let's figure out next steps."

"I can check the registration information once I get back to the station," said Janet. "Unless something else has blown up, I should be able to do that this afternoon. I'll give you a call."

Preston nodded in appreciation.

"I can't do anything else about that until I hear from you," he said. "I also have to speak to Anne Gaudet and give her an update. The car business depends on what John finds out and he said he won't get to it until Sunday."

They both turned to Rashford, who shrugged.

"I've got no plans," he said. "My contact from Halifax is on holiday for another week so there will be nothing happening there for a while. Like you say, Jim, I can't give any more information to Anne either. And I don't really understand this smuggling pirate business."

Janet laughed, shaking her head.

"I don't think any of us do," she said, then paused. She glanced at Preston and then back to Rashford.

"According to Compass last night," she said, "it's going to be a lovely hot weekend. It sounds like you should go and spend it on the beach."

"What's Compass?"

Preston snorted.

"It's the local news show, every afternoon at six o'clock. Something like eighty per cent of Islanders watch it. But their Thursday forecasts are rubbish."

"They are not!" said Parsons.

"They always say it will be a good weekend," said Preston. "They want the tourists who are planning to come here to stick to their plans. Tonight, they'll give a proper forecast and say, 'oh sorry, a cold front appeared out of Ontario and it's going to rain'. But by then the tourists are here, spending their money."

"You're just an old cynic," said Parsons, as Rashford laughed.

"You watch," muttered Preston. He looked thoughtful for a moment, then turned to Parsons with a smile.

"How about you find that registration information for me this afternoon, and we spend the weekend tracking down Muriel Stanhope?"

Parsons scoffed.

"Why should I spend my days off running around helping you with your private investigations?"

"Loyalty and respect," grinned Preston. "And you want to find her as much as I do. If charges are involved, you'll get the credit."

"That's true," conceded Parsons. She thought for a moment.

"Okay, how about this. We'll meet tomorrow morning, not too early, and if it's a nice day we'll go to the beach. If it's raining, we'll go looking up addresses."

Rashford looked at her.

"We?" he said.

She nodded.

"Yes. Where are you staying?"

He told her, and she suggested they meet outside at nine.

"We can go to the Farmers' Market and get some food for a picnic," she said, "and then head out to a beach."

"Bread and cheese would be good," said Preston. "We can eat in the car out of the rain."

They all laughed and stood up. Rashford felt the sun on his neck, the heat of it percolating though the vine leaves. He decided to spend the rest of the afternoon looking for a bathing suit.

～

Rashford got back to his hotel just after six and threw his purchases on the bed. Then he switched on the television and channel surfed until he found the local news on CBC. He was delighted to hear that a pet Fat-Bellied Pig which had run away three days ago had been found, unharmed, and was now happily reunited with its owner. He then groaned as the weatherman appeared and started making a number of stupid pig-related jokes while waving his arms around and laughing maniacally.

The news anchor eventually brought the meteorologist back on track to give the weather forecast. Rashford laughed as the forecast was regretfully changed, an area of low pressure having emerged out of central Canada and now threatening rain for the afternoon. This fact was presented as good news for the agricultural industries on the Island, the implication being that the tourists should 'take one for the team' and be glad they could at least have a morning on the beach or the golf course.

For some reason the forecast closed with a photograph of two kittens, each nestled into the breast cup of a bikini top, an image which the weatherman found both cute and hilarious. He was still waving and laughing as Rashford turned off the television, then picked up his phone and called Anne. She was delighted to hear from him and agreed to his idea of meeting for dinner and a drink. They spent the evening chatting and made plans for him to go out with her and Sandra at the beginning of the week.

"Mom has Monday off," she said. "If you don't mind driving, we'll go east, down towards Murray Harbour. Hardly any tourists get down there and it's just beautiful."

He agreed and was back to his hotel room before ten o'clock.

At nine the next morning he was waiting outside when Janet Parsons pulled up in a bright yellow Subaru Cross-Trek. She waved him over.

"Get in the front," she said, "your legs are longer. Move the seat back until you're comfortable. Jim can sit behind me."

She accelerated away, explaining that she had arranged to pick Preston up from his house on their way to the market. They left the main downtown core and entered an area where detached houses with spacious gardens stood well back from the tree-lined streets. They pulled into the driveway of a low rancher-style building. Jim Preston came out, locking the door carefully behind him, and walked to the car.

"This is where the rich people live," laughed Janet. "Jim hates being teased about it, though."

"What was that?" said Preston, climbing into he back seat.

"Oh, nothing," said Rashford. "Janet was just telling me what a ritzy area of town you live in."

Preston scoffed.

"I'm on the wrong side of the street," he said. "The fancy places are over there, on the water side. I'm only VR."

"VR? What's that?"

"Vicariously ritzy," he laughed, then patted Parsons on the shoulder.

"Come on then, if you want to get to the beach. Rain is coming this afternoon."

She shook her head and pulled away from the curb.

"Market first," she said, "then I thought we'd go to Basin Head. Does that suit you?"

"Perfect," said Preston.

Rashford looked at the map on his phone and shook his head.

"That's miles away," he said. "Anne told me the best beaches were in the national park at Brackley Beach and we would probably go there."

Preston scoffed.

"I'd disagree that it's the best beach," he said, "but it is closer to town. The two problems with it are first that it's always crowded with people, and second that it's nowhere near the addresses that Janet found for us yesterday. Basin Head will be just as crowded as Brackley, so you'll still get the full tourist experience, but this afternoon we can drive around and have a gander at some properties. Okay?"

Rashford agreed that this was okay, and then watched with admiration as Janet navigated a crowded parking lot and followed a woman who was carrying two large shopping bags. She waited patiently while the woman placed her shopping in her car and then turned into the space as soon as it became vacant.

"Parking karma," said Preston, noting how close they were to the building. They got out of the car and stretched, then walked up a short flight of wooden steps. There was an open area crowded with tables under awnings, small caravans, and customers with bulging bags and baskets. Rashford saw one stall that seemed to only sell tomatoes, boxes of multiple varieties being picked over by people with keen eyes and keener elbows. Another stall focused on carrots, displaying large bunches of them with crowns of leaves attached.

They walked inside past an older gentleman who sang songs in Spanish, accompanying himself with a guitar.

"He's been here forever," whispered Janet, as she guided Rashford into the building. "I think he reminds people of their winter holidays in Cuba or Mexico."

Once they were inside, past the toilets and what appeared to be an office, Rashford saw that there was one row of stalls against the outer wall and a second row which formed a central core. The aisle that separated the two sides was about eight feet wide and crammed with shoppers. The air was hot and oppressive, with only a few windows open to let in any breeze.

Jim Preston disappeared with a muttered 'see you in a few minutes' and Janet bullied her way through the crowd, talking over her shoulder. The building itself was an old railway station, Rashford learned, and should really be expanded but there was an ongoing dispute between the Mi'kmaq community and the government as to land ownership. As a result, the market felt almost claustrophobic, a situation exacerbated by two women pushing double-wide strollers through the aisle.

'At least they're in tandem, not parallel,' thought Rashford as he tried to edge out of the way but still had his leg grabbed by a sticky hand.

They passed stalls selling all manner of vegetables that Janet told him were locally grown.

"They have to be clearly marked if they're from away," she said, "but pretty much everything here is locally grown or made."

In addition to the onions and potatoes, beets and beans, mushrooms and kale, this edict apparently applied to the craft leathers and pottery, the hormone-free chickens, and the wide variety of brown and white eggs. Some people were actively selling their product but most simply stood in their booth, engaging in conversation if someone stopped but otherwise not touting their goods.

At the top end of the market, they were held up by lines of people waiting to be served their morning coffee, each cup of which was being painstakingly crafted by hand. The three young people behind the counter chatted with each other and customers alike, and to Rashford's western eye appeared to be functioning at half the speed he would expect. An older man, presumably the owner, stood outside the booth and had his own queue of people waiting to receive half-pound and pound bags of coffee beans, some of which were sold whole, and others which were ground on the spot.

They eased through the lines and started back down the other side. At one stall a vendor in a creased tweed jacket was talking to a man standing off by the wall, the two of them totally ignoring a customer who held two chocolate croissants in one hand and a ten-dollar bill in the other. Eventually the customer gave up, leaving the bill on top of a loaf of rye bread and walking away. As Rashford watched, another customer came by, picked up both the ten-dollar bill and the rye bread, and gave them to the man in the jacket, who nonchalantly gave a five-dollar bill as change. The customer burst out laughing.

"It's no wonder you never make any money," he said, and explained the situation. The tweed jacket man looked confused but took the proffered second ten-dollar bill with a shake of his head, then resumed his conversation with the man to the side of his booth.

Janet was on the other side of the aisle. She tugged Rashford by the arm.

"Are you okay with sourdough bread?" she said.

He nodded, and she bought a round country white loaf, dropping it into a shopping bag that she materialized from a pocket. They crossed the aisle to where a glass fronted case displayed two dozen or more varieties of cheese.

"Any preference?" she asked.

Rashford shook his head and indicated that any type of cheese was fine by him. Janet bought some extra strong cheddar and a round gouda covered in green wax.

"These are both local," she said, and then led him down past a stall selling woollen mitts and hats, another with a wide variety of brightly coloured paintings, and a large, refrigerated display case of chicken and turkey meat. At the end of the corridor, between the pottery and the pork, she bought four bottles of cider which were handed to her in a small cardboard carry case.

"Let's go and find Jim," she said. "He's probably with the coven."

Rashford raised an eyebrow but didn't say anything. They walked past the stalls selling cooked food, the smells of perogies and pizza mingling with spring rolls and samosa. At one stall there were display boxes of small potatoes alongside bags of carrots, but Janet stopped to buy green onions and then, at the next stall, a long green cucumber. They turned into the eating area, a small space reserved for customers who wanted to chat and visit. Here they found Jim sitting at a table. He was talking to five older women, who laughed at something he said and took turns patting him on the arm. He looked up at them and nodded a greeting.

"Sorry, ladies," he said. "My friends are here. I've got to dash, I'm afraid, no rest for the wicked."

One of the old ladies cackled.

"That's what I always found, when I was young. I never got any rest in bed."

The rest of the group guffawed politely, although Rashford was sure they had heard the story before, and Jim smiled at her.

"I bet you were a right looker when you were young, Flo," he said.

She tsked at him.

"What do you mean, were? I still am."

The five all laughed again, genuinely this time, and Preston accepted the rebuke with a nod, laughing with them as he stood from the table. Parsons and Rashford followed him from the table and outside into the heat.

CHAPTER ELEVEN

Once they were back in the Subaru and had emerged unscathed from the car park, Janet spoke.

"Out with it," she said. "What did you learn?"

Jim Preston leaned forward between the seats and grinned.

"Well, he said, "I learned that our friend Muriel Stanhope is indeed Brenda Frizwell, as you surmised from that registration check. So, well done, Janet."

She nodded in appreciation.

"Nobody much likes our Brenda," Preston continued. "Apparently, she's got 'a mouth as foul as a sewer and as big as Darnley Basin', or so I'm told. She's got three sons and they're all bad 'uns according to the ladies, troublemakers since they were in school. None of them are married because Brenda hasn't found anyone who she's willing to accept into the family. One boy runs the farm for her, another has a lobster boat, and the third drives long-haul trucks to Toronto and back, carrying potatoes."

"What does the dad do?" asked Rashford.

Preston scoffed.

"There's no dad around. Brenda is from out Toronto way, originally. According to Gail, she turned up and set her cap to Stu Frizwell, was pregnant within the hour, and moved onto the farm. He disappeared when the oldest boy was about nine, the youngest about three. Gladys told me she'd heard that he went out west on a job and just never came back, but Maida reckons Brenda didn't want any more kids, so she offed him and fed him to the pigs. Take your pick."

"She sounds like a lovely lady," said Janet, chuckling.

"'Tough as an old boot and vicious as a pit pull', or so I'm told," said Preston.

Janet looked across at Rashford and grinned.

"What do you reckon, shall we go and rattle some chains?"

"Sounds good to me," he said, then settled back in his seat and watched the countryside unfurl.

He recognized a few places he had seen on his drive out to Goose River and was kept amused by Preston's stories. Despite changes in ownership and, subsequently, colour scheme, one house was known locally as 'it used to be the purple house'. The tall wooden structure in front of a garden centre was a feeding station for the petting zoo goats, who had to climb to the top to reach the bundles of hay. It seemed that otherwise they got no exercise to offset the multiples handfuls of pellets they were fed by bored children left to amuse themselves while their parents argued over which type of basil would be best for their kitchen garden. The large farm on a hill was owned by one of Canada's longest serving Members of Parliament, who had been dragged kicking and screaming into retirement by his wife.

At St. Peter's Bay they stopped for ice cream, Rashford's suggestion, at what he referred to as 'his' shop. They walked over the road and leaned against the iron balustrade of the bridge, the breeze on their faces a pleasant relief. The river was running out, churning against the estuary, and they watched gulls and terns scream and drop into the bay on their perpetual search for food. Further out, a man in a small boat maneuvered his way along the lines of buoys, every so often leaning over to tug one of the mussel ropes. Apart from the whoosh of a passing car, it was quiet.

Preston finished first, crunching the last inch of cone into his mouth and then pulling out his cigarettes. He offered one to Rashford, who took it, and to Parsons, who didn't. They stared meditatively across the bay.

"I've been thinking," said Parsons. "We're doing this the wrong way."

Rashford glanced at her. Her eyes were still focused on the buoys. He murmured questioningly.

"Well," she said. "It makes more sense to wander through the country on the way to the beach. Afterwards most people just want to get home for a beer. If we take the top road, towards North Lake, we can cut down across the point and ..."

"And ask for directions, as if we were lost," finished Preston, smiling at her. He nodded at Rashford. "Well, you can. With your accent, she'll know immediately you're from away."

Rashford stubbed out his cigarette.

"I don't have an accent," he said. "It's you who speak funny."

They chuntered back and forth as Parsons led them back across the road. She was laughing as she pulled the car back onto the highway and took the top road, up the hill and out along the north shore.

As they detoured over the wooden bridge at Naufrage, a local attraction that Janet Parsons could not believe Rashford had missed on his two previous visits, Preston spoke up again.

"I've had a thought as well," he said.

Rashford maintained his grip on the dashboard, mentally assisting as Janet eased the car over the steep and rattling boards. A car waited on the other side of the narrow channel, unable to cross until they completed the passage. A lobster boat cruised beneath them, returning back from an early morning run to pull traps. It was only when they were back on solid ground, and Preston had waved a casual thank you to the waiting car, that Rashford relaxed and breathed again.

Janet smirked.

"You should have seen the old bridge," she said. "It got damaged in Hurricane Fiona and they rebuilt it, stronger and safer."

"That must have been terrifying."

She shrugged.

"People liked it," she said. "It was a good photo opportunity. After the storm the fishers asked for it to be higher, so the bigger boats could get under it to use the wharf, and the highway people wanted it to be a bit wider and less steep. So, this is what we have now."

Preston huffed.

"Sorry to interrupt this infomercial," he said, "but as I mentioned, I've had an idea."

"What's that?" said Rashford.

Preston chuckled.

"We're a bit like the odd couple, aren't we? You, me, and Parsons here. Hardly your typical tourists, now."

Parsons scoffed.

"Speak for yourself. We're a pair of holidaymakers and you're our cranky uncle who's along for the ride."

Rashford laughed.

"Who'd be related to him? I think he's a hitchhiker we happened to pick up."

"Or a bored guest at our hotel who's glommed on to us for the day."

"Maybe he missed his cruise ship and he's waiting to be repatriated."

"Or perhaps ..."

"Thank you," muttered Preston. "Very funny. As I was saying, three of us in a car looks a bit funny."

Rashford turned and looked over his shoulder.

"What, you think one of us should get out somewhere?"

Preston shook his head. Rashford stared at him, then nodded.

"Do you think that would work?"

Parsons glanced at him.

"What are you two talking about?" she said.

"I'm on holiday," said Paula White, standing resolutely above them on the steps up to the cabin. Jim Preston and Janet Parsons stood below her, while Rashford was off to one side, trying to calm an excited Cilla.

"It'll be fun," said Preston.

"First you said you were taking photographs, then you said you were looking for some pirates. What exactly is going on?"

Janet Parsons pushed gently on Preston's arm.

"Jim," she said, "why don't you go and help Gavin walk the dog around the lawn a bit. I'll chat with Paula here."

He looked at her, then back up to Paula, who nodded. Giving a large sigh, he walked across the gravel and onto the mixed-herbs lawn. Cilla looked at him and growled, edging protectively in front of Rashford, who held her collar lightly and waited until Preston was almost upon them.

"Scratch her ears, Jim," he said. "Then you'll be friends."

Preston huffed but complied, and the three of them set off around the side of the house. They walked out to the picket fence and looked over the edge.

"Don't they worry about the dog?" said Preston.

Rashford turned and gestured behind, to where Cilla lay on the grass, panting slightly, gaze firmly fixed on them.

"There's an invisible fence under here, and she knows it. She won't come any closer in case she gets zapped."

Preston looked over again.

"Smart dog. This is kind of scary."

They stood and watched three gulls angling down towards the beach, wings outstretched to catch the updraught. They gave a final turn and then landed softly on the sand.

"Just as good as the old Parachute regiment," said Preston in an admiring tone. "Perfect landings."

Rashford laughed, then stepped back from the fence. As soon as he was twenty feet away, Cilla got to her feet and bounded over to him, her tail wagging at speed. He ruffled the back of her neck.

"Come on then," he said. "I'll race you."

He started running back towards the house and then sharply turned, zig-zagging to left and right before curving back towards Preston, who sauntered behind them. Cilla lolloped alongside him, barking. They stopped and Rashford bent over, panting, while Cilla sat on her haunches and looked at him quizzically.

"I don't think she even went into second," chortled Jim. "Here, you look like you could do with a smoke."

He passed the packet to a panting Rashford, who took one gratefully. As Preston brought out his lighter a loud voice cut through the air.

"Sorry, this is a no-smoking property. Do you mind?"

"It's Paula's mother," Rashford muttered from the side of his mouth. "Best do as she says."

Preston waved an acknowledgement and took the cigarette back from Rashford, putting the packet and lighter in his pocket. The woman went back inside, and the men continued their slow promenade around the lawn. They had made three circuits before the door opened and Paula emerged onto the back verandah, carrying a tray with glasses and a pitcher of lemonade. Janet followed with a plastic bowl full of potato chips.

Once they were all settled around a table, drinks poured and chips piled on paper napkins next to each hand, Paula spoke up.

"Okay," she said, "I'll go along with this. But only for today, right? I want to enjoy my holiday."

Rashford nodded.

"Thank you," he said. She scoffed.

"My second condition is, Janet is the lead, okay? As far as I can tell, she is the only one of you with anything like jurisdiction here. If things go sideways, I want to be able to say that I was assisting a serving officer, not following on to a pair of cowboys."

Rashford spread his hands.

"That works for me," he said. "I'm just along for the ride, no ownership at all."

Janet Parsons looked across at Preston.

"What about you, Jim? After all, it was your case."

The old detective shrugged and took a drink of lemonade, then crunched some potato chips into his mouth.

"It's yours now," he said, spraying crumbs onto the table. "I'm just helping you with your inquiries, as it were. I'm good with that."

Janet leaned forward and steepled her hands on the table. She ticked off the points on her fingers as she spoke.

"Our cover story is, we're four friends out for a drive. Paula here is our host, they have a family cottage, all that backstory is kosher. That protects us if Brenda Frizwell knows who they are, which is likely. If this is a smuggling operation, then the family will be aware of everyone in the area."

Preston nodded.

"Makes sense," he said. "Are we out visiting from Charlottetown or somewhere else?"

"Gavin is obviously from away, he looks and speaks funny," said Paula, smiling sweetly. Janet grinned, while Preston elbowed Rashford in the ribs.

"I guess you're not forgiven yet," he said.

"Stop it, guys," said Janet. "I worry about her recognizing you or me as police officers, Jim. Especially if she knows that Paula is a member of the Halifax force. So, I think we should be from away as well."

He nodded.

"Are we just friends, or two couples?"

"Paula and I talked about that," said Janet, smiling. "We think that we need to be as confusing as possible. So, if it's needed, we're going to say that we're a couple, and you two are distant cousins who are over for a visit."

Rashford and Preston looked at each other, then shrugged.

"It's as good a plan as any," said Preston. "Come on, let's get in the car."

Cilla barked.

"Yes, you can come as well," said Paula.

They cruised along the coast road with a brief stop at Secret Cove so that Janet could see the place where the fishing boat had pulled close inshore. Cilla took the opportunity to run around and pee on various tufts of grass, then was disappointed at not being taken for a walk and had to be bribed back into the car with a series of treats. She slumped down in the trunk area with a huff and the four humans looked at each other. Janet took a deep breath.

"I want to revise the plan," she said. "To make this seem real."

"Go on," said Rashford.

"It's your case," said Jim.

Paula nodded.

"Well," said Janet. "Two things. First, we should head down to the beach now, before it rains. We'll go round the point and down to Basin Head. Afterwards we can drive up the Baltic Road and have a look at the address I found. If we see anybody, we'll tell them that we were taking the scenic route back to Souris and got lost. Is that okay?

The other three nodded.

"Second, I think that Paula should sit up front next to me," said Janet. "Then we can chat. You two can squeeze in the back. That will look normal as well."

"Can the front seat go forward a bit?" said Rashford, looking dubiously at the leg room he was being offered. Paula reached down and pressed the lever, moving the seat forward a few inches.

"I've got legs as well, you know," she said.

Eventually they were all settled and started out again towards the East Point lighthouse. As the car began to move, Cilla raised herself and leaned her head over the back seat, breathing noisily in Rashford's ear. After he reached his arm back and scratched her nose, she sighed and lay back down on the stained rug.

At the lighthouse they kept Cilla on a leash as they walked around, peering over the fence at the drop down to the ocean. Five seals bobbed in the water where the currents met, and lines of gannets flew grid patterns in their search for fish.

"We get water coming from three directions here," said the older lady in the gift shop, "and that stirs everything up so there's lots of food for the fish. And where there's fish, there's birds and seals."

Her voice hovered slightly beneath the 'I thought every idiot knew that' tone which Rashford had half-expected, just enough that nobody could get upset but clear that she was a hairsbreadth from saying something that might impact sales. He thanked her for the information and felt guilty enough that he bought a Nelly J. Banks tea towel, for whom he was not sure. The sales lady nodded.

"That was a big rum running ship, back in the day," she said, smiling.

"Does that still happen?" said Rashford. "Rum running, smuggling, that sort of thing?"

She looked at him.

"Hard to say, dear," she said. "There's stories, of course, but they don't get shared much in public."

She winked at him.

"You might be a buyer, but you might also be a revenue man. Who's to know?"

Rashford laughed.

"I'm not a revenue man," he said. "But I wouldn't mind some decent rum if there was some around."

The lady nodded, then looked around quickly. She leaned over the counter and crooked her finger to beckon Rashford forward. He stepped up and put his head next to hers. She placed a finger on her lips and spoke softly.

"Now don't you be telling anyone I told you this," she said. "This is just between you and me."

Rashford glanced around. Paula and Janet were over by the postcard and knick-knack collections, admiring a series of earrings made from sea-glass and driftwood. Jim Preston was outside, walking a bored Cilla up and down the picket fence between the gift shop and the lighthouse. There was nobody else in the shop except a young girl who was working as an assistant, gently dusting some small seabirds made from stained glass. Rashford leaned back over the counter.

"You want good rum?"

He nodded.

Her voice dropped even lower, and he had to strain to hear.

"The liquor store in Souris is open until late," she whispered, grasping his hand. He stared at her, then they both burst out laughing.

"Gotcha!" she said, wiping her eyes.

Rashford shook his head, paid for the tea towel, and then left to join Jim for a smoke while they waited for Janet and Paula to finish looking through the shop.

From East Point they drove down through a few small hamlets and then turned off to the left, along a narrow, paved road which led them into a large, gravelled car park. They walked down the hill and onto a platform decked with wooden boards. Grey clapboard buildings lined the edge of the channel that directed a small river, crossed by a narrow bridge crowded with teenagers, into the ocean.

"This is the famous Basin Head beach," said Janet, pointing towards the shore. Rashford looked around.

"What's that?" he said, pointing to a ribbon of corrugated blue plastic sheeting laid across the sand.

"It's for wheelchairs," said Janet. "They kept getting stuck. The idea is that everybody should be able to access the beach."

"That's a clever idea," said Rashford.

"It's a bit crowded," said Paula, surveying the beach with distaste. "Do we have to go down there?"

Rashford huffed.

"I'm going," he said. "I've not come all this way just to look at the ocean. I want to have a paddle!"

Janet laughed.

"I'll go with you," she said.

Jim looked at the crowded sand and shook his head.

"I'm not fighting that mob," he said. "And it's not fair to leave the dog in the car by herself. I'll go back up and sit with her."

Paula nodded.

"That would be good," she said. "Maybe I'll come with you. I'm not a big fan of crowds."

Rashford and Janet looked at each other.

"We need to have wet towels," said Rashford, "just in case."

Janet laughed.

"Well, it does seem crazy for you to come all the way from the prairies and not get wet. Okay, a quick dip. We'll see you guys shortly."

She went first, picking her way through the family groups and the gaggles of teenagers, the couples and the awkward trios, the sleek and the stout, the large and the small. Rashford followed, checking over his shoulder and seeing the other two slowly walking back up the hill. He nearly stumbled over the red and white Lifeguard paddle board that was barely visible in the crush, but the young woman on the tall red chair just laughed at his clumsiness.

At the end of the beach, almost underneath the red soil cliff topped with trees, they found an empty spot of white sand beach. Janet lay down her towel, then looked at Rashford.

"I'm going in," she said. "Are you coming?"

He nodded.

"Of course. I'm wearing my trunks under my jeans."

He kicked off his shoes and pulled off his jeans, then threw his shirt down on the pile. When he looked up, Janet had also shucked off her clothes and was waiting for him. He took in the yellow one-piece bathing suit she was wearing and smiled.

"What?" she said.

He shook his head.

"Last one in's a sissy," he shouted, and dashed down to the waterline, jinking between people lying on the sand.

He was three strides in before he realized how cold the water was, stumbling as he tried to stop and turn around at the same time as lifting his feet out of the waves. With a curse he fell belly first into the surf, water spurting up around him in a great splash.

Gasping, he sat up, only to be hit on the side of his head by the next wave. He rolled over onto his knees and pushed himself upright, wiping the salt from his eyes. Once he could see, he looked to the beach. Janet was standing just beyond the surf line, arms folded, tears streaming down her face as she laughed.

"It's fucking freezing," screamed Rashford, causing her to laugh even more as she raised a hand.

"Language," she said. "There are children about."

Most of whom were laughing just as hard as Janet was, Rashford noted sourly, as he hopped from one foot to another.

Janet walked into the water and stepped towards him. The water was below her knees, and he realized what a sight he must have provided. She patted him on the arm as she went past.

"Most of us walk out to where it's a bit deeper," she said.

~

Later, when they were sitting on their towels, Janet asked him about his work in Alsama.

"I've always wanted to go out west," she said. "I've never been past Toronto."

Rashford laughed.

"There's no ocean out there," he said. "Just miles and miles of prairie. We do have sand dunes, though."

"Really?"

He told her about the Great Sandhills Park and the World's Largest Wheat Stalk Sculpture controversy, which made her laugh. That led into him describing the people of Maple Creek, his work, and the link to Anne Gaudet which had brought him to the Island.

"So, the Amanda Robicheau thing was just coincidence?" she said.

Rashford shrugged.

"Perhaps. Coincidence or karma, take your pick."

She huffed.

"Some karma. Four thousand kilometres from home and stuck on an Island with two ex-girlfriends. You must have done something really terrible in a previous life."

Janet leaned forward and picked at a hangnail on her big toe, avoiding his eye, but he could see she was trying not to laugh. He tried to change the subject.

"That reminds me, Anne talked about her dad once. She said he used to run a small garage in Charlottetown but had more or less retired. Some fellow called Jean was looking after it now. Do you know, has anyone spoken to him?"

Janet looked at him.

"How would I know? This isn't an official case, you know. You'd better ask Jim."

She looked around.

"Talking of who, we should probably go. They'll be wondering what we're up to."

"I doubt it," said Rashford. "There are way too many people around for us to be getting up to anything."

She pushed him on the shoulder, hard, so he fell onto the sand. He lay on his side and watched as she lithely sprang to her feet.

"Not unless you're a closet exhibitionist," he laughed.

"Wouldn't you like to know," she said, flicking her towel at him, "Anyway, you're the one with the body art!"

"What?" said Rashford, confused.

"The dinosaur plasters on your shoulder," she laughed, and started walking away down the beach. He watched her for a moment, convinced that she was flirting with him, then scrambled to his feet. He picked up and shook out his towel, then grabbed his clothes and followed her striking yellow swimsuit through the crowd.

Chapter Twelve

They found Jim and Paula sitting on a grassy bank under a tree, Cilla lying next to them and panting, her tongue hanging out. She wagged her tail half-heartedly as Janet leaned over and scratched her ears.

"The poor thing needs a drink," she said.

Preston huffed.

"I've taken her down to the damned creek seven times in the last hour," he grumbled. "It's me that needs a drink."

Paula laughed.

"She's been playing him," she said, standing up and stretching her arms over her shoulders. "Jim walks her down, she drinks, then he lets her off-leash to run back up here. By the time Jim makes it to the top of the hill, Cilla figures she needs another drink."

The dog stood up and stretched, mimicking Paula by extending her front paws as far as possible and then arching her back. She turned to Jim and whined, dropping her head and looking up at him through her eyelashes.

"Oh, wow, the Princess Di look!" said Janet. "She's really sussed you out, Jim."

Preston grunted and tried to stand, pushing one hand onto the grass for leverage. Rashford leaned over and grabbed his arm.

"Up you get, old timer," he said, pulling him to his feet.

Preston shook him off and glared at the group.

"It's my knees," he said. "They sometimes take a while to get working."

"Nothing to do with the smokes, then?" said Janet, shaking her head.

Preston met her gaze and reddened slightly. She chuffed, then turned and walked over to the car, Jim a few steps behind. Paula and Rashford exchanged glances, then followed, Cilla slouching along beside them.

It was only as they drove back down the narrow access road back to the highway that Rashford posed the question that had been bothering him.

"Jim," he said, "have you spoken to Marc Gaudet's widow, or to that fellow Jean who was running his garage?"

Jim looked at him, then scratched his ear.

"I spoke to Francine LeBlanc, yes. I'm not sure whether she's officially his widow because they weren't married, but she was his significant other. She told me that he was okay, but she was starting to notice some little things. He would sometimes forget what he was doing, or bump into a door, or doze off when they were watching television."

Paula spoke over her shoulder.

"Had he been seeing a doctor?"

Preston laughed.

"I asked her that. Her answer was, 'what doctor?' Apparently, there are no GPs in that area of the Island, and since the government closed the local hospital, people have to drive an hour into Summerside, or two hours if they have to go to Charlottetown. As she put it, 'tu n'y vas que si tu vas mourir'."

"'You only go there if you're going to die'? That's a bit morbid," said Janet, taking her eyes off the road long enough to glance around. "I know the health care system here is in trouble but that's a terrible thing to say."

Preston shrugged.

"It's the new rural reality," he said. "Doctors want a decent work-life balance these days, as well as educational and extra-curricula activities for their kids and a social life for themselves. Being constantly on-call in a small community is nobody's idea of a balanced life."

He paused, looking out of the window. The summer wheat shimmered in the heat.

"I mean, why would you want to miss the opportunity to get out to the beach on a day like today?"

The others murmured agreement. Jim continued to look out of the window as he spoke.

"Now's not the time for a fulsome debate about health care on the Island," he said, "but as a retired person I wish they'd get their act together. The system was set up when we did have rural doctors, mostly men, who were willing to give up their evenings and weekends to go and see patients, make house calls, whatever. The doctors have changed, and the system hasn't. That's the problem. We trying to do the same old same old in a new environment."

Paula laughed.

"Wasn't it Einstein who said that the definition of insanity was doing the same thing over and over again and expecting different results?"

Janet looked across at her.

"You don't need to be Einstein to know that," she said.

They all laughed.

"Anyway," said Jim, blowing out his breath noisily. "The short answer is, yes, I've spoken to the widow, but not to the garage guy, Jean Gauthier. I did go around there but he was away somewhere, fixing somebody's combine, and I haven't had time to go back. Thanks for the nudge. I'll put him on the list for next week."

Rashford nodded his thanks. Just then, Janet indicated that she was turning off the highway.

"Right," she said. "This is the Baltic Road. We go up here a bit and then turn left. Keep your eyes peeled."

"You've got to be joking," said Rashford, leaning between the front seats and peering through the windscreen. "That's a road?"

"According to the map, yes. It's a route vicinale. A local road."

They had turned at the sign and then pulled to a halt, looking ahead at the rutted track. Large red rocks littered the edges of the banks and dark shadow gashes on the road surface indicated the presence of deep potholes. Jim Preston leaned next to Rashford and scoffed.

"Just be glad it's not rained for a week," he said. "Then it would get a bit slippy."

Janet grinned.

"We've got all wheel drive," she said. "Hang on, folks."

She drove slowly, trying to avoid the deeper ruts and larger rocks, but the vehicle still bumped and banged as they travelled. With one hand, Rashford clung onto the handle just above his window; the other he pressed down hard on the seat between himself and Preston.

"Who the heck lives down here?" he said. "There's nothing here!"

Paula half-turned in her seat.

"Yes, there is. Do you not see all the driveways? People live at the end of those, you know."

Rashford scoffed.

"Driveways? You mean those tracks cut into the bush?"

"Yes, each one has a house at the end of it. Well, sometimes not a house, maybe a trailer or a camper van. But it's somebody's home."

"I've heard of off-grid but this is ridiculous. There are no civic numbers or anything."

"Folks out here like their privacy."

Paula turned back to face the front and there was silence for a few minutes, then Janet burst out laughing.

"She's winding you up," she said. "Those are mainly logging roads. Sometimes there might be a summer cabin, or a river where people go fishing, but nobody actually lives here. Look, there are not even any power lines."

She pointed to the edges of the road, which were bare of any kind of pole or other human invention.

"Ha ha, very funny," muttered Rashford. Preston poked him in the ribs.

"You'll always be our favourite come-from-away if you keep falling for those," he said.

They had gone nearly two kilometres when the local road emerged onto another dirt road, this one scraped clear of rocks and debris, trees on each side arching over to form a pergola. The ride became immediately smoother.

"This is a heritage road," said Paula, waving the map. "That means that it has been left unpaved as a sort of museum exhibit. According to the tourist people, 'these narrow, red clay lanes are special places, each with a story.' So now you know."

"What? There are different categories of dirt road?" said Rashford, shaking his head. "The ones they leave unpaved on purpose, and the ones they just leave? Who knew?"

They travelled under the canopy of trees, the sunlight making zebra stripes of shadow on the red dirt. Now and again, they passed what appeared to be a deserted farm field, sometimes with an abandoned building slowly disintegrating back to the land, but usually the view beyond the trees was one of forest. After another five kilometres, the road dropped down to a narrow bridge that spanned a small creek. On the other side they could see a yellow sign indicating that the pavement was broken. Janet pulled over to the side of the road.

"We're getting near, I think," she said. "Let's just go over our plans."

"Can we get out for a minute?" said Jim Preston. "I'd love a smoke."

The road from the bridge was thinly paved, the edges cracked and blistered, numerous cracks and potholes across the surface. They rattled along past what appeared to be fields of low brown scrub.

"Blueberry fields," said Jim. "They're wild. All you have to do is mow them down every couple of years and then take the harvest. Good money if you've got some, though."

A large field had a herd of black cows grazing; one lifted its head as they drove past, but the rest ignored them. There was a narrow windbreak of trees, planted to line a driveway that was bookended by two plastic bins, one green and one black, and a small tidy bungalow. Paula checked the paper which Janet had given her.

"That's 3195", she said. "We're looking for 4013, it won't be far."

They passed a small thicket of trees and bushes, after which there was a field strewn with the broken stems of dried grasses and grain stalks, fringed by an electric fence. A tractor with a rusted bucket was parked at the edge of the field, a tattered For Sale sign hanging from a wing mirror. At the end of the fence was an open-faced building, nothing more than a shed, with a hand-painted sign indicating Fresh Vegitables for Sale. The blue civic number sign was nailed to the corner post of the fence. Janet let out a deep breath, indicated, and turned in.

They bumped along for a hundred metres, the electric fence on one side and a sagging wood and wire fence on the other, marking the edge between the unkempt driveway and an equally unkempt field where three bedraggled goats were hobbled to wooden stakes. Ahead they could see another small shed, this one with corrugated iron walls and a flat roof, a yard dotted with disabled vehicles, and at the end of the drive a low bungalow with a wide verandah. The house looked weathered and worn. There were gaps in the rows of shingles along the front wall, and the surface of those that remained was pockmarked where the wind had stripped the paint.

In the yard there was a yellow school bus missing a front wheel, a nose-down pick-up truck missing two, and three snowmobiles with fractured tracks splayed around. From behind a red sedan with a stove-in front end, two aggressive geese appeared and marched purposefully towards the car, their wings flapping, their necks extended. Janet slowed down as the geese scurried out onto the road.

When she stopped the vehicle they could hear the angry cries of the geese, a sound soon overwhelmed by the deep baying howl of a large mixed breed dog that emerged from behind the metal shed, straining against a heavy linked chain.

"Well, they'll know we're here," said Preston with a snort. "I recommend we stay in the vehicle."

Rashford huffed.

"You think? I'm not going out there."

Paula laughed.

"You western wuss," she said. "Never seen a goose before?"

From the back of the car, Cilla whimpered.

"It's okay," said Rashford, leaning over to scratch her neck. "We'll protect you."

"Quiet, someone's coming," said Janet.

A large man had appeared at the front door of the farmhouse. He paused, scratching his belly, then walked down the steps and across the yard. He was carrying a stick and the dog cringed back as he approached, sinking back on its haunches and staring at the car. The geese moved to the side of the drive, still cackling.

"He's got a gun," said Paula in a low voice, noticing that the stick was a shotgun that the man cradled under one arm. "Fuck."

"It's okay," said Jim Preston. "It's cracked open. And we're just lost tourists, remember."

They sat silently as the man approached, moving towards the driver's side door but scanning the car thoroughly as he did so. Janet pressed the button and her window wound down.

"Hello," she said, as brightly as she could. "I wonder if ..."

"Git your car off my momma's farm," said the man.

"... could help us. We're a bit lost, you see. We were at the beach ..."

The man spat, then leaned to the window.

"Git your car off my momma's farm," he repeated.

"Which way ..."

The man stepped back, clicking the barrel of the shotgun into the stock. He jerked it towards the road.

"That way," he said. "Back out. Another yard further and I shoot your tires, then I let the dog off the chain."

He scratched his stomach, the grimy tee-shirt taut over his belly.

"Thank you for your help," said Janet, putting the car into gear and reversing slowly back to the road.

"He's been watching too many American movies," muttered Rashford. "'Git your car off my momma's farm'? What kind of Island welcome is that?"

"He was quoting the Klan 101 handbook," said Janet, shaking her head. "I'm glad I wasn't on my own."

They drove past three wind turbines and followed the road almost a kilometre in silence before Paula spoke.

"Did you see her?"

Jim grunted.

"At the window, yes. She had to have a look at us, didn't she?"

"Who?" said Rashford.

"His 'momma'. The barely known Brenda Frizwell, AKA Miz Stanhope. She pulled back the curtain in the front window when her boy was doing the whole hillbilly act."

Janet scoffed.

"I don't think that was an act."

"Whatever. The thing is, they've got something happening here. I think we need to ask around a bit. Can you get us into Souris?"

"Sure," said Janet. "At least, I think I can. Why?"

"I think there'll be a Mountie station there," said Jim. "Hopefully he's not out driving. It might be good to have a little word, see what he knows."

Rashford scoffed.

"Why would the Mounties tell us anything? We're hardly official, are we."

"True," said Jim. "I think the three of us should go and have a coffee while Janet drops in for a visit. She can say it's related to a case she's working on back in town, if he asks anything."

Janet nodded.

"That makes sense," she said. "Let's go and see what we can find."

An hour later they were driving back towards Charlottetown, second coffees in hand, as Janet described her visit to the police station.

"I actually knew her," she said. "Corporal Stephenson. She came over here from Nova Scotia a year or two back and we met on a WIP course."

"What, they teach you how to wield one?" chuckled Preston.

"Not 'whip', WIP. Double you eye pea. It means women in policing."

"Ahhh."

"Anyway, she knows the family at forty thirteen, says they're a bit strange even by local standards, but they don't get into trouble much."

"Much?"

"Well, a few noise complaints from neighbours, guns fired at night and that sort of thing, but they did a weapons check, and everything was locked away properly. Coyotes, they said, after the geese and the goats."

"Anything else?"

"One of the boys had a warning a year ago, a bit of an argument in one of the local pubs, but generally they keep themselves to themselves."

Preston leaned forward between the seats.

"You said, 'one of the boys'? How many are there?"

"Three, like the ladies at the market told you. The one we met is George, he's the youngest and looks after the farm. Paul has a lobster boat, and Johnny drives potato trucks to Toronto."

Rashford scoffed.

"George, Paul, and John. Big Beatles fan, was she?"

They all laughed.

"I wonder which one we saw on the beach," said Preston. "He was big, but not as big as Georgie-boy."

"Perhaps it was Johnny, the trucker? I'm guessing it was Paul on the boat."

"Who was his sidekick? Ringo?"

Rashford chuckled.

"Perhaps. The thing is, we know they're up to no good, but what? And how do we prove it?"

Janet rapped her fingers on the steering wheel.

"I might have something to add, there," she said.

Paula turned to her.

"You have our attention," she said.

"According to Helen Stevenson," said Janet, "there's some suggestion of smuggling. The Mounties haven't tried to prove anything but the word around is that the Frizwell's have a long history of rum running. They've been doing it since the farm started, and that was in the eighteen hundreds. Remember that nice route vicinale we followed, and the heritage road afterwards? Well, both those have lots of small sheds, tunnels, and other places where goods can be safely stored, away from prying eyes."

"How do they sell it?"

"You know those vegetable stands you see at the side of the road? The rumour is that the one George Frizwell has, at the end of his driveway, is not self-serve. He's actually there, every afternoon, selling the potatoes. They've got three or four different types. Russets, Irish Cobblers, Green Mountains, Yukon Gold, the usual, all at five bucks for a three-pound bag. But if you ask for a bag of special blend, it's fifty bucks, and you get a five-pound bag. Three of potatoes and a bottle of Barbados dark rum."

Paula scoffed.

"What about during the winter? They only have those stands during the summer and fall."

Janet nodded.

"The thinking is that that's all they do. In the winter they're like everyone else."

"What, they go to Florida?"

Janet giggled.

"No, they just hide inside by the fire and hope that the weather will go away."

Paula laughed.

"That's something they never put in the tourist ads," she said. "Are you saying that the smuggling is a seasonal occupation. Just a sideline?"

"That seems like a lot of risk for not very much reward," said Rashford.

Preston grunted.

"Perhaps. Anyway, at least we're a bit further ahead. Let's keep digging. Hey, where are we going?"

Janet indicated and turned right onto a paved road that ran away from the coast.

"We're taking Paula and Cilla home," she said. "Then we'll go back to town."

The rain started just before they reached the coastal road and they drove the rest of the way in silence.

CHAPTER THIRTEEN

The rain continued through the night and into Sunday morning. Rashford stayed in his hotel room, channel-surfing the television and checking his phone in a desultory way. In the afternoon he shrugged on his jacket and went for a walk, the pavement still glistening. The streets were quiet and when he found himself outside the Irish pub, he went inside. Phillipa the pink-haired hostess nodded at him from behind their dais.

"Sit where you like," they said. "It's quiet today."

He had beans on toast for lunch, washed down with a beer, and watched the dozen or so other customers as they listened to a lone fiddler playing a series of melancholy tunes. The man left the stage to desultory applause and was not replaced. Phillipa came over to see how he had enjoyed his meal.

"That's it for music, I'm afraid," they said. "The band who were supposed to be on next had a big row last night and have disbanded."

"The band disbanded?"

"Yeah. Ironic, really. They called themselves 'Uncertain Future' and now two are in hospital, one is in jail and the fourth has gone home to Miscouche. You don't happen to play, do you?"

Rashford scoffed.

"Missing my big break, am I?" he said.

Phillipa shrugged.

"It was worth a try. Where's Paula?"

"At home, I think. I'm not sure."

"Ah," they said, and pointed at his glass.

"Another one?"

"I'm good."

They left and went to check on another table. He was wondering what to do next when his phone vibrated. He glanced at the screen and saw it was a message from Jim Preston.

"Where are you?"

"At the pub," he typed.

"Can you meet me outside in ten?"

"We have a result," said Preston, as Rashford settled into passenger seat of the E-Type. "I've heard from John the mechanic."

Rashford nodded.

"Go on."

Preston pulled away from the curb.

"He says that there is something we should see. He's waiting for us at his shop."

Five minutes later they turned into the narrow lane, the ruts now full of water and splashing up from the tires. As they pulled up to the building the door opened and the mechanic came out, lighting a cigarette. He waited until they joined him before he spoke.

"Mebbe your client was correct," he said, squinting through the smoke. "There's something a bit off."

"Hello to you too," said Preston.

John grinned, then stubbed out the cigarette with his boot.

"No time for chit-chat. Come and see what I found."

He led them into the small office and through a side door into the workspace. Marc Gaudet's car was up on a hoist and John ducked underneath the chassis. He took a penlight from his pocket and shone it up into the wheel well on the driver's side.

"There. Look."

They crowded around him and peered into the illuminated area. Rashford shook his head.

"I've no idea what I'm looking for," he said.

John snorted.

"I thought you was a detective. Look, there."

He pointed to the chafed end of the hanging brake hose. Preston nodded.

"Yes, I can see that it's torn, like the police mechanic said."

John moved his penlight closer.

"It's torn, yes, but see there."

Rashford and Preston both leaned in, then simultaneously shook their heads. John tutted in exasperation.

"There's a thin scour line in the rubber. The hose burst by itself, yes, but only because someone had weakened it."

Rashford looked again, this time seeing what had been pointed out to him.

"How would that work?"

John turned off the penlight and stepped back into the workshop, stretching his back.

"I think someone did a partial cut, enough to weaken the structural integrity of the hose. Each time the driver used his brakes, the rubber got a little weaker. Then, when he braked hard for that bend, it burst. Suddenly he's only braking on one side, so he'd swerve off the road. If he's going at speed, no chance."

Preston looked from one to the other.

"Shit," he said.

～

John agreed to keep the car under lock and key in his shop until the next day, when Janet Parsons would bring a police mechanic to review the evidence. Rashford and Preston thanked him and returned to the Jaguar.

"Let's go for a drive," said Preston.

He drove carefully down the lane and across town, taking a series of short-cuts though residential neighbourhoods before crossing a bridge over the arterial highway. They circled back onto a street lined with warehouses and building supply stores. Next to a shop selling used and recycled tires was a chain link fence with a double gate, in the centre of which a large padlock was secured with a heavy chain.

Beneath the padlock was a grimy For Sale by Owner sign, one corner loose so it hung at an angle. Three cars and a pick-up truck were parked back-in to the fence, facing across the yard to a workshop with a shingled roof. The main part of the building was a low single-storey affair, with a double-storey addition at one end. A weather-beaten panel over the main door indicated that this was Gaudet's Autobody, but the paint was so worn that it was difficult to discern the original text.

"Gud Body?" said Rashford, opening a cigarette packet.

Preston snorted, taking one and accepting a light.

"This place always used to be spic and span," he said. "It must have broken his heart, the way Gauthier let things go."

"How long has it been for sale?"

"According to Francine LeBlanc, Jean Gauthier put up the sign the day after Marc Gaudet died."

Rashford nodded.

"In a rush for the money, was he?"

Preston shrugged.

"It's as good a motive as any," he said.

Rashford studied the building.

"I imagine there will be a hoist in the extension," he said.

"John said you'd need to have a vehicle on a lift if you were going to cut the hose so precisely," said Preston.

"So now we've got a possible motive and possible means," said Rashford. "The thing is, would there have been an opportunity?"

"I think that's a question I shall have to ask Monsieur Gauthier, when I find him," said Preston. "But that's tomorrow's job. Did you eat?"

Rashford looked at him.

"I just had lunch in the pub, yeah,".

"It's turned into a nice afternoon," said Preston. "Shall we go for a drive around and grab some supper on the way back?"

"Anywhere in particular?"

"Nope. Just put the top down and cruise."

"Lead on," said Rashford, laughing.

The phone woke Rashford from a deep sleep. At first, he had thought it was his alarm, and only after fumbling for a few moments had he realized it was a voice call. He clicked on the correct icon and tried to shake his head awake.

"Gavin?"

"Yes," he mumbled. "This is he."

"It's nine o'clock."

He wasn't quite sure how to respond.

"Ah, good," he said.

There was a distinct tutting sound.

"I'm going to phone back," she said, and the line clicked.

Fifteen minutes later the phone rang again. Rashford, who had managed a quick shower and was in the process of sipping his first coffee, answered brightly.

"Gavin Rashford speaking."

"That's better," said Anne. "Were you out late?"

He grunted.

"You were supposed to pick us up at nine," she said. "We're waiting."

Rashford jerked awake.

"Shoot, I'm sorry," he said. "I slept in. Can you give me twenty minutes to get dressed and grab a bite to eat?"

"Ten minutes," she said, sweetly. "We'll grab something on the way. We didn't eat breakfast either, we didn't want to make you wait."

"Ouch," he said. "Okay, I'm rushing."

According to the clock display on his dashboard, it was nine thirty-three when he turned into the loading zone outside Anne's apartment. She and Sandra were standing outside the coffee shop, talking to an older gentleman who nodded briefly at Rashford before shaking Sandra's hand and disappearing through the glass door.

The two women got into the car, Sandra in the back seat, and Rashford pulled away. He glanced across at Anne, who was looking straight ahead, and caught Sandra's eye in the rear-view mirror. She stared back at him.

"Look, I'm sorry," he said. "I was out yesterday with Jim Parsons, and we stayed late, and ..."

The women didn't move.

"And I forgot."

Anne huffed and turned to him.

"At last, the truth," she said.

Sandra banged him on the shoulder.

"I knew we weren't on your priority list anymore," she said. "Now you've proved it."

"That's not true," protested Rashford, feeling himself blush.

There was silence. He focused on his driving, braking for a pedestrian who stepped out from behind a parked car and started to cross the road. She glared at him, waving her arm. He pointed at the crosswalk not twenty metres further up the street and held up his arms in question. She ignored him, shaking her head.

"Where are we going?" he said.

"Over the bridge and then follow the highway," said Sandra. "We'll show you."

He merged into the bridge traffic, admiring the cormorants perched on a series of massive stone pillars.

"That's the old railway bridge," he said. "What's left of it, anyway."

Sandra huffed.

"Suddenly you're a tour guide?" she said.

Rashford flushed and tightened his grip on the steering wheel.

They had passed the emergency services building and were on the main highway before Anne spoke.

"So, what did you do this weekend?"

Rashford told them about going to the Farmer's Market, then the drive out to the Naufrage bridge, the East Point Lighthouse, Basin Head beach, and Souris. He didn't mention Paula, or Secret Cove, or the confrontation with George Frizwell.

He also didn't mention the meeting with John, and the mechanic's interpretation of the brake hose on Marc Gaudet's car. That news should come from Jim Preston, he thought, and not until Janet and the police mechanic had confirmed his supposition.

Instead, he talked about his long Sunday drive with Jim, a big loop around the central part of the island. He remembered particularly the picturesque village of Victoria-by-the-Sea, the shops in the old railway station at Kensington, and the wharf at North Rustico.

"We came back through the National Park," he said, "and had fish and chips at a place called Covehead. Then we spent the evening at Trailside, listening to music and drinking."

"Who was playing?" said Anne.

"They called themselves the Nineteenth Nervous Breakdowns," he said. "They played covers of Rolling Stones songs all night. I was surprised, there were a lot of young people there. They knew the words as much as the oldies in the crowd."

Sandra broke her silence.

"You've seen a lot of the island," she said. "Today we're going to the quiet part of the eastern tip, down to Cape Bear. Another day I'll take you up west, and we'll go to meet the people, at Lennox Island. Okay, pull over here."

She pointed to a gravelled area in front of a low building. There was a small sign indicating that this was a café, and five vehicles were parked on the gravel.

"Best coffee and breakfast sandwiches east of town," said Sandra, getting out of the car. "Come on."

After they had eaten, they continued round the south-eastern bulge of the island, making detours to see the grand houses on Point Prim, and each paid five dollars to climb to the top of the lighthouse. When they got to Wood Islands, the ferry was just arriving, so Sandra directed him to drive past the toll booth on a slip road that led them up behind the cafeteria. Here they parked and watched the ship as it carefully rounded the end of the breakwater and made its way to the dock. They saw the big door swing open, and the first fleet of motorbikes roar ashore. The trucks followed, and then the cars.

"Won't we get stuck in all that traffic?" said Rashford.

"Not many of them will be going our way," said Anne. "Just watch."

Rashford drove back to the toll booth and waited for a gap in the stream, then a few hundred metres later turned off onto a quiet road which took them back along the edge of the ferry compound and into open countryside. The houses were a mix of new builds with large glass conservatories and old homes with wind-lashed shingles stripped of paint. The Northumberland Strait sparkled behind a series of vineyards, the rows of grapes shining in the mid-morning sun. Horses grazed in fields, and a farmer leaning against the side of his pick-up waved a lazy hand as they passed.

They saw the sign for Guernsey Cove and wondered what the first European settlers to the area must have thought, washing up on this desolate shore so many miles from home. At Cape Bear they walked to the end of the path, marvelling at the view, and saw the old lighthouse platform teetering on the edge of the cliff. The lighthouse had been moved further inland, but a fund-raising notice indicated that continued erosion meant it would soon have to be moved again.

Apart from pausing for a walk on the nearly empty beach at Panmure, they kept driving through the quiet villages and towns scattered along the coast; Murray River and Montague, Brudenell and Georgetown. It was early afternoon when they stopped at a restaurant overlooking the water at Cardigan. Anne chose the snow-crab leg salad and Sandra the scallops, but Rashford stuck to fish and chips, declaring these the best he'd had so far. When challenged by Anne, he admitted that he'd said that after every meal.

As they lingered over their coffee, Rashford spread the map out on the table.

"We're here, right?" he said, pointing. The two women nodded.

"I've been to Rollo Bay and Souris," he said, "but not the bits in-between. Can we go back that way?"

Sandra pursed her lips.

"It's a long drive," she said. "Another hour at least."

Rashford shrugged.

"I'm from the prairies," he said. "We go an hour for coffee."

Anne gave him a shrewd look.

"Do you want to see anywhere in particular?"

He looked more closely at the map.

"There's a place called New Zealand," he said. "I could send Gayle a photo and tell her we got lost!"

Sandra shook her head.

"All the way out there? That's going to add nearly two hours."

Rashford nodded.

"I know, but I don't mind the driving. If we go there and hook back on the north shore road, we can look at the crazy bridge in Naufrage. I never got a photo there either."

Anne looked at him with raised eyebrows, then glanced at her mother,

"We'll still be back by five," she said. "And I've got nothing else planned for today, do you?"

The road was slower than Rashford had anticipated, with narrow bends and large farm machinery conspiring to keep him well under the speed limit. Anne and Sandra chatted non-stop, pointing out interesting buildings and captivating views along the way. Sometimes Rashford was able to glance at them, but mostly he focused on passing the next tractor or braking for the next blind bend on a hill. It was an hour before he saw the sign indicating the road to New Zealand and was able to pull off the highway onto a narrower, but still paved, road.

He had used the time to rehearse what he was going to say and, when the three large wind turbines loomed ahead, he was ready. He indicated and moved over to the side of the road, where he parked. Turning in his seat, he looked at them both.

"I wonder if you could do me a favour," he said.

Anne stared at him, then huffed.

"I knew it," she said. "This is work, isn't it, Gavin?"

He nodded.

"It would be a great help," he said.

"I should have known that not even you would drive us two hours out of our way just to look at the scenery," said Anne.

"I'm sorry."

"No, you're not. You had this planned all along."

Rashford shook his head.

"I didn't, honestly. It was only when we were in Cardigan for lunch that I got the idea."

Anne folded her arms and sat straight in the seat, looking ahead. From the back, Sandra coughed.

"What would you like us to do?" she said.

Rashford turned to her in relief.

"I'd like you to buy me some potatoes," he said. "Please."

Sandra chuckled.

"Long way to come," she said. "They've even got potatoes in Charlottetown now."

Rashford nodded.

"Yes, but these are special," he said.

"In what way?"

Anne turned back towards him.

"Yes, Gavin. In what way?"

He cleared his throat.

"I can't give you all the details," he said, "but this is what I'd like you to do."

They listened in silence as he explained, then looked at each other.

"I'd better drive," said Sandra. "You can hop out and buy them, I'd just burst out laughing."

Anne nodded.

"Fifty bucks, eh?"

"Yes," said Rashford, taking out his wallet and handing her three bills. "Here's eighty, in case they've gone up."

"And what if he asks us if we want a particular kind?" she said.

Rashford had been mulling on that very question, wondering if the choice of variety was a secondary code. He thought he had the answer.

"Ask for Green Mountains," he said. "Apparently they're the best ones to make scalloped potato pie."

She nodded.

"Drive down, do the deed, drive back. That's it?" said Sandra.

"Yes," said Rashford. "I'll wait at the end of the road. I can't take the chance of him recognizing me."

"We'll try to remember to come back for you," said Anne.

Rashford grinned, then got out of the car. Sandra left the back seat and took over the driving.

"Just turn right up there," said Rashford. "Where the turbines are. It's about a kilometre down the road, on the left. An open-fronted shed, you can't miss it. He spelled 'vegetables' wrong."

Sandra nodded.

"Hasta la vista, baby," she said, putting the car into drive and accelerating smoothly away.

Rashford watched her turn, then started walking slowly up the road towards the junction. He could hear the blades of the turbines, rotating at a much faster speed than he had envisaged. There were still black rain clouds on the horizon, but the sky above was a clear cerulean blue. The white towers reflected the sun, and he was glad he had brought his baseball cap. He lit a cigarette and watched three crows wheeling over a field of grain, not sure whether it was wheat or barley or something quite different.

He felt badly for asking Sandra and Anne to step into an active case but felt he had no choice. He didn't think that George Frizwell would cause any trouble, even if he did sense that something was wrong. Nonetheless, he listened anxiously, hoping not to hear the reverberation of a shotgun on the soft island breeze. A monarch butterfly danced lightly along the hedge beside him, its bright orange-red wings delicately veined. A hawk of some sort glided over the fields, hunting.

He waited.

Chapter Fourteen

"Mont Verde rum," said Jim Parsons, holding the bottle carefully in his hands. It was Tuesday morning, and they were sitting on a bench in the smoking area outside Rashford's hotel.

Rashford nodded.

"Green Mountain," he said. "Put it away, we'll get into trouble if someone sees it."

"It's not open," said Parsons. "Sadly."

Rashford took the bottle and returned it to the brown paper bag, which he placed carefully in his backpack.

"This is evidence, this is," he said.

Parsons scoffed.

"Obtained without a warrant by two civilians acting under the direction of an out-of-province cop with no jurisdiction. Fine. I'm sure the defence counsel will have no problem with that."

Rashford placed the bag on the floor between his feet and sipped his coffee. He offered his cigarettes to Parsons.

"Well, what have you been up to?" he challenged.

Parsons sighed.

"It's as we thought," he said. "Janet and her team had another look at the Corolla and confirmed what John had said, the brake hoses had been carefully scored. They can't say it was a plot to actually kill Marc Gaudet, the hose could have gone at any time, and he might have just skidded to the side of the road. But they can say it was manslaughter, even if it was an accident."

"And you think it was that Jean guy?"

Parsons nodded.

"Oh, I'm convinced of it. I haven't had chance to talk to him, of course, the police picked him up right away. But I've spoken to a number of people, and it seems that he's a bit of a fixture at Red Shores."

"What's that?"

"It's our local racetrack and casino. Horses and slots, what could go wrong?"

"So, he owed money?"

"Lots of it. His cards were maxed out, his bank account was empty, and he'd borrowed some 'tide-me-over' money from a very disreputable character, who wanted his thirty-per-cent interest, per day, before he even started thinking about the main amount."

"Jesus."

"Exactement. That's why he was desperate to sell the garage, it was his last hope. But Marc Gaudet wouldn't agree, and he was the senior partner."

Rashford shook his head.

"Have you told Anne?"

"Not yet. She was out with you all day yesterday, remember. I'm going to go and see her later today."

"I don't envy you that."

Parsons shrugged.

"It's all part of the job," he said. "She asked me to find out what really happened, and I did. End of. Time to move to the next case."

"Which is what?"

"There's a half-dozen to choose from. A missing teenager, a possible insurance scam, a land custody argument, you name it. It's amazing how busy I'm keeping. I think the one I'll do next is for a young woman in town, a lawyer, she thinks her husband has been playing away from home. I'm going to see if that's true. It's a small town."

Rashford laughed.

"Ah, the intrigue," he said.

Parsons scoffed.

"You want to believe it," he said. "That should be an easy one, I hope. The others …. I dunno, Gavin. I think I'm going to have to take on an assistant soon. You're not looking for a job, are you?"

Rashford chuckled.

"No, thanks. I've got another week or so here, my boss extended my leave again so I can try and wrap things up. I feel kind of invested in your smuggling case, as well as the business with Anne's dad. Plus, Paula should be back in Halifax now, and I'm hoping to hear from her. But then I'm going home. I miss the prairies."

They smoked quietly for a few minutes. Eventually, Parsons spoke.

"Whatcha' going to do with that?" he said, gesturing to the backpack.

Rashford shrugged, scratching his ear.

"I'm going to have to go for a chat with Janet," he said.

"She'll tear your head off," said Parsons.

"That's why I've not called her yet," said Rashford, pulling out another cigarette.

Janet Parsons asked him to meet her at the police station, which he thought was not an auspicious beginning. He parked in the visitor area and stood under the Safe Exchange Zone sign for a few moments, reviewing what he was going to say. He held the backpack over his shoulder, certain that she was inside, watching him on the closed-circuit camera. Taking a deep breath, he went to the door.

He found himself in a large waiting room area, with a counter extending in an ell-shape. There was a Perspex screen on top of the counter and three chairs on the other side. Two filing cabinets stood against the back wall, in which there was a door. The area in front of the counter was empty. He looked around and saw the semi-circular blue disc of a video camera perched high on the wall, so he waved at it. A few moments later the door in the back wall opened and a young woman in civilian clothes came out.

"How might I help you?" she said.

"I'm here to see Detective Constable Parsons," he said.

She pursed her lips and glanced down at something on the desk.

"She's busy right now. And you'll have to leave that bag outside here, when you see her."

"This is what she wants to see," said Rashford, moving to open the bag.

The lady stood up straight, her right hand moving to the side, her eyes flashing towards the camera.

"Please don't open that in here," she said.

Rashford dropped his hand just as the back door opened again, and Janet Parsons stepped out.

"It's alright, Stella," she said. "I'm expecting him."

The civilian huffed.

"He still has to leave his bag out here," she said. "That's the rule."

Parsons nodded, then opened the glass window and gestured. Rashford handed her the bag. She opened it and took out the bottle of rum, which she passed to Stella.

"Log this in, please," she said. "One 750 ml bottle of black rum, Mont Verde distillery, Barbados. Unopened and with the cap sealed. Time and date, etcetera."

She waited while Stella opened her computer and typed rapidly, pausing only to look at Rashford.

"Name?"

He told her, glancing at Janet, who raised her eyebrows. When the typing stopped, she lifted the bottle from the counter.

"Please note that I have taken possession of this item," she said. "I'll be in Conference Room 3. While we're there, please check the bag to make sure that there is nothing suspicious inside."

She pointed Rashford to a half-door set into the counter, then pressed her ID card against a small panel. The door clicked open and Rashford walked through, leaving his backpack on the counter. He nodded at Stella.

"I've counted the condoms," he said, seeing her face flush bright red before he followed Janet out of the reception area and into a narrow corridor. Once the door had swung closed behind them, she punched his shoulder.

"That was mean," she said. "Poor Stella was only doing her job."

"Whatever happened to positive police-citizen relations," he said, then stopped as she opened a single grey door. The room inside had no windows, just a table and two chairs, lit by a blipping overhead fluorescent tube.

"This is a conference room? How many people work here?"

"We had to rename it, apparently *Interrogation Room 3* scared the punters. You know, 'positive police-citizen relations'."

Rashford could almost see the air quotes, so he said nothing and waited for her to point him to one of the chairs. She did so, putting the bottle on the table, then sat down herself.

"So, tell me," she said. "What have you been up to?"

"It makes no sense," she said. "How many cases did you say they hauled up at the beach?"

"Six."

"Right. And they were each about the size of a Rubbermaid container?"

"Yes."

"Wait here."

Janet Parsons stood and left the room, leaving Rashford staring at the bottle of rum on the table. The door clicked behind her. He was very tempted to open the rum but decided that was probably a bad idea. He waited, turning over his story in his mind. He could not think of anything he had missed. He had just decided that she was right, and his story made no sense, when the door opened.

She entered backwards, pushing against the door with her hip and turning to reveal that she was holding a large grey plastic container. She nodded at him to move the bottle, then placed the tub on the table. Rashford peered inside and saw what appeared to be four large hiking boots. Parsons stared at him.

"Was it this size or bigger? Smaller?"

Rashford scratched his chin.

"About that size, I'd say," he said. "Although I was some distance away, and it was foggy."

"This is the 53-litre size," said Parsons. "They make a bigger one, but I think that would be too difficult to carry. This works well. Look."

She took the bottle and laid it flat on the bottom of the tub, the neck and base facing opposite sides. She laid the four boots down next to the bottle, two on each side. The five objects covered most of the base of the tub.

"Imagine that these are all bottles, and they are wrapped in bubble wrap or something similar," she said. "Look, there's room for another layer, before you seal the top. So that's ten bottles a container, times six containers, that's sixty bottles."

"At sixty a bottle, that's thirty-six hundred dollars," said Rashford.

"Less costs," said Parsons. "You've got to buy the booze, pack it, ship it, take the boat out to meet the ship, drive it back in from the beach, all of that. They'd be lucky to be making two grand from a shipment."

Rashford shrugged.

"Perhaps that's sufficient for their needs," he said.

Parsons shook her head.

"No. There's something else going on here, something we're missing."

Rashford thought for a moment, then made a decision.

"I know a guy in Barbados," he said. "A cop. I can give him a call if you'd like. He might have some local insight into things from that end."

Parsons nodded.

"Why not," she said. "This room is secure. You call him and just ring the buzzer when you're done."

"Buzzer?"

She pointed to her side of the table. Leaning over, he saw a small, black, rectangular piece of plastic flush against the edge. He raised his eyebrows.

"Just in case," she said, laughing as she left the room.

The phone only rang twice before Patrick York answered.

"Is that really you, mon?" he said.

Rashford smiled to himself.

"It is indeed," he said. "How are things?"

"Oh, you know, same old same old. What's up? How's Mandy?"

Rashford had expected this and decided to be forthright. He explained the situation, then paused. There was a moment of silence.

"Sorry to hear that, mon. You were good together. Why the call, then?"

Rashford had decided to be less forthright on this subject.

"I need some information," he said. "What can you tell me about smuggling?"

York huffed.

"To here or from here?" he said.

"From there to here."

"Here being ..."

"Prince Edward Island. In eastern Canada."

"Ah."

Rashford waited. York cleared his throat before he continued.

"Well, traditionally there's rum running," he said, eventually. "We export nearly forty million dollars in rum a year, that's three per cent of the global market. We probably smuggle about another ten million dollars worth. Why?"

"Is it good money?"

"Not bad. It costs about four bucks to make a bottle of high-end rum, so the mark-up can be pretty high. Again, why?"

"What about shipping costs?

"Minimal. You pack it in watertight boxes and the captain gets a back-hander to drop them to a waiting fishing boat outside the line. Again, why?"

Rashford sighed.

"I've been helping with an investigation here and we seem to have found someone bringing in Mont Verde rum, then selling it on for sixty bucks a bottle. Private sales, as it were."

"Sixty? Well, they're probably landing it for under twenty so that's a good return on investment."

Rashford nodded, then realized that York couldn't see him.

"Yes," he said. "It is."

There was another pause.

"Monte Verde is a proper good rum. As long as that's what's in the bottle, not just what's on the label."

Rashford grunted.

"I'm assuming it's the real thing. But ..."

He paused, running different scenarios through his mind.

"But ...?" said York.

"Well, they only seem to be bringing in thirty bottles. It just doesn't seem worth the risk."

York coughed.

"They might just be starting out," he said. "Seeing if the route works, finding the glitches."

"Perhaps. But I don't think so. I think there's something else going on."

"What?"

"I'm not sure, I was hoping you might have some ideas."

He could hear a tapping sound, as if York was drumming his fingers or tapping his teeth. Eventually the Barbadian spoke again.

"Just a sec," he said. "Let me get the door."

A moment later he was back.

"This is pure guesswork and background, okay? You didn't hear it from me."

"Okay," said Rashford, then waited again.

"There's some speculation," said York, "among some of my colleagues, you understand?"

"Yes."

"They think that maybe a channel has opened up between here and the mainland. That's you. Well, you and America. Anyway, they think that the cartels might have started running cocaine through here, as a sort of staging post before it goes north. They were using Haiti, but that place has gotten kind of crazy, and they lost too many shipments to the gangs. That's an even better return on investment, if you can make it work."

"Cocaine?"

"Yeah. And other goodies. Pills, fentanyl, meth, that sort of thing."

Rashford thought about that for a moment.

"So, if you can get rum through, you could use the same route for drugs?"

"If you packed it correctly, yes."

"I see. Thanks, Patrick. You've been a great help."

York huffed.

"What, that's it? Don't I get the full story?"

"One day. It's still not clear to me yet. How's Shyanne?"

"Don't change the subject. She's fine. She's coming down again, in the fall. Can I tell her about you and Mandy?"

"Of course. It's not a secret, everyone knows she's heading off to be a superstar."

"Bitterness don't become you, mon."

"I'm not bitter," said Rashford. "I'll give you a call once this is all sorted out."

They exchanged a few more pleasantries, then Rashford ended the call. He sat at the table for five minutes, staring at the wall, and then leaned over to press the buzzer.

"Cocaine? We've had no reports of cocaine suddenly appearing on the streets."

Janet Parsons paced around the small room, switching her focus from Rashford to the wall, and back again. She returned to the table and sat down, resting her elbows and looking directly at him over her folded hands.

"What are you thinking?"

Rashford shrugged.

"I have no proof," he said. "This is just a hunch."

"Go on."

"Well, what did the Frizwells' pull out of the water?"

Janet moved her head from side to side.

"Six sealed plastic containers full of rum."

Rashford nodded.

"And ...?"

She leaned back in her chair and gazed at the ceiling.

"And nothing. Just six containers, which they loaded into their truck, according to Jim. And you."

"We were wrong," he said.

She brought her eyes down to look at him.

"Go on."

"They pulled out six sealed containers, and six buoys. Muriel Stanhope Frizwell or whatever her name is didn't touch the containers. She wasn't really interested in them. But she was very careful with the buoys."

Parsons stared at him, then suddenly sat up straight, clicking her fingers.

"You think they were packed with cocaine?"

"It would make sense," he said. "That's where the real profit would be. The rum is just a screen, something to keep George happy. He gets to be a big man in King's County, but she doesn't care if he gets caught, that's not the core business."

"But cocaine? Where does she sell it? We've not heard anything about a local supplier. And we would have done. Most of the guys trafficking on the Island are known to us, it's a pretty small place."

"What if she doesn't sell it here?"

Parsons stood up and started pacing again. He could almost hear her excitement when she turned to him.

"Johnny the truck driver," she said. "He drives it to Toronto. She sells it there. Oh, I could kiss you!"

Rashford raised his hands.

"I'll press the buzzer," he said, laughing.

"Only if it's an emergency," she said, and left the room.

Stella brought him a paper cup of weak warm coffee but refused to answer his questions. She closed the door firmly behind her and left him staring at the wall of the conference room. It was nearly thirty minutes before Janet Parsons returned. She stood in the doorway, smiling.

"Let's go for a walk," she said.

Rashford lifted the cup and waved it at her.

"Can we find somewhere that sells actual coffee?"

She laughed.

"There's a place just on the main drag," she said. "Come on."

They went past a small strip mall and crossed the road at the cross-walk, then cut through the parking lot of a drug store. The coffee shop was nearly empty, and they took their drinks to a table in the back corner. Parsons slurped her iced milkshake.

"It's thirty degrees out," she said. "How can you drink that?"

"It's a coffee shop," said Rashford.

He looked at her, then smiled.

"Come on, what have you found out?"

She slowly put down the large plastic cup, then chewed on the end of her straw.

"Cone of silence?" she said.

He nodded.

"Even from Jim?"

Rashford raised an eyebrow but nodded again. Parsons replaced the straw through the hole in the lid of the cup.

"Well," she said. "I was able to run some checks, ask some questions. It appears that our friend Mister Johnny Frizwell does indeed drive pota-toes for a living. He works for one of the big processors here on the Island, and usually makes a run a week. "

"Damn it," said Rashford. Parsons looked at him.

"What?" she said.

"That means we'll have missed him, they won't want to keep that sort of merchandise lying around at home, no matter how big a dog they've got."

"True," said Parsons. "Normally. But ..."

She paused. Rashford stared at her.

"Normally?" he said. "What do you mean?"

Parsons smiled.

"It seems that two weeks ago, on his way home, Johnny got done for speeding. He was already carrying six demerit points for an earlier offence, then he came over the Bridge at a hundred and ten and a Mountie clocked him."

"What's the limit there?"

"Eighty. Anyway, that gave him another three points, so he was interviewed by the traffic folk and his employer suspended him for two weeks. They've put him on a course, because if he gets twelve points, he could lose his licence for three months. His course finished on Friday, so he should be back on the road either today or tomorrow. According to the fellow who assigns the runs, Johnny is scheduled to leave for Toronto on Thursday."

Rashford pondered this information.

"The day after tomorrow? And will this be the first time he'll have taken a load since the boat came ashore?"

"We think so, yes."

Rashford looked at her.

"Janet Parsons," he said. "I think I could kiss you."

She smiled at him.

"There's no buzzer here," she said, smiling.

Rashford looked across the table, then took a sip of his coffee to hide his blush.

"What's the scoop with Marc Gaudet's car?" he said.

Janet looked down at the table and spoke softly.

"Yes, let's stay focused on work," she said. She looked up at Rashford and smiled brightly.

"I think we have most of the facts now," she said. "I've spoken to Francine LeBlanc, the lady with whom he was living, but I've not yet had a chance to talk to his widow."

"His widow? I thought he and Sandra were divorced?"

"Apparently not. The papers had been served and they were both living separate lives, but it seems there was some sort of screw up at the Family Court and the documents never got processed. Officially, Sandra is still his wife and the majority share in the garage now belongs to her."

"Does she know that?"

"I've not had a chance to tell her, no. I don't know whether Francine spoke to her yet."

Rashford shook his head.

"What a mess," he said.

"Indeed. As I'm sure Jim has told you, it seems that Jean Gauthier was hopelessly in debt. He wanted to sell the garage, but Marc wouldn't agree. He has not yet admitted to cutting the brake hoses, but we have enough circumstantial evidence to charge him with at least manslaughter."

"That's good."

She nodded, reaching over to pat his arm.

"And it's all thanks to you."

"Me?"

"Yes. If you hadn't suggested to Jim that he get another mechanic to check the brakes, we would have closed it off as purely an accident. So, thank you."

"You're welcome."

They sat looking at each other. Rashford cleared his throat.

"Umm. I was wondering ..."

"Yes?"

"What shifts are you working this weekend?"

"I'm not. I'm off from Friday until Monday. Why?"

"Well, the Bridge City Rollers are playing in Halifax on Saturday night. It will be the last show of this tour. I was wondering whether you'd like to go."

Parsons stared at him.

"The Bridge City Rollers? With Amanda Robicheau?"

"Yes."

"You have tickets?"

"Yes."

"You're inviting me on a date?"

"Well, yes, I guess I am. You said that you really liked her and that you wanted a signed photograph, I thought perhaps you could get a selfie with her."

"A selfie?"

Rashford felt flustered.

"Yes. I have a pass to get backstage, so we can go and say hello after the show. If you'd like."

"If ... I'd ... like?"

Janet Parsons stared at him, her eyes wide. She gulped, then spoke in a carefully controlled voice.

"Yes, please. I'd very much like to go to Halifax with you and see the Bridge City Rollers," she said. "When shall we leave?"

Chapter Fifteen

Gavin Rashford pressed the buzzer for Anne's apartment at eight-thirty on Wednesday morning. She sounded surprised to hear his voice but invited him to come up the stairs. Wakoshi barked and chased round his ankles before sinking onto the green striped blanket and growling softly. Rashford hugged Anne and gave her a chaste kiss on the cheek. She put her hands on her hips and looked at him.

"To what do I owe this honor?" she said.

He hesitated before speaking.

"Perhaps we should sit down."

Anne clutched a tea towel and held it to her mouth. He could see tears starting to prickle out from the edges of her eyes. She sat down slowly on a chair by the table. He sat opposite her.

"Is it about my dad?" she said.

He nodded, then held up his hand.

"Partly," he said. "But not only about him."

She gulped, then sat straight in her chair and looked at him.

"Tell me about dad first," she said.

"No," he said. "First you have to tell me that you understand this is all unofficial. I'm only telling you this because I know you and care for you. Other people will tell you the official version, once they have confirmed everything. I just thought you would like to know what it's looking like right now, with the caveat that this 'truth' might change. Okay?"

She nodded.

"Say it."

She smiled at him, shaking her head.

"Oh, Gavin," she said. "If it makes you feel better, okay. I understand that what you're going to tell me is unofficial and might not be the full story, it's just what you're thinking right now. Is that enough?"

"Thank you," he said. "Right. First, your dad. It wasn't murder. At least ..."

He stopped, for Anne had given a shuddering cry and seemed to have collapsed in on herself. He stood up and went to her side, putting his arm around her.

"Shush, it's okay, don't cry," he said. "I haven't finished yet."

She gulped, laughing and crying at the same time, then sat back in her chair and wiped her eyes.

"I'm sorry. Go on. Please."

He went back to his chair and sat down.

"I don't think it was murder," he said. "I think that someone, possibly Jean Gauthier, tampered with the brakes. They were weakened but they were not cut through, they broke by themselves."

"Why would Jean do that? My dad trusted him with everything."

Rashford nodded.

"I know. But what your dad didn't know was that Gauthier had a gambling problem and needed money fast. That's why he wanted to sell the shop, but your dad wouldn't agree to the sale. I think that he wanted your dad to crash the car, because he was the only one who was allowed to work on it. Gauthier could then say that your dad was losing his touch and would be better off selling, or giving, the garage to him."

"But that didn't happen," said Anne, sniffling.

Rashford looked at her.

"It wasn't the only thing that didn't happen," he said. He explained about the failure to process the divorce papers filed by Sandra and Marc Gaudet.

"That means that your mum is still his wife, or rather widow," he said. "And, if I understand the legal stuff correctly, his old will still stands.

In that, he left the repair shop to you. He had told Sandra about it and she agreed, she says 'because you were the only other petrol head in the family'."

"She says? You've talked to mom?"

"Yes. I called her before I came over. Luckily, I got her before she went to work. She told me you would be here as you had a day off today."

"That makes sense," Anne said, nodding. She got to her feet.

"Thanks, Gavin. If that's all, I wouldn't mind being on my own for a bit, to process all this."

He stood as well.

"There is just one other thing," he said.

"Is it more bad news?"

She looked at him, gripping the back of the chair. He nodded.

"I had a phone call late last night," he said. "From Bettina. I'm sorry to tell you this, Anne, but Kôhkum Christine passed away yesterday.

Once he had calmed Anne down a second time, he left the apartment and walked slowly back to his car. There seemed to be an inordinate number of pedestrians and he kept bumping into people who suddenly stopped to take a photograph of a particularly scenic window or door. Muttering to himself, he reached his car and opened the door. He pulled out his road map of the island and randomly stuck his finger onto the paper.

"O'Leary," he said. "Right then, off we go."

He drove down towards the wharf and turned onto Water Street. There were even more pedestrians here, and he got stuck behind a wagon full of tourists that was being pulled by two large Clydesdale horses. As he passed the harbour he glanced over and saw not one, but two, large cruise ships tied up to the pier. Buses were pulling away from the welcome barn, as the reception building was known colloquially, and the road was lined with taxi and ride-share cars of all descriptions.

Most of the tourists were heading towards him, going towards the downtown core, but he was surprised to see that one elderly couple was walking the other way, away from town. At the next set of traffic lights, he indicated and pulled into a small side street. He waited until the couple had reached the junction and then got out of his car, holding his map.

"Excuse me," he said.

The couple stopped and the gentleman, who had a full head of white hair and a trim moustache, took a step towards him. He was leaning on a cane, which he waved slowly in Rashford's direction.

"Yes?"

"I wonder if you could help me," said Rashford. "I'm trying to go to O'Leary."

The man harrumphed and looked at his wife, who smiled brightly. He looked back.

"No good asking me, son," he said. "I don't think I can even find Charlottetown, and we're docked here for chrissake."

Rashford pointed back past the couple.

"The city is that way," he said.

The woman smiled even more brightly, and the man harrumphed again.

"Okay," he sighed. "You were right, dear." He turned to Rashford. "That means I have to do the laundry tomorrow. Again."

Rashford laughed.

"How long are you in town for?" he said.

"We sail at five but have to be back to the ship by four," said the woman. "Why?"

Rashford pulled out his phone and looked at it.

"It's not even nine-thirty yet," he said. "Would you like to join me on a drive?"

The man stepped back, waving his cane again.

"Hang on," he said. "You could be an axe murderer or something."

"He doesn't look like an axe murderer, dear," said his wife.

"I'm not, I assure you," said Rashford. "I'm going for a drive out to O'Leary and thought it might be nice to have some company. And I saw that you seemed to be a bit lost. This is where I'm going, it's here, look."

He spread the map out on the hood of his car and traced his route.

"It should take about an hour and a half or two hours to get there. We can have some lunch and then drive back. Don't worry, we'll be here well before four."

"What's in O'Leary?" said the man.

"It doesn't matter, dear," said his wife, "It'll be fun."

"A four-hour drive in a car with a stranger, you call that fun?"

"An adventure."

Rashford laughed.

"I'm a tourist, just like you," he said. "But I didn't come here on a ship. I've been here visiting friends. In my day job I'm a police officer."

He brought out his wallet and presented his ID card. The man nodded.

"Where's your wife?" he said.

"I don't have one," said Rashford. "I'm touring around on my own."

"That must be nice and quiet," muttered the man, then cursed as his wife punched him on the shoulder.

"That hurt."

"I've heard there is a potato museum out there," said the woman. "I saw it in a brochure. I remembered because O'Leary made me think of Ireland, and the potato famine."

"Really?" said Rashford. "I didn't know. The potato museum it is, then. Hop in."

The man insisted that his wife sat in the front.

"I'm ready for a snooze," he said, "and she'll chatter your ear off. We can switch around on the way back, she'll have run out of steam by then."

"Jerry ...," she said, warningly, but there was laughter in her voice.

"I'm Marjorie," she said. "He's Jerry. What's your name, young man?"

The drive to O'Leary took them almost three hours. Marjorie read the map and directed them to various sites along the way, and in between kept up a constant stream of information about her family, her various ailments, Jerry's even more varied ailments, and their previous lives.

At Victoria-by-the-Sea they ate ice cream and walked out to the end of the wharf. Picking through the fabrics and bric-a-brac on sale in a small shop at the end of the pier, Marjorie commented that it reminded her of the shops she used to visit when they lived in Nairobi.

Rummaging through the housewares at the Church Mouse, a shop of 'gently used' items sold to support the local community of Crapaud, she spoke of the impact of high-quality donated clothes on the self-esteem of refugees in the Shatila refugee camp, one of the world's largest and oldest camps.

"It's in south Beirut," she said. "Near the airport. Everyone knows where it is and everyone's forgotten about it, all at the same time."

At Borden-Carlton they drove through the small village full of tourist shops and parked next to an old lighthouse. Grumbling, Jerry followed them up the path that followed the gentle contour of the hill, heaving for breath when he made the crest. They stood looking at the Confederation Bridge, the pillars bright in the sun, the water still and blue beneath the spans.

"It reminds me of the Øresund Bridge," said Marjorie.

Rashford looked at her.

"Where's that?"

"Between Malmö and Copenhagen," wheezed Jerry. "It's longer than this but this is the longest one over ice-covered water, I believe."

Rashford nodded.

"I knew that," he said. "There's a great little museum down here."

They walked back down and spent twenty minutes grilling the young woman volunteer who was on guide duty, learning more than Rashford would have thought possible about the ice boats, which had operated before there was first a ferry and then the bridge. Still wondering what it would have been like to be dragged over the ice, and paddled across open water where the ice was too thin, they returned to the car.

"It's eleven thirty," said Marjorie. "I think we should stop mucking about and go straight to O'Leary."

"You're the one who keeps distracting us," said Jerry.

"What?"

"Nothing, dear."

Rashford smiled and drove back out to the highway.

In O'Leary they quickly found the building which housed the potato museum.

"What was your first clue?" muttered Jerry, standing self-consciously next to the giant model of a Russet Burbank. Marjorie slapped his arm.

"This is the world's largest potato sculpture," she said. "Think of all the fries you eat."

Rashford smiled as he took their photograph, then led them inside. They insisted on paying his entry fee and chatted amiably as they looked at the various exhibits.

"I'm hungry," said Jerry, nodding meaningfully towards the restaurant area as they came back inside from looking at antique farm equipment.

The hostess told them that they would have to wait for ten minutes before a table came free, time which Marjorie used to browse the gift shop.

"Who knew you could make so many things out of potato?" she said, happily displaying a bag full of potato soap, chocolate covered potato chips, and a tee-shirt showing a bright yellow potato with big eyes and the caption, 'potato puns ap-peel to me'.

"That's terrible," groaned Jerry, but Rashford laughed and immediately bought a burnt orange one in a size he thought would fit his colleague, Sheri Hayleyson. Sheri was a Black woman, like Janet, and he had been impressed by the sight of Janet in her yellow swimsuit.

The young woman working in the restaurant came over and told them that their table was ready, so they paid for their purchases and walked into the small eating area.

"What an amazing menu," said Jerry, brandishing his like a baton. "I'm going to have the chili cheese fries."

"Don't forget your heartburn, dear," said Marjorie, then ordered the pulled pork poutine.

Rashford explained to the waitress that he wanted something a bit lighter, but turned down the recommendation of potato soup, settling instead for a seafood chowder. The food came quickly, and in portions that overwhelmed even Jerry's appetite.

"I hope you left room for the Seaweed Pie," said their waitress, but they had to confess they had not.

"Perhaps we can take a slice with us?" said Marjorie.

"Of course, I'll get a take-out box," said the young woman.

Marjorie smiled.

"That can be our snack this evening, Jerry," she said.

Jerry looked sceptically into the box.

"What is it?"

"Angel food cake with a layer of Irish moss, topped with blueberry fruit sauce and a whipped topping," said Marjorie, reading off the menu. "Irish moss is the seaweed bit, I think."

"That's correct," said the waitress. "It's harvested up on the shore north of here. There used to be a big industry, you make carrageenan from it. That's a thickener and stabilizer that used to be used in ice creams. But now there are synthetics that are a lot cheaper, and anyway the amount available for production has really dropped off."

"Why's that?" said Jerry. "Pollution?"

The waitress shrugged.

"Not really. People blame it on climate change, we don't get as much sea ice and there's more storms, more erosion. And there's a new type of seaweed that seems to be taking over the old beds. That wasn't here before and some people say it's invading the shore because the water is warmer now."

Marjorie nodded.

"It's where the land meets the sea that we're seeing the big effects of climate change," she said. "We were living in the Pacific for a while and they're really noticing the impact there."

Not for the first time, Rashford wondered exactly what kind of work Jerry and Marjorie had done. He watched as Jerry carefully added twenty per cent to the bill, as a tip, and Marjorie balanced the cardboard box in one hand and the shopping bag in the other.

"Right, then," she said, once they were all in the car. "Where to now?"

Rashford turned to look at her.

"It's nearly two o'clock," he said. "I think we should be heading back to town now."

Jerry, in the front seat, nodded. Marjorie looked at the map.

"Can we go back along the north shore?" she said. "Isn't Cavendish where Anne of Green Gables was from? I remember our cleaning lady in Kyoto was all excited about that, when she found out we were from Canada. I was embarrassed to tell her that I'd never been here."

"Sure," said Rashford. "But we won't be able to stop everywhere."

"Good luck with that," Jerry grunted.

Marjorie dozed as they drove back down the road which ran down the centre of Prince County, her soft snuffles making both Jerry and Rashford smile.

"At least we know she's still alive," said Jerry.

"Is that something you're concerned about?" said Rashford.

"Absolutely," huffed Jerry. He looked sideways. "Are you sure you want to hear this?"

"Nothing else to do except drive," said Rashford.

"Well, then," Jerry chuckled. "You asked for it."

Over the next forty-five minutes Jerry spoke about the illness with which Marjorie had been diagnosed some three months earlier. His voice quavering, he explained how they had travelled all over the world but had never been to the Maritimes until now.

"That's why we took this cruise," he said. "We've already been to Quebec City and Saguenay and were in Corner Brook yesterday. From here we go round Cape Breton to Sydney, then down the coast, Halifax, Saint John, and Maine. We get to Boston in a week, then we'll fly home."

"Where's home?"

"Right now, it's a little place called Carp, in the Ottawa valley. We've only been there a couple of years, though. It's what they call a retirement village. This getting old business is no fun."

Rashford murmured in what he hoped was a comforting manner. Jerry continued.

"We used to live in the city, in Ottawa. It was a good place, convenient for our work, you know? And after we retired, we had a nice community of friends and neighbours. But after ten years, life started catching up with me. Shovelling snow is no fun at my age, and my knees started complaining about the gardening. We looked around and couldn't find anything we could afford, so we went a bit further out and ended up in Carp. Marj tells me it suits me."

Rashford snorted and Jerry grinned at him.

"I can get a bit cantankerous, I admit," he said. "I reckon I deserve it."

"What did you do? For a living, I mean?"

Jerry shrugged.

"I was just a civil servant, really," he said. "I worked for the government. You know, reading newspapers and interview transcripts, summarizing them for the higher ups, that sort of thing."

Rashford glanced across at him.

"We have people doing similar work in the police," he said. "We call them intelligence analysts."

"Really. How interesting."

Jerry settled back in his seat and looked out of the window. Rashford smiled to himself and waited. Jerry cleared his throat.

"No, it's Marj who had the exciting job, she was a gender education specialist and travelled all over the place with CIDA, as was."

"As was?"

"Yeah. I think it's called Global Affairs now. That's what it was the last time I looked, anyway. They kept changing it, trying to be hip and relevant, and to move away from the idea that we were being neo-colonial do-gooders by providing advice to developing countries. You can't call them that anymore, either; now they are 'emerging economies', although that rather implies that they are emerging from something into something else. I find it all far too confusing."

Rashford chuckled.

"You don't strike me as someone who is confused by much," he said. "So, while she wandered the world, you stayed at home?"

"Exactly. Anyway, enough about us. That card you showed us said that you were a police officer, but in the NorthWest Mounted Police. Correct?"

Rashford admitted that it was.

"So, what's with all this Alsama business, then? What's your take on that?"

Rashford huffed.

"The west was fed up with being ignored by the power brokers in eastern Canada," he said.

"Baloney. That's a political slogan, not a reason. What were people upset about? Specifically."

Rashford thought for a moment.

"They were upset at the idea of the whole oil and gas economy being ripped out from under them in ways which made no sense. All these taxes were going to Ottawa and being redistributed by the feds, and at the same time the west was being told to shift away from oil and gas. And when they were needed, to get the pipelines built to take the product to market, the feds dragged their feet. So that was one thing.

"On top of that, a lot of folks thought that the whole transition to green energy is a bit of a crock. Canada is, was, a big country. You can't drive coast-to-coast in winter and hope you'll find enough charging stations where and when you'll need them. And how do you produce electricity without oil and gas? Wind? Water? Nuclear? The liberal media in Toronto don't want the rivers dammed, their pristine natural vistas spoiled by windmills, and heaven help a nuclear power plant built in their back yard.

"Then you have bilingualism. There were people from Alberta and Saskatchewan who couldn't get federal jobs because they couldn't speak French. Why is that an issue on the prairies? It's more useful to speak Ukrainian, or Cree, or Hutterisch. But there's no points for that in Ottawa."

Rashford took a deep breath.

"It just all got too much, you know?"

Jerry nodded.

"And you? Do you speak Ukrainian or Hutterisch?"

"No," said Rashford. "I speak Cree."

Jerry looked at him.

"Really?"

Rashford nodded, then explained the FILTER program and how it was changing policing on the prairies. Jerry nodded thoughtfully.

There was silence in the car for a few kilometres. Eventually Rashford spoke.

"You were CSIS, weren't you?"

Jerry smiled and shrugged.

"As they say in that television series, you might honestly think so, I could not possibly say."

Rashford laughed. From the back seat, Marjorie spoke softly.

"Don't listen to him, dear. He's a big bag of wind."

Jerry scoffed.

"Why are you sitting behind me, dear?"

"It's easier to speak to Gavin from here."

"Marjorie ..."

She sighed.

"Okay. It's because this is the safe seat."

Rashford glanced at her.

"The safe seat? Like, in an accident?"

Jerry laughed.

"Not in an accident, no. Tell him, Marj."

"Well," said Marjorie. "If we get ambushed, they'll probably shoot you, the driver, first. Ricochets are likely to hit the front seat passenger. If they miss, or use high-calibre weapons, the bullets will probably hit whoever is sitting behind you. Ergo, this is the safe seat."

Rashford stared.

"Go on," said Jerry. "Ask her if she learned that in a gender education class."

Chapter Sixteen

The conversation continued as they turned at Traveller's Rest and drove along the north coast. Rashford faced piercing questions as he defended the decision for Alsama to separate from Canada. As they pulled into the small parking area next to a house advertising itself as the birthplace of Lucy Maude Montgomery, he turned to them.

"Here's an example, right here," he said. "This is the enigma at the centre of the riddle."

"I don't think Churchill said it quite like that," Jerry scoffed.

Marjorie shushed him.

"Let him finish, dear," she said. "Go on, Gavin."

Rashford nodded.

"Well," he said. "All that stuff about Anne of the Island, her red hair, her pigtails, the green gables of her house, her being an orphan, that's all baloney. It's fiction. Dreamed up by a woman who was born here and had a very rough childhood. Her mum died. Her dad moved away to Prince Albert, Saskatchewan, of all places, and married again. She was raised by her grandparents. But not many tourists care about that, about that story, which is actually true. They just want to see the farm where Matthew drove the buggy, wander through the bedroom where Anne slept, smell the flowers in Anne's garden. But that's all fiction, It's not true!"

As Rashford paused for breath, he realized that he had raised his voice. Jerry looked at him in amazement, but Marjorie leaned forward between the seats and touched his shoulder.

"And is that some kind of analogy for Alsama?" she said.

"Perhaps. All I know is that there was something deeper, more visceral. It wasn't just about taxation and pipelines and language, although those were important. It was also a matter of respect, of choice. Of recognizing that the west is different."

Jerry nodded.

"In what ways, specifically?"

Rashford shrugged.

"I read a book about Henry Moore once. Do you know him? The English sculptor?"

They both nodded.

"We had a lovely afternoon at Much Hadham, didn't we dear?" said Marjorie.

"If you like sheep," Jerry chuffed.

"Well, anyway," said Rashford. "The author said something like Moore saw the spaces, not the objects, and tried to make sculptures that reflected what wasn't here."

Marjorie nodded.

"The concept of negative space," she said. "He was famous for that. The hole in the sculpture isn't defining or outlining the structure, it is the purpose of the piece."

Rashford stared at her in amazement.

"Exactly. And I think that's like Alsama and Canada. Places like Toronto and Montreal are different. They're big, busy spaces with a thousand languages spoken by millions of people. They see rural Canada as the space outside themselves, not as a space in itself. They make rules and laws to make their life better. And I understand that. But they assume that everyone wants to be like them, to live like them, and therefore the rules should apply everywhere. And that's the problem.

"Red Deer and Regina are not like Toronto and Montreal, and they don't want to be. It's as though central Canadians simply can't understand that not everyone wants that kind of lifestyle, full of busyness and high-rises. We don't see ourselves as the hinterland that defines and supports the centre. We are the spaces in central Canadian culture and are the purpose of our own existence, our own reality."

The silence in the car lasted for a few minutes before Rashford laughed.

"Sorry for the rant," he said. "At least it gives you a story to take back to your bilingual urbanite friends in high places. Now, let's have a look where Lucy Maud was born."

From the house they detoured to the New London wharf, where Jerry bought two dozen Raspberry Point oysters. He handed one bag to Rashford, telling him to consider it a tip. From the wharf they continued along the coast road, marvelling at the picturesque harbour of Stanley Bridge and stopping briefly to pay their respects at Montgomery's burial place in Cavendish. Jerry opted to stay in the car, but Marjorie insisted on joining the long line of Japanese tourists, mainly young women, who were waiting to take pictures of themselves at the gravesite. The pink headstone was flanked by two closely cropped trees, and inside the fenced off grave itself there was a display of orange geranium and white impatiens flowers.

"Are they cedar or cypress?" asked Marjorie, pointing at the trees. Rashford confessed that he had no idea and was not really surprised when she repeated the question, in Japanese, to the nearest gaggle of tourists. They looked at her in amazement, giggling, then immediately pulled out their phones and started typing into search engines. One by one they shook their heads and gave disappointed smiles. Marjorie thanked them, and then graciously accepted their invitation to move ahead in the queue and have a few personal moments at the grave.

Rashford took them through the national park to North Rustico and at the entrance gate they paid the fee and were given a revised map. As they drove, they marvelled at the swathes of destruction that had been left behind by Hurricane Fiona, and compared the before and after photographs of the Teacup Rock with the view they could see now. They cut down through the rolling hills of Central Queens and arrived back at the Charlottetown wharf at three-thirty. Rashford got out of the car to say goodbye and shake their hands.

"That was a wonderful adventure," said Marjorie, smiling widely, her eyes shining as she gave him a big hug. "Thank you so much, Gavin."

Jerry nodded, then cleared his throat.

"You wouldn't happen to have a spare one of those business cards, would you?" he said.

Rashford looked at him, then pulled out his wallet and rummaged through.

"May I ask why you want that?" he said.

Jerry smiled.

"Oh, you never know," he said. "One day I might run into one of those bilingual friends you mentioned. They might be interested in hearing your theories."

Rashford snorted.

"I doubt it," he said, but he handed over the card anyway. He stood by the car as they made their way slowly across the cobbled forefront to the large wooden departure building. Streams of other passengers eddied around them, all returning to one of the cruise ships, but he kept Jerry's shock of white hair in sight until they reached the door. Here they turned and waved, so he waved back. They disappeared inside and he got back into his car, then drove to his hotel.

The next day was hot and oppressive. Rashford kept the air conditioning in his room blowing at full but still found himself feeling sweaty and lethargic. Just after ten o'clock he called Jim, who whispered that he couldn't meet for coffee because he was behind a dumpster.

"I'm watching the lawyer's husband grope an older woman in the back doorway of their apartment building," he said, incredulity in his voice. "She's got to be at least ten years older than him and they're making out like teenagers. Luckily, I have my silent camera with me. This one is done and dusted."

Rashford chuckled. They made arrangements to meet at six for a beer, then Rashford clicked off and called Janet. He was forwarded directly to voice mail, only then remembering that she was in court on Thursdays. He called Anne, who told him that both she and Sandra were working shifts at the restaurant, and he should drop in for a visit, but they were so busy that they wouldn't be able to chat.

He went to the fridge and took out another can of Club Soda, popping the top and burping when the first mouthful fizzed in his throat. Sitting on the edge of his bed, he phoned Mandy. When she answered she sounded half-asleep.

"How was the show last night?" he said.

She made a yawning sound.

"It was good, but not our best. We're saving that for tomorrow and Saturday, for the Halifax shows. Today I was supposed to sleep in."

Rashford sighed.

"Sorry, I forgot this would be your break day. I was trying to call before the sound checks."

"That's okay. What's happening?"

He told her that he planned to attend the Saturday night show and was hoping to bring a guest with him.

"Sure," said Mandy, "we'll have lots of room. We had to move from the Neptune theatre to the Rebecca Cohn auditorium, there were just too many people wanting to come to the show. Who's the guest?"

"She's a big fan," he said. "She saw you in both Charlottetown and Summerside, and she'd love to meet you."

Mandy snickered.

"And think of the reward you'll get for arranging that," she said.

"No, no," he protested, feeling his face redden. Mandy laughed.

"You've got your pass," said, "and I'll leave another one for your friend. What's her name?"

They made the arrangements and then ended the call. Rashford sent a text to Janet, confirming their 'date' and saying he needed her address so he could pick her up at ten on Saturday morning. He also told her that he would book a downtown hotel for Saturday night and bring her back to the Island on Sunday. Thinking of Halifax, he drank some more of his soda, then called Paula White. She answered on the second ring.

"Hello, Gavin," she said. "What's happening?"

"I'm bored," he said. "It's a hot day and nobody is around. What's happening there?"

She laughed.

"About the same," she said. "It's the middle of summer, nobody wants to do anything energetic. Not even the criminals. Why don't you go to the beach? That's what people do on PEI in July."

"It will be too crowded," muttered Rashford. "You saw what it was like at Basin Head the other day."

Paula huffed.

"There are other beaches, you know. Drive out to Secret Cove, there won't be many people there."

Rashford clicked his tongue.

"Of course," he said. "Why didn't I think of that. Will it be okay, do you think?"

"Of course. It's a secret beach, but it's not a private one. There is still public access for those who know about it. Just wave at people and if anyone does give you a hard time, say you were down there with me last week. Most of the locals know my parents and our cottage. Oh, and keep to the first part of the beach, near where the cars park. The far side, beyond the little creek, that's kind of a more private space, okay?"

"The swimming is safe, I assume?"

"It's perfectly safe. There's a drop-off about thirty metres out but until then it's quite shallow. Most people swim up and down, parallel to the beach, instead of heading straight out to sea."

Rashford thanked her and was about to end the call when she stopped him.

"Actually, I'm glad you called. I've got something to tell you."

"What's that?"

"I'm resigning from the police. I've just put in my notice."

Rashford was stunned.

"Why? What's happened? When are you leaving? Who ..."

"Who is going to look after your file?" she said, finishing his sentence.

He felt embarrassed.

"Yes. That too."

She laughed.

"So many questions. Okay, in no particular order. I'm leaving because I've got a new job, one where I won't be treated as a leper all the time. I think ..."

"Hang on," said Rashford. "What do you mean, treated like a leper?"

She chuffed.

"Why do you think I'm in charge of cold cases?" she said. "Nobody here was supposed to know about my past, but the word got around pretty fast, and you know cops, it's a macho culture. Nobody wanted to partner with me or even work with me in the office. I guess they're worried that sexuality is catching."

"That's ridiculous."

"It is, yes. It's also, sadly, true. Of course, Human Resources said that I couldn't be discriminated against based on my sexual identification, but that didn't make it easier. Eventually Inspector Smithson came up with the idea of putting me on the cold case file. So here I am, stuck in the office, but still officially gainfully employed."

"Can they do that?"

"They've managed so far. I've had enough, though, and thanks to you, I've got a great opportunity, so I'm going to take it."

"Thanks to me? What have I done? A great opportunity doing what?"

Paula laughed.

"Whoa, cowboy! One at a time. Yes, thanks to you, I met Jim Preston. And he's offered me a job, as junior partner in his investigation business. I filled in the forms for a licence on PEI, and the clerk said that because of my police training and military experience that should be approved right away. I can stay at my parent's cottage for the first bit, while I look for an apartment in town, and Jim's got so much work that he wants me there as soon as possible."

Rashford blew out a big gust of air.

"That's fantastic," he said. "It does sound like a good opportunity."

"Yes," she said. "He knows all about me and doesn't care. He said that I'll be an asset because I'll have access to communities where he might not be welcome. And he thinks my time as a meathead might come in handy. Did you know, he was in the parachute regiment, back in the day?"

"I didn't know that, no," said Rashford.

Paula laughed.

"No reason to tell you, I guess. Anyway, I've submitted my letter, so I'll see out my time here and then move up to the Island."

Rashford exhaled slowly.

"I'm pleased for you," he said. "But yes, I am wondering about the Claydon file. Will someone else be appointed to look after that?"

Paula chuffed.

"I assume so," she said. "I've put the information forward and it's an active file again now, so at least it's not stuck in a drawer somewhere. And there's a budget line attached, so that will be monitored. It will be the last thing I sign off on when I finish, and I'll make sure that your name and contact information are clearly noted. Like I told you, we've submitted the request to a judge for permission to contact the ancestry tracking companies. If that is approved before I leave, then I'll make sure the sample is sent to them. That way the process will have been initiated and the results, whatever they are, will be sent to someone here. And that someone will make a notation in the file, and see your name, and hopefully let you know what's going on."

"Hopefully," said Rashford.

Paula was silent for a moment.

"I'm sorry, Gavin," she said. "I know this is an important case for you. But I couldn't pass up the opportunity. I was ..."

"It's okay," said Rashford. "Really. I would probably have done the same thing myself, in your shoes."

"You'd look good in heels," she laughed. They chatted for a few minutes more, then Rashford ended the call. He checked his phone for messages, but there weren't any, so he lay back on the bed and stared at the ceiling. He closed his eyes, briefly, thinking over what Paula had said, then stood up, found his towel, put on his swimming shorts, and walked out of the hotel.

He went straight to Secret Cove, stopping only in St. Peter's Bay for an ice cream, and was surprised to find three cars parked at the end of the narrow trail. He walked down to the beach and found two women sitting on plastic chairs. They were chatting together while supervising five noisy children who were running up and down the sand, splashing each other and shouting with laughter.

Rashford nodded to the women, then decided to go somewhere a bit quieter. He walked through the narrow channel of fresh water that bubbled between the rocks he had seen from the dune when he was waiting for Jim Preston. Pausing, he looked around, and visualized where the truck must have stopped so that the buoys and containers could be winched aboard. Nodding to himself, he walked around the dune on the far side of the creek and found himself on a short but empty stretch of beach. Three large sandstone boulders blocked the end of the strand, so he threw down his towel and stripped down to his shorts. Hesitating only a moment, he walked into the sea and braced himself against the cold. Then he started to swim.

The water was relaxing and once he got used to it, quite warm. He went back towards the small creek and then turned before he was opposite the children. He didn't want the two young mothers to think he was stalking them, so he swam back the other way. He could not remember the last time he had been swimming, but he soon found his rhythm, steadily churning up the water. It was a calm day with only a gentle swell, and he was soon past the boulders. To his surprise there was another, much longer, stretch of beach on the far side, and he swam parallel to that until his shoulders started to ache. At that point he turned toward the shore and swam until his knees hit the sand. He stood up, stretched, and started the long walk back towards the distant rocks.

The sand was warm under his feet, and he splashed through the shallows. It was a perfect beach day, he thought. The sea stretched out to his right, sparkling in the sunlight. A gentle breeze blew onshore, bringing with it a slight coolness to offset the heat. Inland, the beach ended in a squared-off dune; the sand had been sheared by storm surges and resembled a sea wall. Marram grass stalks waved above the battlement, and beyond them a thin line of wind-sculpted spruce trees was silhouetted against the sky.

The sand was a pale cream colour, yellow threading through the normal white of the north shore, and speckled with a miscellany of shells that reflected the light. The sun was reflecting brightly off the water, and he had forgotten his sunglasses, so he had to squint against the light. He was almost on top of the body before he realized it was there.

He stopped in shock, processing the splayed-out limbs, the indented sand in geometric designs around the feet and hands. There were no other footprints, he noted, except those that ran to the body from the sea. It was a woman, wearing a pale pink bikini bottom almost the colour of her skin. Her hair ruffled and shimmered in the breeze. Rashford reached down and touched her neck, checking for a pulse.

She screamed.

CHAPTER SEVENTEEN

Her name was Chrissie, Rashford discovered, and she was the lady from whom he had bought the cyanotype print. He was still burning with embarrassment as they climbed back over the boulders and retrieved his clothes. Chrissie had already recovered hers from the shade of the dunes where she had left them, along with a bottle of water, while she sunbathed.

"It's clothing optional this side of the boulders," she explained, once she had recovered from the shock of coming awake to a large man looming over her. She had sat up and stared at him. He looked away, mumbling apologies.

"It's okay," she said. "I'm sure you've seen breasts before. At least I wasn't going the full Monty today."

Not that she was that far removed, he thought, her low waisted and high cut bikini bottom serving to accentuate rather than conceal. She had large areolae that were almost elliptical in shape and her nipples stood out like a ferrule on a pencil crayon. He looked away again. She looked him up and down and laughed before moving lithely to her feet.

"Just a minute, I'll spare your blushes," she said, talking over her shoulder as she walked away from the water. At the edge of the beach she pulled on a large men's shirt and buttoned the front, wrapped a piece of brightly coloured material around her waist, and walked back from the dune.

"There, now I'm decent. What are you doing here?"

He explained how Paula had told him that it was okay to come to the Secret Cove beach, but that he had forgotten her warning that the area beyond the creek was private.

"It's not really private," Chrissie said. "Not in a 'nobody else can come here' kind of way. It's just that people don't bring their kids up here, and it's kind of understood that topless or even nude sunbathing is okay."

"I'm really sorry for scaring you like that," he said. "In the real world I'm a cop, and I thought I'd found a dead body."

"Oh, I'm still alive right now," she laughed.

He felt his face burn.

"Um, yes, I noticed," he said, pulling on his jeans and shirt. She looked at him, smiling.

"Do you fancy a coffee?" she said.

Rashford followed her car out to the highway and then along past Goose River. He recognized the driveway that led into Paula's parents' cottage, and a few kilometers after that they turned in at the Blue Jay. This was now adorned with a printed sign stating that the gallery was closed until two thirty pm. Rashford automatically glanced at the clock on his dashboard; it was just before one.

Chrissie drove past the mini barn and parked in front of the farmhouse. She got out and pointed that there was a space behind the mini barn, so Rashford parked there. She waited for him at the bottom of the steps.

"We could go into St. Peter's for coffee," she said, "but I have to be back to open the shop and get the kids from the school bus. So, I thought we could have coffee here, if that's okay?"

Rashford shrugged.

"Sure," he said. "It's your house!"

She laughed and led the way up the steps.

"Home sweet home," she said, opening the door. "Thanks for taking off your shoes."

He nodded. She kicked off her sandals and then gestured to the room.

"This is the main living room," she said. "Kitchen through there, downstairs bathroom and a spare bedroom through there, and the upstairs has three bedrooms and two bathrooms."

Rashford looked around. It was a large room, with a high ceiling and windows letting in a lot of light. The walls were plastered and white-washed, and the ceiling joists were exposed beams.

"It's a nice space," he said. "Where do you do your work?"

"In the spare bedroom," she said. "I shoved the bed to one side, so it's accessible if we have guests, but it's mainly my studio space. I'll show you in a minute. Let me just get the coffee on."

She went into the kitchen, and he could hear her opening cupboards, water running, and then the scent of the first whiff of coffee. She came back into the living room, wiping her hands.

"Come and see my studio," she said, walking down the short passage and opening the door. He stepped inside. There was a wooden desk in front of a large window, which looked out on a flower garden full of bright blooms. The desk was clear except for two metal containers and a computer monitor displaying a split-screen image. He recognized two views of the inside of the shop area and a smaller image that showed the driveway.

"That's my security monitor," said Chrissie, pointing, "and these jars contain my chemicals. In here are my materials."

She pushed a large box with her foot and Rashford saw that it was filled with a collection of natural materials. He recognized twigs, feathers, shells, pinecones, and large dried leaves, among many other items. He glanced around and saw a double bed pushed up against the wall. Above it, and indeed all around the room, the walls were covered with a mixture of cyanotypes and pencil drawings, including some that appeared to be nude sketches of Chrissie herself. She saw him looking and laughed.

"Self-portraits," she said. "That's what that's for. Well, one of the reasons."

She pointed up to the ceiling over the bed and he was surprised to see a large mirror attached to the joists. He looked back at her and saw that she had unbuttoned her shirt. She shucked it off her shoulders and walked over to him. She reached up and ran her finger over his lips, then took his hand and held it to her breast. The nipple hardened under his touch.

"I don't open the shop until two thirty," she said. "The kids aren't back until almost three, and my partner is in Ontario this week. Plus, the coffee's not ready yet, and you need to get the sand out of your shorts."

Rashford stood there as she undid his belt and pushed down his jeans. He stepped out of them as she walked backwards and pulled him towards the bed. He kneeled over her, loosening the hem of the sarong and throwing it to one side. She put her arms around his neck, pulling his face down.

"That's the other reason for the mirror," she said, kissing him hard on the lips. "I like to watch."

~

She wrapped the sarong around her waist again before they returned to the kitchen. Rashford pulled on his shorts and joined her, leaning against the granite topped counter as she poured coffee.

"Milk or cream?" she said. He shook his head. She passed him a hand-made cup in the shape of a dragon, the tail curled to form the handle and the neck wound around the rim. She leaned over and kissed him on the cheek.

"Thank you," she said. "I needed that."

He laughed and she smiled at him.

"It's true," she said. "My partner has been away for over a week, and before that he was so wound up about his work that we haven't had sex in ages. You're fit, and when you looked at my tits, I could see you reacting. Those shorts are pretty thin. Plus, you're only a tourist so I won't see you again. It seemed like the omens were lining up."

Rashford shook his head, looking sad.

"That's all I am to you? Just a quickie to scratch an itch? I feel used."

She stared at him for a moment, waiting until he smiled before bursting out in laughter.

"Pots and kettles, I reckon," she said. "You certainly entered into things with enthusiasm."

He laughed with her.

"You're right. What's good for the goose and so forth. Or the blue jay. Or the gannet."

She nodded.

"The gannet's the best," she said. "They just dive straight in, get what they came for, then leave."

Rashford chuffed, smiling at her exuberance and the double entendre. He drank his coffee.

"Do you make a habit of this?" he said.

"God, no," she said, shaking her head. "You're only my third since I moved here. It's a small community, you have to be pretty careful."

"Ah, so that's why I'm parked behind the mini barn," he said.

"Partly," she laughed. "No sense in broadcasting things."

He put down his coffee cup and reached over to kiss her. She placed her cup on the counter and threw one arm around his neck. Breaking the embrace, she turned to face the counter, leaning forward and thrusting back her hips. He saw her breasts were flattened on the stone surface. She looked back over her shoulder.

"A nod's as good as a wink to a blind gannet," she said, unhooking the sarong so it pooled around her ankles. Rashford stepped forward and held her waist.

"That's it," she murmured. "Dive straight in."

He took what he had come for, again, then got dressed and left. He was only a few hundred metres up the road when a yellow school bus passed him. In the mirror he saw it stop, and the red flashing lights come on, then saw the blond hair reflect the sun as she waved her children across the road.

It was late afternoon when he got back to Charlottetown. He showered and changed his clothes before walking over to the Irish pub where he was going to meet Jim Preston. He was waiting outside, smoking. Rashford shook his head at the offer and waited until Preston was finished, then they went inside together. It was still early, and the upstairs bar was quiet. Phillipa nodded at him as they walked in and told them to sit anywhere.

"You're getting to be known like a local," said Jim, laughing. "She'll be bringing you your favourite beer without you ordering it next."

"They."

"What?"

"They're a they, not a she." Said Rashford. "Like Paula."

"Really?" said Jim, looking back towards the hostess podium. "Who knew?"

"Well, I didn't," said Rashford. "Paula told me. C'mon, what are you drinking?"

"Stout, please," said Jim. "I left the car at home and walked over, so you won't be drinking alone."

Rashford laughed, then raised his hand. Phillipa nodded and looked over their shoulder, back into the bar, as they spoke. A waitress materialized and took their drink orders, persuading them that a plate of the crisp and spicy Aer Wingus would go well with their beer. Preston looked across the table.

"So, what did you get up to today?" he said.

Rashford grinned.

"Oh, same old same old," he said. "I went to a beach, got picked up by a half-naked woman who took me back to her place and bonked me, then came home. You?"

Preston shook his head.

"Ah, the dreams and hopefulness of youth," he said. "No, really, what did you do?"

Rashford shrugged.

"I talked to Paula," he said. "She told me that you've offered her a job."

Preston nodded.

"Yes, I have. It's like I told you. I've got too much work for one person to handle, and she's got great experience. She'll hopefully start before the end of summer. I'm knackered. Ah, here we go."

He paused as the waitress placed their two beers in front of them and her colleague put two small plates, a pile of napkins, and an empty bowl in the middle of the table. The waitress returned with a bowl full of chicken wings, the sauces glistening under the lights.

"It's Happy Hour so you get two pounds for the price of one," she said. "Enjoy!"

The two men contemplated the table in front of them.

"There goes my diet," said Preston, ruefully.

"Again," laughed Rashford. He pulled a piece of chicken out from the pile and chewed the meat off the bone, wiping his hands and lips on a napkin when he'd finished. He took a mouthful of beer and watched Preston take a piece.

"Will she be okay up here?"

Preston tossed a chicken bone into the empty bowl and sucked his fingers.

"What, you mean the trans thing?"

Rashford nodded. Preston shook his head.

"Like I told you before, it's not really an issue here, except in a few sub-groups. The religious right and the rednecks. And if anything comes up involving them, I'll handle it."

The waitress came back and asked if everything was okay. Rashford nodded.

"These are excellent," he said, pointing at the wings. "Great choice. Thank you for the tip."

She nodded and smiled, then left them alone.

"She wants to be the one who says that," said Preston, taking another wing.

Rashford laughed.

"What happened out by the dumpster?" he said.

Preston grinned at him, the smear of sauce along his lower lip making him look like a sated vampire.

"Buddy got well and truly outed," he said. "I was there with my camera and got all the proof the lawyer will need."

Preston chewed another chicken wing.

"I just don't understand human nature," he said. "He's got a good-looking wife with a great job, he's doing well himself, they live in a big house in Brighton, on the right side of the street. Now he's toast, and all because he couldn't keep his hands to himself. The other woman is already divorced, maybe they'll be happy together. Ppffft."

He drank some beer and rinsed it around his mouth.

"Anyway, Paula will be a real help to me, and I'm glad to be able to help her get out of that shit hole."

"What, Halifax? I quite liked the city."

"Not Halifax, numbnuts. The police down there. Groningen Street. Treating her like she's a leper simply because she's different. It's not right."

Rashford looked at him, surprised by the vehemence of his tone. Preston looked up and shrugged.

"Sorry, I shouldn't rant. But it gets me so mad. And no, it's not that I'm a closet anything. It's just basic human decency."

He took a breath, and another sip of beer.

"I don't know what it's like out where you are, but here the police are woefully undertrained. All they need is a physical fitness test and completion of grade twelve, and then they get a thirty-six-week program. We need to step it up. In this day and age, they should have at least a degree, and some life experience. They need an emotional skill set as well as a technical one. If our cops were smarter then they'd maybe be more reasonable and less prejudiced."

They sat quietly for a few minutes, eating the chicken wings and drinking beer. The waitress came over and they ordered a second pint each. Preston drained his first glass and looked at Rashford.

"You served, right?"

Rashford nodded.

"Me too," said Preston. "Before I became a cop. I joined at eighteen, served ten years, then quit. I was based in Edmonton and so I hung out in Alberta for a while. Ralph Klein was in power, oil was starting to boom again, there were lots of jobs up in the oil patch. I was young, fit and fearless, it was fun. Then I met a girl at the donut shop in Fort Mac and followed her to the Island, and here I am."

"Who were you with?"

"In the Army?" Preston looked down. "I started with RCR, then got recruited to Airborne."

"Ah," said Rashford.

Preston looked across the table.

"Yup. And before you ask, yes, I was in Somalia. But no, I wasn't involved in the Arone situation. I happened to be on my mid-tour leave when that happened. But ..."

He paused, looking down at his hands, then returned his gaze to Rashford.

"But if I'd been there, who knows? That was a horrible rotation. We were under all sorts of pressure, those kids kept coming onto the base and stealing stuff, we had some very right-wing nutters both on the team and in positions of command, it was not really our type of work at all. And yet there we were, supposedly the best of the best, trying to protect people from the warlords who ran the country. I'm not saying we didn't have bad apples in our crew, what regiment doesn't, but it was unfair that we all got tarred with the same brush."

"So, you quit?" said Rashford, quietly.

Preston nodded.

"When they disbanded the regiment, I went back to the Royal Canadians. They put me and all the other jumpers in the 3rd Battalion, and we did the work we'd been supposed to be doing in the Airborne. I stayed until I'd got my ten years in, then quit and became a roughneck. I started out as a floorhand and made my way up to being a derrickhand. I had been offered a position as a driller when I met Cathy." He laughed. "Long story short, I came down here, joined the police, and took a forty per cent pay cut."

Rashford smiled.

"But you had your woman," he said.

Preston snorted.

"For just under a year," he said. "Then she met someone she'd known from school and went off with him. Back to Alberta, for god's sake."

Rashford laughed.

"But you stayed?"

"Yes. I liked my job, the people, the Island. It's a comfortable place to live. It's not cheap, mind you, and the weather in winter is atrocious, but people make do. I like it here."

~

They finished their beers and decided against a fourth, opting instead for coffee.

"I've still got to work in the morning," said Preston to the waitress. "We're not all lazy tourists like this guy."

She looked at Rashford with interest.

"Are you staying in town long?" she said.

"Just a couple more nights," he said. "I'm off to Halifax on Saturday."

"Enjoy your stay," she said, tossing her hair as she walked away.

Preston chuckled.

"Looks like you could get your own personal tour guide there," he said.

Rashford thought of Cassie in the throes of passion, tossing her long streaked hair. He smiled.

"I'm good, thanks," he said.

They sat quietly for a few moments, glancing around at the newcomers who were drifting into the pub, which was slowly filling up.

"Will you see Paula," said Preston, "in Halifax?"

Rashford shrugged.

"I'm not planning to. I'm taking Janet with me, we're going to see Mandy's band on Saturday night, then come back here Sunday. My ticket home is booked for Tuesday, that stupid five thirty flight. I'll give Paula a call before I leave."

He paused for a moment.

"Have you heard anything from Janet?" he said.

"What about?"

"Don't play the innocent with me. About Jean Gauthier. About Brenda Frizwell. I know these are not my cases, but I feel like I'm involved in them, you know?"

Preston reached out and patted him on the forearm.

"They're not my cases either," he said. "You have to remember that. It's all official now. She'll tell us when she wants to."

Rashford chuffed.

"Can we invite her for coffee tomorrow morning?" he said.

"We? You mean, can I invite her for coffee, and you just serendipitously turn up?"

"Something like that, yeah."

Preston shook his head, chortling, and then took out his phone.

"Sure, why not," he said.

Chapter Eighteen

The heat broke on Friday and Rashford woke to scudding grey clouds. Looking out of his window, he saw paper wrappers whirling around the hotel car park, and pedestrians in tightly fastened coats and jackets leaning forward as they braved the wind. Nobody wore a hat or carried an umbrella. He pulled on a hooded sweatshirt and then zipped his fleece before walking outside.

He was feeling windswept and cold when he reached the coffee shop where Preston was meeting Janet Parsons. It was in what appeared to be a heritage building, a long low terrace of connected houses. The café took up the ground floors of four houses, walls having been knocked out to create a series of interconnected rooms. Rashford went in the first door he reached and looked around.

The room was bright and airy, with five tables scattered about. At one a young woman sat with her laptop open, a coffee by her hand. The others were empty. Rashford crossed into the next room, where there was a counter displaying a variety of pastries. Realizing that he had not had breakfast, he ordered an almond slice to accompany his extra-hot latte. The barista gave him a metal stand with a number on it and told him to sit anywhere, his purchases would be brought to him when the coffee was ready. He nodded his thanks and wandered through into a third room.

"Gavin!" said Janet. "Hello. I got your text, sorry but I was so busy yesterday, I never replied. Ten is great. My address is … Here, give me your phone."

He entered his password and opened it to contacts, then passed it over. She quickly typed, then gave the phone back.

"Name, address and phone number," she said. "I'm so excited. What are you doing today? Sit down and join us."

She patted the stool next to her. Rashford sat down, nodding across at Jim Preston, who raised his eyebrows.

"Morning," he said.

Preston grunted.

"Janet was just going to share what she knows about Anne's dad and the Frizwell woman," he said.

Janet tut-tutted him, waving her finger.

"Not quite," she said, then turned to Rashford. "I'm going to share what I can say in the public domain. Jim here has to remember that he's retired now, he doesn't get the inside story. And neither do you."

"Not even for a face-to-face with Amanda Robicheau?"

Janet grinned.

"That's actually a better reason than 'I used to be your boss'," she said. "But all the same; no."

They stopped talking as the barista appeared and set down a large ceramic cup of milky coffee and a wedge of pastry in front of Rashford, who nodded his appreciation.

"A proper latte, this," he said. "Thank you."

The barista smiled and walked away, taking the metal numbering stick with her. Rashford and Preston glanced at each other, then both turned to Janet.

"Go on, then," they said.

Janet struck a dramatic pose, holding her chin with her right hand and pulling on her ear lobe with the left.

"Well," she said, "what do you want first, good news or bad news?"

"Bad news," said Preston.

"Good news," said Rashford, simultaneously.

Janet looked at them.

"Can't you two agree on anything? Okay, dealer's choice, then. First, the Marc Gaudet case. We've charged Jean Gauthier with a number of things but not murder. As you know, the brake hose was scored, and he has admitted to doing that because he was trying to scare Gaudet into letting him sell the garage. He's desperately in debt. But he is adamant that he hadn't meant to kill Marc, and there's no way we can prove otherwise. The Crown prosecutor thinks that if he agrees to counselling for his gambling habit then he'll get away with a fine and some sort of deferred sentence, either weekends or house arrest."

Rashford nodded.

"Does Anne know this?"

Janet shrugged.

"I assume so. We spoke to Sandra, as she's the widow and therefore the person who has now inherited the garage. I would think she's told Anne, but I don't know that."

"Of course," said Rashford. "Thank you."

Janet nodded.

"Right. Okay, second, Brenda Frizwell." She paused. "I have nothing to tell you."

Preston banged down his coffee cup and pushed his chair back with a screech.

"What? Nothing to ... What do you mean?"

Janet used her hands to pat the air in front of her.

"Calm down," she said. "Let me tell you what I know."

She waited until Jim nodded at her, and carefully pulled his chair back to the table.

"We don't know where she is," she said, eventually. "I might have more later, there's a briefing at three when the chief is going to update us on various things, including this one. What I do know is that they pulled a traffic stop yesterday on Johnny Frizwell and found nothing They looked everywhere, took his cab apart, there was nothing. A few porn magazines, but no cocaine. Traffic had to let him continue on. We asked Corporal Stevenson to go out and inform Brenda Frizwell that her youngest son was helping us with our enquiries, but there was nobody at the farm except George."

"What did he say?" said Preston.

"He said that his mum had gone on a holiday with her friend. He wouldn't tell Stephenson who that was at first, but she wheedled it out of him. His name is Gordon, apparently, and he's much younger than our Brenda. It seems that he's lived with her for the past year or so."

She paused, looking at Jim. He scratched his head, then grinned.

"Since just after the fund-raiser on the ship got robbed?"

She nodded. "George seems to think that Gordon is just after his mom's money, but it might be the other way round."

"Do we know where they went?" said Preston.

"Toronto, apparently. They're going to see the Blue Jays and visit Niagara Falls. Says George."

"Who's ticked off at being left to look after the farm?"

"That's what it would seem like, yes."

Rashford tapped his fingers on the table.

"She's done a runner with the coke," he said. "I bet she recognized one of you in the car when we went out there, and she realized you were onto her. She switched the cocaine out from the truck and went to Plan B, taking it up to Toronto herself. Do we know what sort of car this Gordon is driving?"

Janet shook her head.

"No. And without knowing his last name, we can't trace it either."

"Damn it," said Preston. "Still, you can get her when she returns."

"Get her for what?" said Janet. "Giving police a false name and address when questioned a couple of years ago about a case in which she was not a suspect? I can't see that being prioritized, can you?"

Preston nodded.

"I guess not," he said. "At least you can keep an eye on her."

Janet shrugged.

"Perhaps," she said. "But far-eastern Kings is hardly in my jurisdiction, is it? You'll have to talk to Helen Stephenson if you want to know what's happening up there."

"Damn it," muttered Preston, slurping back his coffee. "So damn close."

~

While they finished their coffee, Janet chattered about the weekend and the forthcoming trip to Halifax.

"It's only a bloody fiddle player," muttered Jim Preston.

Janet scoffed.

"The best darned Métis fiddle player in the world," she said. "I'm so excited."

Rashford smiled.

"I'm sure we'll have a great time," he said. "I'll pick you up tomorrow morning."

"Thank you," she said, patting his arm. "I'll be ready. What do you think I should wear?"

Rashford shrugged.

"I really don't think that matters," he said. "Whatever's comfortable."

Preston scoffed.

"Maybe a beaded jacket and a sash," he said.

Janet slapped at his arm.

"Don't be such a grouch," she said. "You're just jealous."

"Mmmfft," he said.

Rashford laughed.

"Sorry, Jim. If I'd known you were a fan, then I'd have tried to get you a ticket as well."

Preston shrugged.

"No, I'm good," he said. "Just winding Janet up a bit. You two young 'uns go and have fun."

"Oh, we will," said Janet, reaching across and squeezing Rashford's hand. "Won't we?"

He squeezed her hand back.

"Absolutely," he said.

Preston looked at them both and shook his head.

"Get a room, for heaven's sake," he said.

Janet blushed and dropped Rashford's hand.

"Sorry," she said. "I'm just so ..."

"I know, excited," Rashford laughed. "Well good, that makes the trip worthwhile."

He got to his feet.

"I'll pick you up tomorrow, see you at ten. Jim. Good luck with everything. I'm sure we'll be in touch."

Jim stood up as well.

"You're not coming back? After Halifax?"

"Just for a day. I'm bringing Janet up on Sunday, then I fly out on Tuesday morning."

"Oh, right. The early flight."

"Yeah. So, I think I'll spend Monday seeing any important tourist bits I've missed, and then get an early night."

"What about Anne?"

"I'm going there now. She and Sandra are supposed to be off work today and I said I'd drop by." He looked at Janet. "Nothing you mentioned is confidential, is it?"

She shook her head.

"No. We already told Sandra, so you can talk with Anne."

"Thanks."

He shook hands with Jim Parsons.

"Good luck with catching Brenda Frizwell," he said. "Maybe Paula will be able to help."

"Paula?" said Janet. "What's she got to do with it?"

"I'll let Jim explain," said Rashford. "See you tomorrow."

He nodded to them both and left the café.

Wakoshi was glad to see him, barking madly and bouncing on four stiff legs as Rashford entered the apartment. Anne laughed as he eased the dog to one side with his foot and then stepped into the living room. Sandra was already there, sitting on the couch. She looked up from her magazine.

"Kwe'," she said. "How are you."

He nodded a greeting.

"I'm good, thanks. You?"

"Eh-eh."

"Tea?" said Anne, bringing in a pot and a mug. "I already put in the milk."

"Thanks," said Rashford, then sat in the empty armchair which didn't have a mug on the floor beside it. Anne passed him the mug she had carried over and poured the tea, after which she topped up first Sandra's mug and then her own. She placed the teapot carefully on the table, then sat down. Picking her mug up from the floor, she held it in both hands and looked at Rashford over the rim.

"So, what's happening?" she said.

Rashford shrugged, careful not to spill his tea.

"I think you know as much as I do," he said. "I just thought I'd stop in and say goodbye. Oh, and I have a couple of questions."

Sandra straightened herself.

"You're leaving?"

He nodded.

"Yes. I don't fly out until Tuesday morning, but I'm away this weekend, and then Monday I'm going to be a tourist. Actually, that's my first question. Where else do you think I should go on the Island? Places I've not been to yet."

The two women looked at each other.

"When we've finished our tea, I'll find the map and we can look at it together," said Anne. "We'll check where you've been and see what's left. Okay?"

Rashford nodded his agreement.

"Right," said Sandra. "What's the next question?"

Rashford looked directly at her as he carefully placed his mug on the floor.

"Is there anything else you want to know about your husband's death?" he said.

She swallowed.

"I don't ... Maybe, please ... Look, could you just tell me what you know, and I'll see if there are any gaps or differences between that and what I think I know. Do you mind?"

Rashford looked across at Anne, who was nodding, then back at Sandra.

"Sure," he said. "This is what I understand happened."

He spoke for fifteen minutes, calmly and carefully, pretending not to see the tears that appeared on their faces and ignoring their futile attempts to wipe them surreptitiously away. As he came to his conclusion, Sandra sobbed, noisily. Anne walked over and put her arm around her mother's shoulders.

"Thank you for that, Gavin," she said. "We appreciate your honesty."

He looked at her.

"Is it how you understood things?"

She nodded.

"Pretty much, yes. It still seems weird that they can't charge Jean Gauthier with anything more serious, but even if they did, it wouldn't bring dad back."

Sandra sniffed.

"I wish I'd known that those stupid papers hadn't been filed," she said. "I'd have made him sell that garage ages ago. But now ... Well, I guess now Anne will have her own business."

Rashford looked at her and smiled.

"You're really going to take it over?" he said.

She laughed.

"Yeah, you know me. I've always been a petrol head. This will give me lots of opportunity to play with the proper toys. Mom is going to help me with the accounts, that's only part-time work, and Darryl has nearly finished their hours to be a certified Automotive Service Technician. Once they have completed the Red Seal then they're going to come and work with me in the garage."

"That sounds great," said Rashford. "Are there going to be any problems with Marc's partner. What's her name, Francine ..."

"Francine LeBlanc, yes," said Sandra. "No, we've already spoken with her. Marc had a decent life insurance and we're giving her two thirds of that, so no problem there. She had no interest in the garage."

Rashford nodded. Sandra looked at him.

"My turn," she said. "What are you doing in Halifax?"

He blushed.

"I'm going to see Mandy and the band play their last show of the tour," he said. Then, to forestall the question he knew would come next, he added, "with Janet."

The two women looked at each other.

"Janet who?" said Anne.

"Janet Parsons," said Rashford. "She's just a friend, a colleague really, but she thinks Mandy is the best fiddler ever."

"A colleague?" said Sandra. "Is she a cop?"

Rashford nodded.

"Yes, here in Charlottetown. She's the contact Jim Preston had, the one who found everything out for you guys and followed up on what we found at the mechanic's shop. I found out she really liked to listen to Mandy. And as I was going down anyway, I thought 'why not?'"

Sandra rolled her eyes.

"Why not, indeed," she said.

"Why can't we see you on Monday?" said Anne. "You can tell us all about the concert."

"And the after-party," laughed Sandra. "Heh, I remember those, from when I was young."

"Mom!"

"What? It's all a long time ago now."

"I'll get the map," said Anne.

They spread the provincial map out on the table and Rashford explained the areas to which he'd travelled. As he spoke, Anne used a bright pink highlighter pen to carefully colour the roads and towns where he had already been. It soon became obvious that he been all over the eastern end of the island, and had circumnavigated the centre, with only a slight venture into Prince County. Sandra nodded in satisfaction.

"There's your route, then," she said. She picked up a yellow high-lighter and used it to trace over each road as she spoke. "Leave from Char-lottetown and go out towards Warren Grove, then follow the 225 all the way across the middle of the Island. Once you get to Kinkora, hook over to Middleton and rejoin the highway here. Then go past the Bullrush Curtain, all the way up the Old Western Road to North Cape, it's beau-tiful up there. The wind farm is incredible. Come back down the coast ..."

"Hang on," said Rashford. "Bullrush Curtain? The Old Western Road? Where's that?"

"Here," said Anne, pointing. "The Bullrush Curtain is just a joke name, when you get past Miscouche you'll see these swampy areas with lots of bullrushes, and then you're really up west, you know?"

"That's Highway 2."

"Yeah, but everyone calls it the Old Western Road."

Rashford scoffed.

"This place is infuriating sometimes. The other day I met someone who said they lived on the 48 Road. It took ages for me to figure out he meant Highway 3. It's like there are two realities, the official one where things are named on signposts and maps, and the unofficial one where people say things like 'turn left where K-Mart Corner used to be' or 'go up by what was the purple house' or 'drive to the Old Western Road' or whatever. Maddening."

"Three," said Sandra.

"What?"

"There is a third reality, the L'nuk one. Epekwitk we call this place, which means 'cradled by the waves', and all over the Island there are sacred places and names. And don't forget the six parallel worlds which our people, animals and supernaturals can travel between."

"Six ..."

Rashford just stared at her, but Sandra didn't blink.

"The world didn't start when your people came," she said.

"Anyway," said Anne, trying to defuse the situation, "after the Cape then visit the Stompin' Tom Centre at Skinner's Pond, and drive all the way down to the lighthouse at West Point. There's lots to see and do on that shore."

She stopped to take a breath, then continued.

"From there, I'd drive across to Alaska and see what time it was when you got to Portage. If you're pressed for time, go straight back to Kensington. Otherwise, if you've got time, you could wander down the Acadian coast through Abrams Village and Mont-Carmel, here, or stop off in Summerside and look around their waterfront. Whatever you choose, you'll end up in Kensington. From there you come back through the centre of the province, back to Charlottetown."

Sandra huffed.

"Or you can come down the other side, visit Lennox Island. That's the heart of the Mi'kmaq on the Island, right there. There's a museum and a cultural centre, all sorts of things to see. I wanted to take you there, remember? But I'm working on Monday."

Anne nodded.

"Sorry, mom, you're right. That's a good road as well." She looked at Rashford. "Either way, you'll end up in Portage, and come back from there."

"Whichever," said Sandra. "Either way, that's a good day out, that is."

She nodded to herself as she sat back in her chair. Anne smiled.

"That's you told," she said.

Rashford looked dubiously at the map.

"That seems like a lot of driving," he said.

Anne scoffed.

"You'd do that before lunch on the prairies," she said.

Rashford looked at her, then nodded.

"Fair enough," he said.

He folded up the map and put it into his pocket.

"Thanks, Sandra," he said. "You've been a great help."

She nodded. He stood up and looked at them both.

"Good luck with the new venture. Again, I'm sorry for your loss. I hope you're going to be okay."

"You as well," said Anne.

She reached over and gave him a kiss on the cheek, then stepped into an embrace. Sandra rolled her eyes but smiled. Anne spoke into his chest.

"Say hello to Bettina from me," she said. "Tell her I'm really sorry that I can't get back for Kôhkum Christine's funeral next week."

He stroked her hair.

"I'll tell her when I see her," he said. "I'm hoping to be back before then."

Sandra stood and came over, putting her arms around her daughter and joining them in a group hug.

"Thanks for all your help, you," she said. "Take care of your people."

Rashford murmured something that he hoped sounded affirmative. They held the clinch for a few more moments, then he stepped away.

"Right, then," he said. "I'd better go and get organized."

He hugged and kissed them each individually, leaned over the dog blanket and scratched Wakoshi between the ears, then walked to the door. He opened it and stepped out, turning to wave before closing the door. He wiped under his eye with one hand, straightened his shoulders, then walked down the stairs and out onto the street.

Chapter Nineteen

The next morning, he checked out of the hotel and drove to the address Janet had given to him. She was already waiting, pacing up and down the driveway outside her door. She nodded at him as she got into the car. He leaned over to give her a kiss but she moved her head so his lips brushed her cheek. He looked at the bag she had placed between her feet.

"Is that all you've got?"

"It's only a night, Gavin," she said. "And it's not like I'm going to have to dress up for anybody."

"I suppose not," he said, reversing down the drive while she buckled her seat belt.

"Anyway, there're lots of shops in Halifax," she said. "What time's the ferry?"

Rashford scoffed.

"I couldn't get a reservation," he said, "it's too busy. And I don't want to spend the day waiting in line on the off chance someone doesn't turn up. No, we'll drive around. I like the bridge, anyway."

They were soon on the highway and cruising towards the Confederation Bridge. Janet asked if he'd mind her finishing a few e-mails for work and so he watched the road and enjoyed the scenery. They were in Borden-Carleton before she put her phone away with a sigh.

"Well, that's all done. Thanks."

"You're welcome," he said. "Do you want a coffee before we go on the bridge?"

"Sure," she said. "And maybe the washroom as well?"

He nodded and turned at the traffic light so he could pull into a gas station with a coffee shop attached. They both used the facilities and met at the pastry counter. Janet paid for the coffee and honey crueller donuts they each chose, and they walked back to the car. Rashford drove back to the highway and followed it to the toll plaza, where he paid his twenty dollars fee with a grumble.

"Don't be mad, it's great," said Janet. "We used to pay nearly sixty at one time, twenty is good. And starting next January, if you have a PEI driver's license then there will be a special lane and the bridge will be free."

Rashford grunted, then eased himself between two camper vans and a large semi-trailer as the five open lanes where you paid the toll converged to one as you approached the bridge.

It was only as they drove onto the bridge that Janet spoke. She cleared her throat, twice, hesitating long enough that Rashford looked across at her.

"What is it?" he said.

She took a deep breath.

"I think we should have separate rooms," she said. "In Halifax."

Rashford was flustered.

"I'm sorry, I didn't mean to imply anything else," he said. "I invited you down because I knew you liked the band, and I thought it would be a good opportunity for you to meet Mandy. I'm sorry, I didn't ..."

He stammered his way to the end of the sentence. Janet nodded.

"That's alright then. We're agreed?"

"Of course. Of course." Rashford paused. "I'm not sure I understand ... why did you think otherwise? Have I said something to upset you?"

She shook her head.

"No, not really. It's just ..."

Rashford kept his eyes on the road.

"Just what?"

"Well, yesterday afternoon, we had our weekly summary meeting like I told you. No, there was nothing new about either Gauthier or Frizwell. But a case we've been working on came up. Again. It's been on and off since Christmas, but this was the third time we've noted activity and I think it'll be moved up the priority list now."

Rashford glanced at her.

"What case? Can you talk about it?"

Janet shrugged.

"Not really, but I think I should. At least the basics."

He drummed his fingers on the steering wheel, then focused on keeping a safe distance between the semi-trailer that was slowly grinding its way to the highpoint of the bridge.

"Go on, then."

"It's not a big thing, really. At least, not yet. We have someone who is selling access to porn videos online. We're not sure where she is, yet, or who she is for that matter, but we know she's on the Island."

"Selling porn? Are there kids involved?"

"No. Nothing like that. Just adults. But it's amateur stuff. Home-filmed, but in a clever way. And everybody is disguised. Electronically, that is."

Rashford chuckled.

"Go on," he said. "You said it was a 'she'. Is this lesbian sex, then?"

Janet laughed.

"Oh, no. This is plain old enthusiastic heterosexual escapades. Various positions, of course, but nothing illegal or dangerous, it's not even very rough. Quite vanilla, actually."

"What's the problem, then?"

Janet cleared her throat, again.

"Well, first she's charging people to watch. The sex with someone isn't illegal, but asking people to pay to watch, that's different."

Rashford nodded.

"Second, in all three films it is the same woman, but with a different guy each time. We don't know who they are because she replaces the faces of the participants. The man always has a bird mask ..."

"A bird mask?"

"Yes, a long-beaked bird. It's like those masquerade masks they used to have back in the Renaissance or whenever. Only this one has a white beak, with a yellow face. Like those big birds we saw on the shore."

"Gannets?"

"Yes. And she is always wearing a cat mask, so you can't see her features."

"How do you know it's the same person, then?"

"Her hair. It's quite distinctive. And she posts the films under the same name. She calls herself the Gannet Whisperer."

Rashford felt a sense of impending terror but managed to keep his voice even.

"You've seen these films, then? You and who else?"

Janet chuffed.

"Yes, I have. Me and a hundred and fourteen others, at least. That's how many subscribers she has, at thirty-five dollars a show. Mind you, at least two of those are police, us and the Mounties."

Rashford nodded.

"And this show. What does that entail, actually?"

"Not a lot, really. Just her having sex. Basic missionary, sometimes she rides cowgirl style, they mutually pleasure each other orally, perhaps a bit of spanking and some doggy. There's no audio so you can't hear anything, but they're both obviously enjoying themselves."

Rashford stared at the road.

"So, she basically has sex with a guy, then posts film of it and earns about four grand from people who pay to watch?"

"That's right."

They drove another kilometer in silence, before Rashford asked the question they were both waiting to hear.

"I'm not sure I understand what that has got to do with you and me needing separate rooms tonight," he said.

Janet sighed.

"I'm not really into random couplings," she said. "I had thought we might have a kiss or a cuddle as a way for me to thank you for getting me to the show, but I wasn't thinking further than that. Then I saw that film, and I thought you might have different ideas. So, I wanted to be clear."

Rashford looked across at her, then back to the road.

"Which you have been," he said. "But, why?"

Janet blew out an exasperated breath of air.

"She disguised the faces and muted the voices, Gavin," she said. "But she didn't take those dinosaur plasters off your shoulder."

Rashford could feel himself going bright red. He didn't know what to say, so he kept focused on maintaining an eighty kilometre per hour speed as he crossed the bridge. When they were safely in New Brunswick, he indicated and turned right, pulling to a stop in the car park outside the tourist information building. He took a deep breath, still looking straight ahead and gripping the steering wheel with both hands.

"I'm sorry," he said.

She scoffed.

"You're a big boy, Gavin. You can sleep with whomever you like."

"Yes, but ..."

"Did she force you into having sex with her?

"No."

"Did she pay you?"

"No!"

"Did you pay her?"

"No."

"Did she tell you she was filming?"

"No."

"Well then, it seems to me you're as much of a victim as the other two might be. Obviously we don't know who they are, yet."

Rashford took some deep breaths.

"Do I need to tell you who she is?"

Janet shook her head.

"I don't think so, no. Maybe lose the plasters before you take your shirt off in public, though."

She laughed, deepening Rashford's discomfort.

"Look, I didn't tell anyone that I recognized you. To the investigators, you're just Gannet Guy Three."

She paused.

"What you could do," she said. "Assuming you know how to contact her, what you could do is tell her to stop. Like I said, this is pretty low-key on our list. Most of the guys just like to watch for prurient reasons, I think. If there were no more films posted, I think the whole thing would just go away."

"Rashford nodded.

"Thank you," he said.

She punched him on the arm.

"C'mon, let's get going. I need time to buy some decent clothes before the show, and the shops will all close at six today."

Rashford laughed, put the car in gear, and drove back up to join the highway.

The traffic thickened as they approached the city and crossed the MacKay Bridge from Dartmouth into Halifax itself. Rashford followed the instructions from his GPS and exited onto Robie Street, his impatience at all the traffic lights exacerbated when they turned onto Spring Garden Road and within fifty metres faced another red light. Janet was still telling him to relax and calm down when they arrived at the Lord Nelson Hotel.

"Yes, I booked two rooms," said Rashford, and was pleased that Janet had the grace to blush. He did not mention that he had expressly asked for adjoining rooms with a connecting door, and hoped that this fact wasn't mentioned at check-in. It wasn't, and once they had their keys, they took the elevator up to the fourth floor. In the corridor Janet paused outside her room.

"It looks like we're next door to each other," she said.

Rashford nodded, clearing his throat.

"Yes, well, I booked them both at the same time."

She raised her eyebrows but made no comment. As her door clicked open she paused, then turned to him.

"What's the plan, then?"

Rashford shrugged.

"The show starts at eight, but I'd like to get there a bit early. I think it will probably be heaving. If we want to get something to eat first, maybe we can meet in the lobby at ..."

He pulled out his phone and looked at it.

"It's two-thirty now, how about we meet in the lobby at five thirty? That gives us time to find a restaurant and then make our way to the auditorium."

"Sure, but why don't you book us a table somewhere? Then we won't be worrying about finding a place."

"Sure. Any preferences?"

"Nah, I'm good with anything. You choose, but I'll pay. Okay?"

He looked at her.

"You should choose the restaurant, then."

She stared at him and stomped her foot.

"Gavin, you choose. I've got to focus on shopping. Apart from deciding which mall to go to first, I can't make any other decisions. See you at five thirty."

She went inside and closed the door behind her. He shook his head, then went into his own room.

He used the next three hours wisely. First, he checked some restaurant reviews and booked a table at the Wooden Monkey for six o'clock. He also booked an Uber to collect them from the hotel at ten to six, and another to meet them at the restaurant at seven fifteen. Then he found the hotel stationery and a pen and wrote a quick note to Chrissie explaining that her little escapades had been compromised and that the police were looking for her. He signed it 'beach guy' and addressed it to the Goose Bay Gallery Shop, which is what it said on the business card she had given him. He did not write a return address. He took the envelope down to the reception desk, where they sold him a stamp and said they would make sure it got mailed.

Once that was done, he stood outside and had a cigarette, then returned to his room and set his phone alarm for four thirty. He kicked off his shoes and lay on the bed watching a baseball game. When his phone woke him up, he had a shower and shaved, then twisted himself around so he could pick the plasters off his shoulder. He tossed them into the garbage bin and dressed in the clean blue denim shirt he had brought with him. It was a lighter shade than his jeans and he thought they went well together. At five twenty-five he shrugged on his leather jacket, checked that he had his wallet and the hotel room key, and went downstairs.

He sat in one of the white leather-clad armchairs and watched people wandering around the lobby, some checking in and others heading out for the evening. A group of teenage soccer players danced and preened themselves as they waited for the coach to check them in and assign rooms, but they stayed away from Rashford after one inadvertently tripped over his outstretched foot. Rashford didn't say anything, but his stare was enough to send the young man backstepping away.

Rashford tensed when an older man carrying an overnight bag approached the desk, nervously looking around and keeping his right hand in his coat pocket. He watched as the man checked in alone, relaxing only when the guest brought his hand out of his pocket and laid a key on the counter, asking if someone could park his car. The clerk called for the concierge and the guest, still looking nervously around, walked to the side of the lobby where a younger woman stood, holding only a purse. He nodded to her, and she followed him towards the elevators.

Rashford was still watching the couple and chuckling to himself when the elevator door opened, and Janet stepped out. The older man immediately stood to one side and then turned to watch her walk through the lobby. A number of the other people milling around stopped and stared. Rashford pulled himself out of the armchair, which was really too low for his taste, and stood to meet her. He checked to make sure his mouth had closed.

She had curled her hair and stacked it so that the ringlets piled on her head only edged down to her temples. The rest of her face was clear, her long silver earrings and bright red lipstick reflecting the lobby lights. She wore a cream-coloured, tight-waisted sheath dress with a deep vee neckline that plunged to her navel. Rashford had no idea how she was keeping her breasts inside the dress, but she was obviously not wearing a bra. The hemline of the skirt was just above her knees, and then her long legs stretched down to a pair of strap-on stiletto heels that matched the colour of her lipstick. Rashford stepped forward.

"You look amazing," he said. "Wow!"

She bobbed in a simple curtsey.

"Thank you, kind sir. Where first?"

She took his arm and turned, causing the people who were staring at them to hurriedly look away. Rashford smiled.

"We have nearly ten minutes until the car comes," he said. "Do you want to sit here or go outside?"

"Outside, I think," she said, so they went across the marbled floor. The concierge immediately rushed over and held the door open for them; Janet nodded regally as they went through. Once outside a uniformed doorman asked if he could call a cab and, when told they were expecting an Uber, gestured them to sit in one of the all-weather armchairs located on the verandah to the right of the steps. They did so, Janet demurely crossing her legs and Rashford very conscious of his jeans and leather jacket.

"I feel woefully underdressed," he said. "You look absolutely stunning."

Janet laughed.

"This is the first date I've been on in months," she said. "And anyway, it's not for you. I'm meeting Amanda Robicheau!"

She fanned her face with her hand, laughing, and Rashford grinned.

"Fair enough," he said. "I'll just bask in the knowledge that every man in that hall tonight is going to be wondering how he can possibly kill me and take my place."

She giggled softly.

"Do you need a cigarette?" she said.

He shook his head, and they sat quietly until the doorman ushered them down the steps and into the waiting car. At the restaurant Janet was delighted to find that Rashford had reserved a window seat, although she felt compelled to mention that their view of the reflective glass windows on the bank building across Prince Street could have been improved. Rashford agreed, arguing that the food would be worth it because you couldn't eat a view, and as they finished a wonderful meal Janet told him that he was right.

The soft lighting reflected off the wooden furniture and from the highlights in Janet's hair. As they finished the bottle of wine Rashford had ordered, he decided that he could not remember being so relaxed. He raised his glass to her.

"Cheers," he said. "Here's to a great night."

She smiled.

"It's already great," she said. "Here's to an excellent one!"

He laughed and clinked his glass against hers. She took a sip, then reached over and picked up the bottle.

"Burrowing Owl?" she said. "Where's this from? It's good."

Rashford nodded.

"It's from BC," he said. "The Okanagan Valley. Down at the bottom, between Oliver and Osoyoos. I had to go down there a few years ago, on a case, and I got to know the guy who runs the place. You don't often see his wine in shops, he sells most of it from the vineyard. At least, he used to."

"Maybe he's expanding?"

"Maybe. It's good enough, anyway." He looked at his phone. "Come on, we'd better be making a move. Our car will be here in a couple of minutes."

After they finished the wine, Janet paid the bill and they walked out into the warm Halifax evening. Their Uber was a spacious Ioniq 5 and they settled happily in the back seat. The driver grinned at them through the rear-view mirror.

"You must be vipers tonight," he said in a broad Newfoundland accent.

Rashford looked at him.

"Vipers?" he said.

The driver chuckled.

"'at's what we call VIPs from where I'se from," he said, and pulled into the traffic. Janet squeezed Rashford's hand, trying not to laugh, and they spent the seven-minute drive studiously avoiding looking at each other while the driver regaled them with tales of his life in rural Newfoundland before he moved to Halifax. He was just ending a long and convoluted story to explain his few possessions, and to describe why he preferred to be happy rather than rich, when they arrived at the Rebecca Cohn auditorium.

"It's as my old priest always said, you'se never saw a hearse towing a U-Haul," he finished, and Rashford had to laugh as he shook his hand and left the car. He held out his arm for Janet to hold, and they walked into the foyer. There were already a number of people milling around and they joined the queue to the Box Office.

Rashford could sense people looking at them and gossiping to each other; he was sure they were wondering what someone like him was doing with someone like Janet. 'I'll pretend I'm her bodyguard,' he thought to himself, and was smiling at the idea of clearing people out of her way when suddenly he was in front of the desk.

"I have my pass here," he said, proffering the laminated card, "and I think there's a seat ticket for me. Gavin Rashford. Also, there should be a ticket and a pass for Janet Parsons, please."

The young Black woman at the Box Office flipped through the cardboard box in front of her and pulled out a small white envelope.

"Here's one for Rashford," she said, still flipping cards. "Do you have your ID please? Ah, and here's Parsons." She pulled out another envelope and looked up, her eyes glancing over Rashford and then widening when she saw Janet.

"Oh my god … are you …" Her voice dropped to a whisper. "Are you Naomi Campbell?"

Janet laughed.

"Goodness me, no. I'm Janet Parsons. Here."

She handed over her driver's licence, as did Rashford, and the young woman passed them their envelopes.

"It's okay if you're incognito," she said, "I won't tell anybody."

Janet nodded as she retrieved her licence.

"Thank you," she said. "I appreciate that."

The young woman clasped her hands to her face and exhaled noisily, watching them walk away. Rashford heard the next person in line say 'excuse me, Miss? Miss?' in an exasperated tone. He smiled.

"That was naughty," he said.

"What was?" said Janet, her eyes widening in innocence. "I didn't tell a lie."

As they walked into the auditorium, Janet gasped.

"My word, it's huge," she said. "I didn't expect them to be playing in a full-sized concert hall."

"Apparently they had to change venue," said Rashford. "The original one they booked was just too small."

Janet looked around the floor area and up to the cantilevered balconies.

"How many people does it seat?"

"About a thousand, I think. Come on, we're down here."

Their seats were in the third row, C19 and C20. He stood to one side so she could enter the row first. She looked at him.

"I prefer the one on the aisle," he said. "For my knees."

She looked at him.

"Right, you old grouch. It's got nothing to do with perhaps having to chat to someone on your other side, has it?

He grinned at her and made the sign of a cross over his chest.

"Right," she said, smirking, but stepped in and sat down on the second chair, nodding to the older man who was already sitting in the third. His partner leaned over.

"Hello, dear," she said. "Isn't this exciting? Have you seen them play before?"

"Yes, I have," said Janet, smiling. "Twice, actually. You?"

"Oh no, dear. We don't normally come out to concerts. But I was in my garden listening to the CBC, and they said be the third caller in and you can get free tickets, and I was and I did. I think they're from Brooklyn."

Janet looked at her.

"Brooklyn?"

"Yes dear. That's why they call themselves Bridge City. I think."

Janet shook her head.

"No, I don't think so. I think they're from Saskatoon, which is known out there as the city of bridges."

"Really?" said the woman. "How interesting."

She settled herself back into her seat and Janet turned to Rashford.

"We can always switch seats at the break," she said.

The concert was breathtaking. The band played two fifty-minute sets and followed that up with a series of encores that lasted another thirty minutes. When they eventually left the stage for the last time, Mandy stayed behind. She moved to Monica's microphone and stood quietly. Slowly her presence was noted, and the audience stopped putting on their coats and turned to face her. There was absolute silence in the hall. Mandy cleared her throat, then spoke.

"I want to thank you all for coming out tonight," she said. "This was our last night of the tour, and we have had a wonderful time out here. But I wanted to make something official. As you might have heard, I am leaving the band to start my solo career."

There were a few gasps from people who had obviously not heard, and some sage nodding of heads from those who had, or at least wanted to pretend they were in the loop on such things.

"I wanted to take a moment to thank my bandmates, Monica, Jody, Mick, and Gary, I wouldn't have been half the player I am if it wasn't for you. Please guys, come back out."

The four musicians edged their way through the back curtain and stood on the stage, sheepishly looking down at the floor.

"Please, give them a big hand," said Mandy, leading the applause herself. After a few moments, she waved for silence.

"I'd also like to thank the light guys who made us all look good, and the sound engineers who made us sound good as well."

She waved into the darkness at the back of the hall, and the audience clapped as directed.

"And last, I'd like to thank the guy who carries our gear everywhere, and who makes sure that the things we need are where we need them, at the time we need them. Ladies and gentlemen, this fellow never gets any credit, but I'd like a big round of applause please, for our Road Manager and general Mister Fixit, Mister Sebastian Wiebe. Get out here, Seabass."

The young man came out onto the stage, nodding and waving. Rashford clapped along with everyone else, thinking how much the young man had changed since he had first met him at the Majestic. That made him think of Sarah, who had clung to his arm and shouted 'I'm with the band' to anyone who would listen.

"Penny for them," said Janet, nudging him with her elbow. He just shook his head, still smiling.

The applause died down as Mandy turned back to the microphone. She brought her fiddle to her chin, waving her empty hand at the five people on stage.

"I couldn't do what I do if they weren't so good at doing what they do," she said. She looked across at them. "This one's for you, guys."

She launched into the slow entry notes of the Red River Jig, gradually increasing in tempo. The audience stayed on their feet, clapping and cheering, even as she brought the tempo back down and slowly walked off stage, stopping in front of Seabass and then each musician in turn to play a short fast melody. It was only after she had left, and the sound of the fiddle died away, that Mick waved to the crowd, and led the rest of the Bridge City Rollers off the stage.

Slowly, chattering excitedly, the audience filed out of their seats and made their way up the aisle. Janet and Rashford stood aside to let the older couple leave.

"Did you enjoy the show?" said Rashford.

"It was wonderful," said the woman. Her husband chuffed, touching his ear.

"I kept my hearing aids off," he said. "Too damned loud. We're only here because it was free."

"Henry Michael," she said. "Don't be such a spoilsport. Have a good evening you two."

They left and Janet slumped heavily back onto her chair.

"Wow," she said.

Rashford smiled at her.

"We'll wait a few minutes," he said. "Until things have calmed down a bit. Then we'll go backstage. Okay?"

Janet nodded.

"In a minute," she said. "I need to get my breath back."

Chapter Twenty

Their passes were scrutinized twice but they made it backstage to the dressing room area without incident. Rashford knocked and then walked in, surprised at the number of people milling around. Two young women were sitting, one on each arm of a comfortable looking chair, holding wine glasses in one hand while caressing Mick's hair and neck with the other. Gary and Jody had pulled two chairs close to each other and were looking at a guitar that was held by someone whom Rashford did not know. Monica and Seabass were standing by the drinks table, talking to a small group of men wearing jackets and ties. Mandy was laid out on a couch, a cloth over her eyes, giving no indication that she was listening to the man squatting by her side, clicking through photographs displayed on the rear screen of his camera..

Mick saw them first and waved.

"Hiya, Gavin," he said. "What d'ya' reckon, did we do okay?"

"Not too bad, I reckon," said Rashford.

Mick laughed.

"Not too bad? That's high praise, coming from you."

Mandy lifted the cloth from her eyes and sat up.

"Hello, Gavin," she said. She looked at Janet. "Is this your friend?"

Rashford nodded.

"Amanda Robicheau, please may I introduce one of your biggest fans, Janet Parsons, from PEI."

Mandy stood up and held out her hand.

"I'm pleased to meet you," she said. "I hope you enjoyed the show?"

"I, I, I ..." stammered Janet, gulping and shaking at the same time. "God, you were so good. And you're so beautiful."

"Thank you," said Mandy.

"You're not so bad yourself, sister," said Gary, turning away from Jody and the guitar man.

"Come over here," said Mandy, ignoring him. She took Janet's arm and brought her around to her side.

"Gavin, can you take our photograph, please," said Mandy, smiling at him. "It's okay," she said to Janet, "he'll mess up many things but he's okay with a camera."

Janet laughed and relaxed. Rashford raised his phone and took half a dozen photographs.

"One of them will come out, I'm sure," said Mandy, laughing. "Gavin, will you take one of us with the band as well, please."

"Sure," he said, and waited while she called the other four to join her. Janet stood in the middle of the group, smiling, as Rashford raised his phone. He noticed that Gary had insinuated himself into the group so that he was standing next to Janet, his arm loosely around her waist. The man who had been kneeling on the floor next to Mandy came and stood beside him.

"Can I get a couple as well?" he said. "For social media."

Mandy nodded, then turned to Janet.

"As long as you're okay with that?"

Janet nodded.

"This is Phil, by the way," said Mandy, looking at Rashford. "He's my new manager."

The two men nodded to each other and Rashford stepped aside while Phil took photographs with a bulky digital camera.

"What's that?" asked Rashford.

"DSLR," said Phil, proudly. "Digital single lens reflex. It's one of the new Nikons. I just got it a couple of days ago, at Henry's. It's got this sixteen-millimetre fisheye lens that I can stop down to two point eight, can you believe that?"

Rashford had no idea what he was talking about and was starting to glaze over when Mandy rescued him from a lecture on the benefits of single lens reflex cameras over mirrorless ones. She walked over from the group and grabbed hold of Phil's arm.

"I heard that," she laughed. "You see, Gavin, how detailed he is? It's lovely to have a manager who is so precise."

Rashford nodded, hoping that she didn't mention the stage monitor incident again. She didn't, instead saying that she had to go and get her stage bag packed. Phil wandered off and Rashford looked around, hoping to see if Janet was ready to leave. At first he thought she had left already but then he saw her standing in a corner, leaning in close and laughing at something Gary was saying. She turned and waved at him to join them.

"Gavin, Gary and I are going to go for a drink. I'll make my own way back to the hotel, okay? What time do you want us, me, to be ready to leave tomorrow?"

Rashford looked at the drummer, who shrugged. He glanced back at Janet.

"About ten would be fine," he said. "There's no rush. Unless you want to go shopping again before we leave?"

"Great," she said. "See you later."

Rashford knocked on the door into the back room and entered when instructed. Mandy was standing at a table, folding clothes and packing them into a suitcase. Phil lounged on a small couch, checking his phone. He stood up and nodded.

"I'll leave you to it," he said. "Amanda, I'll wait out with Mick."

She nodded. Phil waved at Rashford and then left the room. Mandy stared at him.

"Are you okay?" she said.

Rashford nodded.

"I just thought that I'd come and see you, before I leave," he said, stumbling over the words. "I might not see you for a while, and I thought …"

"Oh, Gavin," she said, stepping over to embrace him. "You big silly soft thing, you."

She hugged him tightly and he smelt the lemon from the shampoo she favoured. He spoke into her hair.

"You were brilliant tonight," he said.

She chuffed.

"Thank you. I hope your new friend enjoyed the show."

"She did. But she's not that sort of friend, she's just a colleague."

Mandy leaned backwards and looked up at his face.

"Really? I don't think I've ever seen a colleague of yours dressed like that. Not even Sarah!"

Rashford blushed.

"That was for you," he said. "She bought that outfit just for the show."

Mandy chuckled.

"That's her story and she's sticking to it? Fair enough."

She released him and stepped back to the table.

"Now, you're not going to get all maudlin on me, are you?"

He scoffed.

"Maybe a little," he said. "You're going off to become rich and famous, I'm going back to Maple Creek."

"Which you like very much," she said. "You'd hate life on tour and, anyway, I'll have no time for men."

He raised an eyebrow.

"What about Phil?"

She laughed.

"Phil? He's more interested in Gary, to be honest." She picked at a loose thread hanging from a shirt collar. "Really, Gavin, it's all about the music."

"Uh-huh."

She turned to him.

"It is. Truly. I might have the odd liaison if I get itchy, but I have to be focused on the music. I don't have time for relationships. Sorry, Gavin, but that's the way it is."

He nodded.

"I know," he said. "I've received that message loud and clear. Don't worry, I'm not going to stalk you. But I do expect an invitation to your big house with a view of the sea."

Mandy sniffled.

"And you shall get one, I promise," she said. She paused. "I've got to pack ..."

He walked over and kissed her on the top of her head. She clung tightly to him and he could feel her shaking.

"It's okay," he said. "You're going to be brilliant." He paused. "You are brilliant," he corrected, "and you're going to be famous."

She sighed, softly.

"And you? What are you going to be, Gavin?"

He laughed, then in a sing-song voice misquoted a song he remembered.

"I'm just a copper in a black and white land."

She laughed with him.

"That's a terrible pun," she said. "It's the kind of thing Mick would say. Now, go on, be off with you. Please."

"You are going to be a superstar, Amanda Robicheau," he said. "And I'll be cheering you on with everyone else. Only louder. Whenever you play Saskatoon or Regina, or even over in Calgary, I'll try my best to get there."

She nodded.

"I'll leave a pass at the door with your name on it," she said. "No stormtroopers, okay?"

"Okay."

They stood quietly, holding each other, then Rashford gave her a final squeeze and stepped away.

"Thanks for everything," he said. "It's been a blast."

She nodded.

"Yes. The best and most enthusiastic sex I've had in a long time."

"Not ever?" he teased.

She blushed, running her finger down his chest.

"One more thing you can do for me," she said.

"Anything," said Rashford.

"Catch Marc Claydon," she said.

~

He said his farewells to the rest of the Band and left the auditorium, waiting until he was outside before lighting a cigarette. A woman walking by stopped and asked him for a light, then wondered whether he was looking for a date. He shook his head and walked back to the hotel.

He stayed on University Avenue, crossing Robie by the Fire Station and passing the immense bulk of the Children's Hospital. The trees were in full leaf and offered a cool shade for his evening stroll. After about a kilometre he turned onto Cathedral Lane and cut across through Victoria Park, past the statue commemorating Robert Burns and over Spring Garden Road to his hotel. He contemplated stopping into the bar for a drink but decided he would probably get either too sad and morose or else too excited and lively; neither option appealed to him, and he went straight to his room.

He had been back about an hour, lazily channel surfing, when he heard the door to the next room open and voices through the connecting door. He could not make out what they were saying and tried to focus on an action film he had found. Suddenly he heard the unmistakeable sound of a woman crying out in ecstasy. When it happened a second time, he came off the bed and stood next to the door; the voice was still indistinct, but he was sure he could hear words like 'more!' and 'harder!'s Shaking his head, he went back to his film, turning up the volume on his television.

The sounds continued, however, and after twenty minutes he had had enough. Muttering to himself, he took his wallet and walked down the corridor to the elevator. The voices were more muffled through the main entry door to the room, but still distinguishable as someone experiencing a long night of passion. The Do Not Disturb sign was hanging from the door handle.

Mumbling imprecations to himself at how the drummer, who must surely be the instigator of the liaison, was able to maintain such a torrid and lengthy pace, he was almost at the bar when he glanced across to a table by the window. There, chatting quietly together, were Gary and

Janet. Rashford stopped, stupefied, then continued to the bar and ordered a double Ardbeg. He signed it to his room, then walked over to the couple. Janet looked up.

"Oh, hi, Gavin," she said. "I hope we didn't ... mmm ... disturb you?"

Her eyes crinkled. Gary sucked in his cheeks, staring rigidly down at his beer. Janet waved what looked like a vodka and tonic at Rashford.

"Come and have a drink with us," she said, smiling.

Rashford pulled over a spare chair from a nearby table and sat down. Janet looked at him, a mischievous grin on her face. Gary kept staring at his drink. The silence lengthened as Rashford took a sip of his scotch, then suddenly realized that he had been played. He shook his head, slowly.

"Bastards," he said.

Janet laughed loudly, throwing her head back in delight. Her carefully arrayed hair wobbled but did not collapse around her. Gary made strange noises and Rashford realized the drummer was crying, his shoulders shaking, and his eyes scrunched tightly closed.

"I'm sorry, Gavin," said Janet, "I couldn't resist it. We got an Uber back and were just getting out of the car when you arrived. We thought you'd come in here but when you went straight to your room, well, it was just too good a chance. We had one drink until we thought you would be settled, and then made our move."

Gary took a deep wheezing breath and sat up straight, looking at Rashford.

"Don't blame me, man," he said, still snorting. "You know I'm gay, right? She picked the movie, it was all icky, but she seemed to know what she was looking for."

Janet slapped at him.

"I did not," she said, vehemently. "Honestly, Gavin, I just picked one that seemed to have no plot other than a guy putting together a hot tub at a house rented by three girls. I didn't watch any of it! Gary's making that up."

Rashford shrugged.

"It doesn't matter to me," he said. "It's all on your room."

She looked at him.

"What is?"

"Well, the bill for the porno movie, for a start. And the noise, everyone walking past in the corridor can hear it, and they all know it's your room."

Janet scoffed.

"How would they possibly know that?" she said.

Rashford grinned.

"Because I taped a sticky note with 'Janet's room' written on it to the door," he said.

Gary burst out laughing again, slapping his knee and shaking his head.

"Oh, you two are beautiful," he said. "Drinks are on me."

The next morning Rashford woke to the sun streaming through the window. Cursing to himself for not closing the curtains when he'd eventually staggered back from the bar, he stood up. The room moved a little, so he held onto the mattress for support, then straightened and walked across the room. He was pulling one curtain towards himself when he noticed the splash of cream on the back of the armchair. He turned around as quickly as he could without falling over and stared at the bed. Janet opened one eye and looked at him.

"Good morning," she said, her voice hoarse and raspy. "My head hurts."

Rashford looked down and checked that he was still wearing his boxer shorts. Janet sat up, the sheet pooling around her waist. He stared at her, noting that she was wearing a plain pink nightgown with a high ruffed neck.

Janet coughed.

"Don't worry," she said. "Your honour is intact. What's left of it, that is."

He walked over and sat on the edge of the bed.

"Umm ... what happened?"

She shrugged.

"Gary," she said. "That's what happened. He got you drinking black rum and you got all melancholic. We listened to your stories for a while, until you told us for the fifth time what a beautiful woman Bettina Black-eagle was, then we'd had enough. We carried you up to your room and put you to bed, then Gary left."

She paused.

"I left the connecting door open because I was worried about you. In the middle of the night, you came through and got into bed. I was going to throw you out, but you started snoring. So, I just left you."

Rashford looked around.

"This is your room?"

"Yes, Gavin," she said, patiently. "Yours is through there."

She pointed to the open connecting door.

"You can close it as you leave," she said. "I'm going to grab a shower."

Rashford hesitated.

"I just snored?" he said.

"Yes," she said. "I kicked your leg and that seemed to stop it."

"That's it?"

"That's it. You had me in bed and you fell into a drunken stupor. I missed the opportunity to become one of Gavin's Girls. Ah well, c'est la vie. Now, scoot. I'll see you at breakfast in an hour."

She pushed him off the bed. He shook his head, slowly, and walked back into his own room, carefully closing the door behind him.

They met in the dining room and ate breakfast, talking about the concert and laughing over the events of the night.

"You look cute when you blush," Janet told him, numerous times, as she sipped her orange juice and picked at an omelet. Rashford just shook his head and focused on his eggs Benedict, smearing the sauce on his toast before soaking up some yolk.

"I'm not the one who welcomed a stranger into my bed," he said.

She scoffed.

"Hardly welcomed! I checked you had your pants on."

Rashford looked at her.

"Keep your voice down," he said. "People are listening."

She giggled, and soon he was laughing with her.

Once she had finished her third cup of coffee, Janet stood up.

"I'll go and get ready," she said. "Downstairs in half an hour?"

"Sounds good," he said. "I'll see you at Reception."

He finished his coffee, then walked outside the hotel and across to the smoking area. He stood quietly, enjoying the warmth and the view into the public gardens. He stubbed out the cigarette and walked back inside to collect his bag before meeting Janet down in the lobby.

Once the formalities were completed, but not before Rashford had leaned over Janet's shoulder to read her bill and asked her if the movie she'd watched was worth twenty-three ninety-nine, they went out to the car.

"Back on the ferry?" she said.

He shook his head.

"If it's okay with you, we can drive round. It's a lovely day and we're in no rush."

She shrugged.

"I don't mind," she said, placing her bag next to his in the trunk and then getting into the passenger seat. She clicked on her belt and then patted his thigh.

"It was a lovely weekend, Gavin," she said. "Thank you."

He nodded at her and smiled, then put the car into gear and drove out onto South Park Street.

"We'll go over the Macdonald bridge this time," he said. "I always try not to go home the same way I came."

Janet shook her head.

"Of course you do," she said.

Chapter Twenty-One

The drive back was uneventful. There was not much traffic, and the road was dry. Rashford smiled to himself as they passed the fast-food restaurant where he had burned his mouth on the scallop. It was less than three weeks since he had stopped there, he realized, shaking his head.

"What's wrong?" said Janet.

"Nothing," said Rashford. "Just thinking about something."

At Truro they turned left onto the TransCanada Highway and stopped for lunch at the Masstown Market. They contemplated fish and chips at the Lighthouse, but the line-up was too long, so they went inside, and each had a chowder and half-sandwich combo. After they had eaten, Janet left Rashford at the table with a second cup of coffee and his phone. She browsed the retail area and returned with a shopping bag full of vegetables as well as a large round loaf of rustic white bread.

"That's my shopping done for the week," she said, smiling.

Rashford turned his phone so she could see the map he had open.

"It's still early," he said. "Why don't we go down the old road, through the Wentworth Valley and then up to the coast and along. It won't be much longer than taking the highway, and it will be a lot more interesting."

"Sure," said Janet. "I always come straight down the main road; I've not been in that area at all."

Once they were off the highway the slower speeds and warm summer day meant they could drive with the windows down. They passed the long expanse of Folly Lake and the chairlifts at the Wentworth ski area. The landscape was a monotonous mix of scrubby brush along the roadside backed by ranks of trees marching up the low-lying hills. Once a black bear appeared on the road and Rashford slowed down so that Janet could snap a photograph with her phone. The bear posed for a moment, then huffed and turned back into the brush.

Just past the village of Wentworth they turned onto a minor road and continued north until they intersected with the main coast road at Wallace.

"This is known as the Sunrise Trail," said Janet, checking her phone. "We're here at the wrong time of day."

Rashford scoffed.

"And going the wrong way!" he said. "We're heading west, not east."

At Pugwash, Janet suddenly squealed in excitement and told Rashford to pull over.

"Look, a gift shop for Seagull Pewter," she said. "Let's have a look."

Rashford obeyed and parked outside the grey two-story building. They went inside and Janet entered into a detailed conversation with the saleslady. Rashford poked around, bemused at the variety, half-listening to their conversation. They went into a small, recessed area and emerged with Janet carrying a package. Rashford met them at the till.

"This is for my nan," said Janet. "She loves pewter and is going to be ninety this year. I've been looking all over for a decent birthday present. What have you got?"

Rashford showed her the small trinket box with a raised grape and vine design on the lid.

"It's for my friend Bettina," he said. "She can use it to hold her smudge sticks when she's not using them."

He paid for his purchase and waited outside, smoking a cigarette, until Janet emerged. In the car she showed him the sculpture she had bought, a pewter angel holding a harp.

"My nan is convinced she will go to heaven and surrounds herself with angels, just so she will feel comfortable when she gets there," she said.

Rashford started to laugh and then saw the serious look on Janet's face, so he simply nodded. After leaving the store and driving across the bridge, they stopped at a gas station and bought an ice cream each before returning to the main road.

Meandering through the small communities of Northport, Lorneville, and Tidnish, they chatted about themselves and their lives. Rashford laughed when Janet told him that her family had originally lived 'at the end of the 48 Road' and explained to her his theory of the multiple realities of place that existed on the Island.

"Sandra's wrong," Janet said. "There's at least four layers. Do you know about Darkie's Hollow, or the Bog, or Blackman's Bridge …"

Rashford admitted he didn't. Janet huffed.

"I was born in Charlottetown and learned the old stories from my nan and my aunties. About how some of our people came here as enslaved persons, not just as Black Loyalists. About the racism and the injustices and the cruelty. Mom didn't speak much of those times because she wanted us to grow up as part of mainstream Canada, but you can't just lose who you are."

He nodded in agreement.

"Have you always lived in Charlottetown?"

She shrugged.

"I went away to Fredericton and did my BA at UNB, with a major in criminology and criminal justice. Then I came back and studied at the Academy in Summerside before joining the police."

Rashford scoffed.

"No wonder Jim liked you," he said. "He was telling me the other day that police training should include academic training as well as the practical stuff."

She nodded.

"Yes, he told me that on the day he fixed it for me to be his partner," she laughed.

∽

They navigated the traffic circle at Port Elgin without difficulty and followed the signpost towards PEI.

"Was that a rotary or a roundabout?" asked Rashford.

"Whichever you prefer," said Janet. "They both mean the same thing."

Rashford shook his head.

"Why can't people just settle on one term?"

"It's more fun this way," she said. "It confuses the tourists."

There was the normal ten-minute wait at a road works where three people in high-viz jackets were watching a fourth look into a pothole, but soon they were crossing the bridge over the Northumberland Strait. As they approached the Y junction where they could choose to go east or west, Rashford spoke.

"Straight back to the city?"

She nodded.

"I think so. I have to be up for work tomorrow."

They followed the highway along the south shore and through the Bonshaw woods before arriving in Charlottetown.

"Home again," said Janet, reaching her arms behind her head and stretching her shoulders. "Thank you for a wonderful weekend, Gavin."

"You're welcome.

"I'm going back to reality tomorrow," she said. "What are you going to do?"

"Tomorrow?"

"Yes."

"I'd planned to go on a trip back this way and up to North Cape, but I think I'm going to save that for another day. I've done enough driving for now. I might go up to the National Park for a swim, but I think I've earned a quiet day before I go home."

"That's on Tuesday, right?"

"Yes."

"Well, if I don't see you before you leave, I hope you have a safe flight back. And thank you again for a lovely weekend. It was fantastic."

She leaned across and gave him a kiss on the cheek, but he reached out his hand and touched her shoulder. She looked at him.

"I'm sorry about the gannet," he said. "Truly."

She sighed.

"Me too," she said, kissing him full on the lips. Breaking away, she looked at him. "Me too."

She got out of the car and walked into her house without a backwards glance.

The next day Rashford paid the day fee at the National Park and pulled into the big car park at Brackley Beach. He slung a backpack holding a towel and a bottle of water over his shoulder and started walking down the old road to Robinsons Island. The bay to his left was choppy in the light breeze but the screen of trees on his right blocked any cooling effect of the wind. It took him nearly forty minutes and before he was half-way down the causeway, he had removed his shirt.

When he reached the end of the road, he left the old parking area and followed the trail to the beach, disturbing a large flock of terns as made his way to the edge of the channel. Across the narrow strip of water were the wharf buildings at North Rustico. The terns chattered and screeched as they wheeled above him, the braver birds dropping down and skimming close to his head. He realized he must be near a nesting colony and started to back away, then turned and followed the beach back past the trailhead and over a pile of red sandstone boulders. The long expanse of sand extended in front of him. He took off his shoes and put them in his backpack, drank a mouthful of water, and started to walk.

It was only when he reached an area close to a lifeguard tower that he paused. There were seven or eight piles of belongings, some accompanied by a person stretched out on a towel and others simply left in the open. Looking around, he saw a group of teenagers splashing in the gentle surf, and further out the heads of two or three older swimmers. He assumed that the presence of the young woman on the top of the tower would deter any random thieves.

He dropped his backpack, covering it with his towel and shirt, then waded into the ocean. The depth was shallow, and he was nearly thirty metres out before he flexed his shoulders and dove under the next incoming swell. He swam parallel to the shore and back a dozen times, then returned to the beach. Sitting on his towel, he was enjoying a long drink of water when his phone rang. It was Paula.

They exchanged pleasantries and she told him how jealous she was that he was spending his Monday on a beach while she was stuck in the Gottingen Street office. Then she got to the crux of her call.

"We got approval from the judge," she said. "I heard back after I spoke to you last, and we submitted that sample to the lab on Friday. I guess someone ran it over the weekend, and they've got an immediate hit."

"You know where he is?" said Rashford, feeling a buzz of excitement.

"Not yet, no. Apparently it's a close match but not an identical one."

Rashford scratched his shoulder.

"A relative, perhaps?"

"That's what they think," said Paula. "The next step is to identify that individual and then to try to figure out the relationship to your man. But it's a step forward."

"More like a leap, I'd say. Thank you so much for letting me know."

"You're welcome. I'm not sure how long the next part will take, if something happens before I leave then I'll be in touch. Have a safe flight home."

"Thank you," said Rashford. "And good luck in your new job."

Paula laughed, then they finished the call. Rashford pulled out his cigarettes and was about to light one when there was a sharp whistle. He looked around and saw the young lifeguard pointing at him.

"No smoking on the beach," she said, sternly. "It's the law."

Rashford waved his hand in apology and put the cigarette back into the packet. He got up and walked back to his car, opening the windows and checking nobody was standing around near him before he lit his cigarette. He leaned back in his seat and smiled.

"Gotcha," he said.

The next morning, he left his car in the designated lot at the airport and dropped the keys into a lockbox on the rental desk. He had checked in online but still had to collect a boarding pass because the printer at the business centre in the hotel had been broken. He joined a line of several grumpy passengers who apparently didn't want the four o'clock check-in time to interrupt their sleep.

He collected his documents then carried his bag to the x-ray machine, standing at the front until the operator waved him away. He lined up for security and, once he was cleared, lined up again at the small café so he could get a coffee. At five twenty they called his flight, and he walked out to the plane. His last view of Charlottetown was of the harbour, the early morning sun glinting on the water and reflecting back from a large cruise ship entering through the narrows.

He had a brief layover in Toronto and bought himself a coffee and breakfast sandwich to go as he walked between the gates. The next flight left on time, and he ate his breakfast as the plane climbed out across Lake Huron. The time zone differences meant that he landed in Regina shortly after nine o'clock and within the hour he was at the headquarters building.

He nodded at the young constable sitting at the reception desk and flashed his identification card.

"Don't phone up," he said. "I want to surprise her."

The constable nodded and Rashford went to the stairs. He climbed easily up the flights and was soon in the corridor outside the Chief Superintendent's office suite. He too a deep breath, then walked into the reception area.

To his surprise the person sitting at Sarah's desk was not Sarah but rather a large, florid white man with a squashed nose and a smear of what looked like eczema or rosacea across his cheek and temple. He was in civilian clothes and peered at Rashford through square lensed spectacles with a blue frame.

"Can I help you?"

The voice was of a much higher pitch than Rashford had expected. He stepped to the desk.

"Staff Sergeant Rashford to see Chief Superintendent Pollard," he said.

The man looked down at his computer screen.

"I don't have anyone by that name on my list," he said.

"I don't have an appointment," said Rashford, "but I do need to see her."

The man shook his head.

"She's actually not here at the moment," he said. "But even if she was, I'm not allowed to just let you in. You have to book an appointment."

"She will want to see me."

"If you have an appointment, then she will."

Rashford took a deep breath.

"Please can I make an appointment?" he said.

The man shrugged.

"You have to do it online, using the GaffersApp."

"The what?"

"The GaffersApp, it's the new app for the Force. I thought you said you were a Staff Sergeant."

"I did. I am."

"Then you should know about the app. The details were e-mailed last week, and it's been pushed on all our social media channels."

"I've been on holiday," mumbled Rashford. "Not online."

The man chuffed.

"I'd suggest you check your e-mail first, then you can sign up for the app. Then you can make an appointment."

Rashford looked carefully around the office. He ran his finger along the wooden slat that served as a rail on the edge of the desk, relieved to feel the familiar notches. Then he walked over to the bookshelves on the side wall, looking carefully into the corners.

"What are you doing?" said the man, a note of nervousness entering his voice.

Rashford continued to pace around the room, looking into each corner, then turned back.

"I give up," he said.

"Give up what?" said the man, in confusion.

"I can't see the cameras."

The man looked around.

"What cameras?"

Rashford smiled at him.

"The hidden ones that you're using to film me. What is this, some sort of Candid Camera operation?"

The man clucked his tongue.

"Look, Staff Sergeant whomever you are. Go online and check your e-mail, then make an appointment to see CS Pollard, then come back. Otherwise, I shall have to call security."

He looked at Rashford more closely.

"How exactly did you get in here, anyway? This is a restricted-access floor."

Rashford smiled.

"Tell the Chief I said hi," he said, and walked out of the office.

He returned three hours later, having logged on and followed the instructions before taking the next available appointment. The Chief Superintendent greeted him with a beaming smile as she shook hands, then glanced at the receptionist.

"No calls or visitors until I'm finished, please, Clarence," she said. "Unless it's the Commissioner, of course."

She ushered Rashford inside her office and then closed the door.

"Sorry about earlier," she said. "Clarence told me you'd been by and he wouldn't let you in. He was quite pleased with himself for defending my door. I told him I would kill him if he did it again."

Rashford chuckled.

"Who is he?"

"He's a temp because silly Sarah broke her arm. She fell or something, and it's rather bruised, so she's had to take a couple of weeks leave. She should be back tomorrow or Wednesday, though."

"I'm glad to hear she's recovering," Rashford said.

Pollard nodded, then pointed to one of the armchairs.

"Until then, there's no coffee, I'm afraid. It's against the rules for me to treat my assistant as an assistant, apparently. I'm not supposed to exhibit any authoritarian gestures that might upset his self-esteem."

Rashford bit his lip as he sat down.

"I'm assuming he's a civilian," he said.

"Oh, very much," said Pollard. "Sarah thinks it's hilarious."

Rashford strove to keep his face expressionless.

"Ma'am," he said.

She glanced at him.

"Right, then. What have you been up to?"

For the next twenty minutes, Rashford gave a summary of the police-related activities that had taken place during his vacation. He did not mention Cassie, or the dinosaur band aid plasters. Pollard listened, at times asking insightful questions, at other times nodding as though she was having some preconceived notion validated. When he had finished, she looked at him.

"That's excellent news on the Claydon file," she said. "It would be wonderful to catch that piece of shit. Josee is still not a hundred per cent, you know."

Rashford kept his surprise out of his voice. He had never heard the Chief Superintendent swear before. He shook his head.

"I didn't know," he said. "Mandy didn't say anything."

Pollard nodded.

"She might not know anything," she said. "I think that Petra and Shyanne are hoping she'll focus on her career stuff right now. I only heard because Bettina gave me a phone call a week or so ago. You heard about Kôhkum Christine, I assume?"

"Yes, Ma'am. I think the funeral is on Saturday."

Pollard nodded.

"Yes, it is. Eleven o'clock at the church in Maple Creek. I'm not sure which one."

"Probably Saint Lawrence," said Rashford. "I shall check tomorrow. But, Ma'am. About the Claydon file."

"Yes?"

"Paula in Halifax didn't know how long it would take for the investigation to identify a specific individual," said Rashford. "I think you should keep communications open with Inspector Smithson, so it doesn't fall off his radar."

Pollard chuckled.

"Oh, don't worry, I have him in my agenda," she said. "Every Tuesday morning, I give him a call."

She looked at Rashford.

"When did you actually get back?"

"Just after nine this morning, Ma'am."

"And when did you leave Charlottetown?"

"About five forty-five, Ma'am."

"Local time?"

"Yes Ma'am."

"So, you were up around four?"

Rashford nodded.

"That would have been one in the morning here. Go to bed, Staff Sergeant. Use tomorrow to get your laundry done, buy groceries, that kind of thing. I'll see you here on Thursday morning, nine o'clock sharp. Understood?"

"Yes, Ma'am."

Rashford got to his feet, saluted, and turned to leave. As he reached the door, she stopped him.

"I got a telephone call about you," she said. "From Ottawa."

Rashford looked at her. She nodded to herself.

"We'll chat on Thursday."

Chapter Twenty-Two

On Saturday, after the funeral, they met for lunch in the back room of the Bel-Air restaurant. Chef Li supervised the staff as they put plates of General Tsao chicken and mushroom fried rice on the table, then shushed them out of the room. She returned and carefully placed on the table a tray which held seven bottles of Tiger beer. She took one herself and stood off to the side.

"Please, everyone take one," she said. "For the toast."

They each reached over and took a bottle. The caps had already been removed.

"I drink to the memory of Kôhkum Christine," she said. "A very good lady who came here many times and always said good things about my food. I drink to wish her well on her journey."

They all raised their beer bottles.

"Kôhkum Christine," they said, except for Bettina.

"Nôhkum Christine," she said.

They all reached over the table and clinked their beer bottles together, then each took a swig from their bottle. Chef Li looked to her left, at Gayle Morgan.

"You next," she said. "We follow the sun, arounding the clock."

"Arounding ..." said Sheri in a whisper, looking at Sarah.

"Clockwise," Sarah whispered back.

Gayle lifted her bottle.

"I drink to the memory of Kôhkum Christine," she said. "I did not know her well, but whenever I needed knowledge of the Nekaneet people, or about what important things were happening in Treaty 4 territory, she would know. I drink to wish her well in the next life."

"Kôhkum Christine," they said.

"Nôhkum Christine," Bettina said.

Gayle looked to her left, to Chief Superintendent Pollard.

"Ma'am?"

The Chief Superintendent raised her bottle, took a deep breath, and spoke.

After the round was completed, Chef Li left the room and the group sat down at the table. Bettina edged in next to Rashford.

"That was beautiful, Gavin," she said. "Thank you for those kind words. My nôhkum would be very pleased."

He shrugged.

"I hope she knew how much she meant to me," he said. "As I said, she was very much part of my life here in Maple Creek. Especially as through her I got to meet this beautiful professor who everyone is scared of, did I ever tell you about her?"

She dug her elbow into his ribs, then put down her chopsticks and clapped her hands.

"Ladies, please," she said.

The group stopped eating and looked at her.

"Ladies, as you know, Gavin is a man."

Pollard smiled; the others groaned theatrically. Rashford steeled himself for what was to come.

"Because he's a man, he does things differently than we do."

"Tell it, sister," said Sheri. Laughing.

"Because he's a man, he can't control his ..." She paused. "Appetites."

"Whoo-hoo," said Sarah, waving a chopstick.

Rashford cringed.

"Because he's a man, he's already had two helpings of chicken and a large plate of fried rice!"

Gayle leaned over and peered at Rashford's plate.

"And finished it all," she said.

"Exactly," said Bettina. "Now, normally, he would have run outside for a cigarette by now. But ..."

"I quit. Again." Said Rashford, sheepishly.

Bettina looked at him.

"Really? When?"

"When I went through security in Charlottetown," he said. "On my way back here."

"Ah," said Bettina. "That explains why Anne thought you were still smoking."

"Anne? How's Anne?" asked Gayle Morgan.

"Who's Anne?" said Sheri Hayleyson.

There was a short period of confused conversation as everyone spoke over everyone else while Rashford looked on, bemused. After a few moments, Bettina rapped a teaspoon against her beer bottle.

"We'll talk about Anne later," she said. "Meanwhile, I have decided, while we ladies finish our meals in a gentile and decorous fashion, Gavin can tell us all about his holidays."

The group whooped as Bettina sat back in her chair, a satisfied smile on her face. Rashford looked at her, then around the table.

"Fair enough," he said. "But to be fair, the reason I eat fast is not only because I'm a man, it's because I grew up with three sisters and I never got any food unless I was quick."

Pollard shook her head and the others just laughed. Rashford took a last gulp of beer and then asked one of the servers for a glass of water. When it had been delivered, he began his story.

"I decided to go to Prince Edward Island for a holiday," he said. "I have to tell you, it's a pretty special place, and I had lots of adventures. The first one started ..."

～

As he finished his account of receiving the phone call on Brackley Beach, Rashford was pleased to see the rapt attention on everybody's face. They had long since finished the food, and after serving a second round of beer, Chef Li had reappeared with pots of fragrant green tea. Rashford stopped talking, then leaned down below the table and brought up a small backpack.

"Here," he said. "I brought you each a little something. It's not a lot, I'm afraid, but I wanted you each to know that I was thinking about you while I was away."

He turned first to Chief Superintendent Pollard.

"Chief Superintendent, you're always complaining that you have to clean up my messes. Here's something to help you with that." He handed her the tea-towel from the East Point Lighthouse.

"Sheri, you are always getting into scrapes, and the old British word for a policeman was 'Peeler', so I figured this would work." He gave her the tee-shirt, which she held up against her chest before leaning over and giving him a kiss.

"Gayle and Sarah, for you I cheated and took the easy option. They're really big on flowers down in the Maritimes, and I know you both have gardens, so I brought you some seeds to try. Here."

He handed out the packets and each looked carefully at the labels.

"Lupin?" said Gayle.

"Yes, they're a really beautiful tall flower that gets everywhere, it's basically a very pretty weed. They sure liven up the ditches, though!"

Gayle looked at him.

"Thank you, I think," she laughed.

"Dicentra cucullaria?" said Sarah. "What the heck's that?"

Rashford chuckled.

"Also known as Dutchman's Breeches," he said.

"What, because they're easy to pull off?" said Gayle.

Sarah reddened as the others laughed.

"No, honestly, they just look like that," said Rashford. "Honestly."

"Methinks the knave doth protest too much," laughed Bettina, looking at him expectantly. He passed her a padded yellow envelope.

"It's for when you smudge," he said.

She opened the packet first and admired the pewter box.

"That's beautiful, Gavin," she said.

He coughed.

"There is one other thing," he said.

Pollard held up her hand.

"Let's save that for when we're having a drink, Gavin," she said.

Gayle shook her head.

"We've already had a couple," she said. "I don't want to have a bunch of coppers done for DUI on my patch."

Pollard coughed.

"It's okay, Senior Constable," she said. "We're here on official business, to represent the force at the funeral of an old friend. I took the liberty of booking half-a-dozen rooms at the Jasper for the night. The Force will pay for those. So, no need to worry about drinking and driving."

She looked around at the chattering group.

"If I might suggest," she said. "Perhaps it would be best to go over there and check-in now, while everyone is still sober enough to find their own room."

They regrouped in the car park behind the hotel.

"Get yourselves organized and freshened up," said Pollard. "Let's meet down in the bar in an hour. Okay?"

"Yes, Ma'am," said Rashford, and led the way into the hotel. A small desk stood in the hallway that led through to the dining room and the bar. They rang the bell and a young woman appeared from the back room.

"Hello, Barbara," said the Chief Superintendent. "We spoke on the phone. Can we sign in please?"

"Sure," she said. "I have all the keys here. Just each sigh the form, please, and if you have a car put the registration number just there, so we know it's supposed to be in the car park."

"And don't search the bogs for a dead punter," laughed Gayle in her strongest Mancurian accent.

"Exactly," said Barbara. "Gavin, you're in 201, on the end."

He signed the forms and collected his key, then nodded to everyone and left. He heard Barbara allocate the other rooms.

"Chief Superintendent, you're in 205. Miz Morgan, you're in ..."

Her voice faded. As he reached his room, Rashford realized that he didn't have a toothbrush with him. He was about to go back downstairs and out to the pharmacy when he noticed a sign saying that toiletries were available from housekeeping. He phoned and someone told him they would be right up with his request.

He stood at the window and looked out over Maple Creek. He had enjoyed his time in the small town and would miss it when he was in Ottawa. Perhaps he could think of it as a possible place for retirement. There was a knock on his door; he walked across to answer.

"Thank you ..." he began and stopped as Sheri Hayleyson gave him a small paper bag.

"I took them off a housekeeping person," she said as she pushed past him into the room. "I said I'd deliver them. You can brush your teeth later."

She was wearing the potato peeler tee-shirt and a short lime green skirt. He looked quickly up and down the empty corridor, then closed the door and turned. She looked at him.

"Do you remember what I said to you, back at the Majestic?" she said. He nodded.

She stepped in and gave him a long kiss, then took a pace back.

"I reckon we've got twenty minutes," she said, peeling off the tee-shirt to reveal she was naked underneath. She held out her arms and he drew her to him. As they kissed, his hand caressed the back of her thigh and he realized that there was only skin under the skirt.

"But Gayle ..."

Sheri scoffed.

"That was never a thing for either of us," she said. "We're just friends. We were just trying to be able to go out without being hassled all the time. Now come here. Nineteen minutes."

He was unbuckling his jeans as he moved her backwards onto the bed.

She was true to her word and eighteen minutes later she stretched, pulled on her tee-shirt, and blew him a kiss as she went to the door.

"You've been practising," she said. "That was almost a nine. See you downstairs."

Rashford lay on the bed, staring at the ceiling and wishing that he hadn't given up smoking. After a few minutes he got up, showered, and cleaned his teeth. Then he went downstairs to the bar. He found himself the last to arrive and took the remaining seat, between Sarah and Gayle. Sheri sat opposite him, between the Chief Inspector and Bettina. He felt a foot rub against his ankle and coloured slightly.

"Did you have a good rest?" asked Sheri.

"Yes, thank you," he said. "Did you?"

"Not really. I only had time to do a few stretches, get my exercise for the day."

She smiled brightly.

Gayle coughed.

"I've bought the first round," she said, as the waitress brought over a pitcher of beer and six glasses. "Cheers!"

They finished the first pitcher and were halfway through the second when Bettina spoke.

"So, what is this news that should wait until we had beer?"

Rashford looked across at Pollard, who nodded. He cleared his throat.

"Well, let me start by giving you this. There's one for each of you. Here."

He passed two small envelopes to each of them. Bettina looked at the seed packets in her hand. "Lavender and Forget-me-not?"

She glanced quizzically at Rashford, who shrugged.

"It seemed appropriate," he said.

"Aaah," she said. The others looked at each other and raised their eyebrows. Chief Inspector Pollard broke the silence.

"We'll come back to those in a minute," she said. "In the meantime, thank you very much for these, Staff Sergeant. And for the other gifts. In between buying us all these tokens of your, umm, appreciation, you actually did quite a bit of work as well. For example, you moved forward the file on Marc Claydon."

The others all started talking at once.

"You helped break a gang of smugglers," said Sheri Hayleyson.

"You helped Anne get her man," said Bettina Blackeagle.

"You pulled the girl, and she turned out to be a guy," said Sarah.

"You got Mandy out of your system," said Gayle Morgan.

Bettina pushed her hair out of her eyes and looked across the table. She smiled.

"Well, if I was making a film of this, I know what I'd call it."

"What?" said Rashford, intrigued.

She took a long drink of her beer.

"You've got smugglers, and cocaine. You've got art, music, and what might have been a murder. You've got what sounds like enthusiastic recreational sex. And you're tracking a sociopath. So, it's easy."

Rashford stared at her. He shook his head.

"I've no idea what you're talking about," he said. "Excuse me. I just need to use the facilities."

He stood up and walked through the back door to the washrooms, weaving slightly. A few minutes later he returned to the table.

"You should all finish your beer," he said. "The next round is mine."

"Are you trying to get us drunk?" said Sheri, coquettishly.

"No," he protested. "I meant we should go and eat, and I'll buy the wine."

"He'll be the first to fall," Bettina scoffed.

She pushed over an envelope that she had taken from her purse while he was in the washroom. On it she had written the key words she had mentioned earlier, but this time capitalizing the fist letter of each word. He read each word out loud, carefully.

Smugglers. Cocaine. Art. Music. Murder. Enthusiastic. Recreational sex. Sociopath.

"I don't get it," he said.

"Read it carefully," she said.

She could almost see the lightbulb go off in his head. He laughed as he decoded the note.

"Scammers?" he said.

"That would be a great title," said Pollard, once they had moved into the dining room and ordered their meals. "Should you ever have time to write a book."

She coughed, looking across at Rashford.

"Didn't you have something else to tell us, Staff Sergeant?"

He nodded.

"Thank you, Ma'am."

He looked at the group.

"It's about the flower seeds."

They looked at each other, but Bettina nodded.

"You're going away," she said, quietly.

Rashford nodded, meeting her eyes and avoiding looking at anyone else.

"While I was away, the Chief Superintendent got a phone call. From Ottawa." He took a deep breath. "They want to second me to a special task force that is being set up. It will focus on not just looking for missing and murdered Indigenous women, but also on catching those responsible. It's going to be just a small team, with representatives from both us and the Mounties, as well as from a number of First Nations police forces. There will be twelve members altogether, and they've offered me the role of coordinator."

Gayle Morgan nodded.

"Will it mean a promotion?"

Rashford smiled.

"Yes. I shall be made an Inspector."

Everybody clapped, including Pollard.

"This calls for another bottle," said Sarah, waving at the waitress. "My turn."

"Where will you be based?" said Bettina.

"In Manitoba, I think," said Rashford. "My understanding is that the Task Force will move around the country, or countries, I guess. But it starts in Winnipeg, that's where I would have to report."

"When?" said Sheri.

"In a month," said Rashford. "The first of September."

They all chattered about his new role, asking questions to which he had no real response. The only one he could answer was from Bettina, who asked him how the task force had identified him for the job.

"Why would they pick you?" she said. "I know you speak Cree, but why pick a white man for a job like this, instead of an Indigenous woman? Surely such creatures exist within the police?"

Rashford shook his head. He thought that perhaps his trip to the potato museum might have played a part in that but was not truly certain.

"I agree," he said. "That's why I turned it down."

There was a moment of stunned silence, broken by Gayle Morgan.

"So are yer being promoted or not?" she said, her accent harsh and slurred. "An' why didja say yer were going away, when Bettina asked yer?"

Rashford nodded.

"Good questions," he said. He took a deep breath.

"A couple of days after I told them I didn't want the Task Force job, a fellow turned up at Headquarters and spoke to the Chief Superintendent. She called me into her office."

Rashford remembered the meeting. The man was white, in his late fifties, of medium height and with no noticeable features except his heavy blue framed glasses. The man had shaken his hand but not given a name. 'I've been told to tell you that we have a mutual bilingual urbanite friend,' he had said. Rashford smiled at the memory.

"I chatted to this fellow and he asked me to go to Ottawa, for a secondment. Two or three years, just to do some analysis work for them. You know, reading newspapers and interview transcripts, summarizing them for the higher ups, that sort of thing. Government work. I've agreed, it sounds like a good opportunity."

Especially, thought Rashford, as the man had closed the conversation by quietly saying that he understood the newly promoted Inspector might be interested in some additional work focusing on undercover operations.

'We need someone who is free to travel,' he'd said. 'Someone who is quick to learn, and who can look after themselves in a tight spot. Not just physically, they can think on their feet as well. From what we've heard, you're that man.'

'Travel where?' asked Rashford.

The man shrugged. 'Wherever is needed,' he said. 'Across Canada, into the States, across the pond. It depends which tail we're chasing.'

There was a pause. The man looked down at his feet, then up at Rashford's face. 'We do whatever is needed,' he said. 'Even gender equity training.'

Sarah's voice broke into his thoughts.

"Does that work start in September as well?" she said.

He shook his head.

"Sadly, no. They need me there on Tuesday. I'm sorry, Bettina, the important thing tonight is your nôhkum, not my situation."

She shook her head, smiling.

"It's alright," she said. "My nôhkum would be pleased to share her farewell party with you."

She looked around, waving her arm.

"Come, Sarah, your bottle is nearly empty. It is my turn to buy more wine."

Everyone took another glass, and peppered Rashford with questions about his now job. He tried to remember his answers, in case he had to repeat them, and made sure that he drank a glass of water after each one of wine.

After a time, the questions became repetitive, and the alcohol took its toll. One by one the group left the table, making their way unsteadily to the elevator. Pollard shook his hand as she said goodnight and helped Sarah up the stairs after she had given Rashford a sloppy kiss. Gayle and Sheri each sat on his knee, nuzzling his neck, until Gayle ruffled his hair and then took Sheri by the hand.

"Time fer bed fer us," she slurred, and the two wove their way across the room. Only Rashford and Bettina were still seated.

"Time for coffee, I think," she said.

Rashford nodded, and Bettina called the waitress over and made the order. They sat in silence until it had been served.

"Ottawa, huh?"

"Yes."

"That's a long way, that."

Rashford nodded.

"There are two good universities there," he said.

Bettina raised an eyebrow.

"There are many good universities across Turtle Island," she said.

Rashford agreed. "Yes, but if you were at one of them, instead of here, then I would be able to see you more often."

"That's what you want, is it? To see me? Why?"

He blushed.

"Well, partly because you're smart. But also, because, well, I like you. And ..."

She reached across the table and put her finger to his lips.

"Shush," she said. She sat back in her chair and looked at him.

"I like you as well, Gavin. But that's all. I don't want to be more than a friend. You play too fast and loose for me."

"What do you mean?"

"Gavin, Gavin," she said, gently. "Since we've known each other, you've had at least four relationships that I have counted. And if you gave her half a chance, Sheri would be number five."

He blushed scarlet and she gasped.

"Five it is, then. Plus, however many you had on your holiday. That's a bit out of my comfort zone, actually."

She shook her head.

"I looked around the table tonight and I saw that any of those women, with the possible exception of the Chief Superintendent, would welcome you into their room tonight. I don't ever want to look like that."

She drank her coffee.

"Anyway, in case you've forgotten, I already have a friend. Cicily. She contacted me when she heard that my nôhkum had passed. I'm flying down to see her once I finish this summer class I'm teaching. We will see what happens then."

She reached out and held his wrist.

"Go to Ottawa, Gavin," she said. "Do whatever they're asking you to do. I know it's not just analysis, you're too good to be left stuck in an office like that. But whatever it is, do it well."

She squeezed his arm.

"I wish you'd taken the other job. We need someone to hunt these monsters who prey on our women and girls. Bring them to justice. Who won't forget those victims. People like Shyanne and Petra, they are so trusting, they are vulnerable. Pia cannot protect them all the time, even if they are his sister and his lover. And strong ones like Anne and Mandy, like Gayle and Sarah and Sheri, they're all women too. Treat them with respect."

She let go of his arm and stood up.

"Remember that whichever room you go to tonight."

Leaning over, she kissed him lightly on the cheek before walking away across the dining room. Rashford sat quietly, drinking his coffee. He thought about what Bettina had said, and laughed quietly to himself when he realized that he had no idea of where anyone else was staying, except for Chief Superintendent Pollard, and he wasn't going there.

For a moment, he thought about practical matters. He would have to cancel his lease in Regina, pack up his things, make arrangements to have them shipped. He had been given two weeks in a hotel room, after which he was expected to have found a place to rent. He started work in three days ... there was just too much to think about. He finished his coffee, the cup banging as he returned it to the saucer.

The waitress asked him if he'd like anything else, but he declined. She brought him the bill, informing him that everyone else had already paid their share. He gave her his credit card, left a twenty per cent tip, and went up the stairs to his room.

Acknowledgments

Acknowledgements

In the writing of a novel, some people develop an intricate plot to outline the major elements of the story, and then fill in the blanks. I start with an idea and then see how it goes. As part of this process, I draw upon some of the many people and places I have had the pleasure of knowing along the way. In *Scammers*, there are a few people who deserve special mention.

First, I would like to thank John Flynn for the help he gave me when I asked him how one might conceivably cut brake hoses without anyone noticing. Not a normal question for most people, of course, but John has been our family's 'go-to' mechanic ever since we moved to Prince Edward Island, and I don't know anyone who knows more about cars. Enjoy your retirement, John, and I hope you enjoy the story.

Second, my thanks go to Sarah Nicole Dart, a cyanotype artist who answered my many questions about the process and showed me examples of her work. You can find Sarah at the Charlottetown Farmers' Market most Saturdays, and on Instagram (https://www.instagram.com/ukeecruthu/) at any time. No, she doesn't live on the north shore, or have a craft shop near Goose River.

The vendors at the Charlottetown Farmers' Market deserve their own special mention. It is a wonderful community of people, and I would like to thank them all for their support and friendship when I was the cheesemonger in their midst. You will no doubt recognize yourselves in the book, but the names have been omitted to protect the innocent!

I would also like to thank Pat Deighan, the owner and operator of the real Trailside Music Hall. During the pandemic, Pat somehow managed to keep the venue open, albeit with reduced capacity, and those of us who spent those difficult days in Charlottetown were given the gift of live music on a fairly regular basis. At one point, I think this was the only place in Canada providing such an option. It seemed an appropriate venue for Amanda Robicheau and the Bridge City Rollers to play.

Lastly, I would like to acknowledge the beautiful island on which I live, and the landscape of which forms an integral part of this novel. Epekwitk (Prince Edward Island) is located in Mi'kma'ki, the ancestral and unceded territory of the Mi'kmaq People. The Epekwitnewaq Mi'kmaq have occupied this Island for over 12,000 years. I honour the "Treaties of Peace and Friendship" which recognized Mi'kmaq rights and established an ongoing relationship between nations. We are all Treaty People.

Tim Goddard
    Charlottetown

About the Author

J. T. Goddard is a retired educator. Born and raised in Yorkshire, his career took him to every province and territory in Canada, and to many countries around the world. He now happily calls Prince Edward Island home. *Scammers* is his fifth book, and the third featuring Gavin Rashford. Find out more at: www.jtgoddard.com.

www.ingramcontent.com/pod-product-compliance
Lightning Source LLC
Chambersburg PA
CBHW022109310726
48972CB00007B/1947